The Curator of Broken Things

Trilogy

Book 3

Resistance in Algiers

A novel by Corine Gantz

ISBN-13: 978-0-9834366-7-6
ISBN-10: 0-9834366-7-3

To everyday heroes

Corine Gantz

TABLE OF CONTENTS

CHAPTER 1

Springtime in Paris

Hot water pounded Cassie's shoulders; water rivulets slid down her neck, her breasts, her thighs as she stood inside above her Parisian hotel bathroom's claw-foot tub. Steam turned the glass of the small window above the tub opaque, and Paris's skyline blurred, mirroring her thoughts. How easy, and natural and lovely it had been with Hervé. Dinner the night before. Conversations about small things. The laughter. The kisses. His skin. His hands on her. How could it be that five years after her divorce, long past the time when she thought she cared about physical things at all, her body suddenly remembered that it felt things, that it wanted things?

And yet, when she had awakened thirty minutes ago, Hervé had already left. A couple of dinners and two nights of lovemaking did not exactly constitute a relationship, and yet it stung. It was for the best. The romance, if that's what this was, was headed for the cliff anyway. Her omissions – okay, her lies – insignificant at first, had grown the size of an entire continent. She had not told Hervé that she lived in the United States and had not lived in France for a good twenty years or that she was in Paris for only a few more days. She had deliberately moved the conversation away from the truth in big and small ways. She had told Hervé that she had children in college, but not that her twins were Americans, in American colleges. She told him that she was a writer and worked with her ex, but not that the career took place in Los Angeles. It had been easier to let Hervé think that she had landed in this ninth arrondissement hotel room because of an imaginary breakup. She had told him that she lived in the United States and would only remain in Paris for a few more days to visit her father who currently drifted in and out of consciousness in the hospital a few blocks away from her hotel.

At first, she had only meant to withhold information from a stranger. After finding herself in bed with said stranger, and finding herself liking him very much, she had not revealed details that might reflect negatively on her, details such as the country where she lived, or the fact that her mother and sister were barring her from her dad's hospital room because they saw her as unpredictable and perhaps even potentially damaging to his recovery. True, her dad had gone into a rage when Cassie entered the room, but it was only because of the drugs; it was because he was confusing her with Marceline, the sister from which he was estranged and whose existence he had kept hidden for over forty years. Cassie blamed the morphine for his outbursts, but apparently, the hospital, her mother, and her sister Odile blamed her. The fact that Cassie lived in another country where she was still in love with her ex-husband, and that she was presently at war with her father, her sister, and her mother, not to mention the entire French hospital, would have been topics on the heavy side for a first date. She did not judge it necessary to elaborate on how much of a nut she was. Anyway, the curated version of her life had not stopped Hervé from running away while she was asleep, so her lies did not matter at all.

Cassie got out of the shower and wiped the fog from the mirror. The day ahead promised to be fraught with drama. Her mother would intimidate her out of asking questions about the past. Her sister Odile would tell her that cozying up to Marceline had been a betrayal of their dad. She planned to escalate her fight with the bureaucrats at the hospital because she now saw it her mission, on behalf of every French patient they had or would callously ignore, to point out how robotic and heartless they were. Perhaps that was the real reason she was in Paris: to be reminded of the infuriating reasons she had left France and her family in the first place.

Cassie put on her last pair of clean jeans, layered two T-shirts, and pulled on the red cowboy boots. Jessica's little gifts to her family were still on the mantelpiece, reminding her precisely of what awaited back home: work with Peter, not to mention his matrimonial bliss rubbed in her face day in and day out. She had no right to resent Jessica. Jessica had won Peter over fair and square long after Cassie could claim any ownership of the man.

She looked at the little packages. Hervé had hated those gifts the minute he set eyes on them, and now she saw them in a new light. He had belittled the frilly wrappings and even pointed out that her ex-husband's new wife had no business giving presents to her parents. Hervé. His skin. His smell. The way he had kissed her. After five years without a man's touch, she was desperate. Had she been too eager? She'd definitely been eager.

In time, perhaps, there would be other lovers. Hervé's materializing into her life, however briefly, was a reminder of what was possible. Maybe her time in Paris was opening her world in unexpected ways. Sabine, her younger sister, was in need of her friendship. And there was Marceline, with whom she started to feel an unexplainable kinship. She had not told Odile or her mother that she planned to see Marceline again today. Estranged or not, betrayal of their father or not, Marceline was the only member of the family willing to speak of the past.

She left her hotel room and went down the many sets of stairs. The hospital was not open to visitors in the morning, but maybe she'd be able to speak to someone more open-minded, someone more human, who would let her enter her dad's room. The horrible people she had dealt with thus far hid their incompetence and natural cruelty behind nameless superiors and nonsensical clerical rules, and she had hit a wall. At this point, her only plan was to continue to hit that wall again and again until she cracked it open.

At the reception desk, the old hotelier, his white hair straight up on his head like Albert Einstein in a fright, stood behind the desk, his eyes closed, so immobile that he looked as if he might be asleep standing up. But as she walked by the desk, he opened his eyes and handed her a dozen scribbled pieces of papers. "That American man," he said sourly. "He called all night. Every hour." He grimaced with contempt. "Always gave me the same number. He thinks I'm an imbecile."

Cassie narrowed her eyes at the handful of notes. It was Peter's number, written over and over on various scraps of paper. She could well imagine Peter, who did not speak French, as he shouted the numbers at an elderly Frenchman determined not to speak English. "I'm sorry," she said. "He can be single-minded."

The old man grunted. "Is he your boss?"

"My ex-husband, calling from California. He refuses to accept the concept of time zones."

The old man shook his head and made a whistling sound of empathy between his teeth. "The new one," he said, evidently referring to Hervé, whom he had seen going up and down the stairs with her. "At least he knows the difference between night and day." With this, he handed her a separate note. The handwriting was atrocious; the letters looked like a succession of tiny waves, but she managed to decipher it. *"Je ne voulais pas te réveiller. Je viens te chercher vers 20 heures. Ce soir je fais la cuisine. Hervé."* Cassie looked up from the note and beamed at the old hotelier. She had not been dumped! Hervé had only meant not to wake her up. He was picking her up around eight p.m. and was cooking dinner! In the span of two days, she had gone from divorced and bitter to having a French lover who cooked for her! "I need to make a phone call," she told the old man.

"Well, it still works for now. We're about to get rid of it. Who doesn't have cell phones these days," the old man said, pointing to the dark corner of the reception hall where stood the bizarre phone booth, the one inexplicably upholstered in mushy red velvet, like the inside of a cake or the lining of a coffin.

She entered the phone booth and slid the glass door closed, remembering that Hervé had mentioned something about making pasta from scratch. Apparently, it was a thing, some sort of French mating ritual new to her. Still giddy, she made a collect call to Peter's number in California.

"Cassie, at last!" Peter exclaimed. "For heaven's sake, what were you doing for the last eight hours?"

"Sleeping," she sighed. "Peter, it was night here."

"And there are no phones in the rooms?"

"Still nope."

"And yet they wouldn't wake you up to tell you I was trying to reach you?"

"Apparently not."

"This is ridiculous, Cassie. You need to get yourself a new cell phone, immediately."

"I don't know; I'm kind of liking it."

"Liking what?"

"Being unplugged. There's something to say about it."

"Well, you better re-plug and fast because we've got a crisis on our hands." Peter was using the urgent tone that usually preceded his turning frantic. "*Women in Black, Part Two* is getting *creamed* by the critics!"

Cassie thought of the movie, how important it had all seemed only a few days ago, and now how trivial, something not worth wasting a minute of mental energy on. "Bad reviews don't mean the movie won't do well," she said.

"Across the board, *The New York Times, Variety, Huff Post*. They say it's formulaic."

"Of course, it's formulaic," she said. "We gave the studio a paint-by-number of what they wanted."

"Same difference. You know how studio executives are. They want guarantees."

"Tell them the usual garbage: reviewers are failed intellectuals who like to hear the sound of their own rants. Although you and I know they are correct in their assessment."

"What? I don't know that!" Peter said, indignant. "How do I know that? It's a perfectly good film in its genre."

"Correct. The genre is the problem."

"Regardless, the studio's freaking out. They're pumping another fifteen million into promotion."

"Really? You can't take a step in Paris without being bombarded with their ads. Besides, I don't see how any of this is our problem at this point."

"Well, here is how it's our problem: they're freaking out about the one we're writing now,"

"They want to pull out of the prequel? *An Inter Galactic Dramedy*."

"They would if they could, but lucky for us there are too many big names attached."

"So, what do they want from us?"

"Take a wild guess."

"They want a rewrite?"

"And we better give it to them, and fast, or else the franchise is in peril."

She chuckled despite herself. "Thank God for that."

"Can you cut the cynicism? What's gotten into you? They want to pump up a few things, the humor, the sex, the violence. Oh, and they hate the subplot."

"I hate the subplot too."

"*Now* you tell me?"

Cassie stated something that was suddenly obvious to her, like a cosmic revelation. "I hate the entire film."

"Which *you* wrote with me every day and never said a word!"

"True."

"They think it's not broad enough."

"It's so broad you could stretch it from here to Jupiter."

"What is it you want, Cassie?" Peter said, exasperated. "This is our livelihood. You want to spit in the soup? Bite the hand that feeds or whatnot? I don't know what to tell you. They want a rewrite, and we're going to give them a rewrite. That's what we do. That's why we're the best."

"It's like being the best at clubbing yourself over the head with a rock."

"It's entertainment! Five days in Paris and you've turned into an intellectual snob?"

"Would it be so terrible if our short time on this planet could contribute to improving it, not making it sink to lower depths."

"Oh, please spare me the existentialism."

"I'll remind you that my dad is unconscious in the hospital. It's par for the course."

Peter was silent for a moment, recalibrating. When he spoke again, it was with an almost cheerful voice. "Listen, I know about your dad and all, very tough. You must be going through hell."

"Actually—"

"I hate to do this to you, love, but you need to get your cute butt back to L.A. I'll call the airline to see if there is a penalty for returning early. How about I upgrade you, huh? My treat. There might be a flight leaving today. Or tomorrow?"

"And leave my dad?"

"You can go back to France as soon as we knock this new draft out. You know what? I have an idea. How about I get a service to buy you a new laptop and deliver it to your hotel in the next few hours. I bet that can be done. France is not the Third World."

"The Developing World," she corrected.

"I can email you the studio's notes, and you can start working on the rewrite on the plane. It's what, a twelve-hour flight? You could make a serious dent in twelve hours."

"What about my dad?"

Peter's voice was humble, pleading. "Well, since they won't let you see him anyway...."

Cassie took a breath. Around her was red velvet, both safe and suffocating at the same time. "Peter, Listen—"

"And like I said; you could turn around in a few days and get back to Paris if need be."

She exhaled, looked at her watch. She had just enough time to get to Marceline's house. "I can't get into this right now. Let me call you back in a few hours, alright?"

"I'll get you a laptop," Peter said cheerfully.

****

Outside felt like springtime. The Parisians had a bounce in their step; an optimistically summery wardrobe had replaced umbrellas and raincoats. Cassie entered the boulangerie at the foot of the hotel and bought a pain au chocolat and an Orangina. She walked to the métro at Barbès-Rochechouart. Just like the day before, the station's walls were covered with posters for *Woman in Black*, and there were three men at work gluing more. The studio had wasted no time in printing new posters, but they must have run out of space because they were being smacked right on top of the old ones. That's what fifteen million bought you these days. She laughed out loud and was surprised by the sound of her own laughter.

In the packed métro, a hand on the vertical metal pole, swaying along with every turn, Cassie ate her pain au chocolat feeling not at all like the grown-up she was, but like an eighteen-year-old with a crush. Hervé was cooking pasta. For her! Could someone please pinch her? She had heard of that fantasy, the man who could cook. And she was about to experience it.

Last night, Hervé had talked more about what he wanted to do with his life: something to do with water purification systems in remote parts of Africa. An evening of pasta making was the extent of Hervé's commitment to her. Her return ticket was four days away, and she planned to use those days well. She would have to explain to Peter that saving him, and by extension Hollywood, would have to wait a few days.

Cassie stood facing the Cité des Fleurs house. The first time she had seen the house, it had felt like a foggy dream. But now, moments of her childhood were unlocking as though they had been hidden away in drawers of her mind and were opening up one by one. The smell of wet stones, the chirping of birds, the grey trunks of sycamores, the distant noise of car traffic. Odile in a yellow woolen hat. Her father, towering above them in his winter coat. Her hand in his. All three of them him looking up at the house.

"Why are we here, Papa?" Odile had asked.

"I lived there once," Father said. "In this house."

"When you were little?"

"When I was a boy."

"Did you have a family?" Odile had asked. She must have been six or seven years old. That means that Cassie was four at most.

"Everyone has a family," their dad had said.

"Where are they now?"

"They're dead," he said.

"Can we go inside the house, Papa?" Cassie had asked.

"Oh, no; there are people living in it."

"What people?"

"Just people," he had said.

He had taken them to the Cité des Fleurs twice, maybe three times. They had stood there, the three of them, never walking through the gate, never entering it, never as much as ringing the bell. What strange compulsion brought her father back to the Cité des Fleurs house? Why show it to his daughters but never tell them what it all meant? Why not describe to them the bullying he had endured as a child. Why not mention the years in boarding school or what it was like to be a Jewish boy during the rise of French anti-Semitism? Why not explain how his family had to flee the Nazis, first to the South of France, and then to North Africa where they lived under a false identity? Why did he not tell them that he had a sister? And why say that his family had died, which was clearly a lie?

Cassie hesitated before pressing the buzzer. She was coming here against her mother's and Odile's wishes and, she was pretty confident of this, against her father's as well. Her dad had made a choice to separate from his family and later to hide his sister's existence. He had chosen to alter his last name and to hide his Judaism. And here she was, unearthing it all.

The bell made a screechy, otherworldly noise when she pressed her finger on it. From somewhere in the house, the wide metal gate was unlocked and clicked open. She pushed on the gate. In the garden, the old North African gardener with the handsome face raked the gravel of the path, a cold pipe at his mouth. "Your garden is enchanting," she said as she walked past him.

He touched his cap and tilted his head. "Merci, merci."

"I have a crazy garden in Los Angeles," she told him. "But it takes discipline to groom a garden, and that's not my forte. I can't even discipline my hair."

"C'est une belle jounée," he answered with a smile. She was not sure if he had understood her and her lame humor at all.

"Yes, a gorgeous day," she agreed. She walked up to the stoop. The front door opened and Armelle, Marceline's stepdaughter, placed herself firmly in the doorway. "Mother has been quite exhausted," she said nervously fingering her pearls. "I'm afraid you might have to reconvene another time."

"Reconvene? But I'm returning to the U.S. in a few days."

Armelle perked up. "Oh, are you?"

"What is wrong with Marceline?"

Armelle's eyes avoided hers. "Oh, nothing much," she said. "She needs more rest is all."

Cassie was about to insist when she heard Marceline's voice from upstairs. "Armelle, for heaven's sake, stop your nonsense, will you."

Armelle sighed and moved out of the way. She reluctantly invited Cassie to come in. "She's in her study," she said.

Cassie walked past Armelle and up the stairs. She tapped at Marceline's door. "Come on in," Marceline called out. "No need to knock. I'm not the Queen of England."

The study smelled of old books, heavy women's perfume, Earl Grey tea, and pipe tobacco. Laure, Marceline's assistant, was up on a stool and moving what appeared to be a family of stuffed owls from the bookshelf. Magazine and books covered every surface. Laure next began to sort through old papers. Marceline wore an orange silk kimono pantsuit. Her hair was wrapped in an orange shawl, and her neck and arms were heavy with bracelets and necklaces covered in charms, beads, old keys, and trinkets. She looked the picture of health and vitality. "Are you feeling ill?" Cassie asked.

"I'm perfectly well, Dear."

"Why did Armelle make a fuss then?"

"Ha," Marceline clucked. "Long story."

"She's quite protective of you."

"Not protective of me, that's for sure."

"Of who then?"

"Of herself."

Cassie shook her head. "I don't get it."

Marceline pointed at the two leather armchairs by the window, and they sat down. "Laure, would you bring us hot chocolate? Is it too early for hot chocolate? Or rather, bring us mint tea, the way they make it in Algiers. To put us in the mood." She shifted her gaze to Cassie. "How is Gustave feeling this morning?"

Cassie had a defeated sigh. "I will try to see him this afternoon."

"Try?"

"To tell you the truth, well … I'm in a fight with my mother and my sister. They're making a problem. They're acting as though I might harm him in some way since that first day when he was so agitated, and well … they've barred me from his room."

Marceline did not appear surprised. "Agitated, when he thought you were me?"

"What is it about me that reminds him of you, I wonder."

"Well, it's pretty obvious. It's because of your spark."

Cassie raised her eyebrows. "I have a spark?"

"Call it what you will. That fire, that curiosity, that defiance, that life force."

"Me? No. I'm terrified of the slightest risk."

"And yet you are here, aren't you?"

What Marceline called a spark, might have been a reference to Cassie's temper. It was a part of her that she strived, and mostly failed, to restrain. It was the part that acted on impulse, that got into fights, the part that kicked out a perfectly good husband and then regretted it, the part that rebelled against injustices, real or perceived. But that was also the part of her with the fire to create, the drive to claim a small part of the world for herself. "I want to know what happened between you and my father," Cassie declared.

Marceline sighed heavily. "Death happened."

"Who died?"

"Things began to take a turn in the spring of 1941," Marceline said. "It's a long story, Cassandra. I haven't told too many people about it. A portion was classified top secret, but who cares now. I have a foot in the grave. Are you going to write all this down?"

"Sure."

"Then take out your pen and paper; what are you waiting for?"

Cassie obediently opened her tote bag, set her pad on the table, uncapped her pen, and listened.

CHAPTER 2

Resistance in Algiers

I was only eighteen, and I did not know my heart. I confused sexual attention for love, and I confused the pangs of unrequited love for hatred. Fernand and I had become lovers. This happened after an afternoon when I had stumbled upon him with an attractive girl at his arm. The two of them were looking through the window of a department store. She was giggling, and I could tell that she was smitten with him. A few paces behind them, small purses in hand, their respective mothers followed. Fernand saw me and quickly looked away, pretending not to know me. The reaction mystified me. I crossed examined him the following day, and he admitted that the girl was his fiancée, and had been for months.

"Why have you never said a word about her?" I asked him. We were sitting at the terrace of a restaurant. Only a year before, the Algiers restaurant scene had been vibrant. Now everything was drab. Menus were shrinking, and prices were going up. We could barely afford to eat out at all and usually shared a few items between us, stuffing ourselves with bread lathered with margarine until even those items began to disappear from shops and restaurants. We were waiting for Béatrice, André, and Émile and were alone until our friends arrived.

"What is there to say?" Fernand answered. "It's a boring story. We are engaged. She's seventeen. We have to wait until she turns nineteen to marry. She's a good Jewish girl. No hanky-panky. Our mothers are always chaperoning. You know how it goes."

"How can you be certain she will still want to marry you two years from now?"

"In all practicality, we've been engaged since we were kids. Our families have known each other for generations. The union has been heavily plotted."

"An arranged marriage?"

"Not arranged," Fernand said with a wry smile. "Merely facilitated."

"Do you love her?"

"She is beautiful and sweet. Her folks are important in Algiers. The families approve. What's not to love?"

"In the street the other day, you pretended not to know me. Who are you embarrassed about? Was it her or me?"

He looked at me with those velvety eyes, both commanding and ironic. "I'm embarrassed by neither of you. Only discreet. So as to hurt no one's feelings."

"Do you think I care? Do you think my feelings would be so easily bruised? You and I are friends, nothing more."

He smiled wryly. "Now it is *my* feelings that are being hurt."

"You are capable of feelings?"

He looked at me in an unmistakably sexual way. "You know all too well how I feel about you, Marceline. I am tortured with thoughts of you day and night. It's a miracle that I manage any sleep at all. You have that effect on men, don't you know?"

"Well, you should be ashamed of yourself," I said, flattered. "You are engaged. Try warm milk at bedtime; you'll sleep just fine. Leave me out of your nights."

"Tell me you are incapable of guilty thoughts yourself. Or rather, don't tell me. I won't believe you."

I played with the straw in my glass. I was capable of guilty thoughts indeed. I too tossed and turned at night, and it had quite a bit to do with lust. Ever since that day in the café's corridor, my baffling, thrilling encounter with Khaled replayed in my mind on a loop. Had he meant to kiss me? Had he wanted to speak to me? Had he intended to frighten me? He had appeared in the dark hallway, wordlessly bent toward me, and I had felt engulfed by all the things he had perhaps meant to convey without words or touch: tenderness, threat, desire, amusement, domination. What drove me mad was that the strange courtship had ended as enigmatically as it had begun. Since that day, nothing. Dozens of times since, I had stubbornly returned to Café Djurdjura, and he had not so much as looked in my direction. I was left not knowing his feelings at all and mine even less. I felt eager, and I felt powerless. I was furious, and at the same time drunk with a sort of secret happiness about the thrill, the hope, the romance of it all. It was an unexplained craving, a feeling of desperation, a sense that it had been a cruel game and that I had lost. Was this how things would end between Khaled and me? Over and done before they had even begun? Often anger would take over. How dare he corner me like that? Who did he think he was? He was nobody. He was my social inferior. He was part of a culture and a religion alien to me.

"There are several sorts of people in one's life," Fernand said. "She is the girl I'll marry, the future mother of my children. But I'll admit I didn't want this to push you away."

"Is that so?"

Fernand put his hand over mine and began to gently caress it with the tip of his fingers. "Perhaps I thought you would like me less."

Fernand was handsome. He and I had played a game of seduction for years, but I had no desire to pretend to love him, and I made sure never to cross a line. He and I had not so much as kissed. But his being engaged, his attachment to someone else, changed things. Perhaps he was just what I needed to get my mind off Khaled. I did not remove my hand. "Maybe it's the opposite," I said. "Perhaps I like you more now."

"Now that you know I'm engaged?"

"To become the mother of someone's children is not every woman's dream, Fernand."

And so, we secretly met in cheap hotel rooms. Although I was just two years older than his fiancée, I felt like I was a mature woman. I liked the thought of having a lover with no emotional attachment, no commitment. I liked that he wanted to keep me a secret because I too wanted to be discreet. We met a couple of times a week. Fernand was an attentive sexual partner, and there was a lot of excitement in the secrecy of those meetings. But in a strange way, I felt closer to Khaled after only a few moments with him in that hallway than I felt to Fernand, skin against skin in bed.

It was during one my secret rendezvous with Fernand that I learned about what was really taking place at Géo Gras.

It had been one of those warm spring afternoons. Sprawled under the white sheets of Hotel de Paris, my head rested on Fernand's chest as the blades of the ceiling fan struggled to move the air, already hot for the season. There wasn't much to do in Algiers in the spring of 1941. There was no school to attend, no work to get paid for, no money, and little available to buy or eat. Fernand and I met in secret from our friends twice a week in the middle of the afternoon.

"My family is onto me," I told Fernand as he absentmindedly caressed my naked body with the tips of his fingers. "I'm pretty certain that my brother is spying on me and reporting to my father."

But Fernand had his own frustration. "They say we're not French," he growled. "They're the ones selling France out to Hitler. They fill their pockets stealing Jewish businesses and emptying our bank accounts. Their hateful little minds have no concept of patriotism. How they love to hate the Jews so that they can plunder us!" Fernand sat up in bed, suddenly incensed by his own words. "I will show them what true patriotism looks like," he said. "To my death, if I must."

I shrugged, "Jews have demonstrated their patriotism time and again. Your dying for France will not prove a thing."

"Regardless," he said, "I'd rather die of a bullet, shot proving my allegiance to France, than from typhus in an internment camp."

"Well, I intend on living," I said, sitting up in bed next to him. "We will accomplish far less by being dead wouldn't you think?" Rays of the sun came through the spaces between the window's shutters. It was already late. I had to dress, arrange my hair, and meet up with Sandra before she needed to get to the apartment to fix dinner so that we could both walk home together. "I want to shape my own fate, not bob along the way I have been," I said. Those were just words. I had shaped nothing and knew it.

"Then you better do something soon before you run out of opportunities," Fernand said. "Look at the Jews of Europe. Their chance has passed. They are trapped. But here in Algeria, you can still act." He added, "If you have the nerve."

Did I have the nerve, when for months now I had done nothing concerning the nature of my obsession? I had failed to speak to Khaled, failed to get his attention, failed to get him out of my mind. But I also knew that no good would come out of pursuing Khaled, or him pursuing me. I knew better than to go down that rabbit hole. "I would join the Resistance in a heartbeat," I told Fernand, not even knowing what that meant. This was not the first time I had mentioned the Resistance, perhaps to push him to act.

Fernand looked at me fiercely. "What's stopping you?"

I shrugged. I took the sheet from the bed, wrapped myself in it, and went to sit in front of the vanity. "How would they know to find me? I don't have any idea how to find them? It's not as though I can place an advertisement in the newspaper."

Fernand propped himself up on one elbow and watched me comb my hair. After a long while, he asked, "And what would you do for the Resistance?"

"Whatever it takes," I answered, not meaning it.

Fernand got up from the bed and came to stand behind me. He put his hands on my shoulders. In the mirror, I watched his face turn serious. "You would not have to place an advertisement in the newspaper," he murmured in my ear.

"You know people?"

The fan's blades turned in slow motion as he whispered, "We are part of a Resistance cell. André, Émile, and I."

"You are?" The questioning in my voice betrayed that I was more dubious than stunned.

He smiled. "What is so hard to believe? That we would be, or that we would be without you suspecting a thing?"

"There is resisting, and there is The Resistance," I said. "It's one thing to have good intentions, and another to be properly connected."

If Fernand had planned to keep things a secret, my lack of conviction goaded him to say more. "Do you have any idea of what is really going on at Géo Gras?" he asked.

"You do calisthenics I thought."

"Do you truly think that we care one way or another how healthy we are? Obedience, honor, discipline, willpower, travail, famille, patrie, all that nonsense. Did you actually believe that we bought into that? No, that has only been our excuse to meet."

It was then that Fernand told me all about the activities at Gymnase Géo Gras. The gymnasium was a cover, a meeting place for the Resistance. While Béatrice and I thought that our friends were parading around in shorts, climbing ropes, lifting iron bars, and fine-tuning their musculature as the world fell to pieces; they were doing Resistance work! They gathered intelligence on Vichy hotspots, kept records on boating activities throughout the region, mapped out the coast and mountains, recruited, established codes, and chains of communication and command, and made plans on how to overtake strategic points in the city.

In many ways, the Jews of Algiers were ideally suited for such clandestine organizing. They were a tight-knit group accustomed to a hostile environment. Their trust in each other had developed from parents to children over generations. The arrests, the humiliations, and the privations that had hit the community in the previous two years had only served to reinforce the strength of their bond.

"In theory, we're preparing to defend ourselves should the situation against the Jews deteriorate. But lately, there has been word that something bigger is on the brink."

"How much bigger?"

"Huge," he said. A thrilled silence lingered after his word.

"Are you armed?" I asked.

"You know how the gunsmith had his shop shut down and his stock confiscated by order of the préfecture? That was after we hid away hundreds of firearms in the basement of the gymnasium. Nothing that compares to the Germans MP43, but enough to put a bullet through a Nazi's head. Enough to capture, or kidnap. Enough for the Allied forces to know they can count on us in the eventuality of an invasion of North Africa."

I was enthralled. "You think that's a possibility?"

"Yes … Especially in light of recent events," Fernand said. "We've received contact. Someone was sent to Algeria by the French Resistance to organize us. They're trusting us! The Jews are the only people they know for certain will never be on the side of Pétain or the Nazis. You see," he said, "the Allies see us as the last true patriots!"

I felt thrilled, buoyed for the first time in months by hope and excitement. "I want to be part of this," I said.

"It's dangerous business. And besides, many men think a woman is a liability."

"We raise less suspicion."

"Being part of this means risking your life. Your father would not allow you to get involved."

"My father would never know about this."

"Chances are that he would be one of the first to know."

I shrugged, "How so?"

Fernand gave me a quizzical look. "Your father is one of the cell leaders."

I laughed. "Of course, he's not. What are you talking about? My father is the most cautious man you'll ever meet, and the most risk-averse."

"Him and that big man, Moshe."

"*Uncle* Moshe?" I asked in disbelief.

"They've been channeling money from England and the United States. They have air routes and drop-off points throughout France and North Africa. Their cell is the one that helps finance all the others. Without your father, there would be no funds."

I felt goosebumps all over my body. Baba, my father! With all his talk of being safe, I had never paid attention to his secretive behavior. Now it all made sense. But as proud of him as I felt, I also wished he wasn't involved. I might have romantic notions of risking my life for freedom, but I didn't want my father to risk his. "It there any way I could help without my dad or my uncle finding out?"

"There is a way," Fernand said. "You could help, and it would just be between us two. Underground in the underground sort of thing. In fact, it might be best. The less you know, the safer you are. This is how the cells have to work anyway. Things have to be compartmentalized. That way, if one of us gets caught, only his cell goes down. He can't give out anyone else's names or confess what they do."

"Do you have something in mind for me?"

"Translation," he said without hesitation. "You're fluent in English."

I looked at him askance. "You had always meant to ask me this, didn't you? You've been planning to ask me, and you knew I'd say yes."

"We need you, sweetie. We translate loads of stuff coming our way, but we aren't always sure of the subtleties."

I had no idea that my next sentence would place me at the center of a mission that could soon change the course of the war. "I can do this," I told him, with all the fervor I felt. "I want to do this."

I left the hotel, careful to leave before Fernand did, so as not to be seen near him. As I stepped into the bright light of mid-afternoon, my head buzzed with what I had learned. But just as I walked out of the hotel, I came face to face with Gustave on his bicycle!

"What are you doing in there?" Gustave demanded to know.

"Have you been following me?"

He straddled his bike. Gustave had turned into a hybrid between a boy and a man. He was tall now and muscular from the incessant push-ups and lifting weights in his room, yet he still had no hair on him, and his eyes were still those of a child. He crossed his arms. "Are you being a tramp?" he asked.

I stepped toward him and grabbed him by the arm. "I'll skin you alive, you little rat!"

He shook his arm from my grip, furious. "Are you telling them not to let me in?"

"What are you talking about?"

"You're telling the Géo Gras men not to include me, aren't you?"

Gustave must have caught wind of what was taking place at Géo Gras, tried to offer his services, and been shooed away. If that was the case, it was most likely because our father had ordered it. "I had nothing to do with that," I said, which was the truth.

Gustave twisted his mouth angrily. "You're lying, as usual."

"You better stay away from trouble," I said. "You've heard what Baba said."

"And you heard what he told *you*," he sneered. "You're not obeying either."

"What are you trying to prove, Gustave? That you're a brave man? A big hero? You'd be nothing but a liability to them. One look at you and they can tell you don't have what it takes."

Gustave looked hurt, then furious. "You're nothing but a whore." He spat out the words and darted away on his bike.

I worried that Gustave would run straight to my father to tell on me. But mostly I wanted to punish him for what he had said. Why could men go to bed with whomever they wanted, but a woman doing so was a whore? At the same time, my rage was partially due to shame. I knew that I was being promiscuous not out of love but out of idleness.

Could I have fallen in love with Fernand if not for Khaled? Would I have been infatuated with Khaled had it not been forbidden? The thing was, sex with Fernand did not feel right. I felt blemished by it. Nonsensically, I felt as though I was betraying Khaled.

My Resistance activity thus began. Newspapers from Britain and the United States were contraband items on which the members of the Resistance depended for intelligence. It was terribly dangerous to be caught in possession of one. No one at Géo Gras was fluent enough in English to know for certain that they understood the contents. Fernand soon put me to the task. For hours at a time, by the light of a candle, while the rest of the family slept, I translated all manner of English newspaper articles, brochures, and annotations on maps. At last, those dreadful British nannies had proved themselves not entirely useless.

From May 1941 to January 1942, when we celebrated my nineteenth birthday without enough flour or eggs for a cake, I translated. My fingertips were raw from flipping through the pages of my dictionary with a fervor I had seldom applied to my schoolwork. I was good at this and got better with practice. My English improved exponentially. I was too busy, and nervous, to wonder what had come of Gustave's own Resistance dreams. To me, he was a child. I could not imagine that others saw this pencil-thin seventeen-year-old as a man.

For a young Jewish woman in 1941, it was unfathomable to hope that the world would recover from its spiraling descent into hell. Hitler's maniacal plans and politics went unopposed. His army was unstoppable. But it wasn't just Hitler. Hating the Jews appeared to be the one point on which the entire world agreed. There might have been righteous and well-meaning people not intent on wiping

Jews off the face of the earth, but they were few and mostly focused on their own survival. So very little was being done to stop the hatred against us. We felt it down to the marrow of our bones: soon, Jews would have no place to hide, no country to run to. The information we received from friends and relatives cemented our understanding that we had become the entire world's prey. How would we ever overcome this, even if Hitler lost the war, which at this point seemed impossible? Hatred was closing in on Jews, squeezing us out of existence.

I needed Fernand because his anger was so much more reassuring than our collective apathy and discouragement. Fernand believed that the Jewish people's fate wasn't written yet. He admonished us not to count on the return of human decency or to hope that the government would set up protective policies. These, to him, were paralyzing delusions. He believed that we would prevail because our fight had only begun. It wasn't prayer or hiding that we needed but guns and grenades.

Another person I depend on for hope was my father. As nurturing to me as air or water was the way Baba found reasons to rejoice. In June 1941, when Hitler invaded the Soviet Union, and the Russian army seemed unable to stop him, my father promised us that Hitler would not be able to sustain a war on two fronts. When Japan attacked Pearl Harbor on December 7th, 1941 and the United States officially entered the war, my father tried to convince us that the combined will and brain power of Roosevelt and Churchill would save us. Now that I knew that my father was a prominent person in the Resistance, I hung on to his words and hoped he knew something we didn't.

And so, in the absence of tangible signs that things would improve, what carried me through these dark times was my father's optimism, Fernand's exhortations, my modest efforts with the Resistance, and, perhaps more essential to me, the mystery of Khaled.

As months passed and he still made no eye contact with me, I had to admit to myself that I had fallen under his spell. When I got up in the morning, he was my first thought. The way I dressed, the way I did my hair: it was all for him. I had only one interest in my day, and that was to see him, even from afar. I had no name for this, for my feelings, but in them, I recognized hope. Hope was a fragile thing, it was all we had in that terrible war, and so I protected mine like a weakly beating heart.

Throughout the rest of the winter, I dutifully translated the papers Fernand gave me. Information never changed hands between us. We communicated via a system he had devised. Every day I went to the market and stopped at the flower stand owned by a Jewish woman who was part of the Resistance. We would then exchange matching straw bags. Hers contained the day's documents to translate. Mine contained my translation from the day before. While I have no doubt that the work Fernand gave me was important, it was also a test to observe my grit and dedication. I did not know this at the time, but this assignment was a way for him to calibrate me, and in many ways train me, for the future mission he had in mind.

This pickup and drop-off of papers went on for months without drama until one day when I arrived home after an afternoon with Béatrice. From the moment I entered the apartment, it was clear that something was wrong. Mother, Father, and Gustave were sitting in the living room, waiting for me in ominous silence. Mother looked vindicated. Gustave stood sheepishly. My father immediately brandished one of my translations and a copy of *The New York Tribune*. "What are these?" he said.

"Where did you find that?" I said, knowing just where he had found them. Gustave, whose nose was everywhere, must have dug them out from inside my bedroom fireplace where they were hidden. I turned to my brother and shouted, "You little rat!"

"Who is your contact?" my father asked without bothering to pretend he did not understand what I was up to.

"Give that back to me," I said. "People are expecting this translation. It's my duty to give it to them."

For a man who worked for the Resistance, my father did not exactly give my demand much respect. "What duty?" he said, rolling his eyes. "Your duty is to mind your mother and me."

"I know who she spends her time with," Gustave volunteered.

"Snitch!" I said.

"Your brother speaks only out of concern for your safety," my mother said.

"He's all too happy to get me in trouble."

"You got yourself into trouble without his help," my father pointed out. "And besides, Gustave understands something you fail to comprehend, Marceline. His loyalty to this family has to be greater than his loyalty to you. That's because a family is greater than the sum of its parts."

"What does that even mean?" I said, exasperated.

"It means that if one of us is wounded, or imprisoned, or killed, the others would never … ever recover." My father choked on his words and paused to gather himself. "What if the police had searched the apartment and found this? An American newspaper and a recent one at that! Do you realize how damning that would be?"

"Then what?" I shrugged. "What would they do?"

"They would interrogate you," my father said. "They would want the names of your contacts."

"I would never speak."

"They would torture you until you did," Gustave said.

"Unlike you, I am not afraid of torture," I said haughtily.

"How can you be so daft?" Gustave said.

My father lifted a palm to quiet us. "The thing is, Marceline, we would *all* get interrogated. They would not have to investigate for long before realizing we're here under a false name. From there they would see that I am a wanted man in France. And they would send me to an internment camp."

This chastisement was unfair coming from my father. He clearly had no idea that I knew of his involvement with the Géo Gras group. As the head of a cell, he put himself, and us, at risk every single day. Either Fernand was wrong, or my father was a fantastic actor. Either way, arguing with him was counterproductive. So I changed my tone, knowing it would serve me better to act contrite and repentant. I begged Father to at least let me give the translated documents to my contacts and tell them I could no longer help. He agreed to this but confiscated the dictionary, which I hardly needed anymore.

It never occurred to me, at any point, to obey my father. Had I not always gotten what I wanted? I resolved to be more discreet, and I convinced myself that no matter how angry my father seemed, he was secretly proud of me.

In early spring of 1942, things started to move fast.

The boys were already at Café Djurdjura when Béatrice and I arrived one afternoon. Fernand appeared to be in a jovial mood. "They are getting rid of him at long last," he said.

"Who?" I asked.

"That worthless Arab," Fernand said watching me intently. He squinted in the direction of Khaled, who stood by the entrance of the terrace, in his waiter's uniform, the usual white shirt, black pants, and long apron, his arms crossed in front of his chest, his expression inscrutable. We all turned to look at him, and he stared straight back at us, or, it felt, straight at me. Then he turned on his heels and disappeared inside the café.

"I heard that he quit," Béatrice said.

"Trust me, sweetheart," Fernand said, "these people are in no position to voluntarily leave a paying job."

"Why was he fired?" I asked, as casually as I could.

"The owner's Jewish," Émile said. "The government is putting a Frenchman from Lyon in his place. The new chap is hiring his own people, all pearly white French. Everyone here is laid off; the Jews and the Arabs."

"And we all know who will be the next undesirables: the Jewish clientele, present company included," André said.

I was stunned. Where would I see Khaled now? I had planned on the cat-and-mouse game playing out in my mind to last forever. "Let's not come to this wretched place anymore," I said. "Boycott the anti-Semites before they boycott us."

Fernand had a sarcastic smile. "How convenient, darling, now that the Djurdjura will have lost all its charm."

"What charm?" Béatrice asked. But the boys looked elsewhere and did not answer.

I buried my nose in my glass of iced lemonade, furious at Fernand, at myself, at Khaled. Had I been that transparent? And if so, did it mean Khaled knew? I was humiliated. Fernand hated Khaled. If he knew my feelings, he must have taken a perverse pleasure in watching me hide them.

As my friends bantered about other things, my mind raced. Khaled was leaving Café Djurdjura. He would forever disappear into this wide city, of which so many parts were forbidden to me.

Would I see him again?

A sense of powerlessness washed over me as the reasoning that I had so far managed to keep at bay suddenly imposed itself: I was being ridiculous. Khaled's silent, brooding good looks had been the perfect blank canvas onto which to project my fantasy, the romantic pull of impossible love. The thing was, nothing could ever take place between us. Had he been interested in me I would have no choice but to reject him. Between our two cultures and classes were nothing but animosity and suspicion. Our worlds only intersected in one place, Café Djurdjura. The café had been the gateway between our two very different lives, and now that door was closed shut. There were powerful rules, unwritten rules and some written ones, that forbade us to be in any form of contact. Muslims boys had to abide by a set of laws and constraints as restrictive as those imposed on French Jewish girls.

Khaled and I never could, and never *would*, become anything.

A lump in my throat swelled up. The notion that I might never see him again was intolerable.

The following day, a wiry boy from Montpellier had replaced Khaled. That week, all the Arab waiters, even those who had worked at the café for twenty years, were replaced one by one with friends of the new owner. That same week, the name of the café was changed to Bistro Belle France, but by then we had stopped going.

I had been feasting on glimpses of Khaled. Now that he was gone, there was nothing to sustain me. That was when I realized how much I had needed his presence, even on the periphery of my life. I had a consuming need for him. I felt depressed and angry at the same time. The thing was, powerlessness was not an emotion I handled well. I needed to do *something*. What, I did not know. I had the sense that, given the slightest push, I might do something irreversible.

All week, I walked through the streets of Algiers in a fog. At the sight of a thin, muscular silhouette, a shaved head, or a white shirt, my heart would race senselessly. Soon I had no choice but to admit the truth to myself: this walking through the street wasn't aimless; I was actively searching the crowds for him. I began to walk in and out of cafés and restaurants like a crazy woman, bumping into patrons. I was in and out of plazas and markets. I looked everywhere short of venturing out alone in areas of Algiers where men could be killed and women raped.

Then I remembered what the boys had said. When he was not working at the café, Khaled was a fisherman.

It took some convincing to get Béatrice to accompany me the next morning. "The fishing port? But why," she whined. "I hate the smell. What's the point? It's a bore."

"Oh, but it's so picturesque: the little boats, the market! I hear it's a lot of fun."

Béatrice looked unconvinced. "Let's go with the boys," she said.

"Must you do everything with them?" I said, exasperated. "Well, I shall go alone then."

Béatrice relented. She was grumpy when I picked her up at seven in the morning. "Why so early?" she asked. She contemplated my outfit. I wore my mother's best navy blouse paired with my new cream trousers. They were tightly belted at the waist, form-fitting at the hips, loose fitting around the leg and came floating down around the ankle. "Are you're wearing trousers?" she said without trying to mask her envy.

"Sandra sewed me a pair from a pattern," I said. This was the new fashion, a more masculine silhouette, although there was a gap between what we coveted in magazines and what was available in Algiers shops. I wanted to look like Ingrid Bergman that morning. I wanted to be irresistible.

Béatrice still pouted as we made our way down to the pier, straw baskets in hand. The market smelled of fresh fish and the sea. People were hungry and standing in lines all over the city for milk, eggs, and bread, but there was still plenty of fish if you had money. All around us were crates of sardines, anchovies, sea bass, red mullets, and groupers. There were cuttlefish, octopus, shrimp, and black sea snails by the bucket displayed over beds of crushed ice and algae. The shoppers were men, Arab women covered from head to toe, cooks of wealthy families, dozens of maids, and French housewives. The restaurant buyers and personal chefs of Algiers's elite loaded crates into automobiles while the rest of the populace, from French housewives to Arab mothers to maids to young kids holding fists full of coins, were left to haggle for inferior cuts.

I walked around the market, Béatrice in tow, scanning the crowd and ignoring the merchandise on display as I made my way closer to the boats.

A group of a dozen Arab men crouched around a long net punctuated with small red buoys. And there was Khaled among them! His focus was on his task, his hands agile as he passed a large needle in an out through the rough netting. I placed myself in front of Béatrice so that she would not see him.

"Oh, goodness gracious, this is awful!" I whispered to her with as much alarm in my voice as I could fabricate.

"What? What?" she asked in the same tone. "What's the matter?"

"I'm into a heap of trouble," I said, signifying to her with eye rolls that my period had just come unannounced: a complete lie. "If I take another step, I will stain everything."

"What do you want me to do?" she asked dully.

"I can't move. Find me a shawl or something to wrap around my waist."

"I don't have anything!"

"Then run home and get one! Quick!"

She looked at me with suspicion. "You want to stay here alone?"

"It's perfectly safe. Look, there are plenty of women here. And the police are here too. I'll stay right in this corner, and I won't move."

Béatrice dropped her straw bag and darted away. When she was out of sight, I advanced out of the shadows and stood about ten feet away from Khaled. Finally, he lifted his face and saw me. He expressed no surprise. He stood up, wiped his hands on a towel, walked away from the net and the crouching men and came towards me. When we were face to face, he watched me with keen interest, waiting for me to speak.

"You work here?" I said, stating the obvious.

"I remember you," he said softly, in his Arabic-accented French.

"From the Djurdjura. Yes." I smiled, fearing I was blushing. "I'm one of your best customers."

He shook his head. "I mean that I remember you from right here."

"The pier? I've never been here before."

He smiled. "You have. With your family."

I was astonished. "You saw us? That was nearly two years ago."

He cocked his head mockingly. "That day I was working. You don't remember? You had a white dress."

"I did?"

"I carried some of your luggage."

I searched his face, haunted by the faint memory. "Is that why you've been looking at me?"

He smiled with his eyes only. "I've been looking at you because you are beautiful." He said this without pretense or flirtation.

My chest swelled up like a balloon. "You know I really can't be here," I said. "I can't be here, and I can't speak to you."

"No, you cannot," he agreed. He seemed amused.

"And you can't talk to me either," I said. "Some people would have your skin for this."

His eyes were smiling. "Including that boyfriend of yours?" he asked.

I looked away. It did not matter how secretive Fernand and I were; everyone assumed we were together. "He is not my boyfriend," I said. Was that a lie? We spent time in bed together. And I sounded so terribly eager. Coming here in the first place reeked of desperation.

He seemed distant for a moment, looking past me. Then he said. "You see that area under the pier, to the right of us?" he said this without looking in the direction he was indicating. I looked to my right. Below the pier, dozens of dark wooden pillars created a shaded area that extended from the sand into the sea. A few men, their feet in the water, stood in the shade of the pier with their fishing rods, the lines taut in the water. "I go there every day to fish after work."

"You work at a fish market and you fish?" I said inanely.

"The fish I catch don't cost money."

"I see," I said, not seeing anything for the summersaults my heart was making inside my chest.

"Come here after six tonight," he murmured. "Meet me underneath the pier."

"I will," I whispered.

"I better return to work," he said.

"Yes, yes of course."

He turned away with a graceful economy of movement and went back to his crouching position working on the net. I watched the back of his neck, the tanned skin, and wanted to touch it. Our exchange had lasted all but two minutes, and already Béatrice was running toward me. "I got it!" she said. "I just remembered I had a shawl in my bag; we can wrap it around your waist—"

"False alarm," I said.

She pouted at my lack of appreciation and then looked at me askance. "Why do you look so happy? Are you playing some trick on me?"

"I just love fish!" I answered, taking her by the arm and guiding her away from the area with the fishing nets. I looked away so she wouldn't see that I was beaming.

At five that same evening, I told Mother I was going down to buy her cigarettes and hurried down toward the pier. Mother was taking her sleeping medication earlier and earlier, and by the time I left, she was already groggy. I had under an hour before my father returned from the office where he and Uncle Moshe worked. If I arrived home after him, he would demand to know where I had been.

It was tricky for a young woman to walk alone in Algiers's streets as curfew approached. Already overzealous French policemen did not need an excuse to stop people to inspect their papers, especially if they were young and pretty. I walked from store to store, pretending to be window-shopping. The police seemed more interested in Algerian men they could harass than in me, and so I went on undisturbed. When a policeman watched me too insistently, I entered a building as though I lived there. I came out again minutes later and continued down the street. Once there were no more shops, I wrapped a shawl around my head and shoulders and hurried down to the pier without being stopped. When I reached the beach, I removed my shoes and walked on the sand toward the fishing pier, more nervous as I got closer. In the distance, I could see a half dozen men, some on top of the pier and some on the beach. As I got closer, I recognized Khaled. His pants were rolled up, his feet were in the water, and his shirt was open and billowing in the warm evening sea breeze. He held his fishing rod with one hand and stood perfectly still, the lean muscles of his arm flexed. He glanced in my direction, and then straight ahead at the water, showing no expression. I stood silently about ten feet behind him with the intuition that if he was acting as though I wasn't there, that meant he expected me not to come any closer.

Someone looking at us from any vantage point would have seen two strangers standing on the narrow beach: a man fishing and a woman watching the sunset. Above the beach, a tandem of policemen on their rounds saluted me from afar. I waited, the wind ruffling my hair. The air and the light were soft. A hundred seagulls swirled in the sky above a tiny wooden boat painted white and blue. I did not feel impatient but expectant. I had the sense that the next moment would change my life.

After a few minutes, once the policemen were out of sight, Khaled lifted his rod and reeled in the line. A foot-long fish dangled from the hook, flailing and twitching, his silvery scales catching the light of the fading sun. Khaled unhooked the fish, dropped it in a bucket, and wiped his hands on his pants. He took his time bringing a cigarette out of a pack and to his lips. Only then did he walk toward me. But he did not come close. He stopped to my left and lit his cigarette. Still ten feet away from each other, we now both faced the sea. The sun approached the horizon, and our skins took on a golden hue. The water lapped the beach. Khaled's shirt billowed, and I caught sight of his smooth chest, his tanned skin. I watched him from the corner of my eyes, making sure not to turn my head toward him too conspicuously.

"I'm happy you came," Khaled said to the sea.

"I'm sorry that they fired you from Djurdjura. We're boycotting it, so that you know."

"Do not feel bad," he said. "It was time for me to leave."

"You were not happy there?"

"How could I have been?" he said.

"We will never be able to speak like two regular people, will we?" I murmured.

"Have you ever visited the Jardin d'Essai?" he asked.

"Yes. It's beautiful."

"Could you come there alone?"

"I think so."

"I will be there tomorrow. In the Allée des Dragonniers. At eleven in the morning."

"Is that a place where we can speak more … freely than here?" I asked.

Khaled's profile moved imperceptibly toward me, and his lips curled into a thin smile. "Up to a point," he said.

"I'll be there," I said.

"One of us has to leave now," he said, taking a puff of his cigarette and bending down to grab the rod he had planted in the sand. "People are watching."

He was right. Up above, standing over the parapet, a European couple there to enjoy the sunset was looking at us.

"I'll leave," I said, and I walked past him, continuing my stroll on the sand as though he and I were strangers, which in many ways we were.

I had been near him for only a minute, and yet those few instants felt so rich with meaning, so palpably exciting. I went home but could barely sleep that night.

The next day, I told Sandra that I was off to visit the Jardin d'Essai with Béatrice and my friends and hopped on the first trolley that took me in the direction of the garden.

The most mundane thing could become the pretext to check your papers and even detain you. Hoping to pass as older, since the police tended to show extra zeal toward unaccompanied girls, I wore Mother's fitted jacket, belted at the waist and widely padded at the shoulders, and my favorite A-line skirt. I had done my hair in the new style: hair parted in the center, small victory rolls on each side, the rest loose above the shoulders. If on the outside I appeared polished and collected, on the inside I was all in knots.

In the botanical garden, I made my way past the ten-foot tall strelitzia and the oleanders in bloom, up the cascading set of stairs, and past the circular lake surrounded by a lawn and flanked on each side by tall, willowy palm trees. From the central pathway, the view of the sea was majestic. It was windier than usual, and the wind carried the crisp smell of the sea. I followed the dirt alleys and made my way past more lawns and fountains, past the ficus alley until I faced the sign that read "Allée des Dragonniers." I thought I had stepped on a strange planet. This alley was a wide dirt path planted on each side with primeval-looking plants, half-trees, half-cactuses, with strange limbs that formed a canopy dense enough to block the sunlight almost completely. The thickness of the vegetation muffled all sounds besides that of my footsteps. There were no birds. The scent of the place was unknown to me, musky and sweet. I was alone in the alley save for an old man sporting an oversized turban who sat on a bench, his unlit pipe in his mouth, his eyes half-closed. I walked slowly, trying to calm the wild activity in my chest when a male voice said. "They call these dragon trees." I turned. Khaled was standing in front of me, tall, thin, beautiful. His eyes were on me, inquisitive. To my surprise, he was dressed in a garden guide's uniform. "The Latin name for them is Dracaena. I would love to tell you more about the Jardin d'Essai if you'll allow me," he said. I only nodded, unable to speak. It was the first time I saw Khaled truly smile, and it was like a beam of sunlight, an urgent happiness he was not trying to mask.

I had to say something to hide my sudden shyness. I pointed to the stout trunks of the trees, the strange knives-like blades atop bare branches. "Why are those called dragon trees?"

"Some species ooze a sort of red resin that has been used as a pigment since ancient time. They call this resin dragon blood."

"How peculiar."

"Surprisingly, these trees are in the same botanical family as asparagus." He lowered his head and laughed softly. "That is all I remember. I am still learning."

We walked next to each other in silence. I felt Khaled's presence next to me so violently that I had to control the shaking of my hands. The trees, the garden, the entire city of Algiers, even the war disappeared, and all I could sense was his body only feet from mine and the abyss that was the short space that separated us.

"Here we can be seen speaking to each other in daylight," he said once we were out of earshot of the old man on the bench.

"Are you actually a garden guide?" I asked.

"For a few hours a day."

"How many professions do you have? When do you ever sleep?"

"I constantly sleep," he smiled. "Usually as I work."

I laughed, "Is that what it is when I see you close your eyes in between taking orders?" He smiled, but I regretted saying this. I did not mean to let him know I spent time observing him. It seemed that around Khaled I had difficulty controlling what I said and did. "You know, I'm not worried about anyone seeing us speak," I said defiantly.

"I worry," he said.

I followed him onto a tiny path, barely a path at all, through a bamboo forest. He offered me his hand, which I took avidly. He guided me through thick vegetation, but I saw nothing; all I felt was my hand in his. We emerged out of the thickness of the bamboo forest into a small clearing the size of a very small room at the base of four tall eucalyptus trees.

"I discovered this place," Khaled said. "I come here when I need to think." The tiny clearing had a sharp menthol odor. The sun filtered through the canopy. Above, the tops of the eucalyptus swayed. A strong wind had picked up, but at the base of the trees, the air was still, and the sounds were muffled like inside a cocoon. Khaled stopped and turned to look at me. He was inches from me. I wanted him to touch me. He whispered, "All I want is to hold you in my arms."

"I want to be in your arms." I nearly begged.

My back pressed against the smooth, white bark of the eucalyptus's trunk, I let him kiss me. His kisses were nothing like what I had experienced before. I could feel them in every atom of my being. "I can't stop thinking about you," he murmured between kisses.

"Neither can I," I said.

He held me in his arms, and I surrendered to his kiss. I understood what should have been obvious from the moment I had first seen Khaled at Café Djurdjura: I would not be resisting him. There was no resistance possible.

All of a sudden, he stopped himself and stepped back from me. "I have to leave now," he said. I looked at him, confused. "If I stay longer, someone will notice that I am not at work." I was still breathless, thrilled. He caressed my cheek. "You stay here for a few minutes after I go so that no one sees us together." And he left.

I managed to make my way across the Jardin d'Essai and back to the trolley station. On the way back home, sitting on the hard leather of the trolley seat, my body swaying with the street car's meanderings, all sense of caution and reason had gone out the door. This was irrepressible. And right. I just wanted more of it; whatever "it" was I could not even name.

As I stepped out of the trolley, a violent gust of wind ruffled my hair. A corrosive mistral wind had appeared in a matter of an hour, frigid and unyielding. It pushed the tops of palms trees with increasing force. I shivered as I walked, and just after I crossed rue Michelet, I stopped, overwhelmed by a sense of catastrophe. Khaled had not made plans for us to meet again! He had not asked me! Doubt hit me with an almost physical force. I walked home against the wind, struggling to put one foot in front of the other.

That night, I lay awake on top of my blanket, replaying our encounter, the wonderfulness of being with him, the kisses, the sense of melting into one with another human being. But I was also gripped with doubt, and fear, and dejection. What if after kissing me, Khaled had lost respect or interest? What if, after kissing me, he had decided he did not like me after all?

The following day, I ran out of the apartment as soon as my father was out of the house. I was unthinking. I did not care if I was about to embarrass myself. I needed to see Khaled again. I took the trolley in the direction of the garden.

I walked around the park for an hour before I finally spotted him. He was guiding a group of older French women. I was quite far away, but I knew that he saw me. I went to wait in the clearing below the eucalyptus trees. There, I waited for fifteen minutes, out of my mind with anticipation and worry.

When he appeared, he advanced toward me as if pulled by my body's gravitational force and took me in his arms.

"You came," he said.

"Did you want me to?"

"I did not dare hope. But this is dangerous for you. Much too dangerous."

"I am not afraid," I whispered, kissing him.

The third day we met again. And again, the following day, and the next days after that.

Khaled could steal only a few minutes away from work before someone might notice his absence. Sometimes five minutes, sometimes ten, rarely more. Each day, I waited for him below the eucalyptus trees, my pulse racing. I burned with impatience, but at the same time, I could have waited in the small clearing all day with a mind devoid of other thoughts. Things that were ever-present sources of anxiety, the war, the oppression of the Jews, the terrible news from Europe, Father's well-being, Mother's bizarre descent into something that resembled insanity, now had recessed to the very back of my consciousness. I had always scoffed at the notion of love. It had seemed to me an invention, something silly girls and poets convinced themselves of, but that was merely self-delusion: an affectation. But now, I knew.

I wanted to be with Khaled more than I had ever desired anything. I knew nothing of him. But I knew his scent, his touch, the eagerness of his lips, the feel of his perfect, smooth, golden skin. And that was all that mattered to me.

Khaled had a system to meet without raising suspicion. I would make my way along the paths of the garden and eventually sit on a bench and read. I even took notes about plants as though I had an interest in botany. As soon as Khaled and I saw each other from a distance, we gave ourselves twenty minutes before meeting in the clearing, which I now referred to as our clearing. Our room.

We never had much time together. We would lie down on a blanket that we hid under thorny bushes covered with fragrant white flowers: Carissa macrocarpa, as Khaled called them. The shrub's flowers and the pungent scent of eucalyptus perfumed our encounters. Between kisses, and in our ten-minute increments, I got to learn about him.

Khaled was reluctant to talk about himself. His chin propped up on his hand, his elbow on the blanket, he spoke while studying my face, as though he was trying to unlock a mystery. I lay on my back on the blanket, my eyes lifted toward him. I too detailed his jaw, his skin, his beautiful eyelids, his brown pupils, the corners of his lips, upturned in a permanent half-smile that balanced the seriousness of his eyes. Above us, the silvery leaves of the eucalyptus canopy rustled in the wind against the bright blue sky.

"I am the eldest," he said. "We are twelve children. I have mostly sisters. My two brothers are five and three."

"What are your parents like?"

A shadow floated across Khaled's eyes. "My father is dead. I am the man in my family."

"You can't possibly be the head of a family of fourteen!"

He shrugged, "who else would be? I have no choice."

"What happened to your father?"

I had the sense that this was not a question he wanted to answer, but that he forced himself to for me. His face turned hard. "They took everything from him," he said. "They imprisoned him; they tortured him to make him talk about crimes he had not committed. Then they released him to die when he was too sick to recover."

"Who did this?" I said, outraged.

"It is in the past," he said, but the bitterness in his tone expressed the opposite.

"Tell me. Who?"

Khaled looked away. "Your people."

"My people?"

"The French," he said. His tone held anger and contempt.

"Those whom you call my people don't see me as one of them."

"Because you are Jewish?"

"How do you know that?"

"Those boys you are with," he said.

I wanted to move away from the topic of religion. I wanted to look for common ground between us, not for what could separate us even more. "How can you support so many, especially with the war?"

"Everyone in my family works, but I earn the most. Often, I sleep on the pier to be assured a morning's work mending nets after the fishing boats arrive at dawn. Afterward, I go to the sea to bathe, if I have time I go to the public bath. Then I take the trolley to work at the Jardin d'Essai. Before they fired me, I took the trolley to Café Djurdjura and worked until closing, sometimes until two in the morning."

"You sleep just a few hours a night?"

"I sleep in the trolleys too. The drivers know my family. They wake me up when I get where I need to be."

"This is much too hard," I said.

He had a bitter laugh. "When the French send me to war, I will be well prepared for it."

"How old are you?" I said, horrified at the thought.

"Eighteen soon."

"They won't give Muslims the French nationality, but they expect you to die for them?"

Khaled peered into my eyes with a burning intensity, as though he was recognizing something he had been hoping to find there.

"My father believed I needed an education as the first-born son," Khaled said. "My friends did not have to go to school, so I fought against it. But now I can see he was right. I was lucky to go to school until I was fifteen."

"But then you stopped?"

"My father was gone. It was my responsibility to earn money. For years at the garden, they only gave me chores: raking, weeding, watering." He shook his head. "I was the Arab, the nobody. Now they have fired the Jewish tour guides, and my education finally became useful."

He looked at me, and thinking perhaps that he had been insensitive toward Jews, he bent toward my face and kissed my eyelid gently. "I showed the boss that I had learned everything about the garden, and that I could read and write in French and Arabic and speak some English, and Italian, and German from working at the café. So, he hired me." He laughed softly to himself, as though this was impossible to believe. "They like me here. They trust me. My supervisor wants me to apply for a position as master groundskeeper. If I am accepted, it will pay better than all the other work I have combined. It would be a real career."

"When will you know?"

"I have to pass their tests. I borrow books from the library, and I am learning botany and biology the best I can. I need to know the names of plants in Latin, their genus, their common name. I have to recognize plants and label them, know how they will thrive, and in which part of the garden." The way Khaled spoke of plants, I could tell he was passionate about this work. And a horticulturist was a respectable profession. Already I hoped that Khaled would impress my father. "Part of it is observing, you know. And there are so many plants and families of plants. Less now with the war, but we receive samples and seeds from different nations all the time. And then we study them in the greenhouse; we grow seedlings, we propagate, we find ways to fertilize them and ways to make the soil better."

I sat up. "I can help you study," I said.

"I can manage," he said, visibly irked. "I don't need help."

"Is it because I'm a woman? You can't accept help from a woman?"

He beamed, and his face lit up. "I have angered you," he said.

"What is so funny?"

He caressed my face with his finger and then traced the contour of my lips. "What are you?" he asked.

"What am I?"

"Are you one of the bewitching Sirens of the tales? You have every power over me."

"I wish I were that magical," I said, laughing.

Khaled's eyes were so expressive, even as his face remained brooding. He began to speak as if lost in a reverie. "After I saw your family that first day at the pier, when I carried your bags, I did not see you again for months, and I did not know where I would find you, but I knew that I would one day."

"You were one of the very first people I saw in Algiers. Did you understand that we were being smuggled into the country?"

"I did not know what to think. But I saw that your family was worn out and afraid that morning. But not you. I knew that moment that you were not like other women."

"Not like Muslim women?"

"Not like any woman." He moved his face to kiss me, and I dissolved in his arms, buried my face in his neck and inhaled his scent.

"I would dream about you," he whispered in my ear. "I searched for you in the streets. I knew I should forget about you. I lied to myself; I told myself I wanted to see you just one more time, to see if the feeling would be there again, and that would be enough. And then one day you appeared at Café Djurdjura. I knew then that it was fate and that Allah wanted this."

I caressed his forearms. I wanted to be skin against skin, but that was out of the question. The risks we were taking were already enormous. We were hiding in the deep recesses of a public park. But if Khaled had discovered this secret place, others could stumble upon it too. For two young people to be found intertwined on a blanket, even fully clothed, was seen as indecent. But I was a French girl, Jewish, and he was an Algerian Arab, a Muslim, and those further transgressions might be enough to put us both in jail. At the very least, he would certainly be fired from work.

A week later, I asked Fernand to meet me on the pier, a public enough setting where we did not have to worry about the police asking us why we were there.

Now that pleasure boats had restricted access to the sea, the pier felt abandoned. I walked toward Fernand, who stood on the dock, smoking. He turned toward me and did not smile. His gray suit and hat aged him. In the nearly two years since we first met, we had stopped dressing like children and made every effort to look older than we were, but Fernand genuinely seemed aged, his flippancy now an affectation rather than genuine playfulness. The airs of his privileged youth seemed to have vanished, and in their place was an air of cold, calculating determination. This edge, this bitterness, was what war and injustice did to people.

I had declined meeting Fernand at the hotel for several weeks now, and he was perceptive enough to know that I was here to break up with him. "Are we to remain friends?" he asked before I could say anything.

"I'd like that very much," I answered. The truth was, friends were hard to come by, especially when you were Jewish, and I was not about to dispense with one if it could be helped.

"It is probably for the best, in the business we're in," Fernand said, "Better to keep the sentiments out of it."

I laughed. "I doubt that there were ever sentiments between us."

"Speak for yourself," Fernand said.

"Fernand, don't turn things around. You're the one with the fiancée."

"I am in love with you, sweetheart, and you know it," he said. "How could I not be? But you're a tough nut to crack."

"How so?"

"You don't need me. You don't seem to need anyone."

"That's not true," I said.

"A man wants to know he is loved and needed. It's never quite felt like that between us."

"Perhaps not," I admitted.

"I can't blame you for breaking up with me, darling. But if there is someone else, you better be clever about it. Choose someone who won't endanger you."

"I have no idea what you're talking about," I said. But I worried that Fernand knew exactly what he was saying, that he might be referring to Khaled, that he knew about us somehow.

He looked around, lit another cigarette, and hesitated. "This is as good a time as any to ask you something. Let's walk" he said. We walked past the moored boats, many of them in disrepair now that money was scarce, and war had shifted priorities. There was no wind, and the Mediterranean Sea was flat as oil. Buoys made dull clanging sounds as they knocked against each other. Above us, seagulls circled, cawing piercingly. "You have been useful," he began. "Your translations are precise. You don't need things explained to you: you get it. You're discreet."

"Thank you," I said warily. With Fernand, there always seemed to be a layering of motives.

"Don't thank me yet. What I'm about to ask you is something you should think twice about. We've been eyeing you for a bigger role. We're looking for...." He hesitated. "A woman's touch. A woman with your particular attributes."

"Which are?"

"There is this fellow, this German officer, in a post here in Algiers. We've been trailing the guy for months. We know his comings and goings. Some of our men have even been placed to be his bodyguards. But we need to know more about him. We need someone to get closer."

"How would that involve me?"

Fernand gazed at the horizon. "We think you might have the right kind of finesse."

"You want me to seduce a Boche?"

"Something like that."

Seducing a German officer: I let the concept sink in. "You might be overestimating my powers of persuasion," I said.

Fernand offered me a cigarette. "How could he resist a gal like you?"

I put the cigarette to my lips, and Fernand lit it. "If I'm as fetching as you seem to think, won't your Boche find it a little suspect that I would be interested in him?"

Fernand gave me one of his crooked smiles. "Darling, never underestimate the idiocy of men. We never doubt those kinds of things. He won't believe his luck and will promptly convince himself that his power and his uniform make him irresistible."

"Men can't all be that conceited."

Fernand lit his cigarette and inhaled. "For the time being, all you need to do is gain his trust."

"You mean his lust?" Fernand's response was to chuckle softly. "Don't ask me to go to bed with a German," I said. "I'm not that patriotic."

Fernand flashed that crooked smile. "We want you not to go to bed with him. As a matter of fact, we want you to resist him. We want his balls blue and his dick in a knot so that he won't be able to think."

"What is the goal?"

"No goal yet. Just thinking ahead in broad strokes. This is espionage, Marceline, infiltrate: inspire trust, all that swell stuff. Any little thing you learn might end up being of interest. How the fellow likes his lamb chops cooked. What's his favorite brand of pomade?"

"What kind of man is he?" I asked. I must have looked more worried than I wanted to appear.

Fernand shrugged it off. "Love, he's no match for you."

"Won't he be put off by the fact that I'm a Jew?"

Fernand brushed away that pesky detail with a swat of the hand. "No need to get into that. You don't look Jewish; your last name doesn't sound Jewish; there is no mention of it on your papers."

"Who is the 'we' you keep referring to? Is there really a 'we,' or is it just you?"

Fernand answered with one of his trademark questions. "You don't think I cooked this up all by my lonesome, darling?"

It dawned on me that what Fernand was asking me to do was much more dangerous than scribbling translations by the light of a candle. If caught, my false identity might be revealed, as well as that of my entire family. "I don't know about this, Fernand."

"We need a gal for this job, and you're the top choice. The clock's ticking, and we need an answer. Think about it, Marceline; the possibilities." He cocked his head and smiled. "The Wehrmacht, fooled. The outcome of the war, tilted in our favor. And at the center of it all, a beautiful Jewess."

I laughed. "Well, if you put it in those terms, how could a vain girl like me resist?"

"I know that if you choose to do this, it will have nothing to do with your ego," Fernand said.

"This entire war has everything to do with ego, starting with Hitler's, De Gaulle's, Churchill's, Roosevelt's, and down to the lowliest clerk in the Vichy administration, and ultimately down to you and me."

That night at home, no one said a word as we sat around dinner. Sandra had produced yet another depressing tagine made with canned vegetables. She had waited in lines for hours, but when it was her turn, there had been no meat or fresh vegetables left, and Father did not want her to encourage the black market. As Mother, already too thin, picked at her food without appetite, and as Father held the week-old newspaper, he was reading in one hand and ate with the other, my mind floated between Khaled, Fernand, and the Boche. We all looked up in surprise when Gustave's voice broke the silence. "I've inquired about enrolling into the Chantiers de la Jeunesse," he said.

We looked at him, incredulous. The Chantiers were a sore subject. Now that the French army had been dismantled, the Pétain regime had thought of creating a sort of military service without the military. Parents would enroll their sons in training camps where for months they were made to rise before dawn, "fortify" themselves with cold morning showers, work on their musculature, and perform "character building" activities. No one would subject themselves to this by choice, or so we thought. My father lifted the palms of his hands in incomprehension. "Why?"

"I want to do something," Gustave said proudly. "I'm seventeen."

My mother patted him on the arm. "Tss, tss, don't be silly now."

Gustave's face closed. "How is that silly?"

Mother used her most patient tone. "People pay bribes to prevent their sons from being subjected to something as strenuous as it is pointless. And besides, hiking for miles carrying bags filled with stones, digging useless trenches, and cutting down perfectly good trees like a regular lumberjack: I'm afraid it might not be in your disposition, darling."

After months of our mother hardly speaking or getting out of bed, the sudden burst of motherly wisdom did not sit well with Gustave. His face reddened. He made a point to ignore her and turned to our father. "The French army is gone, and anyway they didn't want Jews. The administration won't hire Jews. The schools won't teach Jews." Gustave gave me an accusatory look. "The Resistance wants Jews but for some reason is rejecting me."

"Shhh," my father said urgently, "we should never speak of this."

"I can't wait to see you in a Jeunesse uniform," I laughed. "A bouffant pair of pants, a knee-length cape like Zorro, a cravat and a beret that looks virile on no one."

"Many suspect there's a darker design behind the whole enterprise," my father said. "They say that the Chantiers de Jeunesse's purpose was never good health and exercise, or moral fortitude for that matter, but to build the youth into better slaves to dig up German mines and repair German railways."

"That's only a rumor," Gustave protested. "The Vichy government—"

Father interrupted him. "Any organization whatsoever created by the Vichy government we should mistrust."

Sensing rising tension, Mother made a small overture. "Well, I'm sure our Gustave would enjoy the camaraderie."

Gustave turned to her savagely. "No doubt you would applaud any opportunity to have me sent away."

"But," Mother protested feebly, "quite the opposite...."

Red-faced, Gustave stood up from the table, his fists in his pockets. "I know what I'm doing," Gustave said.

"No, you do not," said my father, who was turning as pale as Gustave was red. "What I want from you is that you do nothing risky. Don't act rashly, stay home, be safe."

Gustave's voice rose. "I'm not a child!"

"You are *our* child."

"You can't expect me to stay passive. I have nothing to do."

"There is plenty to do!" Father said. "You don't need school to study. Read books; they are free at the library. Volunteer with Jewish charities; help Sandra find better food for us."

"What's the glory in that?" Gustave snapped. "When men are dying for their countries every day?"

Now Father was raising his voice too. "And so you want to die with the lot of them? What will your death bring to this world? How will it improve it?"

"I am not afraid to die," Gustave announced.

My father sat stiffly at the table, full of contained rage. He spoke to both of us. "War may seem to be all glory and big sentiments in your overheated spirits. But war is a wretched thing! A wretched, wretched thing that tears your soul apart."

"Anyway, the age to join the Chantiers is twenty, so you're too young," I said.

Gustave turned to me. "One can request a derogation to go earlier if they wish."

"We'll see about that," my father growled.

Khaled and I saw each other every day except on the weekends, when the garden and streets were more crowded. I also spent time with Fernand, André, Émile, and Béatrice as we wasted entire afternoons at café tables nursing a single drink, usually syrup and water. Even when the others were out of earshot, Fernand did not mention the German mission. When I asked, he said that things were shaping up and to be ready for a day trip on a moment's notice. But nothing was happening, and so I forgot about it. I was so immersed in my love for Khaled that I couldn't give thought to much else. My entire days were governed by plotting my next escape so that I could run to the garden and see him.

When we were together, Khaled and I were starved for each other's physical presence, even if we had met just the day before. We wanted to learn about each other thoughts and dreams, looking for common desires, for proofs that we were on the same path. Our moments together were too brief. There was the ever-present risk of being discovered, compounded with the logistics of his work. He could not leave his post for very long, and so I spent a good deal more time in our secret clearing alone waiting for him than I spent with him. I was mad with craving for him. But being with him was a mix of agony and pleasure. I wanted his kisses, yes, but I wanted more. As inflamed as our kisses were, Khaled had impressive self-control and remained in every way a gentleman. It would have been inconceivable for me to be as forward as I wanted to be for fear of pushing him away. The frustration we felt expressed itself in arguments. We argued almost from day one, not as adversaries but as two passionate people bringing forth our differences and daring each other to meet halfway.

"I don't care about consequences," I told him one day as we lay down on our blanket. "I am not ashamed of being with you."

Khaled kissed my hair and said, "You do not care about consequences because you have never suffered any."

I pouted. "You sound like my brother."

"Your brother is wise."

"My brother would advise me against seeing you."

"And here again it would be wisdom." Khaled sighed deeply. "I am the crazier of us both. You refuse to imagine the consequences if we are discovered, whereas I know the consequences, and yet it does not stop me."

"And so, what if you are fired from this job. You are educated, intelligent. My father is a foreigner too. He managed. You could blend in if you tried. There is no stopping what you could do. You could become a lawyer, a banker, anything you wish—"

Khaled stared at me mockingly. "Blend in? Your culture is not something I aspire to blend into."

"Why not?"

He shook his head in amused disbelief. "This is the arrogance of the French mindset."

"What are you talking about?"

"I would like you to truly see my people, Marceline. See them when they are not serving the French. Our culture is ancient and beautiful. Or was, until it became one of servitude to the French colonizers."

"Haven't the French helped by—"

"Do you imagine my people want to be under French rule any more than the French want to be under German rule?"

"It isn't the same at all," I said, indignant.

Khaled spoke in a calm voice, but I could feel the rage behind the words. "Do you believe that we welcome happily the injustice done to us? Do you think we are glad that our land was stolen from us, our civilization upended? Do you think we want to be ruled by Catholics?"

"But look at all the positive things the French have brought to North Africa."

He shook his head in dismay. "Name one."

"The architecture, the buildings!"

"Where only the French and the Jews can afford to live?"

"How about museums? Gardens like this one, the education system, medicine?"

"We had our own. We don't want to be French, Marceline. Nothing about it appeals to us – not the way of thinking, not the way of conduct, not the principles, not the customs, not the clothing, not the food, not the music, not the medicine, not the religion, not the industrialization. We have our way of doing things, and we prefer it. Is that so hard to imagine?"

"But civilization!"

"Ha. That word. Here it comes! You call yourself civilized and us barbaric because it serves your purpose not to understand us. We are civilized. We have a civilization! You people have bastardized the word. And your education is not freely given to all. Do you know why that is?"

"No."

"Arab children don't get educated so that we can remain slaves to the ruling class, less than human."

"And why would the French want your people to be less than human?"

"That way you can do everything with us that pleases you. You can tell yourself that our rights and needs are less than your own. You can tell yourself that we can't be educated. You can convince yourself that we do not have the same emotions as you. Human emotions."

"I didn't mean to offend you," I said. "It's only that I see you as different from other Muslim men."

"I don't believe I am any different. I don't aspire to be."

"Usually Arab men aren't as ambitious as you are." As I said this, I already knew that I sounded bigoted.

"Most of us work incredibly hard and still live in near misery. And if we don't work, it's only because there is no work to be had. If we aren't educated, it's because your people have made it nearly impossible to be. We are starving. Families have to put their children to work as soon as they are old enough. No one can afford to have children spend their day in school until they're twenty."

I should have apologized at that point, but I continued. "You seem to aspire to something greater."

Khaled was angry. "My people aspire to greatness just as much as anyone. And we are a great people already, not some lesser class." He spoke with fury. "Do you have any idea of what it's like to be a Muslim in Algeria? Do you know how vulnerable my countrymen feel? In the span of one hundred years, we have gone from a flourishing, vibrant culture to becoming nothing in our own land."

"I was only asking a question."

"The police are French. The laws that rule us are made in France. The politicians who run this town are French people with no sensibility to our land or our culture and no understanding or respect for it. And yet French education is denied to us. The entire justice system is slanted against us. For people like me, there is danger at every turn. I could be arrested just for walking in the street having committed no other crime than to exist. And if I were arrested, what would become of my mother? And my brothers and sisters? It pleases you to see my people as inferior and think of me as the exception. But I am not different than they are. I am who I am because of my poverty, because of my religion, because of the last hundred years of injustice toward my brothers."

"Don't put me into the same bag as the people you loathe," I said. "Remember that I am Jewish. I am their victim as well. So don't be angry with me."

"You have done nothing, it is true, yet your thinking is corrupted. You see the world in terms of classes, and you don't want your thoughts rearranged."

I put my head against his chest, wanting to be forgiven. I knew he was right, but it was not in my nature to back down in a disagreement. "Still, though. You believe your country was better before, but you've never known Algeria without the French. How do you know that it wasn't worse?"

He took me in his arms and said, "Well, maybe the French will learn to feel German one day."

"Never!"

"Your children might. If they have never known it any other way."

"Perhaps Christian children would. Being Jewish, my future children's chance of integration would be nil."

"Then you know how we feel. The French and the Germans have similar ancestry, a similar faith. Assimilation is possible. But Arabs were seen as inferior by the French colonizer one hundred years ago, and today is no different. And that is how they see the Jews now. Meanwhile, Jews and Arabs look down at each other and neither Jews nor Arabs consider marrying each other."

"You don't know that for a fact."

"Ask your parents how they feel about it."

"My mother is not a good example," I said. "To her, no one will be good enough for me. Unless I marry a Baron."

"Who is this Baron?" he said, glowering.

I laughed, "Oh, any baron will do. Even an ugly one three times my age. My mother is not picky in that regard."

"Why not a prince?" he asked. He was laughing now, and I was relieved.

"That's what I say!" I put my arms around his neck. "I already have my prince."

We lay side by side and looked up at the swaying treetops and cloudless sky, holding hands. After a while, he said, "We are here, you and me, in our clearing. And the shade of these trees is for both of us, and the birds sing for both of us. In front of nature, in front of God, we are the same. But in the world of men, things are different. In the world of men, I could never be one of your people, and you could not become one of mine."

"Why are you saying that?"

"I am reminding myself. Sometimes I want to forget."

"First, it's not true. We can be what we want."

"No, we cannot. Look around."

"The world changes faster than we can imagine. That's what my father always says."

"It changes for the worse."

"Not always," I said, not believing it as I said it. "Sometimes the world changes for the better."

Fernand came to me the following day. Instructions, he said, would come at a moment's notice, but I needed to set up a pretext to be gone for the day so I could take a train to nearby Oran sometime that week. "Dress to look attractive but respectable, the kind of girl you introduce to your parents," he had said.

I told my family that I was spending the day with Béatrice. We'd be looking through town for things that were hard to come by: good soap, nail polish, ointments, shampoo. My parents were too preoccupied with their own lives to pay much attention.

Three days later, I was on a crowded train to Oran. At the station, the day before, Fernand had handed me a third-class ticket for Oran, and a first-class ticket for the way back to Algiers. I was to have my 'chance' encounter with the Boche on the way back.

When I entered the third-class car, the Arab men, women, and children around me, pressed shoulder to shoulder, turned silent. I sat in a wooden seat by a window. The air was hot and sticky. I was ridiculously overdressed in my pearls, my small hat tilted to the right, and the gray flannel A-line skirt and belted jacket stolen out of Mother's closet and re-cut, re-sewed and re-purposed by Sandra at my insistence. As crowded as the car was, with many people having to stand most of the way, no one even attempted to sit next to me.

When the train began to move, conversations resumed. I observed the women in their white cloaks and headscarves. Many had children in their laps, and at their feet were bags of belongings. The women spoke to each other but not to the men. The men's faces were profoundly sun-weathered. The adults did not look at me. Only the children observed me by turning around in their seats, although when I smiled at them, they did not smile back. In fact, many of the children looked at me with defiant hostility.

I thought of the Boche, of the mission, a mission I had no doubt would fail. I was an attractive young woman, but I knew nothing of what might seduce a man. And besides, I hated the Germans. Every last one of them. How could my demeanor not show it? To me, there was no such thing as a decent German, no matter how friendly they pretended to be. I saw them as a monolithic block of evil warmongers, and I'd sooner see all Boches dead than have to change my opinion about even a single one of them. As the train bumped along, I tried to keep my mind on the mission ahead, but the angry stares of the children unsettled me. Was that hatred I read in their eyes? I thought of what Khaled had told me, and it dawned on me that I was their invader. I was *their* Boche. Whatever politeness or friendliness I had experienced on their part, and accepted as my due, must have been no more sincere than the obsequiousness most of us adopted in dealing with the Germans. I hated our invaders with all my might. And as I sat stiffer in my seat among these people, Khaled's people, I had the sickening feeling that they felt the same about me.

****

I had boarded the nine-a.m. train for Oran and arrived there a few hours later with no idea what was about to unfold. I could not imagine the stakes being high, perhaps because Fernand and I seemed little more than children. But when the train arrived in Oran, and I saw Fernand through the window, I had a sinking feeling. He had his hands in his coat pocket and his hat pulled down over his forehead. He looked tense, dark, unsmiling, and very much like an adult. I understood in an instant that this was not a game, and if it was, it was the kind that could cost us our lives.

He helped me down the steps and spoke fast, under his breath. "You'll be boarding in two hours. He's already on the train, coming from Tlemcen. We know which car he's in, and we've arranged for you to get a seat there." He handed me a first-class ticket to Algiers.

"I don't know the first thing about him."

"It's better that way. So nothing can slip by accident. We don't know why he's in Algeria. We know he's an engineer. Did he pull favors to get himself a cushiony assignment in Algiers away from combat, or did Hitler send him? Why would Hitler send engineers to Algiers? These are all things we want you to find out."

"How could I? Fernand, this is ridiculous!"

"Just relax. For now, just be yourself. We simply want you to meet and hope for sparks."

"And afterward?"

"Get close to him."

"You know there will be limits as to how close I am willing to get."

Fernand was irritated. "Either you do this, or you don't. I vouched for you. I told people you were the right gal for the job."

"I, yes. I am. I'll do it. But what if the Boche isn't interested in me?"

Fernand dismissed the possibility entirely. "You'll have him eating out of the palm of your hand in no time. One thing, though…."

"Yes?"

"We have friends on the train, watching over you. In case things turn sour."

"I need protection?" I said, stiffening as I scanned the platform.

"Don't look," Fernand urged, but already I had spotted at various distances from us a burly boy on a bench smoking a cigarette, his hat firmly screwed on to mask his eyes, and another young man with his face buried in a newspaper. A third one was conspicuously staring at his cuticles. All three were very young; one of them did not look a day over sixteen. All made brief eye contact with me and then looked away. "They'll be boarding when you do," Fernand said. "You're in no danger; this is just an insurance policy. Remember, you're just a pretty girl boarding a train. If anyone wants to see your papers when you get into his car, let them see them and don't sweat it. He's got bodyguards, but this is not an occupied zone. They have no jurisdiction."

Air got caught in my lungs, and I forgot to breathe for a moment. Was there still a way to back out of this? But the excuses I could think of felt weak. *Just a girl boarding a train*, I repeated to myself. "What's his name?" I asked in what I hoped to sound like a self-assured voice. "Where in Germany is he from?"

"It's better for you to know nothing about him. Let him tell you all this. You're a student. You're a good girl. You have a nice mom and nice dad, a darling little brother. Don't say anything else for now. We'll come up with a solid cover; we'll even sign you up for school if he takes the bait."

I frowned. "So what do I do exactly? Talk to him? Introduce myself? Strike up a conversation?"

"Marceline, you're supposed to make him fall in love with you."

With these words, Fernand retrieved a package wrapped in brown paper out of his coat pocket, pushed it into my hands, turned around, and left.

I stood rigid, alone on the platform. What was I holding? The package was a bit heavy and rectangular, like a book perhaps, but with a small bulge in the center. To my left and my right, the young men were nowhere to be seen. I tried to control my growing panic. I could leave right now. Throw the package in the trash. Take the next train. Go home and forget about the delusion that had brought me here in the first place. But almost immediately, the train entered the station, and when it stopped, I was facing the first-class cars. People came down from the train; others went up the steps and disappeared inside. And for a moment, I stood as if frozen. I looked at the steps. There was no time to think. I took a breath, stood straighter, and climbed aboard.

Inside the first-class car, it was all polished brass and woodwork, as luxurious as the third class had been sparse. Plush green velvet covered the seats. The windows were open to let in the breeze, and it smelled of powdery women's perfume. Each compartment was composed of two rows of three seats that faced each other. The train was full, and each seat was taken, with more people standing in the corridors. Looking at the number above each sliding glass door, I walked to the number of the compartment marked on my ticket.

Two men with square jaws stood in front of the compartment as if guarding the door. I did not doubt that they were police or military. I heard them speak in French. Through the glass, I saw the German officer who sat by the window. The only two other people in the compartment were an old husband and wife. Three seats were left open, the one by the window across from him, and the two seats for his bodyguards, who seemed intent on remaining in the corridor. Right then I lost my nerve, what little I had, and walked right past the compartment. My rookie escorts, if they had not already scampered away, were no match for these men.

Suddenly, the train shook and rumbled. Almost immediately after, it began to move out of the station. I was deep into this now. What else could I do at this point but sit in my assigned seat? I did not have to say a single word. I could sit there and wait for the train to take me to Algiers. I would tell Fernand that the Boche had not even looked at me. Maybe he didn't like women after all.

I headed for the bathroom, my heart beating along with the rhythm of the accelerating train, my fingers gripping the package.

In the bathroom, I opened the package. No gun or bomb, thank goodness. In fact, I wanted to laugh when I saw a school textbook and a tube of contraband lipstick. Chanel! I opened the tube. The intoxicating scent, the sight of bright red plunged me back into the world of before, the world of small luxuries and vanities, the world where people did not fear for their lives. With a surprisingly steady hand I applied the lipstick and smiled at my reflection. Fernand, that scalawag, knew what he was doing. The lipstick changed my look from teenage girl to a captivating cross between a studious young woman and budding femme fatale – or so I hoped!

I exited the bathroom, walking past two of my escorts, who must have climbed on the train behind me. It was nice to know I wasn't alone. I walked toward my compartment with flutters in my stomach. The guards didn't move away from the door as I stopped in front of the compartment. "My seat is in here I believe," I told them.

"Show us your ticket," one of the men said, "and your papers."

I presented the men my ticket and papers, ready to dart away, wishing they would deny me entry. They must not have seen me as too big of a threat because they barely glanced at them before letting me inside the compartment.

The German man I was supposed to seduce rose and saluted me with gallantry. He was not the portly, balding, heinous Nazi I had pictured, but an intellectual-looking young man in his early thirties, acne still haunting his face. I smiled with what I hoped to be sufficient coyness and sat across from him.

The older couple nodded at me, then ignored me. The wife occupied herself with crossword puzzles. The husband promptly fell asleep. In the corridor, the bodyguards stood by a pulled window smoking, throwing their butts out into the dry landscape every so often.

The train ride from Oran to Algiers would take five whole hours. I had no idea what to do next. For fifteen interminable minutes, I stared out the window, seeing nothing, trying to look normal, but not remembering what normal was supposed to look like. I felt the German soldier's gaze on me but could not be sure. Once the pounding of my heart subsided, I took out Fernand's book from my purse. It was an engineering textbook. I pretended to read for a few minutes, but it might just as well have been written in Japanese. I scrunched up my face and soon closed the book with a sigh.

"Forgive my impudence, Mademoiselle," he said, unable to resist such serendipity, "but are you pursuing engineering studies?" He spoke an accented but polished French.

I blinked, appeared hesitant to speak and said, "Architecture, as a matter of fact." Instinctively I had changed the pitch of my voice to sound younger, and I guess stupider. "To be honest, I understand none of it."

"It is a fascinating field, and so useful especially in our times," he said.

I pouted, "How will I become an architect's secretary if I cannot understand all the geometry."

"Oh, but you must not get discouraged," he said, his eyes glimmering with earnestness. "The architect bothers with all this; you only need to learn to support him in his work."

"I just started my classes, and I obviously know nothing yet," I said. "I'm not even certain that this is what I want to do."

"It's a matter of discovering your aptitudes. I am an engineer myself," he said.

I batted my eyelashes. "Did you always know you had aptitudes?" I asked.

We conversed for the rest of the trip. I was keenly aware of the men standing guard on the other side of the glass door. They would glance at me every so often, not with suspicion, but with amusement, perhaps contempt. The German's thrill to speak to me was almost painful to watch. I measured my every word and tried to appear reticent. I had to. He was, after all, the occupier, and any other behavior on my part would have been suspect or else a show of poor respectability. I told him I had visited an aunt in Oran for the day and was going back home in Algiers. I said as little as I could about myself. I was a student. I had a brother. My father was in the import business. He said he was from Heidelberg, describing it as a small paradise. I acted pleasantly and listened with feigned interest to his exposé on the thrills of engineering. What I found trickiest was to act demure. The things women must do and say to appear unthreatening to men are harder to master than one would think.

By the end of the journey, as the train rolled into Algiers, we still had not exchanged names. One thing was clear to me: he had to pursue me, not the other way around. He liked me; this much was obvious, but he was no ladies' man, and I wondered if he would muster the courage to ask me out. Because yes, it was a game indeed. And I wanted to win.

He gave me his hand to help me out of the train and offered to give me a ride home. I declined. No well-bred young French woman would enter the car of a stranger alone. He walked me to the taxi station and introduced himself at last. "*Oberleutnant* Dietfried Von Becker," he said. Here I was, a nineteen-year-old Jewish girl with a fake identity, flirting with a Senior Lieutenant of the Wehrmacht. He offered me his hand to shake. "I – had a lovely time making your acquaintance, Mademoiselle—"

"Marceline Dupont," I said, shaking his hand, but he took it instead and reddened as he pressed his lips to my glove with cringeworthy eagerness. He was just being a shy, awkward boy, courting a girl. He was German, and he was the enemy, but I felt that there was nothing monstrous about poor Dietfried. "It was lovely to speak to you too," I said, smiling for added encouragement. To this, he responded by opening his mouth and closing it without uttering a sound. He held the door to the taxi for me, and I entered slowly to give him more time. If he let me go now, that was it, the so-called mission was a failure, but Dietfried made no move.

"Au revoir, Mademoiselle Dupont," he said.

"You can call me Marceline," I said as pleasantly as I could, though inside I was fuming about his ineptitude. Because now I *wanted* this. It had been the highest of highs, and in the last few hours I had discovered one thing about myself: I definitely had the nerve. The door was shut. The taxi began moving. I was furious. This fool's golden opportunity was missed, and my exciting career as a spy over before it started. But just as the car moved a few meters, there was an urgent rap at the glass. I ordered the driver to stop and rolled down the window.

"I was wondering," Dietfried said, red in the face. "I am new to Algiers. I don't know anyone in the city, and I ... well, you were so kind. I was wondering if you could recommend...." He tried to think of something to add. "Good local restaurants."

"There are many excellent ones. Now, of course, with the restrictions, things have changed. I guess I could write down addresses for you. I don't know them by heart."

"Perhaps I could telephone you some time," he suggested. "Or you could telephone me?"

"Well, I'm not sure how...."

"I apologize, I often forget that not everyone has a personal telephone."

Although Father had a Bakelite telephone installed at the apartment the month of our arrival, I pretended to be impressed. "A personal telephone? I suppose that if you gave me your details, I could call you from a phone box."

"Please do!" Emboldened, he tore a piece of paper out of a notepad in his coat pocket and handed me his number. "Thank you, so very much!" He added ridiculously, "I shall be standing next to the telephone day and night waiting for your call." He tried to make it sound like a wisecrack, but both of us knew he meant it.

"I will call you tomorrow," I said.

As the taxi drove me away from Dietfried, I felt exhilarated with power.

I asked the taxi to drop me off on rue Michelet, and I walked on clouds the rest of the way. When I arrived in front of my family's apartment building, Fernand was leaning against the entrance door, waiting for me.

"I better sign up for school," I said, beaming.

"You talked to him?"

"We practically have a date," I said.

Fernand whistled admiringly. "Good girl," he said. "I knew you'd be great at this. We're going to build you a cover solid as bedrock, I promise."

"You better," I said. "Now I better run upstairs. I'm late for dinner."

When I entered the apartment, Sandra, who was coming out of the kitchen, gave me a forewarning look. Mother, Father, and Gustave were already sitting at the dinner table. "I'm sorry I'm late," I chirped, sliding in my chair. My father didn't look at me, but Gustave's thrilled expression told me I was in trouble. Mother lifted her face mournfully and stared through me with vacant eyes. Since her diagnosis of anhedonia, the cocktail of medicine prescribed by our doctor made her agitated to the point of paranoia during the day and useless by dinnertime. Apparently, the Benzedrine had worn off, and the Barbital she took for sleeping had kicked in. Throughout dinner, the only sounds were the clicking of forks on plates. I would have preferred punishments and admonitions than the strained silence that weighed on me through dinner. Before Sandra bought our mint teas, Mother rose from the table and walked to her room like a somnambulist.

As soon as she had left the room my father said, "I did not want to upset your mother, but now I want an explanation about why you were out in the streets until that hour."

"I was spending the day with Béatrice."

"To go where?"

"We were looking for shampoo."

"Until past dinner time? And where is that shampoo?"

I said the first lie that came to my mind. "We didn't find any, so we decided to visit the Jardin d'Essai," I said. "And then we got held up."

My father would have none of this. "Held up by whom? Bandits?"

"We were just … our trolley broke down, and we had to wait for them to repair it."

Father crossed his arms. "And if I were to call Béatrice's house, her mother would attest to this?"

I looked at him with innocence. "Yes," I said.

"Only I already called," he said, clearly furious. "She said Béatrice stayed home and neither of them saw you all day."

I took the offensive. "I am nineteen. You have no right to spy on me!"

"I have every right!" my father snapped. He was yelling at me but silently, so as not to upset Mother, and the result was almost comical.

"Baba was not spying," Gustave said, taking it upon himself to defend my father. "He was worried."

"Stay out of this, Gustave!" I said. "Baba doesn't need an interpreter."

"You think you can get away with everything," Gustave said.

"I don't want to hear that you have any more involvement with those factions," my father said.

I looked askance at Gustave. "I thought you said never to speak of It in front of him." 'It' was the Resistance, the word that must not be pronounced at home. Gustave looked at me with hatred.

"Those people don't know what they're doing," my father continued. "They're mere children playing with your life."

My father's statement rocked my confidence for a moment. Did he know something I didn't? But the German officer was real. The intelligence about the train, the plan, none of this had been child's play. What if Fernand was mistaken about my father's involvement in the Resistance? If my dad was part of the Resistance, would he try to stop Gustave and me from getting involved in something he believed in strongly enough to risk his safety? If the Resistance was too dangerous for us, wasn't it also too dangerous for him? In a split second, I decided to feign the innocence of the wrongly accused. "I'm late for dinner. When has it ever happened before? Never. And now you're reading me the riot act?"

Gustave chimed in, "If they stop you after curfew and they ask to see your identity papers, you put Baba and all of us at risk."

"Don't be a hypocrite, Gustave," I said. "You do plenty to put us at risk, sniffing in affairs that do not concern you, knocking at every door to join the … group."

My father stood up from the table. He looked at Gustave, his rage barely contained. "I forbade you to go near Géo Gras!"

My father's tone, his outrage, struck me as ridiculously unfair, especially if he was indeed knee-deep in the Resistance.

"If Gustave wants to be heroic, then let him embarrass himself," I said.

"I have every right to help our cause," Gustave snapped.

In one tremendous bang that had Gustave and me jumping up in shock, my father slammed both fists against the table, toppling wine glasses, and sending the salt shaker onto the floor. "Enough! Both of you!" He stood there, red-faced, beside himself with fury, he who was usually so soft-spoken and measured. He shouted, "I'll tell you how you can help our cause! By remaining alive! You want allegiance to something, both of you? Have allegiance to me!" Sandra hurried into the room and looked at him with surprise and pain. Perhaps my father realized then that he was shouting. He lowered his voice, but the fury was palpable in his every word. "Focus on your family. Keep yourself alive! Pointless bravado will never make you a hero. It will make you a dead person." Staring at Gustave, he said, "You want to be heroic? I'll give you a mission: watch your foolish sister's every move and make sure she stays out of trouble."

I jumped to my feet, enraged. "If Gustave puts his nose in my affairs, I will kill him with my bare hands."

My father, at his wit's end, said, "If Gustave doesn't stop you, I will. Starting with forbidding you to take a single step out of this apartment." He looked at Sandra, who was standing stiffly by the door, and he seemed to have an epiphany. "In fact, I am implementing some changes starting immediately."

My father told me to make space in my bedroom for Sandra's things. "Now you will share a room with Sandra," he said in a tone that didn't tolerate contradictions.

"Baba! Why on earth?"

"That way, you won't get any ideas about going out at night."

As he said this, Sandra, looking apologetic, was entering my room with a bag, blankets, and pillows. Following behind was Gustave, dragging her mattress.

I sat on a chair looking falsely contrite. I was not worried about Sandra sharing my room, but it was better if they believed they had won the battle.

After they had left my room, I watched Sandra put her bed together. "You won't say a word about me to anyone, will you?" I asked her.

Sandra looked at me. Her eyes were kind, but she looked torn. "Your father has told me to look over you," she said.

"Whose side are you on?" I said. "You know he has no reason to fear for my safety. So, I have a boyfriend, big deal. You've covered for me before, and this is no different. I'll have you know that I plan to continue to do as I see fit."

"If you do things your father and mother do not like, I must tell them," she said.

"Do you really want to be the bearer of bad news to poor Mother?"

Sandra gave me a pleading look. "Please, Marceline, do not go out at night. It is all I ask."

I put my arm around her. "Let's you and I come to an agreement. You let me do what I want during the day, and I promise to stay home at night."

She did not agree nor disagree, as was her habit.

Prudently I waited for things to settle, and I did not return to see Khaled for three days. On the fourth day, I told Mother and Sandra that I was going to study at the library with Béatrice – my usual excuse – and jumped on the trolley in the direction of the Jardin d'Essai. Just in case Gustave had taken my father's ridiculous orders to heart, I devised a convoluted way to get to the garden, taking four different trolleys and buses, looking behind me to make sure he was not following. I told myself I ought to be more careful. But I was high with euphoria and denial. I was giddy; this was April 15th, the one-month anniversary of our first meeting at the clearing. I was carrying a basket, a picnic lunch that I had managed to sneak out of the house, with real cheese Sandra had found at the market and homemade bread.

There was a new balminess to the air. Khaled and I lay on our blanket, ate our cheese and bread, and kissed. Khaled had been more of a gentleman than all the boys I had met until now. He had not even attempted anything other than a kiss. I could tell this was not out of shyness on his part, but a choice. We were talking about this and that. I lied to him about the reason I had not been able to come and told him that I had been visiting Oran with my family.

"There are many beautiful mosques in Oran," he said. "Have you visited them?"

"I did not know that was allowed."

"Mosques are for everyone."

The subject of our respective religions was one we carefully avoided. I told myself I didn't want to dwell on it, and that it didn't matter, but really, I was worried about the topic. "Do you spend a lot of time in mosques?" I asked tentatively.

"I rarely have the time," he said.

"And so ... you're not very religious?"

"I don't need to be in a certain place to feel Muslim," Khaled answered. "Islam is who I am, how I see the world. Islam is everywhere. It inhabits everything."

"Same for me," I said, relieved. "I'm not practicing, but I know down in my bones that I am Jewish. But thousands of years of beliefs and traditions only define me up to a point. I would not want to be narrowed down to some clichés if I were Christian or Muslim either. Why do people want so terribly to belong to a group? Does that reassure them? It does not reassure me! Is people's sense of identity so tenuous that they crumble if they don't classify themselves and align themselves with one religion or another?"

Khaled looked at me with an amused expression. "You are speaking of the political," he said. "I am speaking of the mystical."

"The what?"

"My connection to Allah."

Khaled had a connection to Allah? I did not have a connection to Adonai or anything of the sort. "Do you ever feel that you might be betraying your religion when you are with me?" I asked.

"No," he said thoughtfully. "Not yet."

"Religion is not significant to French Jews," I said, not even knowing whether it was true. "We mostly had to brush our religion aside. To be French, you know."

"So why do you spend all your time with other Jews?"

"Who else will have us?" I said dryly. "Muslims hate us, Christians hate us. I'm not ashamed of being Jewish if that is what you are asking."

He smiled. He had seen the anger rise in me. He seemed attuned to my emotions and could discern what I was feeling even before I could. He moved strands of my hair between his fingers. "Why would I think that?"

"Judaism is nothing like people depict it," I said. "We are not how the world sees us!"

"Is your faith strong?"

I deflected the question. "Religions bring people further from spirituality, not closer. Immoral men invented religions so that they could rule over the moral ones."

"Even so, humans need God to fill the sense of void we all feel inside. It is a void that nothing else can fill."

"I have faith in men," I said. "I know, it seems unlikely at the moment. But I believe that if a single evil man can alter the course of things and destroy the world, a single good man – or maybe a woman – can repair it."

"Like Jesus?"

"Like Tikkun Olam."

"Who is that?"

"It's not a person; it's an idea. It's not about the heavenly afterlife for us Jews. Tikkun Olam means to repair the world; it's the positive impact we can have in the here and now that matters. Not that I've had much personal success with this."

He looked at me tenderly. "You need to do nothing other than walk on this Earth to make it better," he said.

We lay on our backs, our hands intertwined, watching clouds move briskly in the azure sky between the treetops. Already, it was time to go. How long had we been together? No more than fifteen minutes. It felt like an instant. It felt like a lifetime.

Khaled left the clearing. I waited ten minutes and left too. I walked down the alleys toward the exit in the dizzying state my encounters with Khaled always left me, but today, I also felt uneasy. Per Fernand's instructions, I was to telephone Dietfried that afternoon.

It had been four days since our meeting on the train, and I had had time to think about the mission. If it came about that Nazi Germany swallowed all of Europe, my father's plan was to flee. He spoke of going deeper into Africa, all the way to South Africa if need be. Me, I wanted justice. I wanted to win the war. I wanted to crush them all. I wanted Hitler and all his generals, the anti-Semites, the racists, the bigots, the cowards, the crooks, everyone in the Vichy government, the haters, the monsters of this world vanquished. I wanted them to suffer. I wanted to see corpses and skulls riddled with bullet holes. I would fire those bullets myself if I had to. I wasn't naïve. I knew that I was about to engage in something I would not be able to control. I also knew that I would disappoint people I loved if they saw me with a German officer. My family and Khaled would be devastated to learn that I was spying for the Resistance, but even more so if they thought that I was fraternizing with the enemy, and I would not be able to justify myself without revealing my mission. The thing was, neither my father nor Khaled would take too well to the news that I spent time with a Nazi, whatever the noble reason for it.

I passed the central pond and walked in the shade of the cypress trees. Was I effectively becoming a spy? This would mean paying closer attention to details beyond my narrow field of vision. In the last few years, we had learned to suspect everything and everyone; we made sure not to speak when we could be heard. Now I needed to become even more vigilant. For one, I needed to be certain that no one followed me. I needed to watch people better in case suspicious faces sprang up in too many places. Also, I was too visible, too young, too well-dressed. I needed to dress down, put a shawl over my hair, blend in.

Rather than follow the main path toward the exit, I veered left to the area that cut through a patch of dense strelitzia. As a mental exercise, I tried to archive in my mind all the smells, sights, and sounds around me.

But some smells, sights, and sounds must have escaped me because as I came through the strelitzia and stepped into the alley, I suddenly found myself face to face with my brother! He appeared as shocked to see me as I was to see him. "What are you doing here?" I shrieked.

He had his hand on his bicycle. There was sweat on his forehead, as though he had been riding up a hill. His shorts revealed strong calves from the incredible amount of bicycle riding he did up and down the streets of Algiers, as though he were training for the Tour de France. "Same as you," he said. But the real answer came in the redness of his face and the guilt in his eyes.

"You were following me!"

Gustave tried to sound casual, "Stop thinking you are so special that I would care what you do."

How long had he been following me? No, it was impossible. Not after the circuitous route I took to get here. And then I remembered: the day I had gone to Oran I told my father that I had been visiting the Jardin d'Essai. Either this was a coincidence, and my brother had wanted to visit it as well, or Gustave had come here looking for me. The second option was most likely the correct one, or he would not be here, looking guilty. Anger rose through my body. "Oh, but you care," I said, furious. "You're obsessed with me in fact."

Gustave shoved his hands in his pocket to look unconcerned. Using the tone of a mature man he said, "It's not safe for a girl to roam the city the way you do. You should be appreciative that I keep an eye on you."

I stepped toward him menacingly. "I don't need defending; I'm not a damsel in distress like in a stupid book. Get that notion out of your head. If anyone needs defending, it's you, no matter how many push-ups you can do."

He scoffed at this with an arrogance I wanted to slap off his face. "Why would I need defending?"

"I've been defending you since you were six years old, stupid," I said, spitting out my words. "It's always been like that. You can't get anyone to like you or trust you. People want to beat you up. If it weren't for me, the men of Géo Gras would have given you a beating already."

He seemed taken aback by my meanness. He stuttered, "You – You're – conniving, you – use people. You care about no one but yourself."

"And you're nothing but a wimpy baby with bulging muscles and a scraggly mustache!"

Now his eyes were red, as though he might very well cry. "You don't help Mother at all!" he exclaimed.

I was puzzled by this lame accusation. "Mother needs to take care of herself," I said. "She's the parent and not the other way around. You take care of Mother if you're so inclined, only you despise her more than I do."

Gustave stood taller and said haughtily, "Father does not know half of the ways in which you are degrading yourself, and I am the one you should thank for that."

I wondered if he was referring to the time he saw me leave the Hotel de Paris after seeing Fernand, or if he knew about Khaled, or if he had seen me step out of a train with a German officer. Just what was the extent of his spying on me?

Siblings fight. It's innocent at first. But parents often dismiss children's rivalries. My parents noticed nothing out of the ordinary in the increasing fighting between my brother and me, or if they did, they did not act. "Like oil and water," they would say. "Like nitro and glycerin, those two," as my father used to joke before the war. Parents say those kinds of things. They might refuse to take sides, or are reluctant to take on the role of mediator, or are too preoccupied with their own concerns. Perhaps they see one child as the victim and the other the aggressor, or they consciously or unconsciously favor one child over the other. The result is the same. Over the years, the resentment between the children grows. The original offense, now forgotten, is never digested. The differences become intractable. At times, it can come to the point when siblings turn on each other as viciously as rival countries at war.

My father made a terrible mistake by empowering Gustave with the responsibility of watching over me. Between my mother's illness and my father's relative absence, I had gotten a taste of freedom at a dangerous time. I thought that I needed no one's help and that no one should get in my way. Also, I was in love. Like the fox that chews his own paw to get out of a trap, I would have done anything to see Khaled.

As I faced Gustave, I wondered if he saw me disappear into the clearing and reappear from it. Did he know what Khaled looked like? Had he seen him at Café Djurdjura? Would he put two and two together if he spotted Khaled working in the garden? I hated and dreaded him immensely at that moment. I watched Gustave's uneasy smirk. And I did not see his loneliness, his self-doubt, his desire to gain my father's approval and closeness. I ignored the fact that perhaps he too was grasping at straws in this disintegrating world. I only saw that he was getting in my way, and so I attacked. Not with bombs, bullets, knives, or fists. I struck him with what I had in my possession: anger and words. In the heat of rage, I said things I would come to regret for the rest of my life. "You are the one degrading yourself by following me around," I said. "It's sick! Positively sick! Father would be embarrassed if he knew how obsessed you are with me. He'd be more ashamed of you than he already is. Yes, he is ashamed of you! He thinks you're weak. He told me so himself. Return to Mother or crumble and die for all I care but get away from me!"

Gustave blanched. His body seemed to collapse on itself. He looked at me with an expression of incomprehension and pain that I will never forget. He opened his mouth to say something, but instead, he stumbled back a few steps, turned around without a word, climbed on his bicycle, and left.

I watched my brother's silhouette recede on the dirt path. In my anger, I had forgotten that inside the body of a young man still resided the soul of an anxious child, bullied and rejected, a child who wanted to be loved – my little brother. My stomach tightened, but it was too late. The damage to our relationship was done.

That night, Gustave stayed in his room, and Mother in hers. Father did not return until the next morning. Sandra and I ate in the kitchen in silence. I told myself to suck it up. The times had no use for my crisis of conscience. France needed me.

****

Upon my return from the Jardin d'Essai, I entered a phone booth and called my German prey. It all worked exceedingly well. I gave Dietfried the names of local restaurants. He said he wished to know the city more. He did not know anyone in town, he said, and did not know where to go, and what a shame that was when the city was so rich in history. Would I serve as his guide? Dietfried sounded educated, soft-spoken, and excessively polite. He was also German and the enemy, a fact I had to keep remembering. After feigned hesitation, I agreed to give him a tour of the Great Mosque of Algiers. I scheduled that visit for two weeks later, per Fernand's instructions, to give Dietfried time to simmer and give Fernand time to iron out in his plan.

****

I met Fernand at El Bahdja, a café on a tiny street off rue d'Isly. The place was nearly empty aside from a group of old men who drank coffee and spoke in Arabic. I sat down at the wobbly table across from Fernand. The table was sticky, so I kept my hands on my lap.

"Are you hungry?" he asked.

"Just a mint tea for me."

Fernand ordered two mint teas. The plaintive voice of El Hadj M'Hamed El Anka played over the radio, and as my eyes became accustomed to the dim light and my nostrils to the pungent odors of spices and pipe tobacco, I relaxed in my chair. These days it had become easier to breathe among Muslims, away from the eyes of Europeans. The owner, a small man whose fez absorbed the profuse sweat on his brow, set his tray down on our table and poured scalding tea in our glasses. The aroma of mint and sugar spiraled up between us.

Fernand, who clearly understood the male's psyche better than I did, began to map out my artificial romance with Dietfried. "You let him take the lead," he said. "Men need to feel they are the ones doing the chase. The more demure and morally above reproach the woman is, the more compelling the conquest. Men want to take women to bed, but it's the chase that excites them. Don't believe for a second that he is an idiot. He'll spot your deceptions from a mile away. But he'll be powerless against self-deception. Pursue him, and he'll smell a rat. Resist him, and he'll manage to convince himself that he can make you fall in love with him. You'll see. Here is something," Fernand said as he placed a thick book in my hands. "The Architecture of Algiers. You'd better learn a thing or two about the city you're supposed to know so well."

"Listen," I said, "there's an issue with my brother. He might be following me."

Fernand took a drag of his menthol cigarette and narrowed his eyes. "Is that a fact?" he smiled a dangerous smile. "I'll have a couple of our guys trail him," he said. "If he gets too close, we'll scare him away. We'll just take him off course, that little weasel."

Scare him away? I should have told Fernand nothing. I took a sip of my tea trying to act unshaken. The Arab men were still talking. Two French men entered and then exited. The café must have had a bit too much couleur locale for them. A pale man in his fifties wearing a worn fedora and a crumpled suit walked in and went to sit at the table next to us when so many other tables were available. He looked at me with uncomfortable insistence. Fernand sipped his tea and ignored him. I suddenly wondered if there wasn't something oily about Fernand. I had known him for a while now, but was I an apt judge of his character? Could I trust him? The man in the fedora ordered something and looked at me again. His face was deeply marked. He was not Arabic. Maybe Greek or Armenian. Something about him felt familiar; maybe I had seen him before. "My brother is harmless," I said. "He's only doing what my father asked him to do. My family wants to protect me. They don't even know what from."

Fernand's face hardened. "The sooner they face the fact that you are not a kid anymore, the better for you and them. In this business, you can't worry about bruising the feelings of your family members."

I stared him down. "I'll handle them," I said.

"Just make sure all your protégés stay away from our business."

My protégés? "And what business is that?"

"The business of saving the world, sweetie," Fernand said.

The fedora-wearing man got up from his chair, and on his way past me, he smiled with big white teeth and lifted his fedora to salute me. Did we know each other from somewhere? Did he work at one of the local markets maybe? Did he live near our street? Or was he just being courteous? Just in case, I smiled back. The next moment, the man was gone from the café and from my mind.

Back at home, I sat on the couch and leafed through Fernand's architecture book without much fervor. My thoughts were so much on Khaled it's a miracle I retained anything at all. Sandra walked in, carrying things for her sewing. She smiled the way she always did.

"That's it!" I said, beaming.

"What?" she asked.

"I saw a man this morning! A stranger. But he looked so familiar, I thought perhaps I knew him, but now I know why."

"Why?" she said, smiling at my excitement.

"He had your eyes! In fact, he looked a lot like you. He even smiled like you. He looked so much like you that he could pass as your brother." Sandra at that moment must have tripped. All the fabric she held in her arms fell to the floor. She stared down at the strewn clothes like she was about to cry. I kneeled to help her gather her things, but Sandra just stood there. "Are you all right?" I asked. "You don't look well."

"I don't have a brother," she snapped. She snatched the fabric out of my hands and left the room.

****

When the day came to meet Dietfried, I wasn't feeling the trepidations the situation warranted. Algiers, in a short time, had become my turf. Fernand had repeated to me that I was doing nothing grave, only meeting a man and reporting to him afterward. "Don't ask him a single question about what he does or why he is here. You are only trying to gain his trust," he had said.

I met Dietfried at the foot of the Great Mosque. "Thank you for meeting me, Marceline," he said, offering me his arm.

I mentally consulted the rulebook for Jewish girls pretending to be Christian, cross-checked it with the spy rulebook, neither of which existed, and paused only briefly before putting my gloved hand on a Nazi uniform. "The entire pleasure is mine," I said.

Only when we entered the mosque's grounds did I realize my absolute foolishness. I had no idea where we were or what to say, and I was supposed to be the guide, an architecture student! I scrambled through memories of things I had glanced at in Fernand's book. What were those domes called? What about those turrets, those markings? I had not the faintest idea how to go from one part of the mosque to the other. Why had I not rehearsed this or at least visited the place before? My only preparation had been experimenting with various hairstyles and running up and down Algiers with Sandra looking for the appropriate belt for the outfit I had planned. I banked on the hope that coming here had only been Dietfried's excuse to see me and that he would not ask questions.

"So, Marceline," he said. "What can you teach me about this famed mosque?"

In an unexpected surge of clarity that could only be attributed to alchemy in the brain brought upon by a surge in adrenalin I recited, "It is known as Djama'a al-Kebir. Its oldest parts are nearly nine hundred centuries old."

"And what is this?" he asked, pointing to a mezzanine above the entrance.

"This is the ... sedda." I said, surprising myself again. "That's where the muezzin calls the men to prayer."

We entered the rectangular courtyard and walked along the arcade gallery. We entered a vast prayer hall supported by large pillars. Would more of the information I had read in Fernand's book magically come back to me? I recognized the row of alcoves with Moorish arches and exclaimed in relief, "Those are the naves. They are all perpendicular to the qiblah."

"What is a qiblah?"

What was a qiblah? "That is the — the direction of the Kaaba in Mecca. The direction people must look when they pray!" … Or something like that. It sounded right. Hopefully, Dietfried was as ignorant on the matter as he professed to be.

As our footsteps echoed on the tiled floor, we both stopped speaking. The majestic austerity of the place commanded silence. I wondered why I had not visited mosques in the past. Djama'a al-Kebir was pared down except for the few carvings of stylized plants and the occasional mosaic; its design was sober, which was very different from all the temples and churches I had visited in my life. We walked through the marble columns and down the central path, and I felt the palpable weight of centuries of faith in each stone, each mosaic, each pillar. For a moment, I forgot whom I was walking next to or why I was here. Khaled had spoken about the sense of wonderment he felt before God. Now I pictured him here, removing his shoes and kneeling among a hundred other men.

For an hour, we walked through the mosque. I soon realized that I could have said just about anything, Dietfried was hardly paying attention to the content of my words. I could make grotesque errors; he did not mind. Better yet, he loved it. I was a pretty French woman, and nothing more was expected of me. As Fernand instructed, I remained charming but cold. Polite but hesitant. And the more aloof I pretended to be, the more smitten Dietfried appeared to be. By the time I told him I had to leave, he was begging me to show him more of the city.

My entire first interaction with Dietfried was a lesson I would forever owe to Fernand. It offered me a glimpse into the power of women over men, opening the door for skills that would shape my career and my life.

****

"He never once asked me if I was Jewish," I told Fernand when we met afterward at El Bahdja, which would become our meeting place.

Fernand shrugged, "Those things rarely come up in polite conversations. Just like men wouldn't ask ladies if they have the crabs."

"A comparison in poor taste," I said.

"Your identity papers make no mention of it. If he asks, deny it," Fernand said. A skinny adolescent came to take our orders. Even in the darkness of the café and the haze of pipe smoke, I could see that the boy's neck was smudged with grime. "Are you hungry, darling?" Fernand asked me.

I considered the boy's dirty fingernails. "No," I said. Fernand ordered a café au lait and mbesses, a sweet cake Algerians liked to eat for breakfast. "What if the Boche has me investigated?"

"What crime have you committed, sweetheart?"

"Is it beyond the scope of a German officer to obtain intelligence on someone? I don't want to put my family at risk."

A busboy set coffee, the cake, and a small dish of honey on the table. Fernand dipped pieces of the cake in the honey. "Ersatz flour, watered-down coffee. Even the honey has been mixed with agave syrup," he sighed.

I felt wary. Fernand and I were on the same side against a terrible enemy. He trusted me with a mission; perhaps it was time I made an effort to trust him as well. "There is something you need to know about my family," I said. "We're here under a false identity. My father's a foreigner. We left France under less than pristine conditions. If his real identity is revealed, he could be deported or imprisoned. The police have been searching for him in Paris and the South of France."

Fernand smiled in a way to indicate that none of this was news to him. "Here you are just another family among many," he said. "The police have better things to investigate. Your father is a prudent man. Your mother is emotionally unpredictable, but she does not go out of the house much. As for your brother, he has no friends in Algiers, so that puts him at low risk of indiscretions."

A flutter of anguish ran through me. "You know a lot about my family."

"Enough for us to decide to trust you with all this."

"Who is us?" I asked. "Émile? André? What about Béatrice? Is she part of the 'us'?"

"Béatrice isn't as dumb as you think," Fernand said. "So continue to be discreet around her. But we have enough dirt on the girl should she become a nuisance."

My hair rose on the nape of my neck. How long before my family turned into a nuisance in someone's eyes? "Don't mingle in my family's affairs, Fernand, if you want to keep our friendship."

Fernand dabbed the corners of his mouth and pushed the plate of cake toward me. "Would you finish this," he said. "Algerians consider it a sacrilege to throw out bread, and I have enough enemies as it is." He sat back in his chair and observed me, his expression between amusement and menace. "We're at war, darling. Friendship is irrelevant to what we're trying to accomplish."

Before the war, Dietfried had been a civil servant, of undistinguished physique and meek personality who throughout his life must have failed to impress his professors, his superiors, and women. But here in Algiers, he was impressive. In his carefully pressed Wehrmacht uniform, he represented the Third Reich no less. All eyes, albeit filled with hostility, converged in his direction. He did not yet fully embody his newfound prestige. At times, he assumed an air of self-confidence, but he did this the way a second-rate actor in a theater performance might. The rest of the time, he reverted to what I suspected to be his natural ordinariness, his natural dullness. In the few weeks since I had met him, a sparse mustache had sprouted above his upper lip. He was clearly unused to the sensation of hair under his nose, so he petted it constantly as he spoke. Dietfried appeared to be without malice. Like everyone else, his life and his future had been taken off course by the war. He hadn't chosen this military life. His engineering education, and the fact that he spoke French well had resulted, through an agreement with Vichy, in an appointment as part of a small German military contingent on Algerian soil. Were it not for the accent I was conditioned to despise and the dreadful uniform he wore on most of our outings, I could have forgotten that he took orders from a madman, hell-bent on conquering the world. Under different circumstances, I might have given Dietfried charitable pointers: use less cologne, stand up straight, listen to your date rather than to yourself, and above all, keep your hands off your mustache. But I was supposed to find him irresistible, so I bit my tongue.

Just as I had avoided the topic with Khaled, Dietfried made no mention of religion. Perhaps he had decided that it did not matter. Perhaps he was afraid of insulting me by asking. Or perhaps, as Fernand said, infatuation was a blinder that prevented him from seeing what he did not want to see. Because Dietfried was infatuated with me; this much was clear. He did not try to kiss me, but he was awkward in my presence, which revealed plenty. He was intelligent enough to know that his nationality worked against him, so he did not declare himself and rather attempted to woo me.

To act as though I liked Dietfried, to pretend to be someone I wasn't, turned out to be surprisingly more relaxing than being myself. Unthreatening girls don't try hard to say smart things. They let the men do all the talking. Their opinions agree with whoever is in front of them. They don't take offense. They are apolitical. Béatrice was my inspiration: I would remain steadfastly passive. I would say the occasional naiveté and watch Dietfried glow in his superiority. I giggled. I had contempt for the person I pretended to be, but Dietfried seemed to like her very much.

We carefully avoided the topic of war, and this was no small feat when it permeated every instant of our lives, nearly every thought in our minds, and every fear in our hearts. Instead, he spoke about life before the war: his life in Heidelberg, his studies, his family. We discussed travel, food, nature, fashion, sporting events. Conversing with Dietfried was tedious, humorless, but I made sure to chortle at the appropriate times. With anyone else, at any other time, I would have demanded that interesting things be discussed. I'd have said something provocative to spice things up. Or more likely I would have called it a day. Dietfried was terribly dull. But spies must be chameleons in more ways than one. It is not only about the way you dress and speak. It involves becoming a reflection of the emotions and interests of the person facing you. My dates with Dietfried taught me that there was much to gain by listening, a skill I hadn't cared to develop. It also taught me patience. I burned to ask about his role in Algiers, but Fernand had warned me against questioning him. Useful intelligence would come from Dietfried relaxing his guard, from his boasting.

I let Dietfried think he was in charge. I let him decide where to meet, what new part of Algiers to visit, which park, which museums, which streets. From there, Fernand would mastermind the entire date. He would tell me about the area in question ahead of time, and once there, I acted as though I was familiar with the place, when in fact Dietfried and I were discovering it at the same time. This required gumption, improvisation, cockiness, and fearlessness. The complexity of what I was doing was exhilarating, but I had to act reserved and a little bland.

Dietfried went from trying too hard to acting aloof in the hope of making me want him. He reeked of shyness and insecurity. I watched him get frustrated with himself as I continued to play hard to get. Meanwhile, Fernand continued to be the puppet master. Part of me could not help but feel sorry for Dietfried. As much as I enjoyed the challenge, I was not particularly fond of mental cruelty. It is difficult to completely hate someone you learn to know. I found myself thinking he was not such a horrible fellow. He was educated, soft-spoken, and excessively polite. He was also German and the enemy, a fact I had to keep remembering.

On one of our outings, we visited the Algiers zoo. We leaned over the parapet that separated us from an enclosure where two polar foxes played. The animals were beautiful; their fur was stark white against their incongruous desert settings. "How did a fox from the North Pole end up trapped in Algiers?" I said.

"I often wonder the same thing about myself," Dietfried quipped.

"Do you think those two were born in captivity?"

"I hope for them that they were," he said. "If they've never known freedom, they can't imagine it."

For a while, we watched the foxes play, then curl upon themselves and begin to groom each other with quick licks of their pink tongues. As I watched the foxes, I wondered if tricking Dietfried into falling in love with me was amoral.

He cleared his throat and asked, "Forgive me for asking Marceline, but do you have a boyfriend?"

"I do," I told him. Dietfried's face fell so blatantly I had to suppress a smile. "He's a law student at the University of Algiers."

"Are the two of you serious?"

Fernand had prepared me for this. Expressing a mixture of commitment and doubts was the best way to keep Dietfried at bay and interested. "More importantly," I said, "my family approves of his family."

"That is not the strongest of endorsements."

"French men in North Africa have conservative ideas about women," I said. "Not unlike Muslim men, as a matter of fact. They want women in the house, and they disapprove of higher education for them."

"How illogical," Dietfried said. "Any thinking man would realize how much more enriching it is for his sons when the woman who cares for them is well educated." He looked at me guilelessly. Women, to him, were merely a means to the breeding and upbringing of Aryan sons.

"I hear that the restrictions might force the closing of the zoo," I said. "What will become of the animals?"

"Likely, a couple of white fox stoles are soon to appear on the black market," he chuckled and added, "and somewhere in Algiers, a Jew will just get a bit richer." When he said this, my smile was sincere.

It was a smile of gratitude for jolting me out of complacency. When one got to know him, Dietfried turned out to be easy to despise after all.

****

I had a double life now – a triple, a quadruple life. There was my role as a sister and daughter where I felt childish and aggravated. There were my outings with Dietfried where I pretended to be a regular girl while all my senses were on alert. There was my work with Fernand where I watched my steps and acted more mature and sophisticated than I was. And then there were the few stolen minutes with Khaled where I felt I could be myself, except that I kept my Resistance activities secret from him. I wasn't naïve enough to hope that he would understand or accept what I was doing. Knowing how Khaled felt about France, how could he make sense of my dedication to a country that had turned vicious against people of my religion?

Everything, even my challenging hours with Dietfried, felt insipid compared to my time with Khaled. It wasn't just that I was drunk on our emotional connection. I was drunk on our chaste physical contacts. We kissed feverishly, but it was never enough – not enough time, not enough kisses, and not enough to fill my physical hunger for him.

Over time, I told Khaled about my life in Paris. I described our family's powerlessness as we witnessed the inexorable rise of anti-Semitism. I told him how in the span of a few short years the entire nation had turned against the Jews. Every day was cause for disbelief. It was not only that the people in power used baffling false logic and lies, but it was also the eagerness with which the population embraced them. The nation had become insane before our very eyes. The more absurd a lie, the more it gained ground, the more readily people embraced it. I admitted how insidious hatred was. The propaganda was so successful that it made even the Jews feel different about themselves. It was soul-crushing to see Jews portrayed as vile and disgusting, but what crushed my soul the most was the disgust I had felt. I thought Jews stood out too much, should have blended in more. I thought my brother stood out the most.

It was with Khaled that I could articulate for the first time that Mother and I had wanted Gustave sent away, not because, like Father, we were worried about his safety, but in retrospect because of how Jewish he looked. Mother and I had wanted Gustave away because with him around it was more difficult to pass as

Aryan when we walked in the streets. I told Khaled how I had even been ashamed of my father for being too foreign, how I had felt that it reflected negatively on Mother and me.

"You were a child," Khaled said.

"I was a child, but I still feel terrible guilt about it."

"Tell them how you feel. The truth makes things lighter to bear."

"What purpose would this serve? I don't want them to know I was ashamed of them."

I told Khaled about my mother's disintegration and my rage at her. I told him how much I adored my father, but how he appeared absent most of the time, even when he was physically present. How for a while he had seemed to favor me, and, although I could see how unjust my family had been toward Gustave, how jealous I was when my father had become close to Gustave in Cannes. I told Khaled about Sandra, who had raised us and who loved us, but who might be fired at any time because I had manipulated her into closing her eyes to my escapades. "My brother resents me for good reasons," I said. "My father is disappointed in me, my mother knows she cannot count on me, and I'm betraying our loving nanny."

"You can always ask God for forgiveness," Khaled said as he twirled a strand of my hair and brought it to his lips.

"It is hard to believe in God when one looks at humanity," I said.

"Of course. That would be looking for God in the wrong places."

"Where should I look?"

"Me, I look at the trees and the sea. I look into your eyes." Saying so, he let his hand hover just above my belly. I wanted to scream for him to touch me, but what if too much forwardness on my part drove him away?

His hand hovered for a long minute. Finally, he removed it. "I want to respect you," he said finally.

"Touch me," I implored.

Slowly he lowered his hand and slipped it under my blouse. He let his palm rest softly on my belly as I tried to catch my breath. "I am afraid of what my body wants to do," he said.

There was one thing Khaled needed to know about me. Immediately. "The truth makes things lighter to bear," he had said. I did not want to be apologetic. In my heart of hearts, I did not care what society thought. I had made a conscious decision to have no regrets and no shame about this. Regrets and shame were the opposite of freedom, and I wanted to be free. But this was a conservative world, and his culture was even more traditional. I composed myself. I made sure to speak calmly and clearly so that he would have no doubts about it. "I am not a virgin," I said.

Disbelief at first and then confusion and grief washed over his face. Slowly, as slowly as he had placed it there, he removed his hand from my belly and rolled onto his back. "I have to go now to report to my desk," he said. "It is late."

I forced myself to say, "Fernand was my lover, but I broke it off."

He got up from the blanket and gave me his hand to help me up. He was not looking at me. He folded the blanket and placed it neatly in its place under the thorny bush. I brushed my skirt and flattened my hair with the palm of my hands and placed myself in front of him so that he would be forced to look at me. "I am in love with you," I said.

"You are?" he said, dumbfounded.

I tried hard to repress tears of frustration. I was angry. I had wanted him to forgive me immediately, and now I felt his distance, his disgust perhaps. "Why is this so incredible?"

"I'm in love with you," he said as if surprised to have a name for his feelings.

"Well then, I don't want you to be in love with a fiction of me."

He rubbed his face with the palm of his hands, overwhelmed. "What are we going to do?" he asked.

"Continue to meet here whenever we can," I said firmly. Inside, I was shaking.

Khaled put on his uniform jacket and looked in the direction of the maze of bamboo that led out of the clearing. "If I don't leave now, I will lose my work."

My throat tightened tears seemed a very real possibility. "Will you see me again, or will you not?" I said. "Look at me! Is what I told you so distressing that you can't even look at me?"

He took my face gently between his hands and gazed into my eyes with sadness. "There is nothing you or anyone can do or say that will stop me from seeing you," he said.

On May 29th, a German ordinance ordered the Jews in France's occupied zone to wear a Star of David patch sewn on their clothes. We were past outrage and received the news with despondency. That month, I met Dietfried twice. Twice I walked around Algiers on his arm, with me smiling and chatting and appearing to have a swell time. We met in places where my family would not usually venture, but I was more worried about their disappointment than I was afraid for myself.

"You were right," Fernand told me in late May. "Your brother was seen following you."

I was immediately enraged. "How often?" I said.

"Often enough."

"Does he know about the Boche?"

"Not sure. He follows you when you leave home. But once you get on a trolley, he can't climb on the same one without you seeing him, so he stops there."

"Which means your men are surveilling me?"

Fernand smiled charmingly. "Only to keep you safe, in case the Boche gets funny ideas."

"How much am I being followed?"

"When you are with the Boche." He looked at me, an ironic smile in his eyes. "Why should we follow you for any other reasons?"

I felt hot suddenly. If Gustave was following me, and Fernand's men were following Gustave, who knew about my visits to the Jardin d'Essai? "I don't need your protection," I said.

Fernand ignored my comment. "We've also seen your brother on his bicycle, trying to keep up with the trolley you were on. Our guys had to stand in his way a couple of times to slow him down."

Now I wasn't sure if I was more infuriated with Gustave or with Fernand. "How did you stand in his way? You did not intimidate my brother, did you?"

"We put an automobile in his way a couple of times. Once we stopped him to check his papers."

"Why don't you give my brother a job trailing people other than me?" I said. "He's obviously gotten good at it."

"Give him a role with the Resistance you mean? In my cell?"

My father would never forgive me if he knew I had anything to do with Gustave becoming part of the Resistance. A solution presented itself to me brilliant in its simplicity. "He keeps mentioning the Chantiers de la Jeunesse. He wants to join, but he is too young."

Fernand tapped his forehead with the palm of his hand. "The fool. Why not Hitler's Youth while he's at it?"

"They accept younger people on a voluntary basis. He applied for a derogation but was turned down. Could you pull strings? Could you get them to accept his application? That ought to keep him busy."

Fernand must have read my thoughts. "What does your father think of this?"

"The Chantiers de la Jeunesse is a more benign occupation than Resistance work I should think."

"I'll make it happen, sweetheart," Fernand said. "Anything else?"

The lack of adornment in my relationship with Fernand, in its many incarnations, suited me. Just like we had never complicated our sex life with talk of feelings, our work together was not burdened by sensitivities. There was something I needed off my chest, and I took this opportunity. "Yes," I said. "Quit calling me sweet names. Treat me with respect."

Fernand smiled. "The sweet names are how I express affection. Choosing you for a mission is to show you respect."

"I'm not doing any of this to impress you. You realize that?"

"You impress me nonetheless, sweetheart. And I don't believe you're the kind of gal who needs praise to operate."

****

A few days later, Gustave came home brandishing his approval letter and stamped paperwork. "Screening starts Monday!" he said excitedly.

"What screening?" Father asked.

"The Chantiers de la Jeunesse! My derogation came through. But I need to pass the health test first."

"Hmm …" my father said. Judging from the expression of dismay on his face, I got the sense he was the one who had maneuvered to get Gustave's application rejected.

"What does the screening entail?" Mother asked.

Gustave gave a nonchalant shrug. "Talks about morality and the virtues of work, family, homeland, and further brainwashing, I suppose," he said. "The screening lasts three days. It's in town."

"This is nonsense. Gustave, you are not going!" my father said.

Gustave raised his voice. "I was accepted! I can't turn it down now."

"Then you must fail the screening."

Gustave's face turned crimson. "And be humiliated?"

"He might fail without even trying to," I said to egg him on.

Father glowered at me, and Gustave looked at me with hatred.

"Maybe," Mother said, "it is not such a terrible place for children."

"I'm not a child!" Gustave bellowed.

"What about the S.T.O?" my father said. A rumor was gaining momentum that Vichy was drafting agreements with the Nazis to create the S.T.O. or Service du Travail Obligatoire. Forced labor for young French men to work in Germany in exchange for freeing our prisoners of war. Many suspected that the Chantiers de la Jeunesse might be a secret training ground for forced laborers.

"The Maréchal would never allow it," Mother said.

"Mother! Your Maréchal is who sold us out to the Boches," I said. "Can't you understand anything?"

My father just shook his head in exasperation and left the room.

That Monday, Gustave reported to the Chantiers de la Jeunesse office. While my father further schemed to extricate him from it, I was free to move around the city without the fear of running into my brother, or so I believed.

Gustave, I would learn later, never went to the Chantiers de la Jeunesse. He was only using it as an excuse to be gone day or night without my parents asking about his whereabouts. What he did for those three days, and during the ensuing weeks, I would find out later. He too was being trained. But neither one of us knew of the other's missions – until we did.

The following day, I waited in the clearing for Khaled to arrive, but he didn't. After we had spotted each other in the garden, it wasn't rare for him to join me twenty minutes later, sometimes half an hour. Forty-five minutes, once, when his boss had asked him to guide a visitor. That day, I waited in mental agony for an hour. Each minute that passed cemented the fear that my truth had been irreconcilable with his faith, his culture, his pride. I had been with men. I wasn't a virgin.

When I heard the familiar rustling of leaves, I turned and stood there, rather than run into his arms. He walked toward me and took me in his. "The boss had me trim dead flowers off the hydrangea bushes. I worked as fast as I could."

We spread our blanket and lay side by side. We kissed. I was tremendously relieved at first and then unnerved. It was as though nothing had been said.

We began to talk about the future. This was something we did, despite the war, despite all that separated us, despite how improbable the chance of a future together.

"When the war is over. we can rent a house in the South of France for an entire summer," I said. "And I want to take you to Paris," I said. "We'll bring a picnic to the Parc de Bagatelle." Khaled smiled at this. Those notions were as alien to him as a trip to the moon. He described the Kasbah where he lived. "I want you to see it with your own eyes," he said. "It cannot be described with words. It is a city, and it is a home. Imagine it like a house with many rooms, filled with one family so large that you cannot know everyone, and yet they all take care of you. A house with a hundred kitchens where women cook a hundred meals, hundreds of fountains and balconies, a thousand windows, with streets and steps and shops and mothers, fathers, and children all living together, supporting one another."

"People say it's dangerous."

"Only when the French police arrive to arrest our brothers or search streets and houses looking for someone." He shook his head, angry. "It used to be that if someone wanted to hide in the Kasbah, he could never be found. But now they use spies and informants. Brothers turn on each other. They are corrupting our way of being."

"The police?"

"The French. All people want is to live in peace in the Kasbah, live their life, be happy."

"What about the women?" I asked tentatively. "They can't be that happy?"

He raised an eyebrow. "Why would they not be?"

"Don't they feel ... subjugated?"

I immediately saw the hurt on his face. "You have the wrong idea about Muslims," he said. "This is why I want you to come to the Kasbah. I want you to see for yourself how our women are well cared for and respected."

"But not free."

Khaled sat up and looked at me intently. "No one is free in this world, Marceline. Men or women. Even when we move without restraints, even if there aren't wars or jails, we aren't free. We all have duties."

"Duties?"

Khaled searched for the right words, or else he hesitated to reveal his beliefs. "In my culture, it's our duty to have children," he said. "Our duty to keep things holy, to care for our families and our elders in the faith and tradition."

"And people follow this blindly?"

"These rules, these duties, they were developed over thousands of years. They exist because they are our cement. They are the means by which we can all experience order and joy."

"Laws get in the way of freedom," I said, "with new laws added every day. We don't have a choice about laws, or about wars. Religion is an added ball and chain, but at least we can refuse that burden, walk away, be free."

Khaled got up and began pacing. "Freedom is not what men crave most," he said. "They crave heroism, and purpose, and God, and family. They will happily sacrifice their freedom and their lives in the name of something greater."

I leaned back on my elbows. "Men," I said. "It's always about the men."

Khaled kneeled next to me on the blanket. "Women have the same desire to be part of a whole that is greater than them." The way he looked at me as he said this, I wondered for a moment if it was possible that Khaled knew about my Resistance work. But what he said next was more worrisome. "It is not about me, or what I want," he said, distraught. "I want you. You must know this. It's about my people, my faith. I would never betray either."

"What are you saying?"

"I am saying that I am in love with you," he said, peering into my eyes.

"So why do you sound like you are breaking up with me?" I said stiffly.

"I am part of a community, Marceline. You must understand this. My family depends on me to behave within the rules of the community. That is the way I bring them honor."

"So?"

"Things are expected of me. How I worship ... who I ... marry, it's all part of it."

I felt a pang of nausea. "Who is even speaking about marriage?" I said.

"Things aren't simple. The truth is, my family, my people, they – it's expected of me to keep things holy and to...." He paused and looked away and added, "Marry within my religion."

I stood up in a huff and dusted my skirt. "And I'm unholy!"

He took my hands. "I love you just as you are," he said.

"What makes me unholy?" I said, furious. "Is it that I'm Jewish or that I'm not a virgin?"

"No ... but ... neither. It's just that—"

"I'm not damaged goods, Khaled! Being with me is a privilege. A privilege! If you feel otherwise, I have no desire to be with you!"

We stood in the clearing, facing each other like enemies.

"We are slaves to our upbringings," he said. "I am a slave to mine, as you are a slave to yours."

"Can't you see those notions are inventions? Lies repeated!"

"But there is a solution," he said.

I crossed my arms and faced him. "Is there now?"

"Would you convert to Islam?" he asked. His face was grave, his eyes hopeful.

"In which case, you might be willing to overlook my lack of virginity?"

He brightened. "I would."

I eyed him with something that must have resembled hatred. "What possesses you to think I would consider converting? Why don't you try and convert to Judaism instead?"

"It would make no difference to you," he said softly. "You don't even believe in God."

My face was flushed, and it took everything I had not to shout. "I believe in nothing! I don't believe in God or marriage! I don't even believe in being indignant about what you just said. It's just so ridiculous I will ignore it!"

"Please do not be angry," Khaled implored. He tried to take my hands, but I shook free of him. "I'm only looking for solutions."

"You use the word marriage as though it's the most heavenly thing. I despise the institution!"

"And yet you must marry someday."

"Of course not. Can't you see the world is upside down? The old rules no longer apply."

"There are reasons for humanity to have evolved the way it did," Khaled said. "The same in every religion, with a man as the head of the family and the woman at its heart, under one faith. It has evolved that way because it is the glue of civilizations."

"And here I am, bringing civilization to its knees!" I was trying not to cry. How was it possible to lose control so fast and so irrevocably? Why was it that I could not love Fernand with whom everything was easy, and instead had to fall in love with Khaled with whom everything was impossible? "No man will own me," I said.

Khaled looked at me unflinchingly. "I don't want to own you any more than I want to own the moon or the sun. I love you, and I want to be with you and hold you in my heart. All I want is for us to be together. I know you would love living in the Kasbah. I am certain of it! The women in the Kasbah—"

I interrupted, full of venom. "You have no idea what hides under those veils, behind those lowered gazes. Muslim women are watching European women, and do you know what they think? They don't congratulate themselves on how holy they are. They yearn to become like us! Before long, they will rebel against the veil and everything it represents. Muslim men will have no choice but to adapt. You would do well to change the way you think because, like it or not, you soon will be left in the dust, without a single woman to own."

Khaled's eyes were thunderous. He was insulted, yet he tried to use reason, and as he spoke, the width of our cultural divide widened, and my heart broke a little more. "It has nothing to do with ownership!" he said. "What European women are doing is an experiment, and we have no idea of the outcome.

Traditions evolve over thousands of years. Like plants, species evolve slowly to adapt to variations in their environment. But take a plant and transplant it without giving it time to adapt, and it will most certainly perish. The changes in women you are speaking of are happening too fast. The human species is not ready for it."

"So be it then!" I said. I added dramatically, "The human species is not ready for me!" I grabbed the blanket and shook it off. Khaled watched me, his expression clouded with disappointment. I threw the folded blanket on the ground and added, "Your rules are all in your imagination. You are, in fact, free to do as you wish. I feel sorry for how trapped you are by your conventions. I have nothing but pity for narrow-mindedness. And I don't even care that I am a whore in your eyes."

The expression on Khaled's face went from anger to indignation. "Why would you say this?"

"Admit what this is really about: I slept with a man, and now you see me with disgust!"

Khaled stepped toward me and murmured, "What you did or didn't do changes nothing in my eyes. You are the most sacred thing on which I have ever laid eyes. The most precious. The rarest. I am powerless before you. But I can't promise what I cannot give. I am not a free man and will never be."

I tasted tears in my throat before I felt them in my eyes. "Did you hear me ask for anything?"

"I am the one asking. I want a future with you!"

We were still standing in front of each other, but our anger was gone, and all that was left was the desolation we felt. The truth was I wasn't free of the burden of family expectations either. I knew how one's place in society, whether because of race, religion, or class, could cling to your skin like a personal prison. "Why can't we just live now?" I said. I was sobbing now.

"These stolen moments, they are not enough. They will never be enough," he said.

"You have to go back to work," I said. "They will see you are missing. You've been absent too long."

"Will you come back?" he asked.

"What's the point, Khaled? We can't be together, and you know this. We both know this."

Khaled grabbed my arms and pressed me against him. "You will come back. Tell me you will!"

I melted against him, and all vestige of anger vanished from me. "I will come to the Kasbah," I said. "I want to see it. Just tell me when and how."

He took my hand, brought it to his lips, and kissed the inside of my wrist lightly.

****

With July came unfathomable news. The French government had orchestrated a massive raid and arrested over ten thousand Parisian Jews, a large proportion of them foreign or, just like my father, stateless. Those without children had been sent to an encampment in Drancy, but families were being held captive inside the Vélodrome d'Hiver, an enclosed bicycle stadium in the fifteenth arrondissement, with little indication that anyone in the government knew what to do with them.

A few years ago, our father had dragged us to the Vel' d'Hiv to watch a bicycle competition. The stadium had a glass ceiling. The day was hot, and the temperature inside had been too sweltering to bear. Mother had complained, so we had left. We put ourselves in the shoes of those families awaiting their fate, and they were all that was on our minds. Over the next few days, we held our breath as accounts of what was taking place inside the Vélodrome d'Hiver grew unimaginable. Men, women, children, babies, grandmothers, and grandfathers were parked there like beasts without food, water, or latrines. There were rumors of horrors that defied the imagination, rumors of suicide, filth, and death, of people trying to escape and being shot on the spot.

"It's not possible," my mother kept mumbling as she walked around the apartment in a Benzedrine-induced state of agitation.

"Do you think it's true, Baba?" Gustave dared to ask.

"Of course not," my father said, which cheered me up. This was one more rumor to discount. You could not trust the official news channels, but neither should we rely on word of mouth. But when my mother left the room, my father spoke to Gustave and me. "I do not need your mother be troubled any more than she already is. We need to hide the truth from her."

"They can't let people die of thirst?" I exclaimed. "Surely someone will intervene. How could the Parisians let their next-door neighbors be taken away and killed?"

My father did not look at us as he said, "The average French person is trying to survive under the occupation. Acts of righteousness might save a few, but even a handful of evil people placed in a position of control is enough to annihilate all decency." He shook his head. "It is the nature of the most aggressive and heartless humans to spread terror and control the decent, peaceful ones. It has been the case throughout the ages. In my days, I have seen these kinds of things happen. There will never be enough jails for all the people they hate."

"What do you mean, Baba?"

My father hesitated. "It isn't incarceration they want to achieve, but annihilation. In my youth, they walked people from entire villages in the desert until they died."

I felt ill. "They cannot be killing Jewish families on purpose, Baba!" I thought of other rumors, of starvation, of poisonous gas, and prayed that my father would reassure us.

"Persecutions of Jews have happened throughout history," he said. "You are old enough to hear this. You must be attentive, on guard, always. Jews, Communists, homosexuals: those are the people Hitler is after. He has plainly said so. To think he does not mean to exterminate us all makes us just as delusional as he is."

We let the thought sink in. The world did not only hate us: it was putting a system in place to eradicate us. "Is that why so many Jews are staying in Paris, Baba? You think they're delusional?" Gustave asked.

"Many foreigners and refugees have no friends or family in Paris to hide them. They have no money and no means to flee. Maybe they left their countries because of persecutions there, not thinking that France would become just as bad. They might be trapped in France even if they wanted to leave."

Gustave said out loud what we both thought. "If you had not taken us away from Paris, we too would be gathered at the Vel' d'Hiv."

My father did not answer, but in his eyes was unbearable sadness.

"What will happen to us if they find us here in Algiers?" Gustave asked.

"We're in the unoccupied zone, and our false identity is holding," our father said. He paused, weighing whether we should hear the truth. "But do not think for a moment that we are out of danger. The Vichy government seems intent on developing its own policies against Jews, regardless of what Hitler wants. If Vichy has jurisdiction over non-occupied territories, Jews are in danger here as well."

"So, what shall we do?"

"Don't dismiss rumors, err on the side of caution, plan and prepare for every eventuality. And as sad as it is to say, expect the worst from people."

"French colonies in India, Cameroun, Tchad, and New Caledonia have rejected Vichy and are following De Gaulle," I said. "North Africa might still break politically from Vichy."

My father shook his head. "I don't think that will happen."

A sense of entrapment and fear rose in me, and anger too. "And why not?"

"We are too close to France. If it were going to happen, it would have happened by now."

"That was my last hope," I said, sitting down on the couch and placing my forehead in my hands. Gustave stood at the door, pale and stiff, the way he looked when he was upset. My father looked from Gustave to me. He seemed to hesitate. In a voice barely above a whisper, he said, "You must take heart. There is hope, my loves. There is … I can't give you details, but there are plans in the works. The Allied forces … Things are looking up. The fighting in Egypt is giving Rommel a hard time. If we can drive him out of Egypt, the Allies might attempt something."

His words hovered over us, powerful enough to hold our spirits aloft. Gustave did not cross-examine him, and neither did I. We could not risk discovering that our father was only trying to raise our spirits. For my part, I needed to be buoyed by this. I wanted to be reassured. And in this way, I wasn't so different from those dying inside the Vélodrome d'Hiver because they had hoped for the best until it was too late.

The events at the Vel' d'Hiv devastated us psychologically. Sleeping was difficult. We had nightmares. It was hard, at times, to find a reason to get out of bed in the morning. We cataloged in our minds those we knew who might now be dead. We obsessed about what might have happened to us had we stayed in Paris. Despair and fear gripped us without warning from one moment to the next, and we walked in a daze, searching for ways we could reconcile our sense of right and wrong with what had happened at the Vel' d'Hiv and might happen to us.

My early involvement in the Resistance had been a little girl's game I played; now I glimpsed the significance of my actions. I ached to extract something useful out of Dietfried. The couple of dull walks by the seaside when Dietfried never discussed his work tested my patience. But Fernand continued to warn me against asking questions. "Play it smooth, sweetheart," he would say. "No need to put him on guard. We want him to trust you." But I suddenly felt in a terrible hurry, one that bordered on desperation.

Finally, Fernand let me accept to have lunch with Dietfried. We met at Le Neuilly, a classic French brasserie renowned for its rich patrons and its apparent immunity from shortages in the kitchen.

Dietfried rose to greet me and helped me to my chair. In the gleaming restaurant, filled with mirrors and polished brass, the atmosphere was jolly, perfumed, chatty. A pianist played a lively tune. Everything about the place was meant to make you forget the war. I glanced across the hectic, crowded room and saw that I wasn't the only pretty girl being treated to a fancy meal by a powerful man. I despised the sight of those women with their little out-of-fashion hats, bad rouge, and cheap nylons, who cooed and simpered odiously as Germans in uniforms laughed drunkenly. But then I realized that, to the uninformed eye, I was no different. I was just another girl, fraternizing with the enemy in exchange for a full belly and perhaps more.

Dietfried ordered lamb chops, and I ordered roast chicken and potatoes au gratin. As the war progressed, the meals that Sandra managed to prepare for us increasingly lacked fat and protein. I was always hungry. My stomach churned in anticipation, and I had trouble paying attention to Dietfried's ramblings. When the food arrived on our plates, steaming and delicious-looking, I had to compose myself not to devour the content of my plate, trough-like. With every bite came the nearly physical sensation that my blood was replenishing itself. Dietfried ordered German beers, cold and foamy, and I told him that it was the most delectable beer I had ever tasted, and he blushed as though the quality of German beer was evidence of his own merit. As was his habit, Dietfried pondered on and seemed perfectly happy with my lack of opinion and the fact that I had nothing to say about myself. But the beer loosened my guard, and it occurred to me that Dietfried was always available, no matter what time of the day I said I could meet.

"Don't you ever have to work?" I asked, forgetting that I was not supposed to ask him how he spent his time in Algiers.

"I mostly work at night," he said.

"In that case, shouldn't you be sleeping now?" I asked.

Dietfried seemed to swell with importance and casually said, "I'm a communication specialist, but it turns out there are very few communications to be had. Perhaps one per night, if that much. Mostly, I wait and read. I have been in Algiers for three months and have done little more than read and re-read every book in the library."

The information was critical. I laughed to appear tipsy and to kill the subject before it raised suspicion. "That makes no sense to me whatsoever," I said, giggling.

"How about we catch a movie after lunch," he asked.

Both of us were aware of the only benefit of being in a movie theater in the middle of the afternoon. I pretended not to understand. "Oh, but Dietfried, do you not realize that being seen at the movies with a man would be terrible for my reputation? What would my parents say if they found out?"

Dietfried reddened. "I ... of course not ... that would be improper."

"Quite improper!" I assured him.

When I returned home, Fernand, dressed in a brown suit and matching hat, was already waiting for me inside the apartment building's entrance. He was standing near the mailboxes, next to the dark space below the staircases where people left baby carriages and bicycles. If someone we knew appeared, he could retreat in the shadow and not be seen, and I would pretend to open my mailbox.

"Anything new?" he asked.

"It depends," I said. We were speaking just above a whisper, halting our conversation when we heard a door close or footsteps in the staircase. Seeing those girls at the restaurant, and judging them and hating them the way I had, I sensed that I might not be indestructible. It was not a matter of how people might judge me; I needed to shield myself. "If Algiers ever becomes independent from Vichy and Germany, how will I be protected?"

"What have you heard?" Fernand asked.

"Nothing. But here I am, parading around Algiers with Dietfried. I want to make sure that more than one person knows what I am actually doing with him."

"It's Dietfried now?" he said. "How sweet of you to call him by his Christian name."

"What name do you want me to use? Goebbels and Himmler were taken already."

"Never forget he's the enemy, Marceline."

"I don't need a reminder," I said icily. A man entered the building and nodded hello. We nodded back. He pushed the button to the elevator. Fernand lit a cigarette. The man entered the elevator, the door closed behind him, and the elevator went up. "What if we win the war?" I said. "What if we lose? People won't be likely to forget that they saw me at the side of a Boche."

"I will vouch for you. I will tell everyone about your involvement."

"What if you get killed?"

Fernand pretended to shudder. "That's so very morbid of you!"

"I have intelligence. You either want it, or you don't. Give me guarantees."

"You are getting touchy, darling."

I crossed my arms. "I am getting tired of the condescending."

"Me? Condescending?"

"I'm doing a job. I work for you – under your orders. I need a guarantee that I will be safe when this is over. If you cannot offer me one, then I won't be wasting another minute with this."

"All right," Fernand said. He drew from his cigarette, crushed it on the stone floor, and exhaled a cloud of smoke. "Your code name is Brantôme."

"I beg your pardon?"

"Your involvement as Brantôme is being documented. That information is then encrypted and sent to London. When the time comes, if you're ever questioned or doubted by one of us, all you'll need to do is bring up your code name. Is that enough of a guarantee?"

"I have a spy name?"

He smiled thinly. "You do."

I was Brantôme. I liked that. "How is it that I'm the last one to find out my own code name?" I asked.

"What is the intelligence you spoke of?" Fernand asked impatiently.

"Dietfried is a communication specialist. He told me so today. He broadcasts at night apparently, sleeps during the day."

Fernand stiffened. "From his house?"

"Wherever he is at night. He didn't say."

"That is why his house is so well guarded!" Fernand beamed. "Our patience and efforts are paying off."

"Are they?"

"The Germans are in constant communication with Berlin from Algiers, though we don't know exactly how. We didn't know who was transmitting or from where. The man is a fool to tell you this."

"Unless it's a deliberate red herring. A trap."

Fernand dismissed the notion. He was excited. "Finding where they are communicating from was like searching for a needle in a haystack. But now we can check it out, look for an antenna. Wherever he works from, there should be encryption tools, things of that nature. That's why they have an engineer seemingly twiddling his thumbs all day long in Algiers. He works at night! It makes perfect sense." Fernand clapped his hands. "By the looks of it, your small fry turns out to be a much bigger fish!"

Upon my return to the apartment, Gustave was brooding again.

"Why are you here?" I said. He ignored me, went into his room, and slammed his door. "Why is he upset this time?" I asked Sandra, who was hurrying about the living room, emptying Mother's ashtrays and fluffing throw pillows.

"He is sad," she told me.

Mother emerged from her room, wrapped in her white silk kimono, a long ivory cigarette holder at her fingertips. She was perfumed and made up for the first time in weeks. Benzedrine was quite extraordinary, indeed. When she took it, you'd forget she had been down in the dumps, barely able to use a comb or a toothbrush thirty minutes before.

"You look nice, Mother," I said. "Are you and Baba going somewhere special for your anniversary?"

She took a puff of her cigarette. "Wouldn't you know your father has surprised me with a night at the opera no less," she said, tapping the cigarette to drop the ashes and missing the ashtray.

"Well, you look pretty," I said.

She turned in front of the mirror, pleased, and patted her coiffed hair. "You think so?" she said in the breezy tone she used when her system was soaked with the new wonder drug the doctor had prescribed. "I hardly know what to wear. What a bother not to be able to buy anything new. And my good clothes are nowhere to be found."

"You probably left them in Cannes," I said, knowing full well that I had coaxed Sandra into taking many of them apart to make new, more fashionable clothes for me.

I had noticed lately that the new medication made Mother forgetful and sometimes suspicious. "I brought them here," she said sotto voce, "but someone stole them." She emphasized the word 'someone.'

"Who would steal your clothes, Mother?"

"That one," she said, pointing to Sandra without even trying to be discreet about it. "She steals."

I felt bad for Sandra. "What would Sandra do with your clothes? She wears the same things all the time."

"She sells them on the black market and buys meat for herself."

I sighed. "You're being absurd, Mother. Sandra is more honest than everyone in this family put together. When are you and Baba leaving for the opera?"

"He's picking me up in an hour." She looked at herself in her mirror. "I've lost so much weight," she sighed. "Everything hangs on me like a rag." Her shoulders slumped. "I don't even know that I want to go out anymore."

"Here," I said, guiding her by the elbow to her room. "Let's find you something lovely to wear."

There was no way I was letting Mother stay home. Not after all the maneuvering my plan had entailed. I had convinced Father to make an effort for Mother on their anniversary. I had bought the opera tickets. Tonight, I was meeting Khaled at the Kasbah. Nothing short of the arrival of De Gaulle himself that evening would prevent my parents from being out of my way.

Thankfully, I coaxed Mother out of her mood. Father was on time to sweep her up before she changed her mind, they left for the opera, and I was free, save from the unscheduled presence of my pesky brother. But unlike me, Gustave was allowed to go out after dinner as long as he stayed in the neighborhood and returned before curfew, and in the warm months, he usually went. He was seventeen, and this exotic city was filled with excitement for a boy his age.

Once it was only Sandra and me in the apartment, I told her, "I'm going too."

"You aren't allowed," she said looking upset.

"I'll be out for an hour or so."

"Marceline, you cannot leave in the evening!" Sandra said imploringly. It was true that now that we shared a room, she could no longer look the other way.

"It's not even night yet, not even close."

"I'll go with you," she said.

"Oh, don't be a grump," I said cheerfully. "It's barely six o'clock. Curfew won't be for hours." Before she had time to protest, I kissed her on the cheek. "Don't worry," I told her, "I'm like a cat who always lands on her feet."

In the stairwell, I took out of a tote the long tunic and headscarf I had taken from Sandra's shelf without her knowing and put them over my clothes. I clutched the headcovering around my neck with one hand the way Muslim women did, and I stepped out of the apartment building dressed like the Arab women of Algiers who worked as maids in the French neighborhoods.

Outside, the city's walls still radiated the day's heat. As I made my way toward the Muslim parts of the city, I kept my eyes low. Dressing up like a Muslim woman had been Khaled's idea. The length of the djellaba hampered my steps, and the veil and headscarf diminished my vision, yet moving through the city unnoticed was exhilarating. French men, the rude ones who usually whistled and said things to me as I walked by, and the well-mannered ones who eyed me and tipped their hats, now went right past me as if I were invisible. Policemen who usually harassed me under the guise of protecting young French women ignored me entirely.

I arrived at the foot of the Kasbah. The mysterious city inside a city, against which everyone had warned me, stood before me, oversized and foreboding like the entrance of a treacherous maze. Dozens of people came in and out. Some men dressed like Khaled did, in the western style, with pants and button-down shirts. Many wore burnouses and kaftans, turbans, and fezzes. Women were wrapped head to toe in white tunics and shawls. Only their eyes, strikingly lined with kohl, their hands, painted with intricate henna patterns, and their ankles and feet were visible. The Arab men did not display the subservient demeanor they usually adopted in my part of town. Here they looked dominant, intimidating. My stomach tightened. Perhaps I would do well to turn back. But then I saw Khaled.

He sat on a low wall, waiting for me to notice him. When we made eye contact, he did not smile. He hopped down and moved his head to signify I should follow him.

My heart thumped with anticipation as I followed him through the wide entrance. As instructed, I left several feet of distance between us as we walked.

Because I was with Khaled, I felt safe. At no point did it occur to me that I might be followed. At no point did I notice that all the way to the Kasbah, someone had been watching me.

I had never tried to imagine what the Kasbah was like on the inside. From a distance, it resembled a stack of whitewashed, squat constructions, one atop the other, that clung to the flank of the Bourzareah Mountain. I had not imagined the people who live there. The sinuous, narrow streets and staircases concealed a bustling world of sounds, sights, and smells. We entered the souk, the market, and walked past dozens of coffee shops, some as tiny as an opening in a wall, where groups of men sat at flimsy tables, smoked the hookah, and drank coffee. Shops appeared to sprout out of doors and windows. There were weavers, potters, bakers, pipe makers, tailors, and carpet sellers. Men, women, and children moved through the streets carrying goods, baskets, and live ducks and chickens or pulling a goat or a donkey. The scent of spices, roasted coffee beans, grilled food, and trash was overpowering. The women wore white, the men white and shades of earthy colors. French people were few, aside from the many French policemen patrolling in pairs, and I did not see any French women. Hordes of little boys, some as young as five, their little faces ferocious, moved stealthily through the streets like small armies.

Every twenty steps or so, Khaled looked over his shoulder and smiled at me with his eyes, and mine smiled back. I followed him up a hundred stone steps and deeper inside the Kasbah, away from the souk, where the jumble of streets turned less chaotic. The architecture, far from being primitive as I had assumed, was perfectly designed to keep the heat at bay; because the walls were tall and the streets narrow, the sun rarely reached the streets. Houses had tiny, rectangular or dome-shaped windows. A few had small wooden balconies held up by haphazard pillars. I looked up at the blindingly white walls where the sun reached. Above our heads, laundry hung like flags on clotheslines that went between windows from one side of the street to the other.

The steps that crisscrossed the Kasbah seemed to serve as extensions of people's houses. Entire families sat on the steps, playing cards, speaking, eating, playing reed flutes, smoking, laughing. Everywhere dogs and children ran free, and cats who were perched up high witnessed the scenes with half-closed eyes. From every corner came the smell of tagines and grilled fish. The houses themselves kept the sun out and their mysteries in.

Under my veil, it was a new experience to observe and not be seen. I felt perfectly safe and decided I had been ridiculous. The Kasbah was not dangerous. It was a place where people coexisted peacefully in a throbbing, vibrant life.

Khaled walked ahead of me, turning every so often to smile as we went up several narrow, serpentine streets and through a labyrinth of passages, steep stairs, alcoves, courtyards, and alleys. We walked past more playing children, and soon there were few sounds aside from those of our footsteps and faint music coming from somewhere.

We passed palaces with ornate doors and whitewashed walls with mosaic and wood details. We passed a hammam. We walked in front of a minuscule mosque. We walked past wooden doors and walls ornate with mosaic tiles. I was out of breath from climbing. Khaled stopped, leaned against a wall, and looked into the distance as he waited for me to catch my breath. I turned and discovered the Kasbah from above. Overlooking the immense blue sea and the azure sky was a layering of rectangular terraces that reflected the sun. From where I was, I could see people on those terraces, women pinning laundry out to dry and children playing. The higher we went, the quieter it was. Somewhere, someone played the lute, and a plaintive Arabic melody became more pronounced as we climbed. There were fewer people in the streets and soon almost no one. Khaled spoke for the first time. "Kasbah means citadel," he said. "But it's not fortified; all the gates are open. It's just a medina."

"What's a medina?"

"An Islamic city where people live the way of our ancestors. But a medina is open, whereas the Kasbah was built like a fortress. The pirate Barberousse erected it, they say."

"I was worried that someone here would notice that I'm an outsider," I said.

He smiled. "They noticed."

"How would you know?"

He laughed. "Because everyone I saw pretended not to know me."

"How could they tell?"

He pointed to my feet. "Did you see your shoes?"

I looked down at my leather shoes. The Muslim women wore babouches, or sandals or went barefoot.

"My shoes gave me away?"

"And the way you move, the way you walk: anyone who paid attention knew that you were not one of us. The Kasbah is full of gossips, but it's also very discreet. You would not be the first French woman, or French man, smuggled in."

"What would have happened if I had dressed normally?"

"Normally? You think women wearing trousers and pointy brassieres is normal to the people here?"

"I guess not."

"You dressed in a way that did not stir anyone. The idea was to be left alone, and that's what happened."

We entered through a small wooden door and found ourselves at the center of a vast bright courtyard filled with plants and the crisp bubbling sound of water dripping into a faded mosaic fountain. Light came from above, diffused through a wide opening. The house was built on three levels with balconies overlooking the courtyard. On the floor of the lowest balcony, a young child sat, his hands clasping the wrought iron bars, his skinny bare legs and dirty feet dangling toward the courtyard. He looked down at us. A veiled woman scooped him up and disappeared.

"This is where I live," Khaled said.

"Is this your family?"

"Many families live in this house." He took me to the area his family occupied, a large room with low benches and a hexagonal table. Rugs hung on the white-washed walls; the floor was covered in red tiles and sheepskins. The next room was a tiny kitchen where a stew cooked in a pot on a cast-iron stove. Khaled smelled the contents of the pot. "Eggplant," he said.

"Is someone here?"

"My mother or my aunt. But they must have seen you and chosen to leave us alone."

"Where are the bedrooms?"

He pointed to sheepskins on the floor. "We sleep here, and here," he said. He pointed at the floor of the balcony. "Sometimes here; it depends on the temperature." He smiled. "When it is cold, it's all bodies on the sheepskin at night."

We left Khaled's house, returned to the streets, and continued up the steps. My legs were sore from all the climbing. We reached the highest point of the Kasbah and emerged onto a large terrace. The sun was low in the sky. I realized that I would never be home before curfew. I did not say anything.

I was dying to remove my veil and for the breeze to cool my skin. What was it like for young girls the day they donned the veil for the first time? Did they suffer, or did it become as natural to them as it was for a French woman to wear a brassiere, hose, and heels?

From where we stood, we could see the entire Bay of Algiers, shimmering in the setting light. On the terrace, someone had planted a lush vegetable garden in pots; dirt had to have been painstakingly brought here, pound by pound. There were cherry tomato vines that crawled up bamboo posts, and cilantro and mint tufts bursting out of clay pots. I picked a mint leaf and brought it to my nose as we walked around the terrace.

"You planted this?" I asked.

"Many help care for it. I want to show you my favorite place. Come." We walked on a wide ledge until we reached a stone parapet. We sat, out of sight, our backs resting against a wall, and watched the Kasbah cascading below and the darkening sea and sky on the horizon. In the distance, a dog barked. The sound of a radio playing Arabic music escaped from a nearby window. I removed my veil and lifted my hair to refresh my neck. Khaled kissed my neck, and I did not dare move. He put his arm around me, and we kissed. I rested my head on his shoulder, bursting with happiness, and longing, and love. For a long time, we didn't speak. Then he said, "I look for solutions, and I find none."

Cool air arrived from the sea, competing with the Sahara dry air, and the wind ruffled palm trees below. The sky went from blue to purple, and a few stars lit up. "I think something will happen soon," I said.

"In the war?"

"I think the fighting will come here soon, either from the air, or from Rommel's armies in the desert, or from the sea."

"What will that change for us?"

"If we defeat Hitler, then maybe Jews will be able to return to France. You could come with me."

"Do you know how people from the Maghreb live in France? They are packed into shantytowns. They have no rights. They live a life of misery to earn a few francs they can send to their families who also live in poverty here. All this, compliments of your beautiful colonial empire." He said those last two words with contempt.

"But if you came to France, you'd live like us. You'd live *with* us! Most assuredly, my father could give you work. His business was good before the war."

"It is not so simple, Marceline. When this war ends, our struggle will continue."

"What struggle?"

He looked at me and spoke gravely. "The time will soon come when my people will fight for their independence from the French," he said.

"Another war, you mean?"

"It's inevitable. And if your people and my people become enemies, you might come to hate me."

"I will never hate you," I said, kissing him. "For one, my people aren't the French, but the Jews. Jews and Arabs have no reason to ever be at war. Besides, I'm certain that the French and the Arabs can find peaceful ways of resolving their differences."

"Tell me about a time in history when peaceful solutions were chosen over fighting and destruction?"

We were silent. The wind had died down. Soon my parents would return from the opera. I needed to leave at once. But I did not move. I wanted to continue to feel the warmth of Khaled's body next to mine.

"I have some happy news," he said. "They hired me as a full-time groundskeeper at the Jardin d'Essai."

"Khaled," I said, throwing my arms around his neck, "your dream has come true!"

"That used to be my dream," Khaled said with sadness.

"What changed?"

"Now I have a new dream," he said, searching into my eyes. "But this one is unattainable." Up in the sky, the stars began to come out. Behind us, the warmth of the desert brought with it the plaintive howls of coyotes. "I think about you day and night," he said.

"Then kiss me," I said. "Hold me in your arms."

We kissed; our breathing became heavier. Khaled pulled away. "Even here we have to be careful."

"I don't care what people think!"

"It's not what they'll think that I fear," Khaled responded somberly. "It's what they'll do. I better take you back. It is nearly dark."

I put my headcovering back on, and we rapidly made our way down through the maze of streets and stairs. We got out of the Kasbah through the same door I had entered. "I will walk you to your street, or as far as I can," he said.

"If you do this, you will have to return after curfew."

"I will take the risk."

The clock was ticking. People were rushing to be home before dark, and we hurried our step. A block away from the Kasbah, we walked under a small bridge. The bridge was only a few yards long. Under it was cool, damp, and dark. Khaled said, "Remove your djellaba and veil. Once on the other side, I will follow you at a distance."

"Why change clothes now?"

"During the day, you don't want to be a French woman in the Muslim quarter, but at night it is better not to be an Arab woman in the French quarter." I quickly took the tunic off. Now I was in my cardigan and skirt. In the dark, Khaled's eyes gleamed. I moved to kiss him, but he stood rigidly. "Too dangerous if we are found," he murmured.

"It's not fair," I said.

"We took risks. But I am happy you saw the Kasbah."

"Thank you for showing it to me."

"If you come again, I could bring you to a place that is more private." He hesitated. "A friend's room somewhere. Would you want that?"

"There is nothing I want more," I murmured.

We were interrupted by the sounds of rapid footsteps. Many footsteps. People running.

"Shhh. Don't make a sound," Khaled murmured. He took my hand, and we pressed ourselves against the damp walls of the tunnel, holding our breath.

The footsteps stopped a few yards away from us. From the darkness that concealed us, we saw what was happening on the other side of the bridge, which we only perceived as silhouettes. They were boys, some of them only children. They were holding someone who was trying to scream. They threw the person to the ground and began to beat him with merciless savagery. There were voices in Arabic, the sounds of someone being struck repetitively screaming in pain, and then a weak call for help in French. "À l'aide!"

"Stay here!" Khaled ordered. "Don't move." Before I could say a thing, Khaled had run out from under the bridge and shouted, "Stop," followed by a few words in Arabic. The boys froze up. All noise stopped. Khaled said more things I could not understand. They looked at Khaled, and, perhaps recognizing him, all at once, like a flock of birds that gets startled, moved as one and scattered away.

Instantaneously, the street turned silent. The human shape on the ground was motionless but let out a moan. Khaled leaned over him. I stepped out of the shadow. "We need to call the police, and a doctor," he said.

When I bent over the body, I gasped. "Gustave!" I cried out.

My brother lay on the ground, his face covered in blood. It was too dark to know how badly injured he might be. "Gustave" I called. "Gustave! Can you hear me?" I told Khaled. "It's my brother!"

"We're both in bad trouble now," was the first thing Gustave mumbled before a wave of nausea overtook him and he turned to the side to vomit.

"Why is your brother here?" Khaled asked.

"He's been following me everywhere," I admitted.

"Sit with him. I'll call for help."

After a few minutes, Khaled returned, accompanied by two French policemen who had been doing their rounds. If they were so close, how had they not heard what was going on? By now, it was dark out. I sensed that they had heard the commotion but chosen not to get involved until Khaled asked for help.

"What happened here?" one of the policemen demanded to know.

My lies came out swiftly. "My brother and I were walking back home, and a group of young boys assaulted him." I pointed to Khaled. "This boy here made them run away."

"Do you know the assailant?" the policeman asked Khaled.

The other policeman observed me with suspicion. "They attacked your brother but left you alone?"

"What were the two of you doing near the Kasbah after curfew?" the first policeman asked.

I remembered who I was. I was a French citizen, and they were the police. "What does it matter?" I shouted. "My brother needs to be taken to the hospital immediately!" Gustave was getting to his feet by the time the ambulance arrived. I turned to look at Khaled just as one of the policemen handcuffed him. Khaled was not speaking, not resisting. "Why are you handcuffing him? What has he done? Where are you taking him?"

"It's police business, Mademoiselle."

"This is a mistake! I just told you he's the one who saved my brother! You have no grounds to arrest him."

"We have to conduct an investigation, and he might know the attackers. If he has nothing to reproach himself, he will give us their names and be released."

Khaled and I exchanged looks. We both knew that any kind of resistance would make the problem worse. One of the policemen pushed him forward. Khaled tripped slightly. To my horror, the policeman struck him on the back of his head.

"Why are you hitting him?" I cried out. "Don't hurt him!"

Khaled looked down, expressionless.

"You and your brother should know better than break curfew," the policeman said. "How can I reach your parents?"

I had no choice but to give the police the information. One of the policemen walked to a police telephone set up in the street, and we waited.

Two vehicles arrived. One was a police car, the other an ambulance. A nurse in white uniform and the ambulance driver, with the help of one of the policemen, helped Gustave into the back of the ambulance, and the nurse went in with him and began to tend to his wounds.

I climbed in the front seat next to the driver, a mournful-looking older Algerian man. As we drove off in the night, the ambulance's headlight briefly shone on Khaled, still handcuffed, being pushed into the police car.

"Why are they taking him?" I shouted. "He is the one who saved my brother from being killed! He's a hero."

The driver shook his head slowly. "He's an Arab," he said. He turned on the siren. I could hardly think straight between my sobs and the piercing noise that rattled my brain. How could my brother be so stupid and so fixated on me? Why had he followed me to the Kasbah? What did he know? Did he understand that I was meeting Khaled? Had he realized that Khaled had saved him? I turned to see my brother, who was being tended to by the nurse. I urgently needed to tell him the version of the story I had given the police, but the presence of the nurse and the terrible noise made communicating with Gustave impossible.

I was in the hospital's waiting room when my parents arrived, dressed in their opera clothes: my father in a tuxedo and Mother in her fur and pearls. First, the police spoke to my father while my mother rushed to Gustave's room, brushing past me without looking at me.

My father came to me and, reassured that I was unhurt, asked me to stay in the hallway while he went to see Gustave.

Twenty minutes later, my father came out of the room, livid. He took me aside into a hallway so that we would not be heard. "Gustave needs stitches. Three of his ribs are broken, as is his nose," he said. "But what your brother told me about what happened has nothing to do with what you told the police."

"Baba, you need to call the commissariat!" I cried. "The boy who saved Gustave was taken there!"

"Saved? Your brother was savagely attacked. He does not look saved to me! He will probably require surgery to fix his nose."

"Gustave would have been much worse; in fact, he could have been killed had the boy not intervened when he did."

"The police will find out what actually happened and not some lie you concocted," he said. "You told the police that you and your brother were just walking together after curfew, that you were attacked, and that a boy who was just passing by intervened."

"That's it. That's what happened. Had it not been for this stranger—"

"Gustave said that he saw you leave the apartment, that he followed you, and that he saw you enter the Kasbah right before curfew. He said he waited at the foot of the Kasbah for two hours until you came back with a boy. By then it was dark and after curfew. He then followed the two of you until a group of boys attacked him."

I had no choice but to tell my father the truth. "It's true. I was meeting a boy there." My father's face turned red. "But we did nothing, Baba!" I quickly said. "I swear it to you! He just wanted to show me the Kasbah."

"Who is this boy you will take such ridiculous risks for?"

"He was just – showing me the Kasbah. What harm is there in that?"

My father put a hand up to stop me. "We will stick to the version you told the police," was all he said.

Gustave was kept under observation in a crowded hall full of hospitalized patients and their families. We were advised that he should not fall asleep, as he might have a concussion. My mother and father, still in their opera attire, fretted over him, my father intent on Gustave drinking water, and my mother crying the entire time and panicking and calling the nurses each time Gustave appeared to doze off. I sat in a chair, furious at the spectacle our family was.

Dawn came. We were all exhausted. My father paid for a private room, and Gustave was transferred to it. In the private room, Father, Mother, and I slumped into chairs, thankful to be alone at last. Gustave looked terrible. Both of his eyes were swollen shut, his nose was cut and misshaped, and it seemed that at least one of his teeth was missing.

"This country is a terrible, lawless place," my mother said. "Look what those savages did to my son. His beautiful face is ruined!"

"Right now, Algeria isn't any more lawless than everywhere else in Europe," I pointed out.

"And his face is not ruined," my father said. "Nothing is ruined. He will heal."

"I don't mind a few scars," Gustave said.

"He will look more rugged," I said.

Now that it was just the four of us, my mother, whose eyes were red from crying, turned to me. "So Gustave was following you. What I fail to understand is why you were out at that hour."

"She was meeting a boy," my father sighed.

"A boy? At night? Oh my!" Mother screeched. "What kind of boy?"

"Is he one of those Jewish students?" my father asked.

I widened my eyes. "How do you know about them?" I said. My father just shrugged in exasperation.

"What Jewish students?" Mother bellowed.

"He's a local boy," I said, bracing myself.

"What does she mean by *local?*" my mother asked my father in complete incomprehension.

My father shrugged toward me and said, "Ask your daughter."

"Ask her? When she's been telling us nothing but lies?"

"He's a Muslim boy, Mother," I said defiantly. "He's the one who stopped the attackers."

An icy silence fell upon the room. We heard a mumble come from Gustave's bed. "I've been trying to keep an eye on her," he said. "Like you asked me to."

"You weren't supposed to risk your life," my father said.

"I thought I'd tell her to stop and she would. I just needed proof."

I was furious that they felt entitled to talk about me as though I was not in the room. "Proof? This is not a criminal investigation!" I said.

"Enough!" my father snapped.

"Tell me you did not actually enter the Kasbah," Mother said.

"It's a perfectly safe place. Lovely in fact." I admitted, "And I was dressed like a Muslim woman."

"Oh my," Mother said again. "But why with this ... Arab?"

"His name is Khaled," I said defiantly. "And I'm in love with him!"

Mother slumped in her chair and began fanning herself. "I will die right this minute," she said. "How did you procure yourself those clothes?"

"I took them from Sandra."

Mother went quiet, as she suddenly understood something. Fury passed through her eyes like a maelstrom. "Sandra gave you the clothes! And she let you out, didn't she? How could you have gotten out of a room you share otherwise?"

"It was only going to be for a few hours. If Gustave had not—"

"This is all her fault!" Mother erupted. "She has ruined your reputation, and she's caused Gustave to be nearly killed!"

"Sandra had no idea," I lied, trying to look innocent.

My mother turned to my father and growled between clenched teeth, enunciating each word. "I want that woman out of my house by morning."

I could deny all I wanted; this was the last bit of news Mother needed in her case against Sandra, and there was nothing any of us would be able to do or say to protect her now. Father and Gustave seemed crushed. I lowered my head.

Father, in an empty voice, briefed Gustave on the official version of the story he should give the police: Gustave and I were together, walking, we got lost, he was attacked, Khaled was a stranger passing by, a good Samaritan who stopped the assailants.

Gustave remained at the hospital overnight and Mother, Father, and I returned to the apartment where Sandra was wringing her hands. My father reassured her about Gustave. Mother refused to look at Sandra and stormed into her room, slamming the door behind her. My father called Sandra into the kitchen and closed the door behind them. They stayed there for a long time, with me pacing on the other side of the door. I will never know what he said to her, but when she came out, her eyes were red. Heartbreakingly, my father looked to have been crying too. It dawned on me that the night had set in motion events beyond my control, and I blamed Gustave for that.

Sandra went to the bedroom we shared. Wordlessly, she began to gather her few possessions and set them out on top of her bed. I helped her fold her clothes, crying. "I thought that if anyone found out, I would be the one to get into trouble. I never thought I would get you fired. I don't want you to go. Where will you live?"

"Your father will drive me to a hotel for now, and then I will see."

"Sandra?"

"Yes?"

"I'm so sorry."

Sandra shook her head. "I knew what you were doing. I let you. I endangered you and Gustave. Your mother is right."

"You couldn't stop me. You tried."

"I could have. I did not want to."

"But why?"

She inspected me with her wide-set, unflinching eyes. "You have a wild spirit and no fear. I wish I had no fear."

"That's not true. I'm afraid for you now."

Sandra had a small, sad smile and said, "Tell me about this boy."

"He is a wonderful person, and smart too." As I spoke, a dam broke inside me. I burst with happiness just to be able to tell Sandra about Khaled. I told her everything: who he was, where we met, how handsome he was, and also how there was no future for us because of our races, our religions, and our places in society. "He works all the time. He supports his entire family. He wants to make something of himself, and I know he will. I know it!"

She beamed at me. "You respect him."

"Oh, Sandra, I love him!" I said, and then I broke down in tears because neither of my parents had wanted to know anything about him.

"Does he feel the same toward you?"

"He does!"

Sandra sat on the bed next to me and caressed my hair. "I too fell in love once," she murmured. "Just like you and this boy, the boy I loved was from a different religion, a different world from mine. We could not be together. To do so was to risk our lives. Still, we ran away together. But then there was the fire.

The city was destroyed. So many died. The great fire of Smyrna tore us apart. We were separated."

"How long did it take for you to forget him?"

She took my hands. "I have never forgotten him."

"Was there ever another man after him?" I regretted asking. With her appearance, finding love again would be nearly impossible.

As though she could read my thoughts, Sandra said, "One great love is more than many people will ever experience."

An hour later, Sandra was gone from our lives.

She visited Gustave at the hospital, and then Father took her to a hotel. He paid for a month in advance and gave her money for her expenses. He told us this and said that he would help find her a new position.

Mother had her replaced the same week by a local woman, a wrinkled old thing with no personality. In truth, Gustave and I had long outgrown the need for a nanny. The circumstances of the war had made it difficult for my big-hearted father to leave Sandra behind in Paris or Cannes, postponing the inevitable. It had made little sense to keep her for as long as we had, especially as Mother had made her into the focus of her unhappiness. I felt certain that Sandra would soon find a family with young children she could take care of. She was so wonderful with children.

Through August and September 1942, I saw Sandra a couple more times. I visited her at her hotel once. She looked resigned. Another time I met her by accident at the market, and we walked through the aisles together and chatted. She was distraught, I could tell. I asked if she had money. She said that my father had been generous. I asked her what her plans were; she said she'd be just fine and not to worry about her. But there was something else, ominous, dark. Or do I only think this in retrospect? Because I have since wondered if her troubles were already brewing that day, below the surface.

When we parted, she hugged me tightly and told me that I was a wonderful, intelligent girl, that I was brave but that it did not mean I should be reckless, and that she was proud of me. Were those parting words? Did she know what was about to happen? She also said she was sorry for the pain she had caused. She uttered not a word of bitterness or resentment toward Mother or Father for leaving her in the dust after her devotion to us.

****

Marceline looked at Cassandra. She now looked back at her early forties, the age her niece was, as her infancy. Everything before that had been a wash. Vanity. Selfishness. She had made so many mistakes. She had saved the day a couple of times, but who remembered?

The tea in their cups was cold. Marceline felt drained. She had not gotten around to what she wanted her niece to know. She could not. Not today. She would first need to find the strength.

Cassandra sat upright, riveted, expectant. She was going to disappoint her. "This was the last time I ever saw Sandra," she told Cassandra. "When we heard from her again it was a whole month later and through the police."

"What happened?" Cassandra exclaimed.

"It was all very mysterious, as you shall see. But I'm quite exhausted. Perhaps we can continue tomorrow."

"Yes, or course. I understand," Cassandra assured her, although her expression told a different story.

"You wait till you reach my age, ma chère," Marceline said. "Aging is not for the weak, as you'll one day find out."

"It's only that I'm leaving Paris soon."

"I will try to remain alive a few more days then. So as not to inconvenience you."

Cassandra looked aghast. "Oh, but not at all!"

"Come tomorrow. It will be lovely weather I am told. We'll have tea in the garden."

"But tell me first, what about Khaled?"

"Khaled?"

"How long did he stay in jail?"

"That's part of a much longer conversation," Marceline said.

After Cassandra had left, Marceline turned to Laure. "Do you think she looks like me at all?"

"It's in the eyes, that unusual color."

"But she doesn't have my strength I don't think. She's more of a delicate flower, like her father."

"Few people have your strength, Madame," Laure answered.

CHAPTER 3

The Man Who Made Pasta

Cassie stepped out of Marceline's house enveloped in a cottony feeling of unreality. She walked on the cobblestone pavement, surprised at the song of birds, at the fact that it was spring in Paris and not Algiers of the 1940s. In Cité des Fleurs, only faint, distant street noises hinted at the twenty-first century. The façades of hotels particuliers peeked from above metal gates, just as they had since their construction a hundred years before. Her cowboy boots hit the uneven pavement in rhythmic sounds that brought her back to here and now. These cobblestones had once been trampled on by horses and carriages. They had been under the wheels of the very first automobiles. They had absorbed the blood of soldiers, résistants, and Jews during the Second World War. In the sixties, revolutionary students had unearthed them to use as projectiles against the police. In Paris, to ignore history was impossible. Every wall, every clock, every statue and building reminded you of it. In the mere twenty years between 1918 and 1938, Europe had ended the supposed "war to end all wars," seen unparalleled growth and progress, revealed in the wild optimism of the années folles, only to embark on the most destructive conflict in human history. How precarious was the balance of things? Economic chaos had been the fertile terrain for anger and xenophobia to fester until the world was ripe for exploitation by the kind of leaders that thrived on divisiveness and fear.

Across the Seine, in the fifteenth arrondissement near Métro Bir-Hakeim, a plaque acknowledged the ignominy that had taken place at the Vel' d'Hiv seventy years before. French citizens beyond reproach, policemen, war heroes, politicians, had taken it upon themselves to round Paris's Jewish families and gather them under the glass dome on a sweltering July day. At what point was it decided to let them die by the hundreds from heat and dehydration? Was it the plan? Or had something gone awry? After allowing that carnage to take place, these upstanding citizens had left the Jews to die and had returned to their wives, children, or grandchildren in time for dinner. It was unfathomable because you wanted to believe in decency, in moral courage. You wanted to believe that mankind was good. But history told a different story. Mankind was awful. And without peace-minded leaders keeping our worst nature in check, it had repeatedly all gone to hell.

Cassie thought of fate, of prescience. Which was it that had compelled her grandfather to run away rather than stay in Paris? Her family had narrowly escaped the fate of other Jews so that Cassie could be conceived. So that she could have two beautiful children. How dare she resent her childhood? How dare she brood with ennui and disenchantment while she lived in safety and abundance? Her father had endured so much yet had chosen to hide his childhood's suffering from his daughters. But this too, she thought, had an impact. In a single generation of deliberate amnesia, all lessons had been lost.

Cassie turned onto Avenue de Clichy with its cars, mopeds, people carrying groceries, children in strollers, pregnant women, honking, whistles, métro vibrating below ground, and smell of baked bread and rotisserie chicken. The arrival of sunshine had transformed the city, altering the sounds and smells, brightening the stone façade of buildings, shifting moods. Because the Parisians were liberated from their umbrellas and raincoats, their eyes met, as if to acknowledge the arrival of springtime.

Maybe she could redeem herself. It was going to be up to her. If she was unable to define herself outside her unrequited love for her father, or for Peter, it was her own fault. She needed to take note, to remind herself of her singular existence at this moment. All around, beautiful things were happening: miracles, moments of grace. In the same hospital where her father languished, babies were born. In studios and apartments across the city, artists created, people kissed under street lamps, men and women made love in bedrooms.

Hervé, she thought. His skin, his lips on her. She hurried her steps, embarrassed by that flash of lust. Only days ago, she was certain that she was done with all this. Sex, desire, those silly things, she never thought about. Or only in those occasional dreams that baffled her. And now she was hurrying through Paris, her heart racing as she thought of a man.

Careful, her mind whispered to her heart. Careful. But those were just words, barely a flutter.

****

When Cassie entered the hospital's waiting room, Odile was alone. She had a book on her lap but was not reading. She sat on the edge of her seat, leaning forward as if she wanted as little of her butt as possible to touch the plastic chair. Her hair was pulled back by a severe little headband that gave her the look of a girl who was never given the authorization to play. Odile had always been uptight, self-righteous. Part of Cassie felt sorry for the perpetual imaginary burden Odile carried. But mostly she felt annoyed. There had always been a rivalry between them. They saw the world and everything in it very differently; their brains were not wired the same way, but was this enough to explain why they were at each other's throat? The antagonism between Gustave and Marceline seemed like a big, sad waste, something that needed repair. And yet, she moved through life not giving a moment of thought to the waste of her relationship with her own sister.

Odile looked up from her book and said in a hollow voice, "The antibiotics aren't working."

"What does that mean?"

"They're putting him on dialysis. Something to do with his kidneys." Odile's eyes flooded. "What if Papa doesn't get better?"

Cassie had the vision of her father in that hospital bed in Algiers, after the gang beat him up. She patted Odile on the shoulder. "The dialysis will help. The doctors know what they're doing. Right?"

Odile stiffened in her chair. "Is that a question or an affirmation?"

"Quit thinking that everything I say is an affront."

"You're the one who keeps questioning the treatment."

Cassie closed her eyes, already exhausted after one minute with Odile. "I really wasn't," she said. "At least not this time."

"How long do you plan on staying in Paris?" Odile asked in a tone of reproach.

"My return ticket is for Wednesday."

"So, you're going to leave?"

"What else can I do?"

Odile had a small laugh. "What can you do besides leave me alone to deal with all this, as you always do?"

This wasn't a new argument. Odile took care of their parent's finances; she did their taxes, blah, blah, blah. They called her when they could not fix something in the house. She scheduled their doctors' appointments. When they needed new glasses, when they went to the dentist, it was Odile who took them. In return, Odile got to play the act of the long-suffering victim. "Are you kidding?" Cassie snapped. "First you don't tell me that Papa is having surgery, then you block me from seeing him."

Odile shrugged. "You don't get it, and you never will."

"You're the one who doesn't get it. You've made it so that I can be of no help at all."

"I'm not asking you to help Papa," Odile said coldly. "Even the doctors can't seem to do that! I'm asking you to help me and Maman."

Cassie took a breath before responding. She was not the selfish, irresponsible person Odile was making her out to be, but it was true that Odile's willingness to sacrifice herself allowed for Cassie to be in another country and live her life, a fact that was never far from either of their minds. "I'm here now," she sighed. "What is it you want me to do?"

"You need to help our family instead of running away from home like you always do."

"The United States is my home. It's been my home for the last twenty years. If anything, I'm running away from there to be here."

"You know very well what I'm saying."

"I don't."

"Every time there is an issue, you're all high and mighty. You act so wronged by us. Or whatever guilt trip you're into, whatever story you tell yourself. But this is not the time and place, Cassie. This is a crisis. We have to stick together."

"Is that what you call casting me away from his room?"

"And here you go again! You keep making it about you! I need to protect him. The doctors agreed. I *don't* know why Papa gets agitated when he sees you. I'm not saying that it's your fault, but the result is the same."

"Oh, I get it. It's not about me, and that's because it's about you! Always. *Your* fear, *your* worry. How about the possibility that I might need to be in that room with Papa just as much as you do?"

Odile thought for a moment. "To be frank, no. I don't think you need to be in the room as much as I do. You said it yourself: your home is elsewhere. You washed your hands of him a long time ago."

In the wave of hurt and outrage, Cassie was rapidly succumbing to an old feeling, something in her soul was being torn open, and she had to steady herself. "You think you have a monopoly on loving Papa? I could love him plenty too if only he'd let me." Cassie tried to take in air, but her lungs seemed reduced to useless pockets. She studied the scratches on her hand, still fresh from the gardening she had done the day before coming to Paris. The scratches felt grounding. Whatever this awful moment was, it was temporary. There was normality to return to, elsewhere.

"I'm sorry that things were so difficult between you and Papa," Odile said. "But it was not my doing. The two of you created this. I was in the middle."

"What was I guilty of, Odile?" Cassie asked in a small voice. "Why was he so irked by me? What did I do that rubbed him the wrong way?"

Odile looked away. "Things would have worked themselves out over time. The two of you hit a rough patch, and you left the country. You just picked up and left. How were things going to ever improve between you after that?"

"You know this was not new. He was like this with me from the time I was a kid."

"Why didn't you try to fix things?"

"I tried everything!" Cassie cried out. "But he shut me out! Moving away didn't create the problem. I moved away for self-preservation! When I finally realized that I would never be loved by him. And this after killing myself trying to accomplish that since I was little!"

"You were always trying to be perfect and being so competitive."

Cassie spoke without a breath. "Yes, I tried too hard! And yes, I was desperate! But every movement I made, everything I said and did, it all seemed to annoy him. And you? You could do no wrong."

"Don't be melodramatic."

Cassie looked straight into Odile's eyes, her fury daring her sister to look away. "Are you telling me that he never said negative things about me behind my back? That, in fact, he said loving things about me when I didn't know it? Please tell me that I'm imagining all this because I'll want to believe you. I would desperately want to believe you!"

Odile stared at Cassie. "Why get into all this now? Papa's antibiotics aren't working. He needs dialysis, and you just want to talk about the past."

Cassie looked at her feet. "You're right. It's just ... so many emotions. I don't know how to feel right now."

Odile sighed. "Look, I didn't know why Papa was like that with you back then," she said. "I still don't know."

Cassie felt a deep silence sweep through her. And then, a sensation of brightness, as though all the lights in the room turned on at once. It was real! It had happened! Odile was confirming it. And yes, she was devastated by this truth, but it was the truth she needed to hear. "Thank you for acknowledging this," she muttered.

Odile rubbed her face with the palms of her hands. "I mean ... I thought I knew why he was like that with you, like part of him could not stand you." She was speaking to Cassie but mostly to herself. "It was the way you were, and all, you know ... bossy, annoying, superior."

"Superior?"

"But the way he saw you maybe colored the way I perceived you. It's hard to tell. It's ... I don't know. Messed up." Odile was crying now. Why was she crying? Was it remorse, sadness, self-pity, or the simple fact that their dad was very sick? Cassie was thankful for her sister's tears because she was not able to shed her own. Something in her was blocked. Or perhaps it was that if she began crying, she might never stop.

"All those years, being told it was all in my imagination."

"I'm sorry. I feel like a piece of shit for telling you this. I don't want you to be mad at Papa. Or Papa to be mad at me for telling you."

"It helps actually."

"I feel really bad about it."

"But why superior? I was insecure my entire childhood."

"Well, like when you think you know better than the doctors what to do about Papa."

"I don't think I know better. I just ask questions."

"Same difference," Odile said with a shrug.

"It's not the same! I—"

Cassie stopped herself. What was the point? The way Odile perceived her was too ingrained to change in a day. Instead, she said, "I need you to put me back on the visitors' list so I can be in Papa's room with you guys."

Odile wrung her hands. "I want to, Cassie. I really want to. But I can't take the chance of Papa having another episode. For the moment, he's calm. If he sees you and goes ballistic, they'll go back to sedating him, and you know that it would make his recovery that much more difficult." Odile looked at her feet. "I'm sorry, Cassie."

Cassie was stunned. "Does Papa even realize that I came all the way here just to support him? Did you even tell him?"

Odile spoke uneasily. "What if he sees you and gets into another fit and has a heart attack or something? I'm sorry, but I'd rather insult your pride than take that chance."

Cassie drew a quick breath to control her mounting anger. "My pride?" she exclaimed. "How can you live with the thought that I'm outside his room and not allowed in? How can you sleep at night after you treat your own sister like a frigging leper?"

"I *don't* sleep at night!" Odile whined.

A childhood urge made her want to throw herself at Odile and pull on her hair, the way they used to when they fought as kids. The adult part of her told her that she had better walk away. Trembling with fury, Cassie looked at Odile. "I will come back later or call to see how he is. I guess for now it's better if I just go, or I'm going to lose my shit."

As she left the room, she heard Odile whimper, "I'm sorry. I really am."

Cassie's boot heels clapped down the hospital corridors, her anger fresh and raw. She needed to bite someone's head off right this minute! She charged toward the ICU's reception desk where Mademoiselle Pinçon huddled with the usual weary group of nurses and interns. "I want an appointment, and I want it now," she told Pinçon. "If your Chief of Services doesn't meet me, I'll escalate the hell out of this!" she said.

"More than you already have?" Pinçon said tonelessly.

"I'm writing day-by-day accounts of our interactions. He'd better meet with me before I post them all over social media with the name of this hospital front and center!"

The nurses averted their eyes, but Pinçon looked at her, or through her, with a calculated mix of hostility and boredom. "You can always try eight a.m. tomorrow."

Cassie had not expected Pinçon to cave, and so she doubled down, improvising, "I have videos! Damning pieces of evidence!" Pinçon gave her an uninterested look. "If he doesn't meet me tomorrow at eight a.m., this hospital's ineptitude will go more viral than any of the germs this place is rampant with!"

"I will pass this on, Madame," Pinçon said.

"Eight a.m. sharp! I'll be here. You better count on it," Cassie yelled before turning around with a flourish and leaving the hospital.

Back in her hotel room, Cassie drew a bath and slipped into the hot water. She floated there for a long time, incapable of aligning two thoughts. It all came in a jumble: Hervé, Odile, Albano, her dad and mom, Sabine, Marceline, Lucienne, her children. And then back to Hervé and their night. Hervé and his hands, his…. Be careful, she reminded herself.

She felt numb, curiously detached from Odile's admission of what she had suspected for years. She wasn't destroyed. Would she feel destroyed later, when the numbness went away? It was one thing that her father "could not stand her" as an adult. She could see why: she had opposed him, she had contradicted him, she had cross-examined him. Eventually, she had married an American and permanently left France. But the confirmation of what she had suspected, felt in her bones rather, that he did not like her even as a child, that was too much to process.

She floated in her warm bath, thinking, trying to make the jigsaw pieces of her childhood fit together. Her dad had not been openly hostile. Things that happened were subtle: a slow and steady neglect of her dreams, a failure to notice her talents, a pruning of her self-esteem. The shaping had been bonsai-like. Imperceptible almost. And just like a bonsai, things looked healthy on the outside, but something was off. She had been shaped by him, by the way he looked at her, or rather did not look at her. His indistinct animosity toward her was a poison that had tasted almost like parental love. How he seemed never to see her, never to hear her. His pointed interest in her sisters. The way he delighted in them but looked away when Cassie was trying so hard to do well. It was not aggression; it was pointed neglect. Had he beat her, or screamed at her, she would have been sure. But he was quiet and sneaky about it, and because she was a child and could find no fault in him, she could only hate herself.

She thought of Albano, her grandfather who had instinctively known to take his family away from danger when so many other Jews had stayed behind. In a way, she had done the same. Without understanding the magnitude of the danger or the nature of the enemy, she had packed her things and left. She had moved to the United States, latched on to Peter, not knowing herself at all, but fighting tooth and nail for survival. She had fought to reclaim the lost parts of herself. Only she had gone about it the wrong way. Instead of sitting with her sadness, she had discovered anger. Instead of going deep, she had gone wayward.

Now, maybe, things could start to make sense. She would have to sit with the sadness, at some point. For the moment, it was relief she felt. She was thankful to Odile for validating her experience. She felt relief that perhaps she was not a bitter ingrate, but justifiably heartbroken.

She took her hands out of the water and examined her pruned fingers. Five years after removing her wedding ring, her finger still showed an indentation. Peter had served as her emotional punching bag. That's why he had left her, wasn't it? But she could not quiet the nagging suspicion that this wasn't the whole story. Something about Peter and Jessica's tale of how they had met smelled fishy. She knew that, had always known that, but healthy self-preservation had dictated that she should not confront him about it. As with her dad, she had blamed herself for the failure of the relationship rather than blame the man she loved. One day she would need the courage to look deeper. But not yet. Not now.

An hour later, she heard Hervé's motorcycle in the street below, and she ran down the stairs, making herself forget Peter, Marceline, Odile, her father, and even, temporarily, her children.

They drove on rue La Mouzaïa, and Hervé made a turn into a narrow cobblestone alley with small two-storied square houses on each side. Clematis and wisteria in full blue bloom were tangled in gates and climbing façades. A fat orange cat, stretched out on the cobblestones as if determined to soak up every remaining ray of the setting sun, moved begrudgingly to make way for them. Hervé stopped in front of a small gate and turned off the engine. They climbed off the motorcycle. He opened the gate and walked his bike into a tiny courtyard. "This is home," he said.

"What is this area called?" Cassie said as she removed her helmet. "It doesn't feel like Paris at all."

"This is the La Mouzaïa neighborhood. For a Parisienne, you don't know your city very well."

"My family was like a sect, I told you. We weren't encouraged to expand our horizons."

"Well, there are 250 houses in the neighborhood along alleys like this one. The houses were built in the late eighteen hundreds as housing for the quarry workmen who worked at mining the gypsum underground. Below it's all quarry tunnels and galleries. That's why the neighborhood was never demolished. The ground is not strong enough to build up the way they did with those atrocious buildings all around." Hervé took the mail out of the box and opened the front door. He turned on the light. Inside, it smelled of wood fire and books. The living room was furnished with old things: a battered brown leather sofa, mismatched wooden chairs, frayed rugs, a fireplace filled with the remnants of a fire. There were two electric guitars in a corner. There were shelves filled with vinyl records and books. The wide beams on the ceiling were sprinkled with cobwebs. "This place looks like you," Cassie said.

"I saw you look at that cobweb."

"I meant it as a compliment."

"My ex took all the good stuff," Hervé said. "And the cleaning supplies."

"She didn't take the house?"

"She kept our house in the Lubéron," he said, leaving the mail on an atrocious coffee table covered with glass, set atop a rusty oil can bedazzled with broken mirror pieces.

"You could not convince her to take this table," Cassie asked.

"This was my brother's first attempt at building furniture. He was twelve years old. He's a talented wood crafter now. He makes all sorts of magnificent things. I kept it because it's funny-looking." He leafed through the mail and brandished a motorcycle magazine. "Again, that crap?" he exclaimed. The back cover had a garish advertisement for *Women in Black, Part Two.* Hervé turned the magazine over, to show Cassie the photograph of all the *Women in Black, Part Two*'s cast members in full costume. "I give up," he said, and he tossed the magazine into the fireplace.

"What's your beef with that movie?" she asked, defensively. "It's harmless."

"I don't find stupidity harmless."

"Hollywood writers are actually pretty smart."

"Even more worrisome if intelligent people are deliberately fine-tuning this crap." He took her coat, removed his leather jacket, and tossed them on a chair.

She sank on the couch. The leather was supple and warm under her fingers. She saw no sign of a television. "What's so wrong with a little mindless entertainment once in a while?"

"The word entertainment itself is the danger," Hervé said. "People absorb the output of creative people and forget to produce anything of their own." There was a scratching sound coming from the front door. Hervé went to open it, and the orange cat she had seen in the street walked in, looking put-upon. "I know," he told the cat. "You're hungry. I know, I know."

From the couch, she watched Hervé enter the kitchen and look in the cupboard for a can of cat food. The cat began purring loudly, throwing himself at Hervé's legs.

"What's his name?"

"I don't know. He adopted me, not the other way around. I call him Le Chat." He crouched and scratched the cat's head. "I understand human's desire to escape their thoughts. We're terrified to contemplate the deep questions: morality, mortality, life's meaning, the universe."

Cassie rubbed her temples. "I'm not sure I want to ponder all of that either."

"But isn't this precisely what you're doing now with your aunt?"

"I thought I was pondering my family history."

"It's all too enormous. We think we might implode with despair if we so much as think about deeper questions. But humans are existential creatures. What you call harmless entertainment yanks us in every direction except inward, and inward is the only place where we'll find any peace."

"So, the problem is the cure?"

"You bet it is. Look at people jab at their telephones and computers, desperate for a distraction. Look at them pack into movie theaters to cram down fake emotions, fake relationships, fake dialogues, cramming a fake world down into their starving psyches. People will never find meaning from the passive absorption of vapid Hollywood crap."

"Where would we find it then? Religion?"

"It will come from the opposite of distraction. The ability to sit with one's thoughts, the ability to make things, to create, to move, to get excited about ideas, to dream up something better, to earn a living doing honest work."

"But you hate your job, you said."

"My true work starts when the job ends. My work is to pay close attention to small things, to the process of things."

"What is this process you keep talking about?"

"Maybe there is a better word for it." Hervé came to sit on the couch next to her. The golden light that came through the window shone on his face. "It's about finding mundane things beautiful," he said. "Then it all becomes simpler. Here, I'll show you." She followed him into the kitchen. "Have a seat," he said. He washed his hands at the small enamel sink. The kitchen was tiny, crooked, with a chipped, old-mosaic floor, an antique buffet, a small range, and an old refrigerator. The walls were lined with shelves covered with a disparate assortment of plates, glasses, pots, and pans. "Bon, so here we are," he said. "We are making pasta, yes? But why? It's a waste of time, correct? I can buy a box of decent dry pasta for two euros. I can leave it in the cupboard for a year, ten years; it will not go bad. When I want to eat, I toss it into a pot of boiling water, and it's done. How convenient! What an impressive shelf-life! These are the yardsticks these days."

He went to the shelves. "But look: here is a bowl, and here is flour and sea salt, and good olive oil." He went to the small refrigerator. "And here are eggs. And what we get out of those four ingredients is an adventure." He moved through the small kitchen naturally, each gesture relaxed and precise. He clipped herbs from a planter in the windowsill: mint, parsley, coriander leaves. "Smell this," he said, putting the herbs near her nostrils. "It's for later." He returned to the table and dropped flour onto it. "So, first, you use good, honest flour, none of that refined stuff that looks like crack and is just about as nutritious. Then you make a well. And then you break the eggs into the well, add a little olive oil." He did this, cracking the eggs with one hand with a flourish. He winked at her. "See that? I hope you are impressed. I practiced for so long that by the end, live chicks were coming out of the shells."

"Duly impressed," she said. She peered at the bright yolks in the white flour well. "Why can't you put the whole thing into a bowl?"

"Drama. Danger. If you put this in a bowl, it won't get all over the kitchen, and getting dirty is part of the tradition." He rolled his sleeves up. His hands dove into the flour. Soon he was whisking the egg in the center, folding in the flour, and then going at it with his hands until his fingers were coated with sticky goop. "Can you add a handful of flour please?" She did, and he began pushing and pressing the dough with his palms until it came together into a ball, shiny and smooth. He spread a thin coat of flour on the table and set the dough on the flour. "And now we wait," he said.

"For how long?"

"Long enough for a glass of wine." He poured her a glass of Bordeaux and plucked the fresh mint, parsley, and coriander leaves off their stems. The combined aroma of all three herbs bounced through the kitchen as he crushed leaves between his fingers. He had beautiful hands, masculine and wide.

"What will you do with these?" she asked. "Are they for a sauce? What do you call it?"

"Bah, no name. I just mix in what I have. Sometimes I add ground pistachios or almonds." He took a head of garlic and with a well-calibrated drop of a fist, separated the head into cloves. He took the cloves between his palms and rubbed them together to detach the skins until each clove lay bare on the kitchen table. He placed the peeled garlic into an antiquated, eighties-looking blender, added olive oil, salt, and pepper, and then added the leaves. The air filled with the aroma of garlic and mint.

"I like your kitchen. It reminds me of my hotel room."

"The old doors creak, the handles wobble, the plumbing is mercurial. I can't find the origin of that mildew smell. But the house has personality. The whole neighborhood does. It's bucolic. Cats roam like sentinels. How many Parisians can boast to have bird nests on their windowsills?" He took out a rolling pin, flattened the dough, flapped it over, rolled it thinner, adding speckles of flour onto the dough, and repeated the motion until the dough was very thin. He folded the sheet of dough lightly, and with a knife, cut thin strands of dough the width of fettuccine. The strands were uneven, but he did not seem to care. "Mix those up with a little flour, so they don't stick to each other."

As Cassie tossed flour on the strands of pasta, she felt the resistance of the dough between her fingers, pliable and soft but also resilient. She dipped her hands in the flour, tossed the pasta until each strand separated. There was flour on every inch of the table and a good deal dusted the floor. Soon there was a jumbled pile of blond pasta in the center of the table, each strand self-contained and perfect, like individual small beings. "Et voila," Hervé said, opening both palms toward the result of their effort. "And here is my point. Was this convenient? Of course not. I have boxes in the cupboard. Was it important? Not either. Was it urgent? No. These might not even taste better. But it was beautiful making those, wasn't it?"

Cassie smiled at the mound of pasta. "It was."

"That, my dear, is what I call The Process."

She noticed in herself a sort of softening. Her guard had been up, and now it was down, and that was all right with her. The kitchen smelled of mint and coriander and garlic. The cat sat on the countertop, his eyes half-closed. Hervé had flour in his hair. She smiled. "I get it," she said.

"Good. Now we wait."

"How long do we wait this time?"

He washed his hands, wiped them on his jeans, came to her, and took her chin between his fingers. "As long as we want." He guided her toward the leather couch. He went to the fireplace and placed branches around a log. He scratched a match and tore the magazine apart, crumpled the pages, and lit them on fire. The Woman in Black was set ablaze. He returned to the couch, sat beside her, and began to kiss her neck.

Night had fallen. Cassie had moved to the table Hervé had set outside in the tiny garden. He went into the kitchen while she picked at olives and cubes of goat cheese. Candles flickered on the table. A record played a French song she did not recognize. Wisteria blooms cascaded down from the fence that surrounded the patio.

What she wasn't telling Hervé came to the surface of her consciousness accompanied by the vaguest of ill-feelings. She brushed her uneasiness aside. For now, she'd continue to circumnavigate any mention of the United States or the ticking clock of her return ticket. A romance. At her age. Possibly for the first time in her life. Because to marry your first boyfriend at nineteen on account of being preggers with twins wasn't the definition of romance.

She was amazed to see how, once deprived of a computer and cell phone and taken out of her natural habitat, her life in Los Angeles had receded into a ghostly fog. A week ago, she agonized over what she should donate to the Salvation Army. This had been the extent of her rebellion; the only way she could attempt to let go of Peter was to reject that job he had given her as curator of all the broken things he was attached to but did not want in his own house. Her new reality included different broken things, not just in her past, but in her father's and grandfather's past. She was the product of suffering she hadn't known about: fear, war, rage, jealousy, resentment, self-loathing. And there were the broken things she knew about but had ignored: her relationship with Odile, her children's bond, which was falling apart, Peter and Jessica's relationship and their lies, and Sabine's heart.

She was brought back to her presence inside Hervé's house as he walked into the patio holding a steaming bowl of pasta in one hand and a smaller bowl of sauce in the other. "Are you cold?" he asked. Not waiting for an answer, he returned inside to fetch a blanket. He wrapped it around her, and she felt immense well-being. He sat down next to her, served the pasta on two plates, spooned the sauce over it, and shaved parmesan over the plates. "On mange," he said.

She took a bite. "My God, it's too good!"

"They say that raw garlic should not be eaten in polite company, but I have chocolate cake for dessert. Chocolate cancels out the garlic; that's a scientific fact."

Soon enough Cassie would pop out of this temporary madness and return to her reasonable self. But not yet. Now, the moment was hers. Hervé served her more Bordeaux, and they ate dinner in the purple glow of the moon as it shined through the wisteria.

****

The shrill ring of the telephone awakened her the following morning. Cassie looked at her watch. It was eight in the morning. Hervé flailed around the bed, feeling with his arms for the telephone on the bedside table. "Yes?" he grumbled, sitting up in bed. His hair stood up on his head; he was wearing a threadbare V-neck undershirt and nothing else, and the stubble on his face was salt and pepper. He was gorgeous.

"There is nothing I can do," he told the person on the telephone. "Better yet, there is nothing I want to do. What? No! Then tell her to stop harassing us. I deal with logistics and flow charts, not people, and you know this. That was the deal I made for as long as I'm in this ... purgatory." Hervé ruffled his hair. "Find an excuse. Tell her I'm in meetings all day. Diplomatically, of course. Tell her I'm in a meeting all week. I don't care." Apparently, the person on the telephone was insisting. He put his hand on Cassie's bare shoulder and caressed the side of her body. "Then tell her I'm on a safari to kill baby pandas," he said while smiling at Cassie. "You might as well since she's obviously made me out to be the devil."

He hung up the phone and rolled over in bed to face Cassie. "And you want me to get a cell phone?"

"Headaches at work?"

"Not for much longer. As soon as I can, I'm taking the first plane to Africa to help people with real problems."

Cassie felt the moment tarnished. What had she been imagining? She was leaving. He was leaving. "I'll take a shower," she said.

"I'll make you breakfast."

They took showers, had a quick breakfast, and hopped on Hervé's bike. He dropped her off at the hotel and zoomed off to work. At her hotel, the old man saw her and disappeared behind the reception's counter. After a few "attendez, attendez," he handed Cassie a small flat package. "It came this morning, special delivery," he said in a tone of utter puzzlement, and then looked at her questioningly, as though she owed it to him to open it right there and solve the mystery.

She went up the stairs to her room and opened the box. It was a tablet and a wireless keyboard, compliments of Peter. Not quite the computer he had mentioned, but he must have paid a small fortune to make this happen regardless. Amazing how simple things became once Peter wanted something.

The sleek tablet, all deceptive minimalism and advanced technology, was a thing of beauty, and yet she felt curiously turned off by it. It made her think of shackles and wastefulness or whatever was the opposite of making pasta from scratch.

She put the tablet in her bag, grabbed her coat, and ran down the stairs. In the phone booth, she dialed Peter collect. "I got your package," she told him. "But I can't leave early."

"But I bought a ticket!"

"Peter! I never agreed to this. I need these few days in Paris."

On the line, there was silence. Peter said, "We're in a very tight spot. What you French people would call a case of force majeure. I realize the timing sucks. I totally empathize."

She stiffened, shocked by the arrogance of his certainty. "Do you?"

"Wasn't I the one who wanted you to go to Paris? I insisted, in fact. I had to drag you to the airport."

"You were right, though. I needed to be here."

"I'm sorry, honey, but I can't let you stay longer, unfortunately. Our name is at stake here."

Now she was angry. She felt it inside her belly like a ping-pong size ball of fire. "My name is not at stake."

"What?"

"You're the A-list writer. You're the one getting the big bucks. I have no name at stake at all."

"Goodness, Cassandra," Peter said, his eye-roll practically audible, "the rehashing, again?"

"I—"

"Besides, you said your dad was unconscious. So, he might not even realize that you left."

"Peter!" she shouted. "I'm not doing it! I'm not rushing to the airport just to please you."

"Same old, same old. Don't turn petty, Cassie."

"When I want something, it's pettiness. When you want something, it's ambition."

"It's always the same thing with you. You start being difficult for no reason. Just because you're in a mood."

"This isn't a mood!"

"Yeah, it's a mood. You have a good thing going, and you sabotage it."

"What the hell are you talking about?"

"You ruined our marriage with all this, and you know it."

"If you're making it about the marriage, is it possible that you were neglecting me, that you were taking me for granted? That you were using me?"

"That's fantasyland, Cassie, and you know it. I was devoted to you. I was quite literally the perfect husband."

She thought for a moment. "Really? So, what about Jessica?"

Peter paused a beat too many before asking, "What about her?"

"You leaped out of the marriage and into her arms." She raised her voice. "Not my definition of devotion."

"You kicked me out!" Peter said, outraged. "You wanted the separation, not me, remember? You brought the whole thing upon yourself. I was heartbroken. I was vulnerable. I looked for a place to stay. I happened to meet her when I was house-hunting."

Cassie knew the story by heart, explained and repeated since their separation like a screenplay rewritten too many times until only the words remained, constricted, incongruous, ill-fitting in the new narrative. She said, "It's just too neat a story, Peter."

Now, Peter was shouting. "I have a contract with the studio!"

"And my father is in the hospital!" she shouted back. She hung up thunderously. She stayed in the booth for a minute, catching her breath. She must have been as red as the surrounding velvet. She got up to leave, but something stopped her. She inhaled deeply and made a credit card call to Alex's cell phone. It rang numerous times. She wanted to hang up but made herself continue. A moment later, Alex was on the line. When she heard her baby, she had to fight back tears. She steadied herself. "Alex, it's Mom," she said. "How are you doing, my love?"

"Mom? Are you back in L.A.?" Alex asked. "I don't recognize the number. I'm walking into class now. Can we talk later?"

"Do you have a minute? I'm calling from Paris."

"My roaming charges are going to be crazy."

"Put it on my tab. How are things in New York?"

"What's wrong?" Alex said. "Is French Grandpa okay?"

"He has a nasty lung infection that's resisting antibiotics. But I'm not calling you about that. It's just that … I'm spending time with my parents and my sisters, and, well, something has been on my mind as I deal with them. Honey, I just … I've been thinking about what you have been saying all these years about your sister."

"Yeah?" he said. He sounded hesitant, like someone who knows no good could come out of broaching this particular topic.

"You were right, my love," she said. "I didn't want to hear it, but it was the truth."

"What was?"

"Sometimes one kid is kind of the squeaky wheel that gets the oil, and we didn't treat you and your sister with equality. We lowered our expectations with Jeanne."

"That's what I've been saying for years!"

"I convinced myself that you were pushing yourself because you wanted to."

"I do want to push myself. But it's just so—"

"Unjust?"

"Yes."

"We found excuses for Jeanne. Not because we thought she deserved them. Only because we were weak."

"Weak with parental love for her." There was thick acerbity in Alex's tone.

"Maybe by denying that there was an imbalance I was hoping that the two of you would get along. But it created the opposite. It drew a wedge between you two. The fact is, she's been terribly lazy and we have been indulgent toward her."

Alex was quiet for a moment, as though he was processing it all. "Well, good. Okay. That's the truth. Mom, I'm outside the classroom. I have a midterm starting in, like, one minute."

"Honey, I have just one other quick thing."

"What?"

"When you were five or six years old, you know, when Dad wanted us all to move, and he kept looking at houses. He would take you and Jeanne, and you'd see houses, and then the three of you would try to convince me to look at them, but I never did. Remember?"

"I guess."

Cassie hesitated. "I mean this was a long, long time ago, but … do you happen to remember seeing house after house? This went on for a year at least. Some of the houses you really liked."

"I remember," Alex said, impatient now.

"You do?"

Alex waited to answer this time, as though he too was bracing himself for her question. "Yes," he said at last.

"Do you have memories about the real estate agent?"

Silence. Then, "Yep."

"Do you remember what he or she looked like?"

"Of course, I remember, Mom." He was upset now.

"It was Jessica, wasn't it?"

"Yes."

"You're certain of this? You were so young."

"I am. It's not like we met her just once. We saw her every time."

"But you never told me."

"Told you what?"

"You didn't tell me, later, when Dad and she … I mean…."

"I thought you knew. I mean, what am I going to say? I was just a kid."

Her heart was beating hard in her chest. "Well. Thank you, love. That's all I wanted to ask you. Water under the bridge; no worries. I was just curious. Are you, um, still happy at Columbia?"

"Reasonably so."

"Are your roommates clean?"

"That they are not."

"Alex?"

"Yes."

"You were right about your sister."

"Got it … got it. Thanks, Mom. It means a lot. I got to go now; class is starting."

"I love you."

"Me too. Bye, Mom."

Cassie hung up. She felt dizzy. The red velvet around her looked about to swallow her. She rattled the door manically, and when it opened, she sprang out of the booth, out of the hotel lobby, and into rue de Seine. Only then did she try breathing. Outside, she hurried to the taxi station. A car was there, and she jumped inside. "Cité des Fleurs, s'il vous plaît."

"What is that?"

"A street. Seventeenth arrondissement."

"Never heard of it," the cab driver said.

"Off Avenue de Clichy, corner of rue Guy Môquet."

"Never heard of it," he repeated.

"Trust me," she said. "It's there."

It had all been at the tip of her consciousness, refusing to be formulated. Could it be that she had known all along? But yes, she *knew*. How could she not have? But she had wanted to believe his lie. Peter had deceived her, and she had let him deceive her.

The car careened through Boulevard de la Chapelle. Cassie saw nothing. She was sweating. She was nauseous. There was a sudden, sharp pain low in her belly like a mean knot. "Stop!" she said. "Stop the car now!" The driver did not slow down; he frowned at her in the rearview mirror, but as soon as he saw how green her face was, he stopped abruptly enough to embed deep skid marks on the asphalt. She just had enough time to open the door and move her hair from her face before throwing up.

The cab let her out near rue de la Jonquière. She entered the first café and washed her face in the bathroom. She ordered a Perrier and downed it in an instant. She felt better. She felt cleaned somehow. Lighter. Unencumbered by the sense of guilt she had carried for years.

At Marceline's door, Armelle, the stepdaughter, had her arms crossed over her chest and a tight smile on her lips. She stood in the door, making no attempt to invite Cassie inside. "It is only that, there's been plans made," Armelle said. "And, well it seems as though Mother has been quite upside down about things. You are here after she's been estranged from her brother all those years. At her age, stirring things can be upsetting."

"She wants to talk to me. I'm only interested in the family's story," Cassie said. "My family story."

"And I'm only mindful of her health."

In a Marceline-like display of straightforwardness, Cassie said, "Do you want me to camp on your front lawn until Marceline finds out that you keep getting between us?"

"No, but of course," Armelle said. "I'm only mindful of her needs." She sighed. "Mother is in the gazebo. Go around the house down the path."

CHAPTER 4

Operation Torch

Why did they have to make the print so tiny? Marceline wondered. Only old people read the newspaper anymore, so wouldn't it make sense to enlarge the type?

Under the gazebo, she looked up from the magnifying glass she held over her copy of *Le Monde* and watched Cassandra walk toward her. The girl looked annoyed. What an open book she was, so unlike Gustave.

"What now?" Marceline asked.

"Your step-daughter," Cassandra said as she plopped down on the empty chair across from hers. "She's starting to get on my nerves,"

"Ha! And on mine."

Marceline contemplated her niece: no compulsory hellos, no niceties, and no waste of time. What a relief it was to interact with a straightforward person. She decidedly liked the girl.

"Why does she make it difficult for me to speak to you?" Cassandra asked. "She has all those excuses. You're tired; you're ill, you're upset about the past, blah, blah, blah. If you didn't want to talk about all this you would tell me, wouldn't you?"

"Don't mind her, ma chère."

Cassandra settled in her chair, put her purse down, removed her coat and took out her notepad. She looked up at the gazebo. "This is so nice," she said. "Everything in Paris is so pretty all of a sudden."

"Paris in the springtime," Marceline said, already bored with the weather talk. "Nothing quite like it."

"The thing I still can't understand," Cassie said, "is what you might have done to deserve my father's hatred."

Now, that was more like it. "Getting right down to it, aren't you?" Marceline said.

"So far, I see that you were annoyed with each other, but what siblings aren't? My sister Odile and I are at each other's throat most of the time, but we are still sisters. We have a rocky relationship, but it's a relationship. And my children. They aren't talking to each other right now. But that's temporary. It's salvageable."

"Until it isn't," Marceline said.

Cassandra looked at her, distraught. "It is salvageable," she insisted.

"Today I'll tell you what happened, and then you can decide if I am worthy of your father's hatred, or not. Where did I leave things?"

"My father was beaten, and Khaled went to jail," Cassandra said.

Marceline was going to tell Cassandra everything. Let her decide if anything at all between Gustave and her could have been salvaged.

****

Days after Gustave's beating, Khaled had yet not been released. I was mad with anguish and guilt. I asked my father how much longer he thought the French police would detain him. Khaled may have refused to identify any of Gustave's assailants, my father explained, and they could hold him until he did.

"They still won't say where they put him?" I asked my father.

"No, and it worries me," my father said. "Despite how upset we are about what happened to Gustave, to the police it's nothing. I cannot imagine why they would even bother making this into a big investigation. This is strange." He looked at me with suspicion. "Are you sure there isn't more to the story?"

I thought of Khaled's family, and the job at the garden he would now certainly lose. All because of my stupid brother. "He's just a nice boy who works very hard to support his family. He stays out of trouble."

"Apparently not enough."

"Oh, Baba, we have to free him!"

"There are limits to what I can do without drawing attention to our family."

"But this is so unfair!"

"It would not be the first time an innocent man is detained," my father said. "Listen, I will do everything in my power to help this young man because he saved Gustave, not because I approve of your fling."

Together with my father, we visited every past employer of Khaled I could think of: at the fishing mole, at the Jardin d'Essai, and at Café Djurdjura. We collected letters attesting to his hard work and to his character. I wrote daily letters to him but had nowhere to send them. I cried, and I raged, over Sandra being fired and Father not standing up for her, over Mother for being so unjust, over Khaled, and mostly over myself. I was inconsolable and at the same time angrier than ever at my brother, who was the reason Khaled was imprisoned in the first place.

Gustave and I avoided each other. When we found ourselves in the same room, we yelled at each other. It was awful between us. We blamed each other for getting Sandra fired, and we both profoundly resented Mother, who declared herself inconsolable about my actions and extremely distraught about the state of Gustave's nose, which she felt should be fixed immediately to look, as she put it, less aquiline and more French. For weeks, I was essentially on house arrest. I could spend time with Béatrice, either at my house or hers. But I was not allowed so much as to go down to the mailbox.

By now Mother's mood swings, her anger at Father, her obsession with me, and her fretting over Gustave had taken their toll. We each had our reasons to shut her out. We all began to retreat to our own corner of the house. The new maid would bring food to our rooms on trays and take them away later. We did not talk to each other. I would have liked to speak to my father, but he was never home. He was acting very strange. He was gone all day, and some nights he did not even come home at all and would reappear in the morning without any explanation given.

I lasted three weeks before disobeying. I decided that I would wait for Gustave and my father to leave the apartment and then go to Mother. I would tell her I was at my wit's end, that I was repentant, that I needed oxygen and sunshine. I knew that she would not resist my cajoling and begging for long. At first, I only asked to wait in the breadline in place of the new maid, insisting and crying, or throwing a tantrum until Mother relented. Little by little, I regained my freedom of movement. In the end, my mother was preoccupied with her ailments and angry at Father for always being gone, and she did not put up much of a fight.

I saw Dietfried three more times throughout September and early October: a walk on the beach, a visit to a local church, lunch once. His interest for me grew in direct proportion to my lack of availability.

And then, everything happened.

It was mid-October when Fernand passed me a note through our usual florist. It was brief: I needed to find a way to be out the following night and this time probably until morning.

Béatrice and I had no qualms about covering for each other when we wanted to spend the night with our lovers. She agreed to lie for me.

Where was Fernand taking me? I did not question his motive. I would have done anything. I wanted to help our cause, but mostly I felt powerless about Khaled, and it drove me crazy. Two months had passed since the Kasbah attack, and he was still in an undisclosed jail somewhere.

I begged my father to let me sleep at Béatrice's home. I told him that I had been a model citizen, that I recognized the error of my ways, and please let me do it. He relented, and I returned a message to Fernand via the florist telling him that I would be there. All was set.

"You're back with Fernand then?" Béatrice asked.

"I guess I must be," I told her.

"Does it mean I can be back with Émile, then?" she asked.

"Béatrice, you don't need my permission."

The following evening, I packed my night bag as though heading for Béatrice's apartment, but instead I went in the direction of rue Joinville. Fernand's instruction was to wait at the corner of rue d'Isly and rue Joinville, where a green

Peugeot 202 would pick me up. The days were shortening considerably. The evening was windy. The chill of fall could be felt, and I wished I had worn something warmer. The date was October 21, 1942.

At the precise time it was supposed to arrive, a dusty Peugeot 202 came to a stop in front of me. A man came out to open my door. I stepped inside. Immediately, the car bolted through Algiers's empty streets.

I had expected Fernand to be there, but the two men in the car were French men I had never seen before. The driver, his fedora deep over his eyes and one arm out the window, could have been one of the men who had watched over me on the train where I first met Dietfried, but I could not be sure. He intermittently peeked at me in his review mirror. The other man, angry-looking, sat in the passenger seat, smoking. Neither said a word to me.

"Where's Fernand?" I asked.

"No names!" the man in the passenger seat ordered.

We drove through the dusk alongside windswept palm trees and the darkening sea, leaving the city. I became anxious. My thoughts went to my father. He spent all his energy trying to keep us safe; what would he think of me now? I was in a situation I could not control, zooming away from the city close to curfew, in an automobile driven by unknown men. I had no idea whether I was going to be part of a Resistance mission or about to be raped and bludgeoned to death.

We drove for a long time. The wind made the car sway at times, and the driver tightened his hands on the wheel. Night fell. The police stopped us twice for violating curfew. Each time, they took one look at the driver and let us go.

We had driven for about an hour when we stopped next to a parked automobile. A thin, nervous man got out of it and entered our car. He sat next to me in back, tilted his hat as a form of introduction, and offered me a cigarette. He looked at me intensely, measuring me. Satisfied, he asked in a clipped tone, "They say you can translate French to English and back to French?"

I relaxed. This was no plot to murder me. "I can," I said.

"There's a meeting tonight. We need you to translate what is being said so that people can understand each other."

"I can translate writing. I'm not sure I'm fast enough to translate as people speak."

The man's face hardened. "The meeting is now. We have no one else. Can you do it, yes or no?"

"Are they British? American?"

"No questions," he said.

"I can do it," I told him.

As we drove, it occurred to me that for Fernand's recommendation to have placed me in this place and time, he must have been more influential within the Resistance than he had let on. After another thirty minutes of driving in the dark, I saw a sign for the small seaport town of Cherchell. Minutes later, the driver slowed down and turned off the headlights. This was a nearly moonless night, and suddenly all was dark. I could make out the silhouette, pale against the black of the sea, of an isolated beach house. The automobile left the paved road and drove on a dirt path. The driver rolled down his window and guided himself by putting his head out the window and watching the edges of the path.

We stopped in front of an iron gate. After a minute, men with guns emerged. They aimed flashlights at our faces. The gate was opened for us, and we went through.

Half a dozen vehicles were already parked in front of the house. Silent, armed men stood all around, some by the windows and doors, some on the roof. We stepped out of the automobile, and a strong sea wind ruffled my hair. No one spoke. I heard car doors opening and closing, footsteps on the pebble path, nearby waves crashing on the beach. Someone took my arm and guided me toward the house.

We entered the farmhouse and went through an entryway decorated without frills, in a mixture of Arab and European styles. We walked into a large room. About twenty French men were waiting there, sitting on chairs and couches, smoking, playing cards. Some were old, but I was surprised at how many of them looked my age or younger. All eyes converged on me. I was immensely relieved to see Émile's face, but he averted his eyes. I understood it was best to pretend not to know him.

"Who's she?" someone asked.

"This is no place for a woman," another man said.

An angry old man in a beret and woolen pullover waved his finger at me menacingly. "You better keep your mouth shut! I don't want to hear a peep. It's an order, you hear?"

I decided to respect the "order" by staring him down and not answering.

"She's the translator, dummy," a man said. "How good will it do if she can't speak?" There were laughs, and the man with the beret turned back to me. "Then keep your mouth shut after the meeting."

"Calm down, Pierrot," someone said.

I found a chair in a corner and sat there. We all waited wordlessly for a good hour. The air grew thick with smoke and tension.

Through the window, I saw people sending light signals toward the sea. As the room filled with smoke and the smell of men, some could not resist talking, and I garnered whatever understanding of the situation I could. There was a submarine at sea, and we were waiting for its occupants to make their way onto rafts and come ashore on the beach. The sea was rough, and things weren't happening as smoothly as hoped. They had been waiting for two hours, and still, there was no sign of the rafts.

"Merde," the grumpy one with the beret said. "They better arrive before sunrise, or this meeting is over before it started."

"Why a submarine of the Royal Navy?" someone asked. "I thought they would be Americans."

"You've been brainwashed to think the Brits are your enemies and Vichy your friends," someone said.

"But in Mers El Kebir—"

"Forget Mers El Kebir!"

Finally, we heard the news that four dinghies had pulled onto the beach.

In the room, everyone sat straighter, conversations stopped, men forgot to light their cigarettes. But when the door opened, only three people were asked to go into another room, and I was one of them.

We were in a small, windowless room. In the center was a farm table on top of which was a large map of the area. The only light came from a lamp placed on the table. Two men walked out of the shadow. I was told to memorize their names as I would need to introduce them to our visitors. They were Henri d'Astier de la Vigerie, whom I later learned had been sent to Algiers to head the Resistance, and Colonel Jousse and Général Mast, the two who were dressed in civilian clothing. The men who had entered with me were Bernard Karsenty and José Aboulker. I had never met them, but I knew them by reputation. They were Jewish, and they were at the heart of Algiers's Resistance, a Resistance composed of a ragtag group of Jews, many of them barely old enough to drive.

Minutes later, the back door to the outside was opened, and several men in British and American uniforms were led into the room. They were drenched. Someone hurried to give them towels. Those uniforms, albeit pitifully wet, were the most exhilarating sight. As far as I was concerned, the Allies had arrived, even if only a handful of them. Hope was here. We had not been abandoned.

A British officer communicated with the submarine via an object that resembled a long metal shoebox with antennas. It was my first time laying eyes on a walkie-talkie.

The meeting began, with me translating as the men introduced themselves. There was Robert Murphy, an American diplomat, and General Wayne Clark, who spoke directly for General Eisenhower. The general was in a foul mood after that difficult entry onto French territory. My mouth was dry; my heart beat fast. The smallest mistake on my part could mean disaster. Lives would be at stake. Perhaps even the fate of Algeria. But after months translating newspapers for Fernand, I had become well versed in the vernacular of war in both languages, and my time with Dietfried had prepared me for thinking on my feet. The French men spoke in French, the Anglo-Saxons in English, and with adrenaline helping, I translated.

When more maps of North Africa were laid out on the table, I gasped at the scope of the operation. Here, in this ordinary house, on this extraordinary night, they were preparing no less than the invasion of North Africa with a simultaneous landing in Morocco, Tunisia, and Algeria! We had been descending into what seemed like a bottomless abyss, and suddenly, everything was possible! For a long time, the men went back and forth as I translated. They discussed the towns that should be part of the strategy, listed which Vichy officials might join our side, and who were suspected to remain at Pétain's beck and call. Questions emerged as to who would lead Algeria once Vichy's people were taken down, but no one seemed preoccupied with this. These were military men, who thought in terms of maneuvers and movement of troops, not politics. What the military men wanted to know was the quality of the Resistance infrastructure already in place to facilitate the invasion.

"We have about eight hundred men here in Algiers, and we've identified and infiltrated most strategic posts," Karsenty said.

"Are all your men Jewish?"

"About two-thirds of them are."

The men from the submarine, seemingly reassured by this information, nodded approvingly.

"But we need weapons," de la Vigerie said. "Ours are obsolete, and we have too few, barely enough for four hundred men."

"Weapons will be sent ahead of time."

"How?"

"We'll find a beach for a night drop," Murphy said.

"We will need several months to organize."

"The landing will take place before the bad winter weather," General Clark said.

"Before winter? General, with all due respect! We are almost at the end of October. There is no way to—"

General Clark exploded. "My submarines might be submersible, but my men are not!" We can't wait for the sea to get even rougher than it is now. "The landing must happen in the next few weeks or not at all."

"Our men are ready," Karsenty said. "Cells are already in place."

"How will you neutralize those who might attack us as we land?"

"We have a plan set in place. We are prepared," Colonel Jousse responded.

"Can you give us a date?" Karsenty asked.

"The date will be given to you shortly beforehand to avoid leaks," Murphy said. "Just be ready."

Two hours later, the Anglo-Saxons climbed back in their dinghies, returned to their submarine, and we were left to ponder what had just taken place. Colonel Jousse and Général Mast discussed things with de la Vigerie, Karsenty, and Aboulker. I was not needed anymore, but they did not ask me to leave. I played it cool and professional, but I was thrilled. An Allied invasion was about to take place, and its success was in the hands of very few people, most of them Jews!

When they had thoroughly discussed all of the details, with me doing my best to translate, we returned to the main room where the rest of the men waited. "It's happening," Karsenty simply told the crowd of men. "The first order of business is to identify hotspots throughout Algiers, but I think we know where they are, don't we? Police commissariats throughout the city, the army headquarters, the naval office, all telecommunication centers, and the places of residence of individuals favorable to the Vichy regime. We're setting up teams. The day of the invasion we are to neutralize those hotspots long enough to create chaos, and then we will hold down the fort until the Allied forces arrive."

"For how long?" a voice called.

"A few hours at most."

A voice in the room asked, "Will we have enough weapons?"

"They are sending them." Général Mast said. "They'll be dropped off on an agreed-upon beach beforehand."

A murmur of approval swept through the room.

"Do we have enough men?"

"We're not putting together an army," Colonel Joust said. "Our mission is not to fight, although there may be fighting. Our purpose is to neutralize the hotspots. It will be night. We'll be taking everyone by surprise. The challenge will not be in the number of men, but in the accuracy and orchestration."

Someone dared ask the question on everyone's lips. "When, Boss?"

Karsenty hesitated. Mast answered, "Before winter."

In the room, there was a roar of voices. Fear and excitement swept through this motley crew of men. Everyone was speaking at once.

"The point is," Aboulker said, "Free France and the Allies are entrusting us with a mission of utmost importance. The Allies will be landing, whether we are ready or not. The lines of communications must be under our control. The army and the police cannot get alerted, so they won't have time to mobilize. The Wehrmacht must be prevented from knowing about the arrival of troops, for as long as we can make that happen. And if we fail to do our work, we'll have the blood of French, British, Canadian, and American soldiers on our hands. Our actions can be the difference between success and failure for the entire landing operation."

After that, no one asked another question, and many points floated in my mind, unresolved. General Clark and Robert Murphy had revealed too little for my comfort. Had they not been excessively vague about the arrival of the weapons? How could such a massive operation not have a set date? And did they truly not have a man in mind to run the next government after they toppled the existing one? Like a good little soldier, I swallowed my doubts and did not share my worries with anyone.

I found out later that my suspicions were correct. Only a few in the room had been privy to the truth: the Allies knew precisely what the next government would look like. The invasion date had long been set. Roosevelt had given the order of attack. Ships and submarines were already designated for combat. Over one hundred thousand well-trained soldiers were waiting. The invasion was set for November 8th. Barely three weeks away.

What I did not suspect, but what I hoped with all my heart, was about to come true. The British-American invasion of North Africa, code name Operation Torch, would turn out to be World War II's first successful Allied landing on French territory. And for all my modern ideas about the role of women, it never occurred to me that I was about to be propelled straight into the fire of battle.

The men shook hands, people left. Someone noticed that I was still in the room. "You did a swell job, sweetheart," the grumpy old guy who had hated me on principle said. "La demoiselle needs to be taken back home."

"I'll take her," Émile said.

Minutes later, we were in Émile's car. "Wasn't this just incredible?" he murmured.

"Incredible," I echoed.

"And you were right there in the room with those generals! After we win this, you'll have to tell me how it all went down."

Dawn was breaking through the morning fog. We had missed a night's sleep, but I could not have felt more awake. "You were swell; they said so," Émile continued. "You know that you can't discuss what just took place." He hesitated. "Not even with your boyfriend."

"Don't insult me, Émile," I told him. "And besides, Fernand and I are only friends these days."

Émile was quiet for a moment. Then he said reluctantly, "I meant, your new boyfriend. You're going out with that Muslim chap from the café, aren't you?"

I felt a sharp sense of danger. "Who told you this?"

"Algiers is nothing but a spy nest these days," he said, philosophically.

I watched Émile's profile in the darkness of the car. "Does Fernand know about this?"

Émile, who laughed at everything, wasn't smiling. "If he does, it's not because I told him."

"Fernand doesn't need to know who I choose to see."

"The thing is," Émile said, "I'm not in the habit of keeping secrets from Fernand. He was a brother to me long before you came along."

"Well, I don't report everything to my brother. Far from it."

Émile, who has no hard edges to him, no meanness, and no anger, said, "But why did you have to go out with the *one* chap Fernand despises so much?"

"What does he have against him anyway?"

"He doesn't show Fernand respect."

"Baloney! Khaled didn't show Fernand respect because he doesn't owe him respect! You all think that he should stay in his place because he's an Arab? Because Monsieur Fernand believes himself superior? Anyway, my boyfriend, as you call him, was put in jail for no good reason. They won't let him out or give him a trial, and I'm going half mad about it."

"Maybe…." Émile paused. "Maybe it would be easier if you broke it off."

"Easier for whom?"

"For everyone," he said as he pulled in front of Béatrice's apartment building. He did not look at me when he added. "Easier for your chap, too."

Too much had happened in the last twelve hours to make sense of his words. I was drained. "Can you find out where they have him locked up? Even my father cannot find out where he is."

Émile considered this. "I'll see what I can find out," he said.

He dropped me off in front of Béatrice's apartment building. I walked the few blocks from there to my house just as the streets of Algiers awakened. Sidewalk sweepers and trash collectors said hello to me as I mulled over Émile's cryptic words. Easier for your chap, he had said. What had he meant by that? Now that exhaustion was replacing excitement, I began to feel nervous. What would happen to Fernand, Émile, and André if the landing failed? Did they not risk jail, or worse? What about my father? Would he be involved in the invasion?

The following day, Fernand and I sat in the darkness of the Pathé Cinéma. It was a matinée. We were alone in the theater. The reel of *Film Actualité* was about to start. A nasally voiced announcer extolled the merits of esprit national and patriotism over visuals of Maréchal Pétain parading through a near hysteric crowd, holding babies, and receiving flower bouquets from little girls. We sat lower in our chairs. "They were impressed with your aplomb," Fernand said. "You didn't blink, love. And they took notice."

"How much do you know about last night?"

"As much as I need to. So, say, how's your Germanic romance going?"

I sighed, "He is growing much too adoring for my comfort."

"Learned anything new?"

"The thing is, Fernand, I'm running out of reasons not to be kissed by him. I don't know how long I can keep him wanting."

A couple walked past us as they went down the cinema's aisle and settled in the front row seats. Another couple went to sit in the far back. On the screen, a cartoon depicted a grotesque-looking Jewish man, with a nose the shape of a banana and paw-like hands, bleating into a microphone. "Ici Londre. Les français parlent aux français. London here, the French speak to the French," the man said in an unctuous voice that mocked London and De Gaulle. The propaganda was at work, linking the Jews, which they had so successfully turned into a source of disgust, with the Allied forces.

"There is no harm in throwing your adoring Boche a bone," Fernand said. On the screen, Mickey Mouse, Popeye, and Donald Duck flew planes that dropped bombs on French farmhouses.

"What do you mean?"

"A little kiss has never harmed anyone."

"Who do you take me for?"

He shrugged, "Come on now, princess, haven't you kissed worse frogs?"

Émile's comment rang in my ears. It would be easier if you broke it off, he had said. Easier for your chap. I tried to contain the alarm in my voice as I dropped all pretenses. "Do you have anything to do with Khaled being stuck in jail?"

"Khaled who?" Fernand asked lightly.

"Were you involved with those kids who attacked my brother?"

"The Kasbah is a place for savages. It's not my fault that he and you chose to venture there."

"How come you know about all this?"

"Algiers is a small town."

"How long have you known about Khaled and me?"

"Questions, questions, so many questions," he said. Fernand's eyes shone with the screen's reflection of soldiers in Nazi uniforms lifting their boots in menacing unison. "Here is one I'd like you to answer: what if I told you that your Casanova is the enemy?"

"An enemy of whom? He's not a Vichy sympathizer. He's not a Nazi."

"He's an enemy of French Algerians, of which I happen to be the very embodiment. If he and his little group figure they're going to get their country back to themselves, they got another thing coming."

"Is this all because of me?"

"As lovely as you are, I'm not the jealous kind. All that matters to me is the mission. I know where my interests lie, and they're better served in keeping you happy than in provoking your ire. Although I am just a bit insulted you would prefer an illiterate over me."

"Khaled is perfectly educated, I'll have you know. And if his people aren't, it's because the French won't let them in their schools."

Fernand stared at me coldly. "I see his counter-information techniques are effective."

"If I learn you had something to do with what happened to Gustave, or to Khaled—"

"You'll learn no such thing," Fernand said.

"Then tell me you're innocent."

"I am. But let me tell you something: no one likes the idea of one of our girls fraternizing with Arabs."

"I'm not one of your girls!"

"You're French. You're Jewish. You're one of us. The best thing you can do is forget about him. I'm sure he'll be left alone much sooner than if the two of you persist."

I felt a chill down my spine. Émile had been right. "Are you threatening us?"

"I'm only appealing to your common sense."

I stared at the screen, my heart pounding with fury. Also, I was ashamed. I had been ridiculous, thinking myself smart when everyone around me, my brother, Fernand, Émile, and who knows who else, had known about Khaled all along. My brother was hurt, and Khaled was in jail, and I had no one to blame but myself. And even worse, I had every reason to believe that Fernand might have orchestrated the beating.

"So, what do you say?" Fernand said playfully pursing his lips as if to blow a kiss, "Just einen kleinen kuss for our horny German friend?"

"I won't let those Nazi lips touch mine. And besides, Dietfried repulses me physically."

Fernand laughed silently in the darkness. "So which is your main objection about our friend Dietfried? That he's our mortal enemy, or that he's not as cute as your Arab?"

Before I knew it, I had slapped Fernand across the face. This made such a noise that the sparse moviegoers jeered and whistled. "What have you done now?" one man snickered, and the handful of people in the theater laughed.

Fernand rubbed his burning cheek and smiled as if this has been only a game. "Listen," he said. "There's something I need you to do if you'll get off your high horse."

"You're in no position to expect a favor."

"Not for me, honey. For France."

I crossed my arms. I hated Fernand at that moment and could have murdered him on the spot, but if he had a mission for me in the scope of the one from the night before, I wanted in. "What is it?"

"Not here," Fernand said.

We left the cinema before the start of the film and came out into the street. We walked down to the pier, away from undesirable ears. "My cell was assigned a mission for the big night," Fernand said. "We're in charge of shutting down the communication between Algiers and Hitler."

I looked at him, afraid of what I was understanding. "You're going to shut Dietfried down?"

We sat on a bench that faced the sea. The sky was gray and low. Powerful silver waves crashed against the jetty. "Here are our facts," Fernand said. "He may or may not be their transmission guy, but he's our best bet. All intelligence points to him. We found his antenna, and it's a nice big one, powerful enough to transmit to Germany and beyond. We think that he set up a full transmission facility at his house. The phone lines will be down on the big night, but he could still communicate with the Reich via Morse code, radio transmission, and so forth. We can't have that happen. We can't have the Boshes coordinate anything. They must be kept in the dark as long as possible. At least as long as it will take for our forces to subdue the rest of the town and let the Allies take over."

"What are you going to do? Destroy his facility?"

"That's the tricky part. Hitler expects an Allied offense in North Africa, but he doesn't know when. As long as he receives reassuring news from your Dietfried, he'll think all is dandy for the time being. So, we can't take him down before the attack starts or it would raise a red flag. We have to do it the night of."

"What does this have to do with me?"

"We know how many armed guards circle the perimeter of his house day and night. Some of his guards are with us. If we go in with force, all he'd have to do is lock himself in and send a message about being under attack, which alone will alert Germany that something's the matter."

"So, what are you going to do?"

"Take him from the inside." Fernand lit a cigarette and offered me one. "With God's help." He smiled his beguiling smile. "And a little help from you as well."

"Me?"

I could tell he was hesitant to speak. "On the night of the operation, we want you to get invited inside his house."

"And do what?"

There was a long silence. At last Fernand said, "We need you to neutralize him from the inside before he has a chance to send a message."

"Neutralize him?" I repeated. I burst into laughter. "Have you gone raving mad?"

"Not in the slightest."

I thought of the Cherchell night, the dozens of men armed to the teeth, the American and British officers, the secrecy. "How am I to neutralize him? Will a stern word or two suffice? Or do you envision something more radical, such as chopping him into pieces with a machete? I don't even know how to use a gun, and anyway, his guards would search me for weapons when I come in."

Fernand was serious now, his tone more pressing. "When we get the green light, you find a way to spend the night with him. He can't abandon his night post, so logically he would think of inviting you over to his house."

"All right, let's imagine that's possible. Then what?"

"Then it's phase two."

"And what might that be?"

"I'll let you know when we get closer to the day."

I looked at Fernand. His face revealed nothing. "Please tell me there is a plan," I said.

"There is a plan," he answered. "A solid one."

"How am I going to see Dietfried at night when I am even forbidden to leave my house during the day?"

Fernand snickered. "Can anyone forbid you to do anything? You found a way to be here now. Find an excuse."

After Fernand and I had parted, I did not mull over the risks too carefully, or I would have turned down the mission. For a few days, I was only concerned with setting up a situation that would lead to Dietfried inviting me over to his house on a moment's notice. Did I need to become his girlfriend? The thought repulsed me physically and morally. And anyway, he might want to meet in a hotel room, which would defeat the purpose. An idea came to me. But first, I needed to set the stage.

One morning, I volunteered to wait in the bread line. Once in the street, I walked to the nearest telephone booth and called Dietfried. We met the next day for a walk along the seafront.

That day, in addition to the fragile feminine persona I had fabricated for Dietfried, I added distracted looks, forlorn gazing toward the horizon, and the occasional sigh and nervous chew of my fingernails. At first, Dietfried was busy pontificating on the merits of industrial sea fishing, and it took him a while to notice that his usually rapt audience was being inattentive. "Dear Marceline, you seem out of sorts," he asked at last.

"Nothing I want to bore you with."

"Please tell me."

"My fiancé has been acting overly possessive." I lowered my eyes and added, "And he's not always a gentleman."

Dietfried frowned. "Has he disrespected you?"

"It's just that … he's not taking too well to my showing you the city."

"You told him about me?" he said, unsure if he should be pleased about this or not.

"When he found that I spent time with you, he went into a fit. I told him there was no harm in showing you the city. You and I are doing nothing wrong, but he's quite old-fashioned. And jealous I'm afraid."

Dietfried took the reins of the situation and patted my hand in a fatherly way. "Are you certain it would be a good idea to marry someone so unreasonable?"

"If there cannot be trust between us, and if he's going to have those fits of rage…." I let my voice trail off and added, "You are right. He is unreasonable. And his anger scares me. Oh, I'm sorry Dietfried to burden you with my story. It's only that I have so few friends to confide in, and my parents have their minds set on us marrying and refuse to hear me out."

"Oh, Marceline, I understand. Just know that I am here for you. Day or night, you absolutely must know that you can count on me."

I blinked away imaginary tears. "Do you mean this? Oh, Dietfried, I'm so glad to have you as a friend!"

One thing I had told Dietfried was true. Now that Khaled was in prison, I truly had no one to confide in. Khaled's imprisonment, the terrifying news from the war, the impending Allied invasion, and my mother's behavior were for me to shoulder alone. And if that was not enough, even my father had started to behave erratically.

He had come home the day before, staggering, his face pale and distraught. Since then, he had not left the apartment. He spent hours smoking on the balcony, looking down into the street as if he were awaiting impending doom. He wasn't speaking and barely ate. He explained that he was feeling ill, but to me, he looked confused and scared. If my father knew that Algiers was inching closer to an Allied operation, I hoped that his mood wasn't an indication that things weren't going well.

The following day, Émile came through. I found him at the foot of my building, waiting for me. "I know where they locked him up," he said, not naming Khaled.

"Where?"

"I will tell you as long as you promise not to do anything reckless."

"I only want to send him a letter," I told him.

"He's on the outskirt of town in a suburb east of Algiers," Émile relented. "It's called the Maison Carrée prison. It's not a high-security prison. They put petty thieves there, people awaiting trials."

"Are visitors allowed?"

Émile looked upset. "You said you only wanted to send a letter!"

"You said it's not high security, and that they allow visitors."

"Don't do something foolish, Marceline."

I didn't know if I would be allowed to see him, but I knew I had to give it a try. Khaled needed to know that my feelings were unchanged. He needed to know that at least one person was doing all she could to help him. "There is nothing illegal or even suspicious about a young woman visiting a person who had saved her brother's life," I said.

I thought of a plan. To go this far out of town, I would have to be gone for several hours, perhaps half a day. It was one thing to slip away when only my mother was home, and another to pull the wool over my father's eyes. I decided to dispense with parental authorization and deal with the consequences later. The tension at home was tremendous. Father and Mother were barely on speaking terms ever since Sandra had gone. With a little luck, they would continue to be too preoccupied with their issues to ask each other where I was.

The following day, I went to the Agha train station and bought a ticket in the direction of Maison Carrée. Through the short, bumpy train ride, I sat oblivious to the scenery and the other passengers. It was a hot day, rendered bearable by the speed of the train and the open windows. When we approached the Maison Carrée train station, I noticed that the people on the train were getting up from their seats to close all the windows. An awful stench rose through the wagon, coming from outside. I asked the French woman who sat next to me what was happening. She explained that years of pollution had transformed the river into a cesspool of industrial and animal waste. "One gets used to it, eventually," she said.

When we arrived at the station, I made my way to the center of town where a livestock market was in full swing. I walked across the plaza and my nose stung from the odor of animals combined with the sulfurous smell of the river. I asked for directions to the police station and hurried past the live donkeys and geese, past the rabbits and horses, and past the food stalls, the barrels full of olives, the mounds of dried figs and garbanzo beans, the citrus fruits on mats, the wine barrels. There was a clear racial divide in the market. In the aisles, French shoppers carried shopping bags and opened their wallets. Inside the stalls, Arab men and women, often shoeless, worked at selling their goods. Ever since the onset of restrictions, food prices had gone up exponentially, and the Arab population's buying power had shrunk to nothing. Many depended on their chicken coops and vegetable gardens to eat. But even for the city folks, food was getting difficult to come by. It was everybody's daily struggle to get our hands on fresh milk, eggs, or butter. Desperation grew at the thought that the bulk of the goods sold in the market would make its way to the kitchens of the rich and powerful of the city and to the restaurants that catered to them.

I entered a large, square building with too many windows, too much direct sunlight, and no ventilation. The architecture was ill-suited for the climate; the glass panes magnified the sun and trapped it along with the stench of the market. A half dozen French policemen in uniform and bureaucrats in suits moved about importantly. Meanwhile, no less than a hundred Arab grandmothers, mothers, wives, and daughters sat on rows of seats set around the room, under signs bearing numbers, or stood in various lines where bored French clerks stamped papers without making eye contact. Behind their desks, the French policemen eyed the younger women, elbowed each other, and snickered. I felt the burn of their disrespect for the women who covered their faces as much as possible. Everyone shone with sweat, but the Arab women seemed resigned and waited placidly for their turn. Where were the Arab men, I wondered? As far as I could tell, I was the only European woman in the room.

I waited in line at the information desk for an hour, struggling to breathe. My clothes were too tight, the stench and heat untenable, but I stood firm and stared straight ahead. The French men's eyes were on me now, their bestiality barely in check. I could feel the corruption of the place on my skin. This, I could tell, was not a place where one wanted to show weakness.

As I got closer to my turn at the desk, I could hear what was said. An old Arab man clearly out of his depth stood by the clerk and interpreted questions and requests. It was always the same story. The woman was here to see a father, a husband, a brother, a son. She was usually told that the man she wanted to see was in isolation, awaiting trial, and that visitors were denied to him. The woman would then beg and cry and be told that nothing could be done. I watched with rising anger as the dismissed women left the building, their despair palpable. I also noticed that on occasion, one of the women was given a number. She would then head for a smaller waiting room and sit there. This was the room where I wanted to be sent.

When it was my turn at the front of the line, I presented my identity papers to the clerk. "I'm looking for someone who might be incarcerated here," I said. "Could you look it up? His name is Khaled."

The clerk, a dull man with a drooping mustache, eyed my papers, lifted his face, and spoke patronizingly. "Every other convict here is named Khaled, Mademoiselle. What would be the last name?"

"I – I don't know his last name," I admitted.

"I'm not a miracle worker, Mademoiselle. There is nothing I can—"

I was not about to be sent away. "Could someone here help me look for it. I have the date of the arrest and the location. Perhaps in your files there would be…."

Already bored with me, the clerk gave me a small card with a number printed on it. "Wait there," he said, pointing to the waiting room. "Your number will be called."

Inside this new waiting room, a dozen women sat, stoic, while their children sat around them, playing in silence. This was a windowless room, and the air inside was stale, suffocating. A ceiling fan labored above us but did little else than blend odors of heat, sweat, and the smells of the animal market. The women, who would never have been caught looking at any of the men, made no effort to hide their curiosity about me. I must have looked out of sorts because the woman on the chair next to mine offered me water from a gourd in her basket, which I accepted with gratitude.

It was another hour before my number was called. I was directed to a room where a bespectacled French man in his sixties without a hair on his skull sat at a metal desk. "Sit please," he said. For what felt like an eternity, he purposely ignored me as he laboriously contemplated, and then stamped, documents one by one from a pile of papers scattered in front of him. I watched him select the stamp he wanted, press it into the proper color ink pad, lift the stamp to see if it was inked properly, stamp the document, and repeat the process with the next document. I wondered if he acted this rudely with everyone. "It's the Sirocco," he said at last with a defeated sigh.

"I beg your pardon?"

"The damn wind dries everything in sight," he said. "Those inkpads are useless after mere days. How do they expect me to do my work?" He took a handkerchief from his waistcoat pocket, wiped his brow, and rather pleasantly said, "Pardon the odor. It's the same horror every Friday. Brings in the flies too." To illustrate, he grabbed a fly swatter and whacked it on an unsuspecting fly on his desk, then meticulously moved the dead fly between two pieces of blotting paper and tipped it onto the waste bin. At long last, he put the form request and my open identity card in front of him. He looked at them, then at me, then back at them. "So," he said, "this individual you are looking for, this Khaled, you have no last name?"

"I was told he is kept here."

"Surely you must have a birth date?"

"I do not."

"An address, then? Name of relatives."

"I can only give you the date of the arrest, and the circumstances," I said, realizing how little I knew about the man I loved. To me, he was just Khaled. Had his last name not come up, or had he told me, and I had paid no attention? Perhaps because it was an Arabic name, I had found it hard to remember.

The bureaucrat stared across the room at the metal filing cabinet as though it would be beyond his physical ability to get to it. He seemed to measure what would take the least effort, giving me what I wanted or opposing my request, and appeared to decide on the former. Reluctantly, he shuffled toward the cabinet, leafed through the files, chose one, returned to his desk, sat down heavily, and again wiped his brow. The file was inexplicably thick. He opened it and with unbearable slowness proceeded to read it page by page, licking his thumb copiously before turning each page. At last, he took out a document and handed it to me. "Is this the individual you are looking for?"

My heart leaped. It was a photograph of Khaled. His face was closed, stubborn, his eyes dull, and because of that expression, he hardly looked like the version of him that I knew. "It's him," I said in the calmest, most indifferent tone I could manage.

The bureaucrat closed the file and looked at me askance. "And what would a young French lady want with a known radical Algerian nationalist?"

I was taken aback but continued to act nonplussed. "He saved my brother and me from a brutal aggression."

"I see," the man said.

"And he's still being detained in error while the perpetrators got to run away."

"The only reason those perpetrators, as you call them, got to run away is that this man pretends not to know who they are." He tapped at the file with his index finger, taking his time to observe me. "This is a very thick file, Mademoiselle. And most of what's in it has nothing to do with your story."

"There must be an error. He's an upstanding citizen."

He squinted. "How well acquainted are you with this man?"

"I am not. But his action toward my brother speaks for itself," I said haughtily. "His past employers have vouched for him. That's probably why your file is as thick as it is."

"Indeed, there seems to be no shortage of people willing to vouch for him. This only confirms our belief that he is a man of importance."

"Of importance to what? He defended us, that's all!" I said, furious.

"Maybe so, but for now he is awaiting trial."

"Trial for what? What is his crime?"

"That is for the jury and judge to decide."

"That's a complete travesty!"

"Mademoiselle," he said in an exhausted tone, "why don't you simply tell me what you want from me."

"I – I want to visit him."

He seemed genuinely surprised. "But what for?"

"I want to thank him in person, quite naturally. As well as bring him every reassurance that my family will testify in his defense during his trial."

"In these difficult times, we have to proceed swiftly so as not to congest the system." He continued to observe me, his words saying one thing, his expressed another. "I would love to help, but I am not sure how."

I clenched my teeth. "I must be misinformed then," I said. "I was told that you had the authority."

The man smiled unctuously and gave his tone layers of significance. "I do have a range of authority," he said.

At last, I understood. I took my wallet out of my purse; I was prepared for this. I knew of the system worked. "I would be happy to contribute to the commissariats' widow fund," I said, taking a hundred-franc bill out of my purse.

"Your generosity is much appreciated," the bureaucrat said, snatching the bills from between my fingers. "I am glad we could come to such a mutually satisfactory agreement."

An hour later, I was one of perhaps a dozen women sitting in a row of makeshift booths inside a long, gray room separated in its center by metal bars. Desks and chairs were set against the bars and on each desk were two sets of metal partitions for privacy. I couldn't see the other women's faces or those of the men they were here to visit, but I could hear the voices, the guttural melody of spoken Arabic and the muffled sobs.

I sat facing the metal bars and waited, my stomach in a knot. My skull ached from dehydration. I fought to push away the loop of fear that moved from my head to my belly and back. By coming here, I could no longer live in the delusion that Khaled's case was following a process that resembled justice. This was clearly a place where the local authorities parked people they intended to forget. Vichy was a parasite that corrupted all decency. The worst of human nature had been dormant, but Hitler had given it the fertile ground to find new vigor and blossom. The basest instincts of men now had the perfect terrain to wander unchecked. I held on tight to my memories of the Cherchell night, the sight of those American uniforms.

A door on the inmate side periodically opened, and a guard entered the room pushing a chained inmate. The inmate was always an Arab, pale, weakened, defeated-looking. What were they doing to those men? My anxiety rose as I waited for Khaled.

Suddenly, he was in the room. My chest tightened. He, already thin, had lost a tremendous amount of weight. His hands were handcuffed together at the waist. He was unshaven, pale, with dark circles under his eyes. There were bruises on his face, a deep cut to his lower lip, and his expression matched the one on the photograph; hardened, dull. He squinted as though his eyes were not accustomed to the light and I had a chance to compose myself.

The moment he saw me, he froze, made a gesture to leave the room. The guard had to push him in my direction and then push down on his shoulder until he sat on the chair that faced mine. He hooked Khaled's handcuffs to the metal bars that separated us. "You have ten minutes," he said and went to stand against the wall.

"Why are you here?" Khaled said. He was whispering, but his tone was full of fury.

I had expected loving words and effusions, and so I had to fight the onslaught of tears. "How are you?" I asked. "Are they treating you well? I am doing all I can to get you out of here. As is my father."

"You should not be here," he said coldly. "Leave. Return to Algiers."

I saw in his eyes a kind of despair and buried rage that had not been there before.

"What are those cuts and bruises? What is happening?"

He whispered urgently, "You must not act like you care about me. And you cannot cry. Not when they are watching us." He was right. I was a fool. I took a deep breath and swallowed up the emotions that risked betraying me. Once I had composed my face, Khaled could relax. "I have been thinking of you night and day," he said softly. "How is your brother?"

"He is free, and you're not," I said between my teeth. "Why are you injured?" I demanded to know. "Who is hurting you?"

"Institutionalized cruelty," he said, shaking his head.

"I will get you out of here. You know I will."

"I need to ask you something," he said, looking at his hands. "People say they have seen you around town with a German officer."

I could not help but smile. Khaled was jealous. The guard was ten feet away. I came closer to the bars and put my chin in my hands so that the guard could not read my lips. "You have to trust me," I said. "Things are happening soon that will change everything. Before long, this government could topple, and they'll have to set you free."

"You are working with the Germans?" he asked, shocked.

"Quite the opposite."

He stared at me with a burning intensity. "Are you in love with a German man?"

"It's nothing like that. But I did hide things from you," I admitted. "I only wanted to protect you. I spend time with him to get information, that's all. I despise him. I promise."

"You are spying?"

"But don't worry; he's not dangerous."

"Everyone in Algiers is dangerous. You are naïve if you think otherwise."

"I am protected."

"Whoever it is that gave you this assignment cannot protect you or will only protect you as long as it doesn't endanger them. I know how these things work."

I stiffened, defensive. "Do you?"

"You should stop at once. Stay out of this, Marceline. They only care to get what they want and are using you."

"I work for the French Resistance."

He shook his head angrily. "Why have allegiance to a country that betrays both Jews and Muslims?"

"Vichy is not France," I said. "If we can get rid of Vichy and Hitler, then things will get back to normal."

"Who is making you do this? Is it Fernand?"

"No one is making me do anything. I chose to do this." Khaled clenched his jaw. My chest tightened. I was done discussing this with him. I would not get his approval. "My father has come to see all your past employers and asked them for letters of recommendation," I said. "We are mounting a defense for you."

"You must tell your father to stop," Khaled whispered.

I blinked at him in incomprehension. "Why?"

He lowered his eyes. "I have not told you all the truth about me either. There are men in this prison who think the way I do. Algiers might one day be liberated from Vichy, but it will not help *my* people. New French men will take the place of the present ones, and those will enforce the same policies against the Arabs that have been going on for a hundred years. Removing the Germans will change nothing for us."

"Some French politicians believe in equality for the Algerians. Including the right to vote. After the war, they will fight for it."

"That's not enough, Marceline," he said, shaking his head. "There is a man imprisoned here. I cannot tell you his name. He's a visionary man. He's been condemned to sixteen years in jail. He's the first one who had the courage to demand the independence of the Algerian nation. Every government has asked him to collaborate with them because they need his power, but he's rejected them all. He is intransigent about our right to sovereignty. For our people, he is ready to spend his life in prison. And with each day, he refuses to negotiate, and for each day he spends in prison, his prestige grows. People in the streets are gaining hope."

"What does it have to do with you?"

"I have worked for this man. The police knew that immediately upon arresting me."

"What work are you talking about?"

"We are learning to shape the future of our country. And I've decided the only way for me to learn from this great mind is to stay here."

"Here?"

"In this prison."

I was horrified. "Have you been indoctrinated?"

Khaled smiled at my outrage just as I had smiled at his jealousy, and for the first time since I got there, I saw that the man I love was intact. "Not any more than you have been. Can't you see we are the same, you and I? Each of us fighting for what we believe."

"It's not the same. France was invaded! We are fighting to get our country back—"

"It *is* the same, Marceline," he interrupted softly.

"What about your work? What about your mother, your brothers, and sisters, the Kasbah? What about us?"

"This man is a hero. His ideas will make it possible to have a future for my people."

I felt chilled to the core. "How will your family survive with you in jail?" I said.

"They are being helped by people on the outside, now that I have joined the cause."

I looked deep into his eyes. "Where does this leave you and me?"

"You are the woman I love," Khaled whispered. "That is all I know. It is simple, and nothing can change that. But when the revolution comes in Algeria and my people fight to retake our ancestral land, we will be in opposition to the French. When that time comes, which side will you be on?"

"The only side I can be on!" I said, irate. "The side of France Libre! Anything else would be to betray my country."

"But what if France Libre become Algeria's enemy?" he asked. "A whole lot can happen in a war. The heroes of today can become the traitors of tomorrow."

"Time's up!" the guard said. In a few steps, he had his hand on Khaled's shoulder and was unlocking his chains from the bar. Khaled and I could only lock eyes for a few instants as he was jerked up to his feet, his wrists were handcuffed together, and he was pushed out of the room.

I sat in stunned silence. There had been no chance to say goodbye, no time for a promise, or for words of love. I stood up, shaken, and left the room. I left the jail. I left the police station, with the stench and the heat, and took a train back home in a state of shock. The Allied operation had to succeed. Vichy had to be annihilated. Because with each passing day he spent in this jail, the forces from within would have a pull on Khaled that I would be increasingly powerless to influence.

I took the train back in a state of rage. I hated that prison. I hated what Khaled had told me. I hated that he had put a seed of doubt in my mind about my mission, and I hated that he was dismissing my country. I walked home from the train station at dusk sullied by the experience in too many ways to count.

I walked into the apartment where Gustave, my father, and my mother waited for me. At first, they seemed relieved to see me in one piece, but at the same moment, they were ready to pounce. Mother was agitated. Gustave sat on the couch, ostensibly leafing through an old book but not about to miss a moment of the cross-examination about to begin. My father only sat slumped in an armchair.

"Marceline, I don't know what you think you're doing but this time you've gone too far," Mother said.

"What have I done?" I said coolly as I took off my jacket.

"You've gone to the prison to see that boy," my father said. So much for secrecy. How did they know all this? My father seemed to have no energy left in him. I did not know if he was seething, or exhausted, or perhaps heartbroken because of me.

"Let me guess," I said, "Gustave was following me again?"

"Guess again," Gustave said. His bruises had healed except for some swelling around the nose and a yellowish hue around his eyes. "Why do I care what you do anyway."

"A friend saw you at the prison and made a phone call to Uncle Moshe," my father said. His voice softened. "Ma petite, you have to trust me to help this boy through proper channels. Through influential people we know. We must do this without attracting attention to ourselves. The situation is complex and getting more so every day."

"The situation with Khaled?"

"The situation with … everything," Father said. "I am working on getting this boy out of prison. Please don't let your stubbornness make it impossible. Apparently, there are people in Algiers who intend to keep him there. He has affiliated himself with a dangerous extremist."

"How are his ideals any different from ours?" I said. "He believes in returning Algeria to the Algerians, just like we want France back for us. But in his case, it's called extremism?"

My father shook his head wearily and was about to say something but my mother, vibrating with indignation, said, "Are you aware of the reputation you are acquiring for yourself?"

"I'm speaking of politics, and once again you worry about my virtue?"

"Just don't talk about politics," my father said. "It's as simple as that."

Mother said, "What if people learn that you are involved with a … Muslim, for goodness sake?"

"What people?"

"The – the good people," she stammered.

"Wake up, Mother! The old world is gone! How can you expect me to live by rules and values that no one heeds or respects? Look no further than those good people you speak of, and explain to me what it is they are doing to the Jews? Doesn't that shake your sense of values just a bit? And women are changing too. They're in factories building weapons, and even in the Resistance, using those weapons."

"A woman's role has never been in battle. You're being completely irrational," my mother screeched.

"Women are fighting this war every bit as much as the men. The only reason they're not piloting airplanes and submarines is that men won't let them."

Mother ignored my cris de coeur and pulled out all the stops. "You're taking advantage of my illness to run around town with god knows who!"

"Illness? Oh, please! You've acted like a victim ever since you set foot in Algiers."

My father raised his voice. "Marceline, I'm warning you!"

Mother plopped down on the couch looking crushed.

I softened my voice and added, "I'm made of stronger stuff than you are, Mother."

"How would you know what you are made of?" my father asked with exasperation. "You haven't been tested. What if you discover that you are, in fact, made of flesh and blood? As fragile and vulnerable as everyone else?"

I shrugged, "I shall cross that bridge when I get to it."

"How can I blame my children," my father mumbled, so low that I wasn't sure if he was speaking to us or to himself. "I have created them this way. I had a dream of a life for them that would be free of fear. I coddled them so that they would not have to witness the ugly things I have seen. I should have prepared them better. I should have taught them fear, instead of that dangerous sense of invincibility and entitlement they have."

Gustave chimed in, "She's been sheltered and pampered her entire life. She thinks she can do anything she wants."

"Like you haven't been coddled," I said.

Gustave gave me a murderous look. "I was sent away if you remember."

"Not this again," I said. "Everyone goes to boarding school, you dunce. It's not a punishment."

"Not everyone goes," he said. "You didn't."

"Blame Mother and Father! They're the ones who sent you and kept me at home. And you've resented me ever since."

"Enough, the two of you!" my father roared. "The point is, you must stop all of this at once, Marceline! The visits to the jail, the translations, the nonsense with the Resistance. You're not helping anything, and you're endangering us all."

"I'm trying to save us!" I said. "I am not about to sit in a room behind closed shutters and hold Mother's hand. If I must perish, then I want to do it fighting for our country!"

"I have heard this kind of rhetoric my whole life," my father said, shaking his head in disgust. "And for what? Death and destruction and despair. Patriotism is a poisonous beverage, my daughter. Soon enough you'll have your own children, and you'll understand that everything your mother and I are trying to do is to keep you safe. I took you and Gustave out of France to escape danger, and you both are throwing yourself toward it. We sent Gustave to boarding school for his safety. We want you to marry the right kind of man who will provide for you and protect you and for Gustave to find a nice young woman who will love him and care for him. You'll one day understand what governs mankind. It's not fear for ourselves, but fear for our children."

"Who in their right mind would want to bring up children in this world?" I said.

"You'll have children someday. You will see."

"I won't. Nor do I intend to live in the shadow of a self-important Frenchman. I have no desire to model myself to society's expectations of what it is to be a proper wife. I've spent the last nineteen years learning to be polite, believe me, and I found no joy in it nor reward."

"Perhaps I am the one who has been wrongheaded," my father said. Was he addressing me, Gustave, my mother, himself? "Perhaps I am trying to do something that is impossible, keeping those I love safe. People have their paths to take, the course of their own lives to follow."

I'm not sure what my father meant when he said this, but Gustave became incensed. "So, that's it? You agree with her? You wouldn't let me join the Chantiers de la Jeunesse, but you'll let her do whatever she likes? This is what she does. She lies, and she manipulates. She puts thoughts in people's heads. She's the most two-faced—"

"Who asked for your opinion, Gustave?" I shouted. "Can't you see you don't matter? Don't you see you're a non-entity? You're nothing but a weak little boy."

Without warning, Gustave threw himself at me, head first, like a bull, and struck me with his head in the solar plexus. I fell to the ground gasping for air.

"Marceline! Gustave! Stop this!" my father shouted, grabbing Gustave by his shirt collar and pulling him off me.

Gustave retreated to one corner of the room. He was red-faced, breathing hard, and beside himself with rage. My back was against the opposite wall. I sat on the floor and tried to catch my breath. My entire chest hurt. Mother wrung her hands, muttering, "Oh my God, oh my God."

"What's the matter with you?" Father shouted at Gustave. "You cannot hit your sister! You cannot hit a woman, any woman. Ever!"

"She's no woman! She's a beast," Gustave screamed. "She's the worst human being. Everyone in this family thinks she is great. You refuse to see her as she truly is."

"She is your sister."

"I hate her!"

"I forbid you to say this," my father said, not in anger, but in deep sadness. "I forbid you to think this. We are family."

"I hate her, hate her, hate her!" Gustave screamed, tears flowing from his eyes. Mother, her fingers shaking, opened her pillbox. I got to my feet, resolved never to speak to my brother again. Gustave stood at the other side of the room, panting.

"I cannot make this family listen to reason against their will," my father said, defeated. "I cannot tell you who to choose to love or to hate. You won't hear my advice. You refuse to learn from my experiences. I cannot try to make you happy if you constantly do the opposite of what I ask. I cannot make you think of the future when all you think about is the present or the past. God is my witness that I have tried." He walked out onto the balcony and leaned over the handrail. He seemed to gaze at the horizon, the sea in the distance, the myriad of tiny boats. I could see him from the back. He had both hands on the handrail, and his back shook lightly. Was he crying?

Mother closed her pillbox, sank onto the couch, and closed her eyes. I got up, flattened my hair, and smoothed my clothes with my hand, thinking of what I could tell Gustave to destroy him, but I worried about upsetting my father even more. Gustave, red-eyed and still breathing hard in his corner of the room, seemed about to consider jumping at my throat again.

Suddenly there was a tremendous knock at the door that jolted us all to the core. We all looked in the direction of the front door and at one another. This was entirely out of the ordinary. Visitors needed to buzz downstairs to be let in. No one ever knocked on the door.

There was a second knock, just as forceful.

My father took a moment on the balcony as if to gather himself for the inevitable, as though he knew who was at the door, which, of course, he could not have. He left the balcony and headed toward the door. There he took a deep breath and opened it.

On our doorstep was a policeman in uniform accompanied by a man in a dark suit. They presented their badges. The man in the suit was a police detective who introduced himself as Detective Poitras of the Algiers police. Could he please take a few minutes to speak with us? "I have a few routine questions," he said, adding that he wanted to speak to the whole family. The word routine, if it was meant to calm us down, had the opposite effect. For years now, routine identity checks, routine vehicle stops, and routine questioning were precisely what sent entire families into trains and off to deportation or forced labor camps all over Europe. My mouth turned dry; my legs were heavy. I shot a look at Mother. Would she be able to pull herself together for this?

We invited the detective and the policeman to sit. The detective sat in one of the armchairs. The policeman declined to sit and stood by the living room door, looking at nothing. We offered them mint tea and almond cookies, and the detective accepted a glass of water. Gustave went to fetch the glass of water and placed it in on the coffee table in front of the detective who drank avidly.

Detective Poitras was a Frenchman in his mid-forties. His skin was pale, as though the Algerian sun had never touched his skin. He had a thin body, a narrow face, and eyes that seemed to take in everything at once. He peered from my mother to Gustave, to me, to my father, and back to me. Could he sense that he was arriving in the middle of chaos? Mother was jittery. Gustave was red in the face, and I was probably still disheveled from our fight. Only Father was composed, at least on the outside. But I knew his calm was an act, his air of surprise and innocence a complete fabrication. To me, he looked terrified. He spoke slowly and made an effort to lessen his accent. Did he think that his identity had been revealed and he was about to be apprehended? Perhaps we all would be arrested today.

Father sat on the couch beside Mother, Gustave sat on the second armchair, and I on the arm of the couch, next to Mother. We were all guilty. We had false identities, fake names. Mother was guilty of sending her maid to buys things on the black market. Gustave was guilty of roaming the streets after curfew. I was in the Resistance, and until evidence to the contrary, so was my father.

Then Poitras's eyes rested on me, and I thought he was here for me, that he knew of my involvement in ... something.

"We are investigating a homicide," Poitras finally said. We all gasped at him in surprise. The sensation of relief was physical. Whatever the reason Poitras was in our living room, it obviously had nothing to do with us. "We believe that your maid was involved," he continued. We all looked up at the new maid, a gray person devoid of age or personality as she brought a bowl of olives and set it on the table, oblivious to the fact that we were speaking about her. "Your name is Xandra, isn't it?" Poitras asked her. The maid looked at him blankly.

"Oh, so not that one?" Mother exclaimed shrilly, pointing to the new maid. "You must be speaking of our past employee. Her name was Sandra with an S. A homicide, you say? Are you saying that she was murdered?" Mother had taken her calming pill, but it had not yet taken effect. She was still on edge from the fight, and I worried she would become glib and say something idiotic.

Poitras said, "Not murdered, no. She is the suspect."

"The suspect?" Gustave and I echoed. The notion was so outlandish that I let out a laugh and all eyes were on me.

"I do not see what is amusing about this," Poitras said.

"It's just impossible," I said.

"You must have the wrong address," Gustave said.

Poitras looked at his note. "Sandra-Xandra, whatever her actual name might be, is being investigated for murder. You are listed as the employer."

"Well, yes, but she was fired," Mother said. "Over a month ago. I certainly cannot fathom this."

I realized that we were doing all the talking and that my father was silent. Poitras told us that a man had been found dead in her hotel room and that Sandra had vanished.

"I can think of a dozen theories why she had no involvement in this!" I said.

"With all due respect, Mademoiselle, we are not interested in your theories. Only in what you know." He turned to my parents, "How long was she working for you?"

"Two years," was the answer my father gave. These were my dad's first words since the policemen arrived. I could see now that the entire time he had listened to the detective, he had prepared his lies. He needed to lie about when Sandra had started to work for us to avoid being asked about the time before we arrived in Algiers. She was Armenian, he said. He had no idea how long she had lived in Algiers before working for us. She had resided in a maid's room on the fifth floor. We had to let go of her recently.

"Why did you terminate her employment?" Poitras asked.

"My wife no longer felt comfortable with her."

Mother, Gustave, and I listened carefully, taking cues from my father. He told the detective how Sandra had been expected to watch me and instead had allowed me to go out at night. He told him about the ensuing attack at the Kasbah. About her subsequent firing. I admired my father's smooth lie and the way he incorporated the truth that the police already knew or could verify. The inspector looked at me with amusement.

"Breaking curfew, the Kasbah at night, or in daytime for that matter. It seems that your children are quite disorderly."

I clenched my teeth at being dismissed as a mere child. *The government you work for is about to be toppled,* I thought, *and you'll have this disorderly child to thank for it.*

"I can assure you, Detective, that we are keeping them on a tight leash now," my father said, which was ironic considering that I had just been caught in the flagrant act of disorderliness of taking a train to a nearby jail to see a boy I loved.

"Smart of you. Especially in these times," the detective said. He turned to me and added, "Mademoiselle, if I may, as a police detective, I see all kinds of terrible things happening to young French women who take the chance of walking freely in the streets. Especially at night." He said this in a way that felt more threatening than protective. "The police cannot be everywhere. Prevention is the best defense." I nodded obediently. His gaze had been fixed on my chest the entire time. "You mention that you were not comfortable with your maid," he asked my mother. "You no longer trusted her with your children. Do you believe her capable of murder?"

My mother answered with a shrug. "She is certainly careless, but I doubt she is dangerous."

"Could you give us a physical description?" Poitras said as he took a small black notebook and a fountain pen from his pants pocket.

"Black eyes, I think," my mother answered. "About four foot nine. But all that people see is that scar on half her face. Trust me, she will not be missing for long. She has the kind of physical description one cannot alter. You shall find her easily."

Unable to contain myself I said, "Mother, Sandra is innocent, evidently!"

Poitras asked, "Would each of you tell me when you last saw her?"

"At the market," I said. "About three weeks ago. I ran into her, and we spoke for a few minutes. Then we went our separate ways."

"I have not seen her since the night my poor boy was nearly beaten to death due to her irresponsible behavior," Mother said.

"I saw her last at the hospital the night I was attacked. My parents had just fired her. She came to say goodbye to me," Gustave said, lowering his eyes.

My father said, "I know nothing past the time when I brought her to that hotel."

"Besides the man who was murdered, there was another man," the detective said. "He might have lived with her, but his name was not on the register. People saw him come and go. No one has a good description. And you know how they all dress the same, those Muslims. Medium built. No beard. That's all I have. Have you any idea who he might be? He was her lover, most likely. We think it might have been a lover's quarrel. Some sort of romantic triangle."

Mother and I scoffed in unison.

"Is this so difficult to imagine?" Poitras asked.

"It most certainly is," Mother said. Her medication was taking effect, I saw, from a slight glazing of the eyes. She had stopped fretting, and she looked sleepy when she said, "The notion of two men willing to kill each other over her is simply ludicrous."

"Besides, Sandra is a devout member of Armenian Apostolic Church," I said. "She is a quiet person, very religious, conservative. Hardly the type who would generate intrigue, or a lover's dispute, let alone a crime of passion."

Poitras smiled as though I was the cutest thing he'd seen in days. "A feisty daughter you have here, Dear Monsieur," he told my father. "Keep her on a tight leash indeed." I stared him down. He turned to my mother. "Would you concur with this?"

"Her … proclivities were not of interest to me," my mother said. I recognized the now familiar slowing of her speech, like a light that first flickers before slowly dimming. Her pill was taking effect. "If she did have a lover, I would be the last one informed." She added, "She was indeed quite … religious. She's an … assiduous churchgoer."

"Are you Christian?" the detective asked, addressing my father.

If my blood weren't already boiling, it would have turned to ice. My father's response came, unflappable. "We are Catholic," he said.

"Ah, yes," the detective said, but it was clear that he did not believe him for a second. He jotted something down on his pad. "I better put 'rectify this' in your file."

"We have a file?"

Poitras answered in a syrupy tone, "This is 1942, Monsieur. *Everyone* has a file."

"Who is this man who died?" my father asked.

"I was going to ask you the same question. Do you have any idea about this? We cannot identify him. He was possibly a vagrant."

"How did he die?"

"He was stabbed."

The notion was so preposterous that I relaxed. "Sandra is incapable of anger, let alone that sort of violence," I said.

"The woman you know and the woman she is might be two very different people," Poitras said. "All we know are the facts: a man found himself in her room, invited or not. She is the one who stabbed him. We are certain of this."

"How can you be?" I asked.

"She took the time to wipe on her dress the blood that had been on her hands and then change out of her bloodied clothes, fold them, place the weapon back into its case, and the case in a drawer. Not only did she kill, but she did so with a chilling amount of cold blood."

"Could it have been in self-defense?" I asked.

"If it were, she would have had no reason to run away."

"Innocent people are put in jail every day," I said, with an arrogance I regretted when my father silenced me with one look.

"Detective Poitras," my father said, "is it possible that someone stabbed the man and that Sandra ran way because she was afraid for her life?"

"This is an excellent question, which she will be at liberty to answer when we find her." He turned to my mother to say something and froze. We all watched Mother in embarrassment. She had dozed off on the couch. Disconcerted, but polite enough not to call attention to my mother's bizarre behavior, Poitras turned to my father. "Please do not leave town. We might have more questions as the investigation progresses."

"We won't," Father assured him.

After the policemen had left, Gustave and I bombarded my father with questions. "What do you think happened, Baba?" "Do you think it's really Sandra they're talking about?"

My father did not want to discuss any of this. "Gustave, you are grounded for a week for hitting your sister," he said. "Marceline, if I hear that you've gone anywhere near that jail, I will hire a bodyguard to camp outside your door, and you will spend the rest of the year looking at the street from your balcony."

"But, Baba," Gustave and I protested in unison.

"Can't you see that this city is terribly dangerous, and about to become more so? Did you not hear this policeman? Did you not see what happened to your friend and now to Sandra? Innocent people are being accused of crimes, and there is nothing we can do to help them." With this he added, "I'm going to work," and he left the apartment, slamming the door.

Mother was jerked out of her stupor by the sound of the door. She adjusted her clothes. "Where has that nice man gone?" she mumbled, presumably referring to the detective.

****

On November 6th, 1942, less than three weeks after the Cherchell meeting, I received a message from Fernand to meet at café El Bahdja. I sneered at Gustave, who was still grounded for hitting me, and left the apartment.

Café El Bahdja was a deserted, grimy place which had become our default meeting spot. There we could speak without being heard, although we coded most of what we talked about. Fernand and I sat at a back table. He ordered olives and anisette for us both. He lit a cigarette, exhaled and whispered. "It's happening," he said.

The hair on the back of my neck prickled. "When?"

"Tomorrow night."

I was knocked down by the news. "But they said before winter!"

"Tomorrow night," he repeated.

"How can we be ready?"

"We're ready." He added grimly, "That's the good news."

"What else?" I asked, trying to mask the trembling of my hand as I put the cigarette he offered me between my lips.

Fernand leaned toward me to light my cigarette. "The package arrived at the wrong beach and sank."

I knew what Fernand meant. What he referred to as the package was the delivery of weapons promised by the Americans. I felt a hollowness in the pit of my belly. "How then—"

"We will manage with what we have."

"It will never work without the package."

"We have a trick up our sleeve. If the plan works, we will barely need the package at all."

"How?" I asked.

"Not here."

Fernand paid the bill, and we walked in the streets of Algiers until we knew we were entirely out of earshot and he could explain the plan. "At the start of Pétain's administration, the Algiers government put a system in place in the eventuality of an attack or a coup. It's designed to relieve the police of their function or assist them in the case of an attack. That system is valid for the mairie, the commissariat de police, the houses of commanding officers, the Nineteenth Corps headquarters, the arsenal, Radio Algiers, and telephone switchboards. Let's say the city is under attack, a special force comes in with specially signed papers, and takes control in order to protect it." Fernand smiled and crushed his cigarette on the pavement. "What will happen is this: we are turning the emergency procedure created to protect the city from an invasion into a way to facilitate an invasion."

"How?"

Despite Fernand's tension, his excitement was communicative as he spoke. "Our men will arrive in the middle of the night dressed in the uniforms of reservist officers and present ordres de mission stating that they are the emergency force set in place to take over."

"How in the world will you get your hands on those orders of mission?"

"The two officers you saw at the Cherchell meeting, do you remember them?"

"Colonel Jousse and Général Mast?"

"They are above suspicion from Vichy. In an exquisite twist of irony, it is those two that Vichy has put in charge of signing the orders of mission."

"So, the orders will be perfectly authentic?"

"Isn't it a thing of beauty? Tomorrow evening, our men will dress as reservists. At midnight, with orders and weapons in hand, they'll knock at all the strategic points and take them over. Not a drop of blood shed. In fact, the people in place will feel protected by us the entire time." He laughed softly. "From there it will be a perfect lockdown. No command will be given or received. Without the police, or a mayor, or any way to get directives from Vichy, no one will know how to react once they realize we're in the middle of an Allied invasion. They won't know if Vichy is for it or against it. They won't know if they should consider the landing an act of liberation or an act of war."

"What if someone suspects the orders to be fake?"

"The phone lines will be cut off precisely at midnight, so they won't be able to reach anyone to verify. They'll have an easy choice to make: either disobey written orders and risk their career or go along with them. And don't forget that even if they work for Vichy, they are French above all. It will be easier to let themselves be relieved of their duty. The alternative would require a sense of initiative most bureaucrats don't possess."

"A perfect plan ... if they buy it."

"If they don't, we will be armed. Once inside, it will be easy to neutralize any resisting bureaucrats. And remember, they are pencil-pushers. Not trained or armed, the way we are. The crucial part is to cut communications. We're counting on confusion and the effect of surprise. With the phone lines down, it will be chaos. The only ones in Algiers with any sense of what's happening will be our men. As all this is happening, other cells will be at work throughout the rest of the city, gaining control of access in and out of the Algiers by taking over bridges and roads." Fernand inhaled deeply from a new cigarette, exhaled, and inspected me with half-closed eyes. "And then, there is you."

"Me."

"Early tomorrow evening you will call your Boche, tell him you need to see him, some sort of emergency. Can you do that?"

"I have a plan. I think it will work."

"That-a-girl."

"What happens then?"

"Tomorrow night, you are the one who will prevent your Boche from contacting the Wehrmacht."

Fernand's commanding tone nearly knocked me out of my chair. "But I can't – how would I?"

I took a measure of Fernand's cold expression. No matter how much he professed to care about me, he was willing to sacrifice me for this mission. "This is crucial, Marceline. The Resistance's single advantage is the element of surprise. If the Boche rings the alarm bell, Berlin will alert the Afrika Kopf. Rommel's troops are already at the Tunisian border. The Italians in the Syrian airbase could deploy their air force. Our job is to prevent the Nazis from making their move a moment too soon. We must stop this Boche from sending or receiving messages, and you're our ticket in. There is no one else." I looked at Fernand, speechless.

"Two possibilities," he continued. "You can lure him out of his house, and we'll kidnap him, or you have to subdue him from inside the house."

I was speechless for a moment. This sounded more like fiction than any sort of reality. "Why not simply kidnap him now?"

"Because they would put someone else in his place. Someone who has no reason to let you close. And his kidnapping alone would be a warning sign to the Germans."

"Oh my gosh, Fernand, how could I possibly do any of this?"

"If you follow the plan, the poor fellow will never know what happened to him."

"What *will* happen to him?" I asked.

Fernand took my hand and placed in my palm two large capsules. "A terrific night's sleep," he said.

I stared down at the capsules and felt the fear like a punch in my gut and understood a whole lot at once. I understood what Fernand was asking me to do. I understood that everything had felt like a game to me up to that point and that my father had been right: I had been in denial about the gravity of it all.

I also understood that I was far too deep into this to refuse.

****

I spent the following day in a state of abject panic that I made every effort to conceal from my parents. Fernand had not given me the mission because of skill or talent, but because the German officer I was assigned to had turned out to be more valuable than expected. As the only person with a connection to Dietfried, I was all the Resistance had. I had no doubt in my mind that I would fail, and the weight of this responsibility was too much to bear. But everything was happening the following night, and there was little time to ponder the risks for myself or my family.

On November 7th, 1942, the eve of the planned Allied landing, I told Mother that I was spending the night at Béatrice's. It was easier to get out of Béatrice's place than to leave my own apartment in the middle of the night. As we had done many times, Béatrice helped me get out of her apartment without her parents seeing, and then she went to her room and closed the door so that her parents thought that I was with her.

I went down the steps of her building shoes in hands. In the street, I walked to the end of the block and entered the wooden telephone box. The phone rang and rang. With each ring, I desperately wanted to hang up.

When Dietfried picked up the telephone, he seemed astounded to hear my voice. "I hope I have not awakened you," I said. I did not have to pretend to be distraught. I was.

"Of course not; is everything all right?"

"You said I could call you anytime and I...." I changed the pitch of my voice and made a sound as though I was muffling tears. "It's just that I didn't know who else to call."

"Marceline, calm down, I urge you," Dietfried said in a commanding but soothing voice. "Tell me what's the matter?"

"I just needed to hear a friend's voice, that's all," I said, sounding, I hoped, pitiful.

"Please tell me what's going on!"

"It's my fiancé." I broke into false sobs. "You were right about him. He's not a gentleman. He got so upset that I was spending time with you. He had a terrible anger fit. He's nothing but a jealous, irate boy."

The thought of my imaginary fiancé being jealous of him opened a door inside Dietfried's subconscious. "Has he hurt you?" he asked, and from his tone, I could tell he was already feeling a sense of proprietorship toward me.

"I'll be all right."

Chivalrous Dietfried took control. "Marceline, has he put his hands on you?"

"It was awful. I don't know what he will do next. I ran away."

"Are you safe from him right now? Where are you?"

"I am near my apartment, but he is standing in front of the entrance. I'm afraid to go home. My family is away, and he knows this. I'm scared, Dietfried. I'm scared that he will force his way into my apartment."

"Can't you call the police?"

"The police?" I repeated. I had not thought of the police. In a flash of creativity, I improvised. "He is a policeman himself. That's his work. That's why I cannot call the police."

"Marceline, just tell me how I can help."

"Could you, would you come down here?" I asked in a small voice.

Fernand had told me that the chances of Dietfried accepting this were slim, but it was worth a shot. If he came, Fernand's men would kidnap him as planned, long enough for Dietfried to be unable to transmit a signal. There was a silence on the line. Finally, Dietfried said, "I am sorry Marceline. I absolutely cannot leave my house at this hour. For reasons I cannot explain just yet."

"I completely understand," I said. Part of me hoped that he would leave it at that. But a stronger urge pushed me to succeed. If I did not find a way to see him tonight, the entire mission might fail.

"We're in a state of alert," Dietfried hurried to add. "Rumors. Absolutely nothing you must concern yourself with, but I cannot go anywhere. It would be tantamount to abandoning my post."

"I should never have bothered you," I said, breathlessly.

There was more silence on the line. Dietfried was processing this. "I do have an idea!" he said at last. "Perhaps you would like to come over here."

My heart beat faster. "Come where, Dietfried?"

"My house. There is a guest room. You'll be safe until morning when your parents return. Would you like that?"

"Do you really think so?"

"Yes, definitely. Just tell me where to send my chauffeur."

I could still turn back. I could still say no. But a process had been set in motion, and I was no longer an individual but a crucial cog in a terrifying machine. "I would like that very much," I said.

We planned for his chauffeur to pick me up at the corner of rue d'Isly and rue Joinville. Next, I dialed Fernand's telephone number. "The dove flies to the nest," I said when I heard his voice, and I hung up.

From the phone box, I dashed to the courtyard of our apartment building. Father's car was parked in its regular spot, as was my bicycle and Gustave's. Curfew time was approaching.

I pedaled away through the emptying streets. My breath was heavy, my heart pounding. The tires made whooshing sounds on the pavement. Night fell, and lampposts lit up one by one. By now, I thought, the Allies must already be positioned a short distance from the shore. Soon enough, a boat, or a submarine, or an ally carrying M1 carbines would be spotted. A bridge would explode. There would be an exchange of gunfire. Everyone in the city would be alerted. Hopefully, by then it would no longer matter. A few hundred Jews bearing obsolete weapons would have wreaked havoc on all communication systems and rendered the police force useless. I pedaled frantically.

I hid the bicycle out of sight just as Dietfried's driver pulled into the street. The chauffeur came around and opened the door for me. He was a French man, burly and violent-looking. Although he worked for the enemy, the contempt on his face displayed how he felt about a young French woman on a nighttime rendezvous with a German officer.

I sat in the back, and the automobile made its way out of the center of Algiers. I thought of what Fernand had told me would happen tonight. At this moment, our men, young and old, prepared or not, were taking their weapons out of hiding, donning reservists' uniforms, badges, and armbands, scurrying around the city with their precious ordres de mission. At the city's edge, others were placing explosives under bridges and getting ready to block roads. Everywhere, our men were preparing to shut down phone lines. And I was about to face Dietfried.

So much could go wrong. An alarm could ring too soon. The local Vichy forces could know in advance of the Resistance's subterfuge, and orders would be given to open fire on our liberators. If I could not stop Dietfried from sounding the alarm in Germany, the entire landing operation might be compromised. If the Nazis found out about the landing before we had Algiers under our control, they could move to mobilize their forces in and around North Africa.

And then, there was the ignominious possibility that the Allies had changed their mind, for whatever reason, without notifying us and that our group was heading towards a suicide mission.

Of all the doubts that assailed me as the automobile headed toward Dietfried's house, it had not occurred to me that my inexperience, my hubris, my stupidity, and my sense on invincibility were matched only by my brother's.

Gustave too had been given a mission that night. He too was out past curfew. He too was about to risk his life. And with this, the fate of my family was sealed.

It was a fifteen-minute drive to the outskirts of town before Dietfried's driver pulled in front of his house.

Armed guards opened the gate, and we drove into the courtyard. In the night, I could only see the outline of the house and the date palms that framed it. It was a two-story house, painted white and surrounded by a wall and a garden. I looked up at the windows; all the shutters were closed.

There were guards everywhere, dark silhouettes against the night. I counted about ten. Fernand had explained to me that the security provided for Dietfried, compliments of Vichy, was composed of Frenchmen, each outfitted with a Wehrmacht Karabiner. Some of those men were secretly with the Resistance and on our side. Some of them were not. I could not tell who was with whom, and it felt as though it was just me, surrounded by enemies.

And then I saw him: Gustave, my brother, standing guard by one of the palm trees.

He was wearing a dark turtleneck, and there was a leather strap across his chest, holding a Karabiner.

Gustave, my brother, impossibly, was one of Dietfried's guards!

My legs went limp, my mouth dry. Our eyes met briefly and widened in horror at the sight of each other. Immediately, we both looked away. I felt ill.

Outside the front door, one of the guards searched me with deliberate roughness, groping my breasts as the others looked me up and down, sneering. To them, I was nothing but a French tramp about to spend the night with a Nazi. I wondered if Gustave had seen this. I felt ashamed.

At that moment, Dietfried stepped out of the house, greeting me effusively as though I were a guest at a cocktail party. "Dear Marceline, please do come in," he said. He took me inside the house. Inside, I collapsed into his arms, and I did not have to pretend.

"I am so glad you are here and safe," Dietfried said once we were inside. Instead of his usual uniform, he was wearing casual pants and a shirt unbuttoned at the neck.

I let him guide me into the living room. I don't know what he was saying. All I could think about was Gustave. What was my brother doing here? I felt rage and panic all at once. How could my brother be guarding a Boche unless he worked for the French Algerian government – in other words, for Vichy? But Fernand had said some of the guards were in the Resistance. For sure, Gustave had to be on our side! Either way, the implications of his presence here were too dire to fathom. If my brother was with the enemy, he might be shot to death tonight. If he was one of us, Dietfried's Vichy guards might shoot him. Whichever it was, Gustave was in terrible danger.

"Are you quite all right?" Dietfried asked. I thought I might throw up. I'm certain I now looked as distraught as I had earlier pretended to be.

"You have a lot of guards," I told him.

He smiled apologetically. "It does seem overkill, doesn't it? Nothing ever happens in Algiers." He looked at my worried face and added quickly, "I mean, in your case something *did* happen, my darling. It's terrible, this unfortunate aggression by your fiancé. Do you not prefer being surrounded by armed guards at this moment?"

I smiled weakly. "I guess I do."

"No harm can come to you as long as you are with me."

The living room was a well-furnished space with high ceilings, crown molding, comfortable sofas, and expensive furniture. This was someone's home, requisitioned, just as our house in Paris had been. I thought of our home, swarming with Nazis, who slept in our beds, took baths in our tubs, ate out of Mother's delicate Limoges china.

In the fireplace, someone had started a fire. A bottle of Bordeaux and two wine glasses were set on the coffee table. The setting was transparent as to Dietfried's intentions. Here I was, allegedly terrified and upset, and he was about to take the opportunity to try and seduce me. "Please do sit and relax," he said mellifluously. "You must be exhausted after the evening you've had." He pointed to the wine. "Please relax. Do sit down on the couch; yes, right here. A glass of wine will strengthen you."

"Thank you, Dietfried, for being so attentive," I said as I sat on the too-soft couch. It was a good thing that I was supposed to be afraid and upset because now I truly was. I thought of my father, of what he had said about his fear that something might happen to either of us. And now both his children were in great danger and might even die on the same night.

Dietfried sat on the sofa too close to me. He poured wine into one of the glasses and offered it to me. I was about to take a sip when I saw that he had not filled his own glass. "Aren't you going to have wine?" I asked.

"I'm very much on duty at the moment," he said.

But Dietfried needed to drink something right now. Had to or else none of the plan would work! "Perhaps its best that I don't drink either," I said, jumping to my feet and walking agitatedly around the room as though I was suddenly able to realize that I was a proper young lady in a compromising situation.

Dietfried must have seen that he could make no headway with me unless he found a way to calm me down. "A glass of wine would help your nerves," he pleaded.

"Oh, a glass of water will do," I said, uptight.

"I will drink with you," he sighed. "But only if you promise to sit down and relax." He poured a glass for himself and raised it. "To our friendship," he said.

We drank, and he listened to me with rapt attention, leaning ever closer as I fed him a tale of domestic abuse and womanly distress. I cried too. Not because of my lies, but because of Gustave, because of my dad, because I might not see morning come, and I was too young to die. Dietfried, perhaps noticing that it gave him courage, filled both our glasses again.

My opportunity was here. I had to seize it. "Dietfried," I said. "Do you mind? All this wine on an empty stomach. Would you have anything to eat?"

He jumped up. "Forgive me. I'm an appalling host. I shall fetch something to eat at once!"

He disappeared into the nearby kitchen. I heard dishes clang and cupboard doors being opened and shut. Everything happened in an instant: I reached into my purse, took the capsules Fernand had given me, opened one, and dropped its powdery contents into Dietfried's wine. I watched the glass in horror: the whole thing had begun to fizz violently. I added the content of the second capsule, and it fizzed some more. An instant later, the wine was still, and I could breathe. I marveled that my fingers had been steady enough to carry this out.

Another moment and Dietfried was back with a plate of olives, cheese, and bread. He sat next to me, urgency on his face, as though his time in the kitchen had resulted in renewed determination. He offered me my glass.

"Let's have some food first, shall we?" I said, thinking that the taste of the cheese might mask any odd taste in the wine.

We ate our cheese and bread. Mine had the feel of quicksand in my mouth. "Have I told you about my childhood holidays in Rügen, off the Pomeranian coast?" he asked. "It is in the Baltic Sea."

He had. "Tell me about it," I said.

He embarked on one of his soliloquies. I heard nothing. I only watched his lips move and tracked the glass as it went from his hand to his mouth. I also noticed something: as Dietfried spoke, his eyes kept veering toward a narrow wooden door to our right. A bedroom? Was this where his equipment was set up?

My attention kept returning to the fireplace mantle where an imposing marble clock indicated that it was already past ten at night. Where was Gustave right now? Where were Fernand and his men? Would Fernand recognize Gustave and make sure no one shot at him?

Dietfried did not seem to notice anything strange with the taste of the wine, but neither did he seem affected by it. Doubt gripped me. What if the product failed to work? Or what if Fernand had lied to me and it was, in fact, poison and Dietfried was about to drop dead? What if there was no Allied landing, and I was found in this room with a corpse?

Dietfried downed the rest of his glass to muster the courage to do something. He took my hand in his. "Dear Marceline, I am so glad you came here tonight. You are so ... You are, lovely and...." He blinked twice and looked at me with puzzlement. I watched him intently, my hand stiff in his. Dietfried looked confused as he went on with his courtship. "You are so...." He leaned toward me as if to kiss me. I leaned away from him, and he made a nosedive into the throw pillow. He pushed himself up, shook his head, and leaned in again to kiss me. I got up from the couch. He looked confused and got up. He staggered toward me, flailing his arms. I took a step back. "Dear Marceline," he said, grasping for my dress. "That pig fiancé of yours ... does not deserve...." His speech slurred. He squinted with great effort and passed his hand over his face. He was sweating, shaking his head. I went to stand by the window and looked through the spaces between the wooden shutters. I wanted to see signs of our men, signs of Gustave, but all I saw was the night. Dietfried set out to pursue me, but at a snail's pace. He got close. I stepped away. He followed me around the room, stumbling, his shoulders slumped, still not realizing that he had been drugged. "You were correct," he mumbled. "One mustn't have wine on an empty stomach." The marble clock on the mantle marked fifteen minutes past ten. I heard something at last: a commotion coming from outside. There were shouts. An instant later a gunshot tore through the night, then another one and a third and a fourth in rapid succession. Gustave! Where was he? My heart began to beat violently in my chest. Dietfried stumbled to the window. "Was ist das?" he exclaimed drunkenly just as a machine gun roared into the night.

"Move away from the window," I yelled. We both ducked. Our faces were inches from each other, and he looked at me. I looked at him, expecting him to fall face first, but he did not.

An expression between disappointment and disbelief passed across his sweaty face. "*You* did this?" he said, stricken.

As gunshots and men's voices pierced the night, Dietfried and I, in unison, looked at the narrow door to the right of the room, confirming my intuition that something important such as his radio equipment was in that room.

Dietfried and I moved at the same moment, me jumping up, him stumbling to his feet. I got to the door to the room first, but he pushed me out of the way, hard. I was thrown against the wall, and I fell to the ground. The honeymoon was over. My blood laced with adrenaline. I got to my feet. Dietfried was at the door, but his cottony fingers did not obey him. He fumbled with the key. Had the door been opened, he would have gotten inside the room and locked himself in, but he had kept the door locked. While he failed miserably in the simple task of inserting a key into a keyhole, I bolted to the mantle, grabbed the heavy marble clock as though it were no heavier than a loaf of bread, rushed toward him, lifted the clock above his head, and brought it down on his skull with all my strength.

I thought I heard the breaking of bones. Dietfried looked at me in shock. He wavered, and his body just tilted forward. His eyes wide, he collapsed to the floor with a loud thump.

He lay on the rug, motionless. There was a large bloody gash on the side of his head.

I could hear more gunshots outside. Tears began to stream down my face. All I could think of at that moment was Gustave. I imagined him dead, my father and mother heartbroken for life.

I kneeled next to Dietfried, not knowing if he was alive or dead, and took the key from his clenched fingers. I stepped over his body, unlocked the door, entered the room, and locked myself inside as the sounds of gunshots continued to tear through the night.

In the room were a metal desk, rolled-up maps, and more maps taped to the walls. There were folders and documents everywhere, shelving, office furniture, a typewriter. On a table set against the wall were all kinds of wires and equipment, a microphone, something that looked like a Morse code machine. Fernand had told me what to do if I found myself in this exact situation: damage as much as I could, as fast as I could. My heart thumped. I hurried around the room pulling wires and smashing things to the ground. Gunshots continued outside, dozens at first, and then fewer. As I broke things, my mind raced. What if Fernand's men were outnumbered? What if they failed? I had, by some miracle, managed to take Dietfried down, but would I live past the hour?

Outside the window, I heard someone shout, "We're all brothers. An Allied landing is underway. Allied ships have entered the port!" Was the man bluffing? No matter; it sounded convincing to me. "Surrender!" the man shouted. "We don't want bloodshed. The Allies are at the city's door. Do the right thing and join us!" From that point on, there were no more gunshots.

Holding on to the hope that Gustave was either with us or had surrendered, I darted around the room, grabbing and shoving maps and documents into an empty briefcase. My focus kept returning to a bizarre-looking typewriter, which had a keyboard, but also a strange pull board and small rotors. Next to it was a wooden case with a handle that fastened perfectly over it. I packed it together and waited.

For many interminable minutes, I stood with my ear to the door, the briefcase in one hand, the wooden case in the other. I heard no sound, no voice, no stirring. Dietfried was unconscious on the other side of the door. The men were no longer firing. There was no sign of Fernand. I set the wooden case on the floor and turned the key ever so slowly. I cracked the door open.

I leaped backward. Dietfried was standing in the middle of the room, blood running down his face, looking like a rage-filled wounded animal. He snarled and rushed forward. "Hure!" he roared. I had just enough reflex to slam the door inches from his nose, turn the key, and lock myself inside. I leaned against the door, breathing hard. I stepped away from the door just in time: in an instant, there was a deafening series of explosions and the wood of the door burst in several places. Sweet, attentive, love-struck Dietfried had found himself a gun and was shooting at me through the door!

I took cover under the metal desk. There was nothing else I could do. Dietfried shot again, and again, each conflagration making a bigger gash into the wooden door. I curled on myself and held my breath.

The sound of a different weapon blasted on the other side of the door, and then silence. A moment later I heard a voice.

"Marceline? Are you in there?" It was Gustave's voice! "Are you all right?" he asked.

"I'm in here," I said feebly from under the desk. I looked at the door. The wood was riddled with large gashes.

"It's safe now," Gustave said. "Are you wounded?" I got up and went to open what was left of the door just as Gustave pushed it open. He was pale, disheveled, the Karabiner by his side. I was shaking so violently I could barely stand. "Did we win?"

"I *think* so," Gustave said.

"What side are you on?" I asked.

"He's on our side!" said a voice. It was Fernand who was entering the room. He looked just as scared as Gustave and I. "Did you stop the Boche from sending a signal?" he asked.

"I can't believe I did, but yes." My knees buckled unexpectedly from under me, and Fernand caught me.

He, Gustave, and I walked out of the room. I clutched Fernand's arm as we walked past Dietfried's body sprawled on the Persian rug. He lay on his back, his eyes open, a bullet wound to the heart. "He's dead. He's really dead," Gustave said, overwhelmed.

"Did you shoot him?" I asked Gustave. He just nodded.

As I looked at Dietfried's body, I had the strong sense that it was I, not Gustave or Fernand, who was responsible for his death. Dietfried was dead because he had trusted me.

"We need to get you back home," Fernand said. He took the briefcase from my hand and pointed to the wooden case. "What is this?"

"I haven't the faintest idea," I said, wiping my eyes with my sleeve. "Maybe we should leave it behind."

Fernand picked it up. "I'll take it," he said.

Outside, Dietfried's guards had been rounded up in the dark. They were kneeling in the dirt, their hands atop their heads, as a half dozen of our men stood around them. Gustave went to join them. I climbed into an automobile, and Fernand took the wheel. "What about my brother?" I asked.

"He's part of another cell."

"Are we leaving him behind?"

"He will come back with his team, when their mission is complete, as per their instructions."

We drove off into the night. I was trembling, but I did not know if it was because of the cold, or the shock of it all. Fernand lit a cigarette and offered me one.

"What will happen to the guards?" I asked.

"They're prisoners for now," Fernand said.

"Have the Allied forces arrived?"

"They'll be here," he assured me. "Soon they'll be landing."

"But you don't know for sure?"

"The Brits, the Yankees, the Canadians," he said with forced cheer. "You'll see."

"Who recruited him?" I asked.

"Who?" Fernand said.

"You know very well who."

"I did," Fernand said.

"Why Gustave!" I exclaimed. "He's only seventeen years old. He knows nothing!"

"He knows enough. We needed all the bodies we could get."

I was livid. "I asked you to do the opposite! I asked you to keep him safe!"

"Not at all. You asked me to make sure he left you alone. This was the best way I could think of to keep him from trailing you so you could do your mission. That kid was tenacious about following you. So I had to give him something to do."

"Did he know I would be here tonight?"

"Even I didn't know that he'd be there tonight. We are in different units," Fernand said.

"So my brother saved my life," I said.

"He shot the Boche. He did what he had to do. We all did." And in his tone, I sensed that he felt entitled to get some credit for what Gustave had done.

We arrived in downtown Algiers and still nothing. There was hardly any moon and no light in any of the windows of the houses or apartments we drove past. The streets were so quiet it seemed hardly possible that anything out of the ordinary was taking place at all. I found the courage to ask. "Why is no one in the streets?"

"We've done our part," Fernand said. "We better hurry home. If things fall to shit, we'll need to act as though we were home the whole time."

"But should the streets be this quiet?" I asked again. Fernand did not respond. My spirit sank. I thought of Dietfried, his love for Heidelberg, his quiet manners — at least until he began shooting at me through that door — and I hoped that his death wasn't for nothing. I closed my eyes and sank into my seat, drained of all energy.

We reached the heart of the city, and there still was no signs of activity. I wanted to hear sirens, gunshots, tanks rolling in, but the only car on the road was ours.

Fernand understood something. "It's too quiet!" he said excitedly. "Where are the police? The place should be swarming with them looking to apprehend people after curfew."

A buzz spread through my body. "Do you think we have the police on lockdown?"

"Something is happening for sure," Fernand said, beaming.

At that moment, a massive explosion tore through the night, so powerful that it rattled the car. The sky above the sea illuminated like fireworks. Fernand pushed on the brakes abruptly. We looked at each other, hopeful, excited. "What was that?" I said.

"That," we found out later, was the Vichy forces shooting a canon at two U.S. destroyers that had arrived in the port.

Within minutes, it was mayhem in the city. All around, windows of apartment buildings lit up like a Christmas tree. Forgetting all about curfew, entire families, awakened by the noise, stepped out onto their balconies, squinting at the dark sea. Men and women, having noticed that no phone lines functioned, descended, frazzled, into the streets to ask what was happening.

Fernand started up the car. We passed the commissariat, where a crowd had congregated in search of information. The same scenario was taking place in front of the préfecture. Once we arrived at the foot of my apartment building, I jumped out of the car. Fernand smiled at me and drove away into the night.

I ran up the stairs, opened the door to our apartment, and found Mother in her bathrobe and curlers standing in the middle of the living room. "There are explosions!" she said, frantic.

"I heard."

"Did you just come back from Béatrice's in the middle of the night?"

"Yes," I lied.

Her voice shrill, she asked, "Where are Gustave and your father?"

My eyes widened. "Baba isn't home?"

"Nor is Gustave. Would I be asking if they were?" Mother whimpered. "I'm all by myself in this horrible apartment, in this horrible country, and something scary is happening in the city! On top of it, our telephone is out of order. Alban must not have paid the bill. Oh, look!" she exclaimed. She pointed outside.

We rushed to the balcony. On the darkened balconies around and below us and in the building across the street were the pale silhouettes of people in their pajamas craning their necks to see what might be happening. In the street below, dozens of men stood conversing in hushed voices. Suddenly an explosion, distant but powerful, startled us all and briefly illuminated the street. The men who had been standing in the street ran for cover. "It's the Nazis," my mother shouted hysterically. "They are coming for us!"

I gripped Mother by her shoulder and steadied her. "Mother!" I whispered, "it's the opposite! We're being liberated!"

She gave me a confused look. "Liberated from what?"

At that moment, the front door opened and Gustave appeared. Seeing me, he looked relieved. "You're back," he said.

"Goodness gracious, Gustave! You're safe!" Mother sobbed. "Where were you?"

"I was on a mission for the Resistance," he said.

"I would not be trumpeting that quite yet," I said.

"Well, you should be glad I was."

"What an idiot! Do you realize how dangerous this was?"

"Do *you?*" he asked, furious.

"I did, as a matter of fact," I said.

"What is happening out there?" Mother interrupted. "Things are blowing up all over the place. And the telephone isn't working."

"If I hadn't been there, we wouldn't be having this conversation," Gustave said. "You'd be dead."

"If you hadn't been there, Fernand would have been, and I'd still be fine."

"You're a monster, do you know that!" Gustave shouted. "You can't even say a simple thank you!"

"I don't understand what you two are talking about," our mother cried out. "Where is Alban?"

"Do you know how terrified I was when I saw you?" I shouted back at Gustave. "I thought you were on the Vichy side. I thought our men were going to kill you!"

"I was placed there by my cell. That was my mission. That's where I was all the time you thought I was doing stupid team-building exercises at the Jeunesse. As if I would ever join those idiots."

"But where is Alban now?" my mother said.

"I was trying to complete my mission and subdue a *German officer*, and I could hardly concentrate because I was terrified that you might get killed."

"Your mission—"

"WHERE IS ALBAN?" Mother suddenly shouted at the top of her lungs.

I turned to Gustave. "Do you know where Baba went?"

Gustave looked dumbfounded. "He's not home?"

"He must have heard the commotion and gone into the street to look for you," Mother told Gustave.

"Why would he be looking for me and not Marceline?" Gustave asked.

"Because he knew that Marceline was at Béatrice's house. All I know is that I jumped out of bed when I heard the explosion, and no one was home." Mother slumped onto a chair and spoke in a ghostly voice. "I know that your father is involved in this nonsense."

"Baba is in the Resistance too?" Gustave asked. It was obvious from his tone and expression that he had no idea.

A new succession of explosions shook the walls of the apartment. The chandelier swayed. "We're being bombed!" Mother shouted. "We must go down to the cellar at once!"

"They're blowing up bridges, Mother," I said. "The Allies are landing. And Jews are leading the Resistance!"

"Oh my God. Where is Alban?" my mother said, whimpering.

As the sun rose, we learned that the Resistance's ploy had been a success. Our men had walked into every government building and agency, presented the official paperwork saying that they were assigned to take control, and they took over. The landing and subsequent occupation of Algeria by the Allied forces took place with a minimum of fighting or casualties. While the commissariat, the préfecture, the Grande Poste, the telephone company, and most public buildings were under the control of our men, the landing progressed unhindered. As it turned out, though, our men didn't get help from the Allied forces until much later than expected. The sea was rough, and it took many more hours before the American and British forces could land on beaches and enter ports and march into the city. For hours, our men had stood their ground until the soldiers arrived, without being certain that they would arrive at all.

Throughout the day, elements of the French police and the French army continued to shoot at the Allied forces and members of the Resistance, but that effort quickly ended.

By five p.m., all of Algiers was perched on apartment balconies, witnessing the arrival of the American soldiers in open cars sporting the American flag. It was a sight to behold! Gustave, Mother, and I, along with thousands of the residents of Algiers, descended into the street. The sight of the American flag was just the happiest thing to see. It represented the hope of an entire nation, an entire continent. Still today I get goosebumps remembering those young soldiers, so brave and so thrilled as they let us kiss and hug them.

But as the American jeeps were driving under our balcony, Father still hadn't returned.

There was tremendous confusion following the invasion. The telephone lines were still down, the police force was under arrest, all local government officials were under military guard, and there was no place to inquire about anything. At first, we were able to soothe ourselves. We reasoned that if Father had been captured, since he was a Resistance operative on the winning side, he soon would be released. But by sundown, our optimism of the afternoon had turned to anguish. Once the Allies had the ceasefire secured, and Father still wasn't back, we began to fear the worst. Between my fear for Baba, the loss of sleep, the trauma of narrowly escaping being shot, and the persistent memory of Dietfried's dead eyes, I unleashed my bottled-up emotions onto Gustave. "Baba went looking for you," I told him. "Why did you have to get involved?" I very much believed that it was Gustave's fault. Perhaps I *needed* to believe this. I needed to believe that it was he, not I, who might have put my father at risk.

It took five days for the Allied forces and the local authorities to decide who in Algiers should now be in charge. Everyone, from the police to the local army, was afraid to counter Vichy's orders. After all, no one knew for sure if the Allies would keep their hold on North Africa, and everyone in Europe still believed Hitler unstoppable.

Mother, Gustave, and I spent two days frantically searching for my father. Once the telephone lines were restored, Uncle Moshe, Fernand, André, Émile, and our family made dozens of phone calls. We knocked on every door; we asked everyone we knew. In those few days, I completely ceased to think of Khaled.

On the sixth day after the landing, there was a rap at our apartment door. Gustave, Mother, and I rushed to open it, but it was not Baba. Two men stood glumly on our front step, hats in hands, and asked to speak to Mother in private. Full of dread, Gustave and I stepped away, as she let the men into the living room. Gustave and I were behind the door, holding our breath. We heard Mother let out a muffled cry like the moan of an animal. We rushed in. Mother was hunched over, a hand over her mouth as if she was about to vomit. One of the men stopped her from falling and helped her to a chair. The sight of her was enough for me to know the worst had happened. I hung on to the doorframe, too stunned to react. Mother buried her face in her hands; her shoulders shook violently. Gustave's face was white, frozen in distress.

The taller of the two men turned to us. "It was an explosion," he said.

"We found this," the other man said opening a cloth from which he extracted the blackened remnants of two objects. We recognized them immediately: they were my father's wallet and his hat. I stared at them unable to speak. "Close that!" Mother ordered. The man wrapped the hat and wallet back into the cloth and set them on the dining room table.

"We are very sorry," one of the men said. "His remains are at the morgue. We are required to ask you to identify the body. Unfortunately, the explosion was followed by a fire so…." He paused, then changed his mind about completing his sentence. Instead, he said, "Please accept our condolences."

And then they left us to our grief. On the table were Father's scorched belongings and a piece of paper telling us how to get in touch with the mortuary.

****

Under the gazebo, a large cloud passed in front of the sun. Marceline felt a bit of a chill.

"But it wasn't him in the end. Right?" Cassandra asked her.

Marceline looked at Cassandra and then looked away. The young woman who sat across from her did not resemble Gustave one bit, but Marceline had to be mindful that she was his daughter indeed. She mustn't get carried away by resentment. The girl loved her father and whatever fiction of himself he had given her. She would try to be fair. She took a small breath and said, "We did have confirmation of my beloved father's terrible, useless death the next morning."

Cassandra let her pen fall on the table. "Baba was killed?" she exclaimed. "That can't be!"

Marceline tried to compose herself by taking a sip of her tea, but emotion overtook her, and her hands trembled violently. She set her teacup in the saucer. "Forgive me," she said. "Even after all these years."

"What happened?" Cassandra asked, her eyes clouded with tears.

Marceline composed herself and took a sip from her cup.

"Uncle Moshe accompanied us to the mortuary. He was the one who identified my father's remains. We could not do it. We were told his body had been scorched. It was beyond our strength to look at him. After we left the morgue, I began to weep and could not stop for days.

"Through Uncle Moshe, we learned what had happened. My father was indeed the leader of a Resistance cell in charge of destroying a bridge. Something had gone wrong. The bridge was set to explode at three a.m. with the others, but there was a misunderstanding, and it was blown up an hour too soon when my father was still too close to it. Moshe told us that no one could explain why our father was there in the first place. The explosives had long been installed; someone else oversaw the detonation. Our father should have been safe at home. Had he wanted to make sure that things went smoothly, Uncle Moshe wondered? We would never know Baba's reasons, he said.

"We did not have the desire to tell Uncle Moshe that Mother, Gustave, and I knew the reason. We knew all too well why my father was at the bridge: he had been looking for Gustave. Not finding Gustave at home on the night of the invasion, my father must have worried. He had headed to the one place he knew for a fact was set to explode. He had wanted to make sure that Gustave wasn't there. He had wanted to protect him."

Marceline stopped speaking. If she said any more, she might be unable to contain her tears. Laure offered a welcome diversion by appearing through the door that led from the kitchen to the backyard and headed for the gazebo under which they sat, carrying a three-tiered silver tray filled with tea sandwiches. She set the tray on the table and gave Marceline a quick look to make sure she was all right. Marceline nodded at her to tell her she was. The top two levels of the tray were filled with pastel-colored macarons, the bottom one with small sandwiches. "I've always thought cucumber sandwiches to be a culinary aberration," Marceline said with forced gaiety. "Whoever thought of putting a slice of a tasteless vegetable between two slices of plain bread and calling it a delicacy?"

"I guess," Cassandra said. Marceline appreciated how the young woman had listened attentively and quietly, taking notes like a studious child. She was a good listener. Nothing was quite so annoying as being interrupted when trying to tell a story. Now Cassandra was very still as if processing what she had just learned required complete immobility.

"It's lovely weather, isn't it?" Marceline said to break the uncomfortable stillness of the moment. "I'm told this should be an exceptional year for climbing roses."

"I can only imagine what it will be like in your garden when all these roses start to bloom. Your gardener is a magician."

"My gardener?" Marceline repeated. She sighed deeply and nibbled on a pale green macaron. "I hardly ever see them in bloom. I prefer to spend the warmer months away from Paris. I go to my country house. I am heading there soon, in fact."

"And so, my dad blames you for the death of your father," Cassandra said. "He has blamed you all this time. That's why he hates you so much,"

Marceline nodded, "That's correct."

"And you've blamed him?"

Marceline pondered the moral obligation to describe the facts not as she had perceived them, but for the first time perhaps, as they were. "Also correct," she admitted.

"What happened to you after all this? How could the three of you manage?"

"It was all a blur," Marceline said. "We buried my father just as the entire city was in a state of jubilation. It was so surreal. Algiers was free. Jews were safe, at least in Algeria. This was precisely what my father had dreamed of, hoped and fought for, but he was not here to enjoy it. We were in shock and too devastated to experience relief at being liberated. Soon thereafter, things turned erratic at home. Mother immediately suffered a mental breakdown. She was hospitalized for months. I guess you could say that her falling apart was years in the making. As strained as her relationship with my father was, she was utterly lost without him."

"You did not want to return to Paris then?"

"Remember that this was only November 1942. Paris and France would not be liberated for another three years. While our mother was hospitalized, Gustave and I lived together in the Algiers apartment without exchanging a word. We blamed each other for everything that had happened, and neither of us was willing to support the other one in grief. It was all quite ugly."

"And you were children, orphans, and left to yourself at a time of war."

"Not children. I was nineteen, and your father was seventeen."

"My twins just turned eighteen," Cassandra said. "Trust me: they are babies."

"In times of war, you become an adult much faster."

"Did you ever find out why the bridge exploded early?"

"A death in wartime becomes part of the statistics. My father's death, the explosion, Sandra's vanishing act, the circumstance of the murder of which she was accused: none of that was ever examined. In the months following Operation Torch, the Algiers government officials and the city's entire administration resembled a barnyard full of donkeys and headless chickens running amok, and those of us in the Resistance kept a low profile. There was no investigation."

"I wonder why I never heard of Operation Torch before. Shouldn't it be as famous as D-day?"

"History is conveniently murky on those few days in November 1942. There is some mention of the patriotic stance of the French of Algiers who bravely defied Hitler and Vichy and sided with the Allied forces. What they never talk about is the handful of Jews who held those alleged patriots at gunpoint so that they would not shoot at the Allies."

"But without all of you, the landing might not have been possible!"

"The truth needed to be altered into a narrative that would make the new government shine in a better light."

"What do you mean?"

"Deals were made. Someone had to govern Algiers after all. The government officials had been humiliated by the deception that had tricked everyone into inaction on that fateful night. So, after all was sorted out between the Allies and the local authorities – the Commissaire, the Préfect, all the military and police personnel, the very people who had been subdued by our men so that they would not shoot at the Allies – they all recovered their original posts. Only now they were on *our* side. Enemies just a few days before now shook hands and began to work together against the Wehrmacht."

"You mean that the police and the local government took credit for the success of the invasion?"

Marceline could not repress a laugh, which was more of an expression of disgust. "It was better for morale that they portray themselves as part of the Resistance, from the first hour. History must rewrite itself in more palatable bites. I made peace with that, eventually. Although at the time, the injustice was hard to swallow. In war and in life, you have to be pragmatic."

"What about you? You must have received a medal?"

"Don't be absurd."

"A recognition of some sort?"

"To this day, my involvement in Operation Torch was never revealed. In the end, it was more useful that I stay undercover."

"Why?"

"Because it was only the start of my Resistance work."

"And so, my father did save your life."

"He did shoot Dietfried. But if he hadn't, Fernand was right behind him and would have shot him…." Marceline paused. This was all so ridiculous: hanging on to a narrative, being right at all costs. And for what, for whom? "Yes," she admitted, "Gustave did indeed save my life."

"Was Sandra ever found?"

"I'll never know if she died, if she was caught, or if she found a way to leave the country. And I don't know if she ever found out that my father was killed."

"What about the boys?"

"Fernand, Émile, and André enrolled in the Seventh Battalion of the Corps Francs d'Afrique. Shortly after that, Gustave was old enough to enroll as well, and he did."

"And you?"

"I spent the rest of the war in Algiers, taking care of Mother and working for the Office of Strategic Services."

"The OSS? Really?" Cassie exclaimed. "So you were an actual spy!"

"When the OSS was dissolved and turned into the CIA after 1945, I was promptly recruited by the French intelligence. First, the Direction Générale des Services Spéciaux and then, the Service de Contre-Espionnage. In the years that followed the Second World War, there was an urgent need for someone with my demonstrated experience and skills. Where one war theoretically ends, another quagmire begins. There was the Algerian war, the cold war, and so forth. My work through the years will remain classified until long after I'm gone."

"So, no medal."

Marceline laughed. "No, no medal."

"To devote yourself to your country like you did: I don't think most people would be so brave."

"Call it what you want," Marceline said. "I only did what I had to do."

Marceline was tempted to tell Cassandra the truth of how she had felt at the time. She who had dreamed of independence, who had wanted to feel all grown up, was suddenly propelled into a forced adulthood. Nothing had prepared her for the loneliness and despair it entailed. Her father was dead, her mother had become unglued, her brother and all her friends had joined the army, and Khaled was transferred to an undisclosed jail somewhere deep in Algeria. There was no one left to bicker with, no one left to give a purpose to her life, no one left to love or care for her. She was perfectly alone when the OSS recruited her.

"Eventually, once the Germans were defeated and the war ended, things were reabsorbed."

"Reabsorbed?" Cassandra asked.

"I can't say that things returned to the way they were. How could they? The entire world was adrift in trauma: seventy million civilian and military deaths, an entire generation lost. There were trials, to restore the beloved illusion that justice prevailed, and to provide the human psyche with clear villains and heroes. In actuality, most of us had had no choice but to turn into a bit of both. As for the few Jews who had managed to outlive the carnage, everything had been stolen, so everything needed to be rebuilt from the ground up. Jewish students were able to resume their studies. Jewish teachers, bureaucrats, and lawyers were reinstated. And everyone was anxious to pretend that life was back to normal and that nothing like this could ever happen again."

"Selective memory loss must be a way to heal," Cassandra suggested.

"Especially for the perpetrators," Marceline said. "Returning to Paris was a surrealist moment. Imagine humanity's worst instincts being given free rein for nearly ten years and then everyone hurrying to forget. They call it rebuilding, but I call it reabsorbing. The hatred, the bloodlust, the anti-Semitism all shoved back into the psyche and muffled, silenced, at least temporarily."

Cassandra smiled. "Permanently, I hope."

Marceline contemplated the crushed macaron on her plate. "You must be more of an optimist than I am," she said.

****

Under the gazebo, Cassie nibbled at her cucumber sandwich, found herself incapable of swallowing, and set it down. Had her dad wanted his daughters to know the truth, he would have told it ages ago. Odile was right in the end: by learning something her father had wanted to keep secret, Cassie was betraying him. The question remained, why had silence been easier for him? He could have spun the story to his advantage and made Marceline the villain. With his silence, he had taken the high road and protected Marceline – if pretending not to have a sister could be considered the high road. Could his silence reveal that he outwardly blamed Marceline for his father's death but inwardly believed himself responsible? And if he felt guilt, how much of that did he carry around with him?

Cassie did see a commonality between Marceline and Gustave: neither seemed big on feeling their emotions. They found different ways not to feel: where Marceline acted out, Gustave became aloof, where Marceline deployed sarcasm, Gustave retreated in silence. She wondered if those mechanisms weren't two sides of the same coin.

The old gardener appeared in the backyard dragging a tall wooden ladder. He propped the ladder against the stone wall that surrounded the garden and, a heavy metal trimmer in hand, climbed it methodically, one step at a time, resting a moment between each step. Once at the top, he began to clip bare remnants of Boston ivy that climbed the walls. The clippers made a little rusty sound with each cut.

"At what point were you able to return to Paris?" Cassie asked Marceline.

"Mother and I stayed in Algiers through the end of the war," Marceline said. "She in her pension, a euphemism for the private mental institution where her doctors and I had placed her, and me alone in the dreadful apartment where everything reminded me of my father. As much as I hated to, I visited Mother every day. I had to; there would have been no one else. While Gustave was in the army, he communicated with us less and less. The mail service was terrible, and the relationship was strained, to say the least. I resented Gustave for not being there for Mother. I think part of him felt vindicated by her internment. She wrote him a letter incensed about having been 'put away,' in a mental hospital, to which he responded that now she knew how he had felt when she did the same to him. We stopped communicating after that."

"And what about Khaled?" Cassie asked.

Marceline wistfully looked out on the garden, at the old gardener up on his ladder. "They sent him to an internment camp where he stayed for the remainder of the war," she said. "A place deep in Algeria where there could be no visitors. With Father gone, there was no one to testify in his favor, and no one would take me seriously. After years of enduring typhus, semi-starvation, and mistreatment in jail, Khaled was freed, eventually. But his time in imprisonment had hardened him." Marceline had a little laugh. "Nothing quite like putting an idealist in jail to turn him into an extremist."

"An extremist?"

"When we had our meetings in the clearing, Khaled still believed in a peaceful resolution to his country's independence. But there was no peace to be had. There always seems to be so little peace to go around, have you noticed? It's exhausting. He became part of the FLN while in prison. Because, as you know, Algeria's troubles did not end with World War II. Quite the opposite. In fact, in 1945, at the same time when people all over the world celebrated the unconditional surrender of the Nazis, there was in Algeria a pro-independence protest in the town of Setif that turned into a bloodbath. The next twenty years or so remain a dark phase of our respective countries' histories. Just as Khaled had predicted, he and I found ourselves on opposite sides of the conflict. As an undercover agent for the French forces, I was on the side of France, a country that had just emerged from the ruins of war determined to hang on to its remaining colonies. Khaled became a leader of the Algerian independence movement. This made any sort of romance life-threatening for both of us."

"What did you both do?"

"We risked our lives. I was heartbroken on more than one occasion. But that's a much longer story."

Cassie had the urge to ask Marceline how she had recovered from her heartbreak, and how long it had taken her, but she decided against it. Marceline had lost Khaled to war and geopolitical conflicts, whereas Cassie's heartbreak over Peter could only be attributed to her own stupidity. "Did your mother get better?" she asked.

"She did, eventually," Marceline said. "And as soon as she was back on her feet, which was a full year later, I moved in with Béatrice."

"Your mother was well enough to live by herself?"

"It was ruthless of me to leave Mother to fend for herself, alone in Algiers. I realize that. Eventually, I made it up to her."

"How so?"

"By marrying well."

"Really?" Cassie interjected. "But what about Khaled?"

"You seem disappointed?"

"I was hoping that love would conquer all, I guess."

"In love, it's often a matter of the risks you're willing to take. And at that time, there were a great many barriers between Khaled and me."

Cassie thought of Hervé, of all the reasons she felt she needed to nip the relationship in the bud. But did it not also all boil down to her unwillingness to take risks? Was it really about the logistics of living in different countries or rather about the logistics of risking a broken heart?

Marceline took a blanket from the chair next to her and set it on her lap. "After the war ended, Mother returned to Paris. Because our house had been used as a Nazi habitation, it was in good shape, although everything not bolted to the walls was stolen. The house an empty shell with only the walls, the roof, and the plumbing remaining. The silver, the bedding, the artwork, the furniture had vanished, to say nothing of Mother's precious things passed down through the years. Uncle Moshe helped us retrieve our money hidden in Swiss banks. We fixed up the house, bought what we needed, and went on with our lives. Gustave never lived in the house again."

"And then you married."

"Not immediately, far from it. Not until fifteen years later, in 1960, after I had traveled the world and lived life to the fullest, and arguably the most precarious. One day I will tell you about those years if you're interested. The point is, I was in my forties when I began to aspire to a more conventional life. I also felt that I owed Mother a bit of happiness, and nothing could delight her more than my joining that elusive and exclusive segment of the French elite."

"Nobility?" Cassie said.

"It was, after all, her dearest dream. A common friend introduced me to Victor de Pontieur, a wealthy man who happened to be a count, or rather a count who happened to be a wealthy man. He courted me aggressively, and I went along with it. Mother was over the moon. Poor Victor wasn't happy with me for long. I made a terrible wife. I traveled constantly for the French secret services, but he could never know about my whereabouts for classified reasons. I had no desire to give him children. The man was left to take mistresses and attend society salons without me."

"What about my dad? Where was he during those years?"

"Gustave traveled the world as well, and we crossed paths on a few occasions. We only knew of his comings and goings through Uncle Moshe, who was aware that we were estranged and did everything he could to serve as a liaison and repair our relationship. But how could he, when he never knew what was at the root of it all?"

"Where did my father travel?"

"He never told you?"

"No."

"I don't know much. Once, he was stranded in Patagonia."

"Patagonia? My father was in Patagonia?"

"Allegedly. He had not given signs of life for years but remembered he had a family only long enough to demand money. We did not send any. So, he wrote us a letter riddled with insults, the kind of diatribe best suited for the wastebasket. We did not hear from him for another five years. Uncle Moshe undoubtedly extended him a lifeline each time he acted irresponsibly." Marceline must have seen Cassie scrunch up her nose. "I apologize," she said. "I forget he is your father."

"My dad is many things, but never irresponsible," Cassie said defensively. "He worked all his life to provide. He never bailed on us," she said, omitting to mention her resentment over his bailing on her emotionally. "Do you know what he was doing all the years between the end of the war and meeting my mother?"

"I honestly have no clue. If Uncle Moshe were still alive, he would tell you everything, but unfortunately, he passed away years ago."

"Did you and my father communicate much at all over the years?"

"There was no real conversation. But I did invite him to my two weddings."

"You had two weddings?"

"Count Victor de Pontieur was my first husband. That lasted a few years. And your father didn't attend that one. Then I married the Count de Bécasel D'Alompe."

"Both were counts?"

"When you are a part of certain circles you tend to meet the same kind of fellows. To my surprise, Gustave came to the second wedding. Although I'm sure his presence had less to do with making peace with Mother or me and more to do with showing off his pretty wife, a Parisian twenty years his junior and gentile as could be."

"My mom," Cassie said. "She mentioned meeting you at your wedding."

"Your father was very proud of her; this much was obvious."

"How about his name change? Do you think it was to reject his Judaism?"

"I can hardly blame him if that was the case. What had Judaism ever done for us? It certainly never helped us. We weren't religious, so why burden ourselves with five thousand years of alienation and suffering? The difference between your father and me is that I was never ashamed of being Jewish and never attempted to hide it."

"Maybe by not telling his daughters he wanted to protect us. In case something terrible happened again. To the Jews I mean."

"Whomever and whatever people choose to reject of their past is their mysterious business. I won't entertain any guesses about my brother's motivations. You will have to ask him. We received birth announcements when you and your sisters were born, but that was the extent of our communication. I suspect your mother is the one who sent the announcements and possibly without your father's knowledge. I responded with a card and proper silver-engraved baby cups, as was the custom at the time. I hardly know what else was expected of me.

"In later years, as Mother got older and became ill, I particularly resented Gustave's callousness toward her. For my part, once I was past the initial blinders of youth, I wanted my mother to be happy. And one of the things preventing that happiness was the absence of her son and grandchildren. I know, too little too late, but people can change. That was a moot point; your father wanted nothing to do with her. That cruelty sealed my opinion of him. Mother might not have been the warmest of mothers, to say the least, but the years had been hard on her, and she suffered greatly from Gustave's rejection and from being forbidden to know the only grandchildren she had."

In a flash, Cassie shuttered to imagine what life would be like if either of her children decided they wanted to have nothing to do with her or if they had children, but she wasn't allowed to know them. It would destroy her. "It would have been so good to know you both," she said, betraying her father again by siding with Marceline.

"When Mother passed away in 1972," Marceline continued, "Gustave did not come the funeral. Your mother and you and your sisters did not either. I figured you all chose not to attend."

"My sister and I were little girls then."

"That's true," Marceline said.

"And we never knew of her death. We didn't know she was still alive to start with."

"I realize this now." Marceline shook her head. "One thing you might have learned by now about the people in your family is that we know how to keep a secret. But this, the idea that your father would tell you absolutely nothing, about your roots, about his past, about his mother, his father, and sister. It defies reason."

"Did you see my father after that?"

"A few times. Once was shortly after Mother's passing. And again during the lawsuit."

"A lawsuit?"

"There was the matter of the will. Eventually, I bought out his share of this house."

"When was that?"

"1974."

"I was ten years old," Cassie noted. It was at this time that her parents had moved to their present apartment. They had bought nicer clothes, gone on more expensive vacations. It had never occurred to her that her father had inherited money.

"The house was all the wealth Mother had. I could afford to buy back his share of it because by then I had married Bécasel D'Alompe, who had money."

"Armelle and Jean-Bernard's father?"

"He was a widower. Those two were adolescent when we married. He died this year, and now those two worry that their fortune and mine will be plunged into new uncertainty with my refusal to give them power of attorney. Not to mention the pesky fact that new relatives are coming into my life."

"New relatives?"

Marceline peered at Cassie. "Well, you for one."

Cassie had an epiphany. "So that's what they're worried about?"

Marceline giggled. "You bet."

"I have no interest in your money. I hope you can reassure them."

"Why do so when watching them twitch and sweat is so much more entertaining?"

Cassie looked out at the beautiful garden. Her father had spent his boyhood in this lovely place, and then it was robbed from him by war, the Holocaust, and family hatred. "Did you love him?" she asked Marceline.

"Who?"

"Your new husband?"

"I was fond of both my husbands, but Khaled remains the love of my life."

"And yet you married them and not Khaled."

"Marriage is a matter of practicality. Love is something else entirely."

"How French of you," Cassie said.

Fifteen yards from them, the old North African gardener laboriously moved the ladder toward the portico, slowly climbed to the top, and, unfurling string, began to attach roses to the pillar. Cassie pointed to him and frowned. "Isn't this a bit dangerous for someone his age?"

Marceline smiled. "I've never been able to stop him from doing anything he wanted to do."

As though he had heard them, the old gardener waved at them. Marceline smiled and gave a wave back.

"I brought a little something for you," Cassie said. She foraged inside her tote bag, took out the tablet Peter had just sent, and set it on the table among teacups and plates of macarons.

Marceline adjusted her glasses and looked at it with interest. "What is this thing?"

"It's a tablet. But mostly you can use it as an e-reader."

"An e-what?"

"Like a tiny flat computer that can do all sorts of things. You turn it on like this," Cassie said, demonstrating. "You can use it as a camera, if you like, and take pictures with it. But the best part is that you can read books on it. You can increase the size of the letters. You'll never again need a magnifying glass to read. You can have your favorite books and newspaper subscriptions in it. It's quite easy to use; you flip through pages by moving your finger, like this, and it even remembers what page you're on."

"How do books appear in this thing?"

"You download them."

"Download?"

"It comes in via … the airwaves or something, and then it pops right into the tablet, somehow."

Cassie spent the next hour connecting the tablet to the Wi-Fi, downloading books, apps, and games, and teaching Marceline who sponged it all up with the excitement of a child, saying little ohs and ahs when something appeared on the screen. Laure took notes about passwords and account numbers and helped set it all up.

"How much longer will you be in Paris?" Marceline asked.

"Three more days."

"I'm off to my house in the Loire Valley. I won't return to Paris until summer when everyone goes on holiday. Paris is so much more pleasant without Parisians cluttering it up. Oh! I nearly forgot. I have something for you as well." Marceline called for Laure who appeared from inside the house. She whispered something in her ear. Laure returned inside the house and came back to the gazebo a few minutes later carrying something wrapped in black fabric and put it in Marceline's hands. The old lady untied the strings of what appeared to be a felt pouch and reached inside. "Tadah!" she exclaimed. In her hands was the twin of her father's finial.

Cassie was incredulous. "For me? No…."

"Quick take it before I accidentally drop the dang thing."

Cassie took it, moved it at arm's length into the light. "Yep. It looks exactly the same. Amazing."

"Bring it back to America when you go. Or give it to Gustave. I'll let you decide."

"I can't accept this," Cassie said. "It's too valuable."

Marceline shrugged. "Its greatest value lies in its meaning."

Cassie held the finial awkwardly. She thought of her father and felt her chest constrict. "I don't know why I am getting so emotional about this."

"Your father wanted it. That's what made it valuable in my eyes. Even as far as a week ago I'd sooner have thrown it down the Seine River than give it to him. But now that I know you, telling you his story, well … It's allowed me to think differently. You are right; we were children. And we were coping the best we could. I did reckless things, but I never meant harm, and I realize now, neither did Gustave." She shook her head as if she were chasing away painful thoughts. "I doubt Gustave would accept an apology from me. Not after all these years. But he can appreciate this, as my acknowledgment to the wreckage of it all."

"Your step-children won't object to your giving this to me?"

"It's just one more knick-knack to them. To be sold at auction as soon as I croak."

"You have to stop saying things like that!"

"Fine. I'll write a letter to go with it, so you have proof that it's now yours." She turned to Laure. "Type up the letter Laure, will you? Blah, blah, blah, sound of mind and spirit, all that jazz. You as witness, and I'll sign it."

"I've meant to ask you," Cassie said. "How did you and my father come in possession of the finials if the Nazis stole everything?"

"It's a strange story actually. It was Uncle Moshe. Moshe had them all along. We had no idea. For years, he kept them. We had assumed they had been stolen. He should have returned them to us when he retrieved the rest of our fortune from the Swiss account, but for some reason, he kept them without telling us. As a memento of my father perhaps. Who knows? Or because it was a Jewish artifact he was attached to. Uncle Moshe did things in mysterious ways. He was a man of many secrets. Quite an extraordinary person, in fact, at a time when being a homosexual and a Jew was no small feat of survival.

"After our father's passing, after the war, and even as Gustave and I made up our minds never to set eyes on one another, Uncle Moshe kept in touch with us both. He always had a camera with him. Later it would be a Polaroid camera. He would take me to lunch and ask every detail of my life and insist on taking my portrait. I think he did the same with your father. It was as though he was making a record of our lives. I never knew what he did with all of that. One of his chief concerns remained that Gustave and I should make up. It was his obsession. When he died, he left the entirety of his considerable fortune to Jewish causes. Gustave and I were at the reading of the will, and you can imagine our dismay when we learned that he had left us merely the twin finials, that they, in fact, had been in his possession the entire time. The will stipulated this very annoying thing: that Gustave and I would each get one. I think in Uncle Moshe's mind, the idea of splitting the pair was so intolerable that Gustave and I would have no choice but to make up and come to an agreement about who should keep both. Suddenly Gustave remembered he was Jewish, that old rascal. The male son. The Kohanim. He used this as an argument that he should have them both. Well, you can imagine that this did not sit well with me. I told him that I was the firstborn and therefore I ought to be the Kohanim. In the end, we each kept one."

"But why did my dad say that you *stole* the second one from him? You split them equitably. That's not stealing."

Marceline chuckled. "Well, I *did* steal it from him. I was a brat about it, I'll admit. After Mother had become sick, Gustave did not once visit or offer to help. As I mentioned, once she passed, we both inherited the house. Again, something needed to be split in two, but this time it was something impossible to split unless we sold it and shared the money. Gustave immediately said he wanted to sell the house. Of course, he would; I lived in it, and he had not since 1939. He wanted to see me lose the house. Think of it: a house that had been in our family for three generations, and he thought nothing of letting strangers have it. Eventually, I bought out his share of the house, for well over its value I might add. Part of the deal we made, which he insisted on, was that he should sell me his half and he would get both finials in return. I agreed to it all, but I never gave him my finial. I kept it."

"Why?"

"Out of spite, just as he had been spiteful about selling the house, or not visiting Mother. He started a lawsuit over that stupid finial. I turned vicious and countersued. I was the one who had taken care of Mother until her death, while he had done nothing! He did not have my means, so he eventually gave up on the lawsuit."

Cassie contemplated the small crown-looking object, turning it in her hands. "And now after all this chaos, you want me to have it. Are you certain of this?"

"You know, what infuriated me the most about my brother? It was his unrelenting refusal to forgive." Marceline sighed and brought her shawl tighter over her shoulders. "Only as I spoke to you have I come to the realization that I might be guilty of precisely the same thing."

Cassie decided not to make another comment. Marceline's confession, her repentance, was more than her father had ever expressed, and that was enough. She caressed the finial as though it were a magic lantern. "It is beautiful, thank you."

"So," Marceline said pointing to the tablet "can you play games on this thing?"

"Absolutely. Card games, crossword puzzles, memory games. What kind of game do you want? Sudoku?"

"No, not that game. The other one."

"Chess?"

"No, that funny one."

"Scrabble?"

"There is the word bird in it."

Cassie scratched her head. "Not Angry Birds?"

"That's right," Marceline clucked approvingly. "I want to – how do you say? – *download* angry bird."

CHAPTER 5

Holy Grail

Cassie walked onto rue de Clichy, and the honking of cars and roar of jackhammers brought her back into the 21st century. She hurried past bar-tabacs, salons de coiffures, fleuristes, and boulangeries. There was heavy construction in the street, something to do with the sewer system. Men in orange vests and helmets disappeared into deep trenches dug into the pavement and emerged from manholes like the inhabitants of a parallel civilization happening underground. Each time she heard the roar of a motorcycle, the nape of her hair tingled ridiculously, and she found herself mentally in bed with Hervé. The noise of jackhammers intensified, and the ground shook under her feet. She cut through a thick cloud of dust and walked a few more blocks before it was calm again. She was on a quiet street somewhere in the seventeenth arrondissement. A small park had sprouted before her like a tiny oasis of calm, and she entered it. She walked on the dirt path feeling the sun on her face. She sat on a bench. There were candy-colored houses on an impasse that looked down at a small playground where a young dad helped his daughter navigate the monkey bars, while his other daughter went down the slide, arms first, shouting, "Attention!"

She should come here with Hervé, she thought, and then kicked herself for thinking that. She removed her coat and took the finial out of her tote bag. A romantic, superstitious part of her told her that the spirit of her grandfather had wanted her to have it. She had worn her grandfather's coat, hadn't she? She had miraculously found Marceline and learned her family's story all without much effort, and she now was in possession of his finial. *Are you here with me, Albano?* She mentally asked the finial.

What was she supposed to do with this thing? It was a funny little object. It looked exactly like the one in her parent's apartment. It was the same weight, hollow in the center, like a small crown made of silver, with some gold parts. There were tiny bells that did not make much of a sound. As she moved it between her fingers, she wondered why, of all things, it had been worth hiding and saving.

On closer inspection, there was one thing that was different: the engraved inscription inside. Instead of the address of the bank that was engraved inside her dad's finial, in Marceline's finial was a series of numbers and letters.

454B5743589112A.
What did that mean?

She had just enough time to get to rue Bonaparte, where she was meeting Sabine for lunch. Maybe her sister would have some ideas about what all those numbers might mean.

She hurried toward Place de Clichy and down the steps to the métro. Thirty minutes later, she emerged onto the street at Métro Saint Germain des Prés. There were cars and people, the latter seemingly being dragged on leashes by their cell phones. But the architecture, the cafés, and the restaurants, even the cobblestones she stepped on, must not have changed much since 1942. Cassie walked past the Deux Magots terrace, filled with people basking in the spring sun. Back in 1942, the terrace must have crawled with Nazis. Parisians, their army now powerless, their leaders having betrayed them, lacked everything. The country's riches were being pillaged. All the food produced was sent to feed the German army while Parisians, ration tickets in hand, waited in hours-long lines for a few eggs or a liter of milk. On the other side of the street, inside Église de Saint Germain des Prés, women must have prayed for the safety of an imprisoned son or the return of a husband forced to work in a German factory. If there were Jews left in Paris in 1942, they would not be there for long, unless they had found a way to hide. Had her grandfather not left for the South of France, and then for Algeria, would her family have survived the rounding up of Jews? Cassie had the sense that she owed her grandfather her life in more ways than one.

At the corners of rue Jacob and rue Bonaparte, she spotted Sabine, who was waiting for her. They kissed twice on both cheeks. "Where do you want to eat," Sabine asked.

They walked in front of La Durée and pressed their faces to the window, detailing the macaron arrangements. "How about an all-dessert meal," Cassie said. "It's the new thing, I'm told."

"Don't you start with the subversion," Sabine said.

It was just warm enough to eat outside. They sat on the terrace of the Pré aux Clercs and studied their menus. Their waiter appeared. "Bonjour, Mesdemoiselles," he said.

"Bonjour," Sabine and Cassie said in unison.

"What will it be for the petite demoiselles?" he asked.

"I want this," Cassie said, pointing to the foie gras and fig jam platter, cautiously adding, "s'il vous plaît."

"Excellent choice," he said.

"Eight hundred calories," Sabine noted. "I'll have the Pré aux Clercs salade, s'il vous plaît, Monsieur."

"What's in it?" Cassie asked.

Sabine read: "Lettuce, smoked salmon, avocado, poached egg, crème fraîche, and blinis. I think my calorie count beats yours."

"Merci, Mesdemoiselles," the waiter said.

"Merci, Monsieur," Cassie and Sabine answered.

"I can't believe the amount of time and energy French people spend saying hello, please, and goodbye," Cassie said as soon as he left. "I had forgotten that. I mean, get to business already! Jeez. Right?"

"Eh?" Sabine said.

"Practically years of our lives spent in politeness and niceties. And to think that French people are supposed to be the rude ones!"

Sabine shook her head in incomprehension. "You are so weird," she said.

"I spent the morning with Marceline," Cassie said. "It was pretty incredible. I've got the whole story now. Straight out of a World War II espionage novel. She told me why she and Papa hate each other, and you won't believe it: all this time, Papa, among other things, has been blaming her for their father's death."

Sabine looked stunned. "His father's death? Our grandfather?"

"And Marceline blames him!" They were interrupted by the arrival of their lunch. Cassie spread foie gras onto toasted bread, took a big bite and moaned with pleasure. "I haven't had this in forever. Foie gras is cruelty to animals in California," she said with a full mouth.

"I'm pretty sure it's cruelty to animal everywhere," Sabine pointed out.

As they ate, Cassie told Sabine all about Operation Torch, their father and Marceline's involvement in it, and their grandfather's tragic death.

"That's flat-out incredible," Sabine said. "If you believe Marceline's story."

"Why wouldn't I?" Cassie asked.

"She could be senile."

"Marceline is more with it than both of us put together."

"Still, you'd think she single-handedly freed Europe from the Nazis," Sabine said. "You don't think she could be exaggerating?"

"She does downplay Papa's role in saving her life. She told me the facts, but I certainly interpret them differently. I mean Papa was a badass hero, and she won't give him that. At seventeen, being undercover in the Resistance, killing a Nazi to save her life! And then he never bragged about it. If you ask me, that's the most heroic part of the whole thing: him keeping his mouth shut. He did not try to make himself look good. And you know what? He might have been an annoyance to Marceline, but he never gave up on trying to protect her, and he never told his parents about what he knew."

Sabine shook her head. "The strangest part is to reconcile this past with the person he is now. Have you ever met someone more risk-averse than Papa?"

"And yet he did all this. And he was barely older than my twins are now."

"I think that his memories and all his emotions of the time had to be pushed back inside. Swallowed and never digested. Maybe he is risk-averse and uncommunicative because he lived with PTSD his whole life," Sabine said.

"Imagine Papa growing up in the shadow of a sister like Marceline, where he could do nothing right," Cassie said. "The one memory he sure hung on to was his rage and resentment against her. And the best way to not change his mind was to make sure never to see her. That way, his perception could not be challenged."

"Also," Sabine pointed out, "there is no risk of us meeting Marceline and maybe liking her."

"I couldn't help but see parallels with the way Papa raised us. He had an idea of how I was and how Odile was, and that was pretty much set in stone. In the end, Odile and I fought because there was not enough love from Papa to go around."

"Papa's not that bad. He never was violent, never was without a job; he didn't drink or chase women."

"Okay," Cassie said. "He was not a serial killer. That doesn't mean he didn't neglect me as a child. I loved him so much growing up, but it was a desperate, unrequited sort of love. Trying to jump through flaming hoops, and missing, and getting burned, time and again. And it's not just me that suffered from that. You weren't showered with attention either."

"Not all fathers are warm and fuzzy," Sabine said.

Cassie was stunned by Sabine's neutrality. Their father had been emotionally absent with her too. Did she truly feel no anger about it?

"At least one person was pretty perfect: our grandfather. At least according to Marceline. It's sad that we did not get to meet him. Had it not been for him, our bloodline would have probably ended in Auschwitz or Drancy."

"There must have been more to him than perfection," Sabine said. "Why else was his family so messed up? I mean, his wife was a wreck, his son broke ties with them, his daughter is a complete bitch."

"Marceline doesn't strike me as a bitch, just very sure of herself."

"Or a narcissist who played spy games," Sabine said.

"If she hadn't played those spy games, it might have changed the course of history."

"Hmmm ... let's not get carried away."

"I like Marceline," Cassie said. "In fact, I like her a lot. She doesn't sugarcoat things; she is forthright. I wish she and Papa had not been so stubborn. We could have grown up with an extended family: a grandmother, an aunt. We could have had gatherings in that big house, birthdays parties, Christmases together."

"Christmas?" Sabine said.

"So, okay, maybe not Christmas. Maybe we'd feel Jewish, instead of nothing. It might be nice to have some religious upbringing, don't you think? It would have given us something to lean on when we were sad or scared."

"Like prayer?"

"Like a set of rules and traditions to hang on to when the emotional seas are rough."

"I guess I could have used that," Sabine said.

"Well, now we know what happened between them. It had to be something big for a relationship between siblings to sour to this extent. Although, on second thought, I'm not sure it takes that much," Cassie said, rolling her eyes. "Try spending five minutes in a room with Odile and me."

"You and Odile don't hate each other like that," Sabine said. "Not to the point of telling your children that the other doesn't exist."

"It pretty much felt like hatred, growing up. You were younger. You were not in the thick of it."

Sabine looked out onto the street. "Two angry, uncommunicative parents, two big sisters at war. Having to take sides." Sabine forced a smile. "And after you left, there was nothing at home but suppressed emotions."

Cassie was genuinely surprised. "You never acted upset back when I lived at home."

"I'm more like Papa," Sabine said. "I internalize."

They ordered espressos and the bill and Cassie said, "You want to see something cool?" She unzipped her tote bag and, still keeping it inside the bag, she uncovered Marceline's finial. Sabine's eyes widened. "How did you get that from Papa and Maman's house? They're going to be furious!"

Cassie beamed. "It's not theirs. It's Marceline's! It's the twin of the one we have. Papa was right: there was a second one. And it had been stolen. By her!"

"You stole it back from her?"

"I'm not that brave. Marceline gave it to me. Returned it to our family, to be specific."

"Why?"

"She seemed to feel magnanimous suddenly."

"Maybe you could have a second career as a snake charmer," Sabine said, setting the bag on her lap to see the finial better while still keeping it inside the bag. She turned it around in her hands. "I don't know why I'm trying to hide it. It looks like some trinket bought for three euros at a flea market."

"I know. I feel the same way. We've been brainwashed to think it's a mythical object."

"Papa's going to freak out when he sees it," Sabine said, laughing. Her laugh was communicative, or maybe it was the relief Cassie felt hearing her laugh. It was good to see her sister capable of lightness.

"So, you think I should bring it to him?"

"Hell yes!" Sabine said. "And complete the mission. Return the finial to its rightful owner. The Kahobib, or kohasomething."

Had this been the United States, and had Sabine been one of her American friends, Cassie would have told her how happy she was to have lunch together, and how wonderful it felt to connect with her. But this was France, and Sabine was her sister. She had to be careful not to scare her away with her puppy-like American enthusiasm. "I wish we could have lunch more often," she said tentatively. "Get to know each other more."

"That should be no problem at all since you only live five thousand miles away," Sabine said. "And speaking of long-distance relationships, have you seen that man again?"

Cassie felt herself blush. "Hervé? Oh, yeah!"

"What is he like?"

"He's a character."

"Like Peter?"

"Peter is a character?"

Sabine shrugged. "I never understood your passion for him."

"What don't you like about him?"

"He's … I don't know. Oily."

"Peter is oily?"

"I don't know. Slippery. Not trustworthy. It's hard to put into words."

"Hervé is peculiar in his own way. He rides a vintage motorcycle. He cooks. He's always philosophizing about one thing or another. He doesn't believe in cell phones."

"He's a typical French contrarian. Nothing peculiar about that."

"I guess the peculiar part is how handsome he is." Cassie hesitated "Shouldn't he be interested in a more suitable woman?"

"You're not suitable?" Sabine looked surprised.

"I might have my own brand of sexiness. But it's not that Barbie doll look."

"Newsflash," Sabine interrupted, "little girls are the ones who like Barbie. Boys hate them. Unless they can tie them to rockets and shoot them up in the air."

"There is that other small detail. I – ahem. I still haven't told him that I live in the U.S."

"Are you serious?"

"I was afraid he'd run away. I kept postponing."

"That's a disaster in the making."

"I didn't want to jeopardize the first fun thing that had happened to me in, what … a lifetime? Should I deny myself this moment? Out of high moral principles?"

"Don't ask me," Sabine shrugged. "I've made nothing but reasonable choices my entire life."

"I was the picture-perfect, selfless, bake-sale, little league kind of mother, and now my kids are gone, and I have little to show for it. I stayed in a marriage that wasn't working for either of us out of principle, and Peter moved on from me without batting an eyelash. I let myself work in his shadow because I was too principled to demand proper credit, and now I don't have a career to my name. I could have done with fewer principles and a bit more self-worth."

"Why did you ever give Peter so much power?"

"I kept waiting for him to tell me that I was good at what I did. I was waiting for his encouragement, his authorization to shine, I guess."

"Like with Papa?"

Cassie looked at Sabine dumbfounded. "Yes. Just like with Papa!"

"Ha!" Sabine said. "Full circle."

"Yep. Crawling for crumbs of acceptance and love. Peter leaving me was the ultimate rejection, after all those years trying to impress him by being deserving and selfless. But at the same time, I was overbearing and constantly furious at him. And I *did* kick him out in the end."

As she said this, Cassie realized that, in fact, she knew what she needed to know, about herself, about Peter, about Jessica. She would not be able to return to the lies to which she was a willing accomplice – deception and self-deception. She had been so afraid of losing Peter's approval that she had been willing to bury all her suspicions. The doubt had been there, and it had slowly poisoned her. That's why she had been so overbearing and furious.

"And then this Hervé character drops from the sky," Sabine said.

Cassie shook her head. "It's nothing. It's just a sex thing. He plans on traveling the world, and my life is in L.A."

Sabine raised an eyebrow. "Except you've fallen in love with him."

Cassie paused. Stunned. "I didn't – whether I did or not is immaterial. I don't believe someone can fall in love with *me*."

"You and I are in the same boat," Sabine said sadly. "Feeling hopelessly unlovable."

"I'm sorry. I keep whining about myself when you've just gone through this momentous heartache."

"My life veered off the path," Sabine said. "I don't know what the next chapter is. I keep thinking about the chapter that was not written."

"You know what you should do?" Cassie said. "You should come to California."

"For a vacation?"

"American men would be lining the streets to meet your cute tush and your exotic French accent. Take a leave of absence from work. Come stay in Los Angeles for a few months."

Sabine sighed. "That sounds perfectly unreasonable."

"Has being reasonable made either of us happy?"

"It's made us feel safe."

"But has it actually *made* us safe?"

"I see your point," Sabine said. And in her eyes, Cassie thought she could detect the birth of an embryonic sense of possibilities.

****

Thrilled with the content of her bag, Cassie walked down rue Bonaparte toward the Seine. Odile might well be the favorite daughter, but Cassie was the one bringing back the frigging family's Holy Grail!

She veered right and walked up onto the Pont des Arts to cross the Seine. The bridge was replete with tourists and couples in love. Cassie stopped walking and leaned against the banister. A péniche glided under the bridge. The people on the open platform waved to the people up on the bridge, so she waved back. It made her think of her dad, the way he was always hunched over a table, carving little sailboats out of balsa wood. Now she understood his hobby for what it was: a retreat to his childhood, to before the war, to a time when his dad was alive, to a time when being Jewish wasn't a death sentence, when he did not yet hate his mother, Marceline, and himself.

She looked out on the water. On the left bank was the dome of the Beaux Arts School, on the other side of the river, the Louvre. The Seine, wide and shimmering, curved through the city, reflecting the monuments and the sky. A few riverboats moved lazily along. She felt a flutter inside her chest. She took notice of how she felt. She felt different. Nothing had changed, really: she still had no husband, her kids had grown up, her mother and father all but shunned her. But she did not feel lonely or sad. It was a strange feeling, that realization that she did not, at that moment, feel lonely. Could the finials, now reconnected, magically erase her dad's hurt and self-blame and everything that trickled down from that? Her own hurt? Her own self-blame?

What had taken place in Algiers, the death of Albano, the guilt over it, the mutual blame, had set the course of all their life. Because of one ugly secret, no one in her family knew where they came from, where they belonged, or how they fit into the narrative of history. Shame was unconsciously taken from one generation to the next, festering into a cesspool of neurosis.

She could see now how the familiar hollowness in her chest, that usual, unnamed emptiness she filled with drama, and frantic activity, had in fact been loneliness. Coming to Paris and meeting Marceline gave her the unexplained sensation that her life had just been jump-started. For the first time in a very long time, things felt possible. She had been trapped inside a tunnel and had not even known to look for a light at the end. And suddenly, she was on the outside, in broad daylight, in the most beautiful city in the world.

****

Later, she faced the entrance to the hospital. Having stepped on Odile's fragile toes and crossed her mother's line in the sand, she knew that she would not be getting their permission to enter her dad's hospital room. So what she decided to do was go there anyway. But how, without being stopped by them or the staff? Her eight-a.m. appointment with the Chief of Services had slipped her mind, and this would not help her already tenuous credibility.

But if nineteen-year-old Marceline could be brave enough to visit the man she loved in an Algerian prison in 1942, Cassie decided to give this a shot. The worse thing that could happen to her was humiliation. Focusing on the finial in the bag, her golden ticket, she took a deep inhalation and pushed through the hospital gate.

The waiting room was densely packed. There were at least ten people in line at the reception. Miraculously, the dreaded Pinçon was not at the desk. Her heart beating a little too fast for a grown woman, Cassie crept from person to person, hiding behind them. She moved fast, and she hoped stealthily. In thirty seconds, she was at the double doors that led to the patient area. She ducked and pushed the doors open. Once on the other side, she zoomed to the changing room. Inside, visitors were fumbling with their paper outfits. She rolled her hair up into a bun, removed her coat, expertly put on a paper gown and boots, and even helped a woman figure out which way of the gown was up. She then tied a paper mask over her face, waited for a group of visitors to go out, and went out with them.

She headed toward her father's room unmolested. Amazing how much easier things were when you dispensed with authorizations!

Inside her father's hospital room, the light was dim. She had half-expected her mother and Odile to be there, but her dad was alone in the quiet room, with only the beeping of the monitors for company. The sight of him broke her heart. He lay on his cot, his arms covered in taped IVs and tubes that connected him to bags of liquid and machines. His eyes were open, and he stared at the ceiling, blinking rapidly. He had the panicked expression of a man who dreams that he is the victim of a scientific experiment and awakens to discover it is not a dream.

She approached tentatively. "Papa, it's me," she whispered. He turned his face toward her and blinked some more. She slowly put down her paper mask so he could see her face. To her relief, he looked surprised, not angry. The beeps of the machines remained steady. She relaxed. "You breathe without an oxygen mask now. Fantastic!" she said. Her father looked at her haggardly. Again, she was struck by his growing beard. Dignity was a fragile thing, as skin-deep as a shave. All her life, she had desperately tried to impress her father. Was she still trying now? But the man on the cot was no longer just the father who kept her at a distance, but the suffering boy, the teenager, trying to survive a war, the young man whose father had been killed perhaps because of him. In his eyes, she saw a whole lifetime of fear, injustice, sadness, and rage, the veneer of distance between him and his emotions about to crack.

Cassie's composure plummeted. There was a floodgate of tears, stuck somewhere between her heart and her throat, and she was not sure how long the dam would hold. "I brought you a surprise," she said with forced cheer. "You won't believe this, but I got my hands on the second finial! Look!" She unzipped her bag, took it out, and held it out. Her father's eyes widened at the finial. Finally, he opened his mouth and mumbled something unintelligible.

She came closer to him to listen. "What, Papa? What did you say?"

"That bitch," he said laboriously, as though he were giving painful birth to each syllable. "She … stole it."

"But I got it back, Papa! You have both finials now. They're both yours. Isn't that amazing?"

"She … she wants to steal it."

"Not anymore," she said, using the soothing-but-firm tone of a kindergarten teacher. "See, one is safe at home, and the other one is right here." He closed his eyes. She did not know if this was in acquiescence or exhaustion. "I got it back for you. I did. Are you happy?"

"You," he said, his eyes closed.

Cassie felt herself dissolve. It was the first time he acknowledged her presence since she arrived in Paris. "Me?"

"You always … fall back on your feet."

She smiled, shaken, and tapped his hand gently, "I didn't, Papa. Not really. Not any more than anyone else."

"You're … ruthless."

Cassie's smile faded. "That's not the way I am. You have the wrong idea about me. I'm … I'm really nice … usually."

"I saved your life."

"Wh-what?"

"I shot the Boche …" he said laboriously. "The bridge … It's not my fault."

Cassie brought her hand to her mouth. Her throat constricted. He still thought she was Marceline! She fought back her tears, but it was a battle she was rapidly losing. She wanted him to see *her*. She wanted him to accept *her,* to love *her.* But in his eyes, had she ever existed without the shadow of Marceline tainting everything? She wiped the tears that pooled in her eyes. The only way he would be able to make peace with her would be to make peace with Marceline. And so, although when every bit of her wanted to contradict him and remind him of who she really was, she whispered, "You're right, Gustave. You saved me."

"I wanted to … protect you," her dad said. "Baba asked me to."

Cassie crushed an angry tear on her cheek. "You were heroic. I was reckless. Baba's death was an accident. But it's really all my fault for being selfish."

Her father nodded weakly. "That's what I've been trying to tell you, and Mother," he murmured.

"Mother knows that you are not to blame. She … she's proud of you. For your bravery. We all are."

He smiled tiredly. Cassie took his hand. "I want us to love each other, Gustave, just like when we were little. We used to be good friends, remember? Can you forgive me now?"

"Ah, yes," he mumbled. He seemed peaceful now, as though a weight had been lifted. He closed his eyes.

Cassie was weeping silently. She had a thought. "And … do you remember Cassie?" she asked. "Your daughter?" She felt sickened by what she was trying to do. "She loves you very much, too." Suddenly her father opened his eyes wide, his face washed with panic. He raised his arm, pulling all manner of tubes and IV. His pulse shot up. A loud alarm began to ring shrilly. "Shh ... Papa," Cassie said, frantically. "Calm down ... shh ... it's me!"

"Go away!" he roared.

Cassie looked back at the door. In a minute, someone would walk in. "But look! I brought you the second finial," she said urgently, showing it to him in a last-ditch effort to soothe him. "I got it back for you!" Gustave was waving his arms spastically, pulling tubes and wires with them. His IV pulled out; blood began to spill. She held the finial in one hand, and with the other, she held his arm down. "It's okay, Papa; it's okay," she said, feeling mounting panic. He was hollering now, out of pain or rage she did not know.

The alarm blared. There were hurried footsteps in the hallway. A moment later two nurses were inside the room, tending to him and pushing her out of the way. "I can't believe this!" one said, as she added a syringe of fluid into his IV bag while the other nurse held him down, "You're not supposed to be in here." She shouted, "Security!" Cassie cradled the finial and watched powerlessly as the nurses struggled to restrain Gustave's jerking movement and to reattach him to his IV. One of the nurses turned her head to look at her. "You better leave!" she said. The other one shouted again, "Security!"

Cassie shuffled backward toward the door. "I'm leaving," she said, just as Mademoiselle Pinçon entered the room. In righteous indignation, she looked even more horrible. "Yes, you certainly are leaving!" she blurted out. "You have no place being here. Look what you did!"

Cassie's panic transformed into fury. "You're the one who has no place here. I'm his daughter! What have you done to him? Poke and probe at him like a lab rat. It's monstrous! And all these drugs you're giving him: they're making him crazy. He doesn't know where he is! He doesn't even know who I am!"

"Leave! Security!" Pinçon shouted.

"Bye, Papa! I love you!" Cassie said. Still cradling the finial, she turned back to look at her dad one last time. She saw him turn his head away from her, but through the tears that blurred her vision, she could not be sure.

At the door, she bumped into two interns, geeky young men but tall and strong nonetheless.

"That one!" Pinçon told them. "She's a big problem. Make sure she is under control."

Pinçon had not finished her sentence when the interns had their hands on her. They tried to each hold one of Cassie's arms, but she curled over the finial to protect it. "Take your hands off me!" she yelled. They continued jerking at her arms. "You better not break this. It's a museum piece. You'll have to pay for it, you hear me?"

"Ma'am, stay calm."

"I'll follow you. Stop trying to hold me! I'm warning you – if this thing falls…."

"If you calm down, we won't call the gendarmerie."

"I'll calm down when you stop grabbing me!"

They let go. Cassie straightened, and, clenching her teeth through tears and fury, she carried the finial like a baby as she walked, now accompanied by four interns, past the people at the reception desk.

At that very moment, Odile and Raymonde were entering the reception and stopped in their tracks in shock. "Goodness gracious. What have you done?" Raymonde said. Her eyes dropped to the finial. "Did you steal it from the apartment?"

"Come off it, Maman! That's not your damn finial. This one's mine!"

"Yours?"

"Please follow us, Ma'am," said one of the interns.

"It was given to me," Cassie told her mom.

"By whom?" Raymonde mumbled.

"By … myself! Since Papa thinks I'm Marceline, apparently."

"You're not making any sense," Odile said.

"No one in this family makes sense!" Cassie shouted.

"We have patients here. You need to stop yelling!" Pinçon hissed.

"Please, Mesdames, we need to sort this out," an intern said. He turned to Cassie. "Madame, if you would please follow us without creating more chaos."

"Follow you where?" Cassie asked.

"To sort this out with the Chief of Services."

Cassie shook her head in disbelief. "You have got to be kidding me!"

"Do you want us to come along?" Odile asked limply.

"Oh no," Cassie said savagely. "This is too good!" She turned to Pinçon, whose mouth looked reduced to a thin downward line. "I would be delighted to meet the Chief of Services at long last!"

They arrived at a large wooden door, and Pinçon knocked. "Come in," said a male voice. They opened the door, and all pushed in, two interns, followed by Cassie, followed by three more interns, followed by Pinçon.

They were in a large, bright room lined with wooden bookshelves heavy with medical reference volumes.

"What is this?" asked the man in the suit who sat at the desk by the window.

It took Cassie several seconds to compute inside her brain what she was seeing. "What are you doing here?" she exclaimed.

Hervé looked up at her in incomprehension and got up from his chair. "Cassie, what's going on? Why are you here?" He pointed to the finial. "What is that thing?" He pointed to the interns and asked them. "Why are all of you here?"

"I don't get it," Cassie said. "What are you doing at the hospital?"

Hervé shrugged, "Working, what else?"

She shook her head. "That can't be."

"What?"

"You can't be the Chief of Services of the ICU," Cassie said, her brain buzzing to reconcile the mess this was. "I've been trying to see you for days!"

Hervé looked utterly confused. "You saw me this morning."

Pinçon looked from Hervé to Cassie and blinked. "Should we call the gendarmerie?" she asked meekly, suddenly not too sure of where this was headed.

"The gendarmerie? Why in the world would you?" Hervé said.

"My lord!" Cassie said.

"This is the cra – the lady who's been wreaking havoc for days," Pinçon explained.

Hervé widened his eyes. "You? You're the crazy American?"

Cassie now understood the incomprehensible. "I must be," she said. It was all coming back to her. He was a doctor. He had a suspended license. He was now stuck in purgatory doing bureaucratic functions. That was the reason he came to the Jument Bleue where they had met. It was close to his work because the hospital *was* where he worked! What an idiot she had been! The phone call from the office this morning when they were in bed: it was *her* they were talking about! All along, it had been *her* that Hervé was avoiding and ditching. The Neanderthal who so rudely refused to see her had been Hervé.

"But how can you be American?" Hervé said. He was standing in front of her now, looking at her with profound confusion. "I don't understand any of this."

"Do we cancel the gendarmerie then?" one of the interns asked thickly.

"Of course, cancel the gendarmerie!" Hervé shouted. "Everyone out of my office! Now!"

Pinçon scampered out of the room. One of the interns took Cassie by the shoulder. "Please follow us, Ma'am."

"Not her!" Hervé said.

"She could be dangerous."

"She's NOT dangerous!" Hervé bellowed.

The door closed behind the mayhem with a hollow thud.

Now Hervé and Cassie were face to face, each trying to process what was happening. Cassie was the first one to speak. "How could you be the asshole who has been giving me the run around for days?"

"I told you I was terrible at this job. I'm a physician. I don't know how to babysit loonies."

"Such as myself?" she said, livid. "Loonies who are sick with worries and are not getting the least bit of humane treatment from this crappy hospital? All I asked for were honest answers and some humanity. Instead, I got contempt and red tape."

"You made up that you were American? Why?"

"Well, I did not make that up. It's the truth."

"You're obviously French; what are you talking about?"

Cassie rolled her eyes. "I am French. It's just that I live in California. I've lived there for the last twenty years."

"What? You live in Paris and—"

She decided to rip the bandage, interrupting him. "My return ticket to the U.S. is on Wednesday."

"You're leaving?"

"Wednesday," she repeated, speaking slowly so that he understood. "Because I live in the U.S. Not here."

"This Wednesday? The Wednesday three days from now?" he asked.

"She nodded." Yes.

"But I made you fresh pasta!"

"I just … I didn't think there was any need to … I had no idea where this was heading."

"You must be joking!" Hervé exclaimed. "Where could this ever go if your ticket back is Wednesday!"

"I told you my situation was complicated," Cassie said. "You're the one who said, oh no, no, no, this thing between us, was, AND I QUOTE: 'an uncomplicated thing.'"

"Well, it's complicated now," Hervé said angrily. "Why didn't you tell me your father was dying?"

Cassie received the news like a punch in the solar plexus. "My father is *dying*?"

Hervé backtracked too late. "I … hmm. I need to consult the file."

"My father is dying?" she said, realizing how obvious this was for the very first time.

"He's in kidney failure, Cassie," Hervé admitted. "And the antibiotics aren't making a dent in his pneumonia."

Her father was dying. This might have been the last time she would ever speak to him, and he had not once acknowledged her. "Let me uncomplicate things for you," she said. "You're the big heartless a-hole who made it impossible for me to be at my father's deathbed. How about that?"

"And *you* lied through your teeth and played with my heart."

"Heart? Oh, perfect! Now you're the wronged party? How convenient! Yesterday you were all penis, and today you have a heart?"

"So, what other lies did you tell me?" Hervé said spitefully. "Are you in fact happily married to some American imbecile?"

"Well, you know that movie you despise, that film that embodies all that's wrong with humanity? That piece of garbage that's a disgrace to mankind?"

"What about it?"

"Well, I'm the one who wrote it!"

"Why am I not surprised?"

Cassie looked at him. There was nothing left to say. She turned around, walked to the door, opened it, and slammed it shut as hard as she could before leaving.

She ran out of the hospital, and Hervé did nothing to stop her.

****

She glanced at her watch. It was 4:20 p.m.

She had a hunch to follow and only about forty minutes to do so.

She grabbed her tote bag with both arms and ran down rue de Maubeuge and then down rue du Faubourg Poissoniere, where she hopped on the métro.

She was standing shoulder to shoulder with dozens of zoned-out commuters as the subway weaved through the underbelly of the city. Thoughts of her father, of Hervé, of Peter, of Marceline, of her sister, her mother, the hospital and the finial senselessly crackled through her mind like popcorn. Nothing made sense and everything did, like disparate, unconnected elements that were also mysteriously linked. She was disappointed. She was heartbroken. She was a mess. She kept glancing at her watch. The bank would be closing at five.

She emerged at Métro Chaussée D'Antin, ran in the direction of the Galeries Lafayette and crossed the street. She was the last person let into the Société Générale before a guard closed the door.

The only change in the twenty years since she had last been at the bank was the thickness of computers. The beautiful art deco glass roof above and the patina of the wood counters looked exactly as they did when she was a teenager. She waited in line, tapping the heel of her red boot against the mosaic of the flooring. When it was her turn, she slammed a piece of paper in front of the teller: 454B5743589112A. The number engraved on Marceline's finial.

The teller typed in the number on his keyboard. "Would you like to access your safety deposit box now?"

Goosebumps rose from her legs up to her neck. "Yes, I want to open it," she said, breathless.

"May I see the key?" he asked.

Cassie's smile turned rigid. "The key?"

"The box can only be opened with your key."

"I don't have it."

"Ah then, Madame, you'll need to bring it tomorrow. Unfortunately, we are closing for the day." Already, the teller was picking up things on his desk.

"What if I, hmm, lost it?" Cassie asked. "Can't you break the safe open or something?"

"That is not how this goes," the teller said with the lack of patience of someone who is five minutes away from going home. "Unless you have the password. If the key was lost."

"I have neither."

"In that case, there is nothing we can do. Not without a notary and an attorney." He pushed in front of her a form she'd need to fill out. "The process takes six to twelve months."

Cassie looked around her at the beautiful building, and up at the dome-shaped glass ceiling. She muttered, "I can't believe how stupid I am."

"I beg your pardon?"

Cassie sighed, shook her head dejectedly, "Nothing. Thank you for your help."

Perhaps the teller felt sorry for her at that moment. "All our keys have the bank's monogram, B. S. G., Banque Société Générale," he said helpfully. "But this is an account in the old vault. It would be an old-fashioned looking key like they made in the old days."

****

At the reception of her hotel was an envelope from Peter waiting for her. It contained a first class return ticket to Los Angeles, leaving three hours later.

It took her no more than fifteen minutes. She wrapped the finial with as many clothes as she could fit in her bag. She shoved the rest of her clothes into the broken suitcase, including the lingerie she had bought with Hervé in mind, and set the whole thing by the wastebasket. She grabbed Jessica's four little packages from the mantelpiece and slipped them inside a plastic Monoprix bag. She looked down at her feet. Those red cowboy boots were never really her, only some optimistic fictionalized version of her that was rapidly disintegrating. She placed the boots on top of the broken suitcase near the wastebasket and slipped on the Uggs.

She came down the stairs with only her tote and her purse, paid her bill, told the old man at the reception that everything she had left in the room was trash, and took a taxi to Charles de Gaulle airport.

CHAPTER 6

Two Boys from Smyrna

When he was a small boy, Albano had wandered alone on Mount Pagus. It was 1910. A month earlier, his entire family had perished in the cholera pandemic, and now he was an eight-year-old orphan raised in the Jewish quarter of Smyrna by his Uncle Jacob and Aunt Sadie. The heaviness in his heart had grown impossible to bear, especially when he first woke up in the morning and found himself in a strange house, sharing a room with sleeping cousins indifferent to him.

That morning, he had awakened before dawn, crept out of the bedroom, left his uncle and aunt's house, and carefully opened the wooden door and closed it behind him. In the Jewish quarter, everyone was asleep. Above, the moon was bright and cast long shadows as he set out on the dirt path that led outside of town. He had left the Jewish quarter without plans. He had not even truly meant to run away.

For a long time, he wandered in the mountain guided by the light of the setting moon. All was quiet; the birds hadn't awakened yet. Even the crickets were asleep. Only the occasional calls of coyotes bounced around the empty mountains, distant at first, and then very near. Under his bare feet were rough pebbles and dirt. The air was dewy and smelled of wild sage.

The sun was rising, and the sky had turned pink when Albano arrived near the top of the mountain. From where he was, he could see his way back to the Jewish quarter, to the place that wasn't his home.

Something moved. Albano stopped, startled. A moment later, a rabbit scurried near his feet. He watched it disappear into the bushes at the foot of a tall rock formation. The rabbit must have its nest in the bushes, he thought. He also thought that if he were to find a baby rabbit, perhaps he could bring it back with him and Aunt Sadie would let him keep it as a pet. His mother would have. But Aunt Sadie was mean, and it wasn't easy to keep a rabbit in a crowded home.

Albano squatted to look between the bushes at the foot of the boulder where the rabbit had disappeared. He moved thorny bushes out of the way and discovered an opening in the rocks. Curious, he went on his hands and knees and crept inside.

What he found on the other side of the opening took his breath away. He was inside a large cave! Just enough light came in from the rising sun through a crack between the rocks for him to see how large the cave was. It was a true castle! It was at least twenty steps across in all directions and tall enough for Albano to stand and still have about ten feet above him. Inside, the ray of sunshine bounced against the smooth rocks and made the walls of the cave shimmer like gold. The air smelled of wet earth and fungi. The only sound, echoing eerily, was a trickle of water. When he found the water stream and put his hand in it, it was cold and clear as diamonds.

That day, Albano curled upon the cave's dirt and allowed himself to sob with grief, but also with relief because for the moment he felt protected by God.

****

It was thirty-two years since the discovery of the cave but Albano, now almost forty years old, remembered that day vividly. He remembered his joy, his relief, the feeling that God had guided him there. The cave would become the center of his life. It was the place where he would hide the finials passed down from his dying father and the money that he and Hagop earned selling newspapers on the quays of Smyrna. The cave was the place where he had protected Hagop and then lost him. The cave was the hidden temple where he and Xandra had loved each other, where they had stayed in hiding as her belly grew with their child.

Today, the secret room where Albano was hiding felt more like a coffin than a castle. It was narrow and windowless, concealed between two walls. It smelled of mildew and old papers. The room was equipped with everything a man in hiding could need: running water, a toilet, shelves lined with food provisions. This was the room where he and Moshe put friends who needed a few days of safety, and today it was Albano's turn to use it. This room was like a coffin also because today was the burial of his old life. He could still change his mind, as long as he was inside the secret room. But once the decision was made, it would be a death of sorts. Or rather a rebirth.

Outside, the Allies had begun the invasion of North Africa. Their success or failure would decide his fate.

Albano listened and heard not a sound.

Years of planning, and, as Moshe liked to call this, "constructive pessimism," had led to this moment. This day. After two years spent in Algiers and working tirelessly to help finance the Resistance effort, Albano was proud of his involvement. Their operation guaranteed a financial lifeline to Jewish groups in North Africa and elsewhere, as well as that of many Resistance cells in occupied France. But Albano's involvement in all this ended today. Freedom would come, he hoped, as a result of tonight's Allied invasion by sea and air – freedom for his family and freedom for the French people of Algeria. But for him, it would lead to freedom of a different kind, one he dreaded and feared, but one he was choosing.

No one was making him do this terrible thing.

One did not have children to possess them, Albano reasoned, but to eventually release them into the world. And whether the world was ready for them or not, his children seemed ready for the world. When they were little, Albano had been able to keep his brood around him. But now, Marceline and Gustave were young adults, and the war had changed them. This city had changed them. Lucienne was incapable of parenting; she had become like a child herself. Marceline and Gustave were wayward and unruly, as futile to try and contain as a running spring. They wanted to risk their lives for their ideals, and there was nothing he could do about it. If the invasion turned out to be a success, the city would be freed, and his family would no longer need his protection from the Nazis. If the invasion was a success, they would be safe.

Xandra had tried to open his eyes. She had demonstrated the courage he lacked. Ultimately, she had been the one to commit the unthinkable act instead of him. But ultimately, they were only peons. It was all the will of God.

The tiny, coffin-like room was built to be soundproof. If the fight had already started, Albano had no way of knowing. If there were gunshots, explosions, men and women screaming, children crying, those noises did not reach his ears. This also meant that no sounds inside the room could be heard from outside. Albano sat on the cot, and, just like he had as a child, thirty years before, he began to weep, over Lucienne, over Marceline, and Gustave, and Hagop, and Moshe, and Xandra, and over what he was about to do.

****

Nine months earlier: March 1942

As was his daily habit since he and the family had come to Algiers, Albano had washed, dressed, and walked down rue Michelet to get his coffee and newspaper before the rest of the family awakened. He had always loved being up at daybreak, a leftover habit from his years selling newspapers on Smyrna's quayside. Algiers was a beautiful city, which seemed to have gotten the essence of two cultures right. It was like Paris, but with the sunshine. It was like Africa, but with European architecture. The seaside even had the feel of Smyrna. As he walked down the streets, he wondered if he should worry Xandra with the upsetting news he had recently learned: according to Moshe, Hagop was no longer in Nice. Not only that; they had no idea where he was.

As he walked through the streets of Algiers, he thought of how, at first, he had been pleased with the swiftness with which his children had accommodated to their new life in North Africa. But now, be it due to their adolescent moods, or their endless conflicts with one another, he was appalled by their poor judgment.

Marceline slipped away every chance she got and spent time with boys. The whole translation business he had managed to thwart, but even if he were to ground Marceline for a week, on the eighth day, she'd head straight into the next mischief. And there was Gustave's obsession with joining the Resistance or the Chantiers de la Jeunesse. The children were on edge, disobedient, lashing out at each other over the merest slights. True, Lucienne's condition helped nothing. And how could Marceline and Gustave not want out of the apartment when he himself could not bear to be anywhere near her?

And now they were all turning against Xandra, she who selflessly served them without expecting, or receiving, an ounce of appreciation or recognition. From Lucienne, he expected this, but the children? He had overindulged them, and so he could only blame himself now that they were spoiled. Just last week he had believed the children would remain on Xandra's side, and he had been devastated to discover that they weren't. He had hoped to enroll Marceline in an intervention, as she was still her mother's favorite. "Your mother keeps telling me to fire Sandra," he had told Marceline. "I hope you can make her listen to reason."

"All the same," Marceline had said, "I can see how Mother feels."

"What do you mean?"

"Mother has been in a state, and maybe not having Sandra around would be best."

Albano had looked at Marceline with incomprehension. "Fire Sandra? Is this what you're asking of me? You agree with your mother?"

"You can't impose her on Mother for the rest of time," Marceline had said. "If she's so miserable with Sandra, why keep her?"

"But wouldn't you miss Sandra?" Albano asked, aghast.

Marceline answered in a paternalistic tone that surely had no place in the mouth of a child. "Baba, we really don't need her. At least, Gustave and I don't. Not as a nanny. And Mother doesn't want her as a maid. What are we to do when Mother is adamant about it? Choose Sandra over her?"

"But Sandra is like a member of this family."

Marceline frowned prettily. "With all due respect, she is not."

"We're the only family she has!"

"I'm not saying leave her destitute. We can find her another family to work for. I'm just thinking about Mother."

Albano saw Marceline for the callous, selfish girl she was. "If you were truly concerned with your mother's well-being," he said, "perhaps you would not lie to her again and again and put her through so much grief!"

"I'm sorry, Baba."

"I'm sure your brother feels very differently about Sandra," he said defensively.

Marceline shrugged. "I think he would agree." She patted Albano on the back, and her touch felt like an electric shock finding its way all the way down to his bone. "Sandra's time has passed, Baba," she said. "It really has. We're nearly grown."

Albano, full of righteous indignation, marched into Gustave's room. Surely Gustave, for whom Xandra was more of a mother than Lucienne had ever been, who knew she had believed in him from the moment she set eyes on him, and believed in him still to this day when he did nothing much but grumble and resent the entire family, would want Xandra to remain. Gustave, at least, would be on her side. "Your sister and mother want to let go of Sandra," Albano told him upon entering his bedroom. "What do you think about this?"

"I'm a man," Gustave answered without lifting his head from the train set he was working on. "I don't need a nanny."

Albano was in disbelief at first, and then he felt angry. "And so, you think I should let Sandra go?" he said, raising his voice. "In the middle of a war? In a country she hardly knows?"

Gustave shrugged. "I didn't say that. I just said I don't need a nanny. It's not my decision. You can keep her if you want to."

"It's not about what I want!" Albano exclaimed. "It's about – about...." Albano was so distraught that suddenly he could not describe what any of this was about. It was about his eternal love for and devotion to Xandra. He could hardly expect his children to share his feelings.

"You're the one who keeps saying we need to save money," Gustave said.

Albano was disgusted. Disgusted with his wife, with his children, disgusted with himself. What would he tell Xandra now? He would not tell her that the children she loved as though they were her own were ready to dispose of her like a spent item. Xandra had done nothing but take care of them, and this was all the appreciation they had for her? Did they not realize her selflessness? Her sacrifices?

And in truth, how could they?

They had been deceived for over ten years. And yet, to think that Xandra mattered so little to them! They would have shown more loyalty to a pet. Or perhaps children grew up, and their love for their family needed to dull for them to move on with their lives. One day, they would feel the same way about him. Perhaps it had happened already.

****

Albano sat down at the terrace of Le Beaugrenelle, a nice café-brasserie that looked in every way like the kind one could find in Paris. He sat at his usual table. Pierre, the terrace's waiter, was an older man, grumpy and arrogant with Arab customers, obsequious with French ones. With Albano, he wasn't sure how to feel and alternated between the two. For a few moments, he and Albano talked about the weather, careful to avoid the topic of politics because spying eyes and ears were everywhere in Algiers. Albano knew how to be careful and how to appear ordinary. Even those at the highest echelons of the local Resistance must not know what he did. The system had been set in place long before France had entered the war. The money, channeled through England, came from all over the world, especially America. He and Moshe had experienced war as civilians before, and so they had understood that setting up escape routes, developing connections, and designing systems to channel money was best done before a war, not in the middle of it when communication became extremely difficult. They knew that communication was often intercepted, which in turn risked the money ending up in the hands of the enemy, not to mention the risk of lives. They had found a way to bypass communication. Their contacts could expect airdrops at irregular intervals on dates prearranged and memorized far in advance. The contacts didn't know each other and had no knowledge of other drops or other dates. No one in Algiers, or elsewhere, knew how the money to finance the Resistance was channeled, not even those in the Resistance.

Pierre brought his usual coffee and croissant, and Albano told himself that next time he would get toast instead. Small pleasures were becoming too much of a luxury. He drank his coffee and ate his croissant and forced himself to concentrate on the newspaper, which was mostly Pétain propaganda and contained no truth whatsoever about the war. His mind kept returning to Hagop's disappearance from Nice. Half of France was occupied by the Nazis, so he doubted that Hagop would have the stupidity to head north toward Paris. If he did not get the idea of heading south, and perhaps crossing the Mediterranean and going to North Africa, there was no reason to worry. And even if he did, North Africa was a vast place. For Hagop to look for them in Algiers would be like looking for a needle in a haystack. Still, he and Moshe had hired people to inquire about his whereabouts and were hoping to find more information soon.

Albano folded his paper, paid, and left. He needed to do something about Marceline, he thought, as he walked back to the apartment. His daughter's latest transgression was the last straw. He had lost his temper the night before when she had arrived well after curfew, her mouth full of lies, professing that she had been at her friend Béatrice's home when he knew for a fact that she was not. What had she been doing, and with whom? This had turned into a family fight. The children took the opportunity to turn on each other like scorpions, and Lucienne had swallowed more pills to numb herself. At some point, Albano had slammed his fists on the table, thus acting like a child himself. Was it the right thing to do to give Gustave the mission to keep an eye on Marceline, he wondered? But what else could he do? He could not have eyes everywhere. It would make Gustave feel like a man while keeping Marceline out of trouble, God helping. He was aware that this decision might exacerbate their mutual resentment.

The living situation in Algiers suited no one. The small apartment had only three bedrooms. Marceline and Gustave each had their own, which meant that

Albano had to go back to sharing a bedroom with Lucienne, while Xandra lived in a maid's room on the top floor of the building.

In Algiers, he and Xandra had no privacy. During the day, she worked in the apartment. But Lucienne, who lived in terror of the city and its inhabitants, was always home. Visiting Xandra up in her room was out of the question. It was not done to go up to the servant's floor where only women lived. The corridors and back stairs that led to the maid's rooms were always filled with women, and his comings and goings would spur a wave of gossip that might find its way to his family's ears. Albano felt terrible about this. In Paris, even in Cannes, Xandra had had her own room in the house. But here, the apartment was too small. He loathed how the worlds of servants and masters were kept separate. In the morning the servants, most of them Muslim women, went to work in the French people's apartments, and at night, they went back up, like things taken out of a cabinet to be used and then placed back inside when one was done with them.

Albano had never seen Xandra's bedroom in all the months they had lived in Algiers. He and Xandra had had only brief moments of true privacy in the last two years. They had to content themselves with a few words exchanged in the kitchen, a smile, a furtive kiss, a quick squeeze of the hand. Maybe once a month, they saw each other at Moshe's. But Moshe's Algiers apartment served as a hub of Resistance activities. It was more often than not crowded with men and thus hardly a suitable place for a lovers' rendezvous. Lovers. If that's what they were. They loved each other; that much they knew. And they lusted for each other – at least he did for her. But Xandra had never wavered on her resolve to refuse intimacy. He was a married man, and she was a pious Christian woman. Ever since she had materialized in Paris twelve years ago, that was that.

Albano walked back on rue Michelet toward his apartment building, looking up at row after row of windows. Behind those windows, housewives put water to boil on stoves. Businessmen shaved in their bathroom mirrors. Students prepared for school. Lovers had a last embrace. Mothers combed their daughters' hair. As a boy, when he and Hagop sold newspapers on Smyrna's quayside, Albano always liked to imagine how people lived behind their windows and doors. Back then, he believed that those who had wealth were by essence happy. He had been wrong about this and many other things.

He entered the building and walked up the stairs to his apartment thinking of Xandra, his beloved, so close and yet so out of his reach. He craved to speak to her, to hold her in his arms. He missed her. Life was a disjointed whirl of activities, full of urgencies and risks, without a moment to pause or think, and, at the same time, cloaked in wretched loneliness. Without quite knowing what he was doing, he found himself passing the floor to his apartment and continuing up toward the fifth floor and the maids' living quarters. A moment later, he was searching for her door in the mildew-smelling corridor. He found it and knocked softly.

Xandra opened after a few moments and widened her eyes. "You know people will talk," she whispered, taking him by the arm and pulling him inside.

As soon as he was in her room, he took her in his arms, and they held each other without speaking.

"What is happening with Marceline?" he asked finally. "Where did she go yesterday?"

Xandra's face closed, the way it did when she had decided not to speak about something. The strain of the last two years was even affecting Xandra, although they never discussed it. Xandra, his anchor in life, his bastion of certainty, was impatient at times. Little things she said and did. A new stubbornness. Sometimes she seemed to be on the children's, or even Lucienne's, side more than she was on his. "I don't know where she went," she said.

"Do you think she was with a boy?"

"It was probably for a boy," Xandra said. Albano contemplated his beloved. She was wearing a nightdress made of thick white cotton. Her braid was undone. Her hair, lustrous and black, fell on her shoulders.

"Marceline is with men, and it doesn't make you upset?"

Xandra looked at him meaningfully, not letting him pretend that he was ignorant of this. "You know this has happened before."

"I cannot understand my own daughter," he said, distraught. "How can one have so much intelligence on the one hand and so little brain on the other?" He looked around the room for a place to sit, but there was no chair in the pared-down room. He had been told the room was furnished. Where, then was the furniture? All he saw was a thin mat set on the bare floor and three rattan trunks; one at the foot of the bed and one on either side. There was the small rug he had given her for a birthday. There was her Jesus on the cross above her mat. She had pinned postcards of Paris to the wall and draped bright shawls on a string that ran from one corner of the room to the other, and this gave the place a warm feel, but there was no dresser, no desk, no chair, no lighting except for an antiquated oil lamp set atop a lace handkerchief. And there was no chimney either, so where would the heating come from?

He felt a wave of unease. In Paris, Xandra had a beautiful room. In Cannes, she had a pretty room with her own bathroom. Now she lived as she had in the cave, no better. And alone. All those hours, alone. For two years, she had served them during the day and been alone in this terrible room at night. And not once had she complained. "Maybe if Marceline becomes pregnant, she can marry," Albano said absurdly. He leaned against the wall self-consciously. Xandra was sitting down on her mattress, looking up at him. "Lucienne will not like that very much," he continued, "but at least she would be a married woman."

Xandra answered nothing and looked at him strangely, as though she had the capacity of seeing straight into his soul. "What do you think of those Jewish boys?" he asked. "You would not want her to become a widow. They are taking risks, spending their time at Géo Gras."

"*You* take risks," Xandra pointed out.

"Moshe and I started something, and now the Resistance counts on us to organize the finances. If I were to quit now, a large part of the Resistance funding would stop flowing." As Albano spoke, he became aware that he was looking for an excuse, a reason why he had been unaware of Xandra's living conditions. He had been working for the Resistance. And this was true. He was under a great deal of stress; this was also true. "I take these risks for Marceline and Gustave, for their future. And all they do is attract trouble."

"They are a young man and a young woman in a world at war," Xandra said. "They are idealistic. Could your family ever stop you from doing what you wanted, what you needed to do? My family could not stop me. Not even my brother could stop me."

Albano rubbed his eyes, confused, and blurted out, "This room is terrible, Xandra! Why did you not tell me? I would have brought in decent furniture. A mattress worth sleeping on!"

Xandra smiled. "The happiest days of my life were spent on a straw mat in a cave."

"Where is the bathroom?"

"At the end of the hall. There is a toilet."

"You and the other maids share a toilet?"

"Have you forgotten the time when no house had one?" she said, smiling. "And we had to walk to the terrible bathhouse to wash? I go to the hammam. It's a beautiful one."

The idea and the solution to two problems sprang into Albano's mind unexpectedly. "You will come to live in the apartment!" he exclaimed. "And you will share a room with Marceline. I will tell Lucienne that it is so that you can keep an eye on her. She will have no choice but to accept this, she who is so worried about Marceline's honor." He beamed. "Yes, this is perfect!"

Xandra crossed her arms and shook her head. "Albano, do not make me Marceline's jailor."

"Your presence will dissuade her, that's all. You'll tell me about her goings on, and everyone will be much better off."

Xandra pinched her lips stubbornly. "I will not be her jailor or your spy. Marceline is like a daughter to me. I will not betray her trust."

"But it's not for this reason," he implored. "It is an excuse. The real reason is that I need you to be comfortable." He gestured at the room. "Not living here. Not like this. And yes, I need Marceline to be safe. It will serve two purposes."

"What is safe, Albano?" Xandra asked softly. "Is safety to remain alive, but not taste life at all? Marceline will not bear to be deprived of freedom when the world is turning to dust and rubble. Not her. Not your daughter."

"If she works for the Resistance, I have to stop her."

"But what about the work she does?" Xandra asked.

"What do you mean?"

"How about its importance?"

Albano looked at her in incomprehension. "How could a nineteen-year-old girl influence the outcome of the war?"

"Not a girl," Xandra insisted. "A woman. Look at her: fierce, intelligent, full of passion. Who is to say what she can or cannot accomplish?"

Albano was astounded. "Tell me you do not approve of all the things she does?"

Xandra answered with that air of stubbornness he knew not to contradict. "I think my own thoughts, Albano."

Albano wanted to tell Xandra that she was defending a selfish girl who was entirely unwilling to fight for her. "The children are taking you for granted," he said. "You deserved children who consider you their mother, not their maid."

Xandra laughed. "Every mother wants this; few obtain it."

"And you are Lucienne's equal, and she should treat you as such."

Xandra dismissed the improbable notion with a shrug. "Even those who Lucienne considers her equal, she doesn't treat as such."

Albano paced the few feet between the door and the window, frustrated that he was getting nowhere. "Still," he said, "you are more of a loving mother and caretaker than Lucienne ever was and ever will be, but you receive none of the credit. You deserve to be in the light. You should not be here, forgotten, but in my life, as my wife!"

"Albano, you are my man, and I am your woman," Xandra said tenderly.

"In almost every way but the one that matters most," Albano said in a tone more bitter than he had intended. Xandra frowned as she did every time he alluded to the fact that she refused physical intimacy in the name of his marriage's sanctity. "I have put you in an impossible situation," he added quickly so that she would know that he was resigned to this. "I've asked you to do something, and you accepted. It was a terrible pact. A terrible request."

Xandra got up from her mat, walked up to him, and touched his cheek softly. "But it has made me happy, Albano. Do you remember when we sold pastries together in the Levantine quarter? It seemed impossible that we could ever be together, you a Jewish boy and me an Armenian girl. I have loved taking care of your home and your children. It did not matter to me if this was not our home and our children. It nearly felt as if it was. Lucienne is the one who suffers the most. To love a man who loves another is the cruelest of fates."

"I have kept my pledge to Lucienne," Albano said. "But what about my pledge to you?"

"What pledge to me have you not kept? You took care of me; you gave me your support; you made me feel beautiful when the rest of the world saw me as a monster. You took me into your life when no one else would. You have kept me safe and adored."

"I also promised you a beautiful house, and look how you live."

Xandra peered at him. Albano looked away. "What is it?" she asked.

"What is what?" he answered.

Xandra crossed her arms and scrutinized his face. "Something else is upsetting you," she said. It was a statement, not a question. "Albano, speak to me."

"It's only that … I received some news. I did not want to bother you with it until I had some answers. We received a call from the custodian of Hagop's apartment in Nice." Xandra stiffened perceptibly. Albano paused, gathering himself so as not to betray his emotion. "Hagop is not living in the apartment anymore."

Xandra brought her hand to her neck as she took a quick breath. "Where did he go?" she murmured.

"The custodian cleaned the apartment weekly, but for the last few weeks, nothing was dirty. His clothes were gone, too. She did not think much of it because her wages were paid for the whole month. She thought he had gone on a trip. When he did not return at the end of the month, she called to inquire about him."

"A month," Xandra said. Her face had turned pale. She sat back down on the mattress, and Albano sat next to her. "Could something have happened to him?" she wondered.

They looked at each other with the same thought, but neither dared express it. Could Hagop be looking for them?

"The bank account in Nice where I left him money has been emptied," Albano admitted.

"Was it a lot of money?"

"Enough to live for about a year if he paced himself. Maybe he was tired of France. He never liked it much."

"You were too generous," she said.

"Look, he does not know where we are. He has no idea. I never told him a thing about Algeria. There is no cause for alarm. The custodian only had the telephone number of a trusted friend of Moshe's in Paris. That's who she called, and the friend then called Moshe."

Xandra did not say anything. She walked to the rattan trunk at the foot of her mat, crouched next to it, and opened it. She took out a folded piece of cloth and put it on the mat, stood up, and stepped away from it as if it contained a live snake. "I have this," she said.

"What is it?"

"Look."

Albano unfolded the cloth. Inside was a leather sheath, and Albano immediately knew what it contained. He slid the seven-inch blade out halfway and quickly slid it back into the sheath and dropped it on the mat. "Xandra! what is this?"

"In case my brother finds us," she said.

"He'd have to look for us in the whole world, so there is nothing to worry about." He was staring at the knife, unable to touch it or take his eyes away from it. "Where did you get this?" he said, his voice shriller than he intended.

"I bought it."

"But why?"

"For my protection."

"From what?"

"Things happen to women who are alone."

"Xandra! Now you tell me this? This horrible room, and now I learn you do not feel safe here? That you are scared? This is one more reason not to be in this room another minute." Xandra did not respond. She carefully folded the cloth over the knife and put it back into the trunk. "And what would you do with this knife?" Albano asked. "You would not know what to do!"

She answered with an impatience that betrayed her anguish. "Who do you think butchers the meat on your plate or empties out those fish you and Gustave insist on scooping out of the sea? I know how to use a knife, Albano."

Albano stopped her anger by taking her hand. As always, the contact soothed them both. "Hagop might just as easily have emptied his account and drank himself to death," he said softly. "He is self-destructive."

"He is destructive," she said, voicing her anger without hesitation. Unlike Albano, Xandra did not feel ambivalent toward Hagop.

"Even if he were to find us, he would not want to harm us. Not physically."

"He has in the past."

"How so?"

"He pushed me and beat me, remember?"

"Oh, yes."

"You have to go, Albano." She got up from the bed and nudged him toward the door. "You have stayed here too long already. People will gossip."

"Let me take you in my arms before I go," he said, coming close to her.

She let him, and as he held her, she softened. "A single kiss," he begged.

When Albano returned to the apartment and walked into the living room, the curtains were down, as Lucienne preferred it, and so he did not see her right away. What he saw first was a thin serpent of grey smoke rising from the embers in the ashtray. Lucienne was sitting at the dining room table in the dark. She brought the cigarette to her lips. After almost two decades of marriage, Albano knew what to read in Lucienne's apparent self-assured composure. Her rigidity had never been much more than a wall to keep fear at bay. She fought fiercely about every small thing, and he accommodated her, but that was because they both knew that the important decisions would be up to him. With Lucienne, it was better not to express doubt. If he left her any room to decide what she wanted, she filled that space with an anxiousness that distressed them both. Ever since he had been proven right about leaving Paris, and then leaving France for Algiers, she had been relieved to defer to him on most decisions.

Albano pulled up a chair and sat across from Lucienne. He dreaded speaking to her. He dreaded her reactions, her emotions, her accusations. "I decided it is best that Sandra shares a bedroom with Marceline," he said. Lucienne remained wordless and motionless for a long moment. In the dim light, he could only make out the outline of her face and the red tip of her cigarette. Finally, she reached into her pocket and produced the tiny silver box that contained her pills, swallowed one, and took a quick sip of water from a glass. "Our daughter doesn't obey us," Albano continued. "She is childish and reckless and puts us all in danger. With Sandra sharing her room, she won't be able to run out into the streets when we're asleep."

Lucienne continued to sit, very erect and tense. She exhaled a puff of smoke. "I am not sleeping under the same roof as that woman," she calmly said.

Albano had expected complaints, not opposition. He was immediately furious. "What difference does it make to you where she sleeps? She slept under our roof in Paris and Cannes."

"That was before," Lucienne said.

Albano did not ask what she meant for fear that she would tell him. Ever since they had left Cannes and come to Algiers, bringing Xandra, Lucienne suspected something that was never discussed. "She is here during the day doing all the work, cooking our meals, cleaning our home," he said.

"Oh yes, Saint Sandra, saving us all," Lucienne said bitterly.

Albano had no other option for Xandra. He could hardly afford this apartment and was in no position to get her a place. But the horrid room upstairs would not do, especially when the Hagop situation was not under control. And besides, what he said about wanting to protect Marceline was the truth. "Do you want our daughter to get hurt?" he said, more aggressively than Lucienne deserved. "Or abducted? Is this what you want?"

"I'll be the one sharing a room with Marceline," Lucienne said, her voice quivering. She was about to cry. Perhaps she was crying already, but Albano could not see her eyes in the dark.

"You are drugged most of the time. You don't even see when people go in and out of the apartment during the day, let alone at night." He was shocked by his meanness. But this also was the truth.

"Those are medications I must take so as not to lose my mind in this wretched place!" Lucienne said. A month ago, this was the point where she would have started to scream and bawl, but her medication dulled everything, even sadness and rage.

"All the same," Albano said.

The pill Lucienne had just swallowed was taking effect. Her speech slowed. "Why can't Marceline and Gustave share a room?" she asked sluggishly.

"They resent each other enough as it is."

Lucienne got up slowly, dropped her cigarette in the ashtray and ambled to her room, her gait uncertain. "The day will come when I can no longer bear this," she murmured so softly that it wasn't clear if she had meant to say this out loud. "I will simply jump off this balcony."

"Lucienne! Must you resort to this every time?"

She stopped, steadying her body by pressing a palm on the wall, and without turning or speaking any louder, she said, "When I am found dead on the pavement five floors below, you will have yourself and her to blame."

"If you throw yourself off the balcony," Albano said. "The only person who can ever be blamed for it will be *you*."

The next day, to his daughter savage indignation, Xandra moved into Marceline's bedroom.

All through the month, Lucienne refused to speak to Xandra or look at her. April was otherwise uneventful until one day when, upon returning to the apartment from Moshe's place, Albano found Xandra looking pale and distraught waiting for him by the front door. With her eyes, she signified to him that they needed to talk later. Albano immediately assumed that Lucienne had done or said some mean thing to her. But she and the children did not seem particularly out of sorts.

When they needed to speak about something, Albano and Xandra would arrange to bump into each other in the stairwell or on the street. A couple of minutes were usually sufficient to exchange a few words. That day, though, Xandra appeared so distraught that Albano just walked into the kitchen to see what might be the matter. She was washing the dishes, and when she saw him, she immediately said in Armenian, in a murmuring, pressing voice full of anguish, "Something has happened! Marceline came to me today. She thought nothing of it, but she said that she saw a man in town. A man who she says looked so much like me that he could be my brother!"

Albano felt dread fall upon him like a heavy cloak. "That's … simply not possible," he said.

"He is here, in Algiers, Albano," Xandra insisted. "He found us!"

At first, Albano found nothing to respond. Then he mumbled, "We left no trace."

"We must have."

"We have to be logical about this," he said, his confidence waning as he spoke. "How would he have found us when the French police couldn't?"

"My brother has his ways. He is clever."

"Even if he knew where we are, which he cannot possibly, how would he have managed to leave France in the middle of this war, come all the way to Algiers, and find us?"

"But what if he did?"

"Marceline saw a man who looked a bit like you. That means nothing."

Just as he said this, Marceline walked into the kitchen asking in that haughty, breezy tone that made her sound both detached and amused, like a femme fatale in one of those motion picture films she loved, "What's all the mystery?"

Xandra turned away toward the sink to hide her distress, and she plunged her hands into the sudsy dishwater.

"Not much," Albano answered as he left the kitchen.

That night, Albano lay rigidly in bed as the rising moon cast growing shadows on the ceiling, the dresser, the lamp, slowly creeping down the wall like ghostly figures. In the distance, the sound of an Arabic melody entered the room through the open window. In her bed, not four feet from his, Lucienne softly snored while the woman he wanted slept in Marceline's room on the other side of the apartment, out of reach of his embrace and his love.

In the morning, he would speak to Uncle Moshe. He was perhaps making too much of this. Moshe would be able to reassure him. Moshe would tell him it must be a coincidence. A look alike. A man in Algiers may or may not have had a family resemblance with Xandra. Or Marceline could have just made up the whole thing to make herself sound interesting. The chance of Hagop being in Algiers was minuscule. But as Albano struggled to find sleep, an alternate thought intruded, a thought impossible to quiet. If it was indeed Hagop that Marceline had seen, then it could only mean one thing: if Hagop was in Algiers, it was not by accident. He had looked for them and taken risks to track them down. This would mean he was even more obsessed and desperate than Albano had feared. This would mean that an undoubtedly deranged, possibly dangerous man had been following his daughter.

The following day, Moshe was not as reassuring as Albano had hoped. "Still though," Moshe said, "it might have nothing to do with you. He might have chosen to come here because Algiers has the feel of Smyrna. The pier, the town, the people, the climate. People know this. This is why many come here."

"Emptying his bank account? Leaving a paid-for apartment? Suddenly finding himself in my daughter's path? No, Moshe, I have come to understand that Hagop leaves nothing to chance."

"We have to find him," Moshe said.

"And then what?"

"And then give him what he wants."

Albano shook his head. "Over the years, I have given him my help, my friendship; he wanted none of it."

"Every man wants something."

"He wants my demise, Moshe," Albano said. "I'm afraid he wants that and only that."

Through May and June, Moshe and Albano deployed considerable resources and contacts looking for Hagop throughout Algeria and found no trace of him. No one had recorded his arrival by boat or plane. No one in the Armenian community had seen him or heard from him. As time went on, Albano relaxed. Had Hagop been in Algiers, they would have found him by now. Hagop perhaps had feared the volatile situation in France's free zone and decided, because of his immigrant status, to return to Syria, or to make his way to Italy or Spain, or any of the Greek islands.

One morning in late July, Albano awakened at dawn after a dismal night's sleep. The news from France was so distressing it was a miracle he had slept at all. He got up, washed, and dressed, careful to let Lucienne sleep, and came down the stairs of his apartment building. He stepped onto the street and walked past the city's workers and merchants, hard at work as they prepared the city for the rest of its inhabitants. He had always enjoyed walking through the streets as the city awakened, but these last few months, stepping away from the apartment felt like an escape; as though he were running for his life. He could barely stand to be home at all. They were all reeling from the terrible news from Paris, and there was nothing he could tell his children to reassure them. There were terrible rumors about the conditions in the Vel' d'Hiv, of families without food, water, or sanitation, of people shot for trying to escape, rumors of filth, of death by dehydration, of little children and old people expiring under the glass dome, when the temperature inside had risen to a deadly level in the summer heat. No, it could not be true. No French government would carry out a horror of that sort. Even Pétain's terrible government could not allow such a thing to happen.

Albano felt powerless. All he could do at this point was to continue to channel money to the Resistance, continue to hope that what the Resistance was saying was true: that they would soon see an Allied push into North Africa.

He headed for Le Beaugrenelle for his morning coffee, walking past housewives throwing soapy water at the curb, grocers arranging meager produce in neat piles, young men carrying burlap bags. The smell of freshly baked bread wafted out of the bakeries' basements. A baker and his apprentice, covered in flour and slick with sweat, took a break and shared a cigarette. Already, sleepy-faced children as young as five waited in the bread line. Today again, because of the shortages, the city would run out of bread before noon.

He thought of his happy times in Smyrna when, his pockets heavy with newspaper money, he would wait for Xandra at the street corner and help with her route to distribute pastries to the Levantine families. Where were the Levantines now? What was their country? Did their wealth and connections spare them from the worst?

Albano stopped at the newsstand just as it opened, and took the first newspaper on the pile. He arrived at Café Beaugrenelle just as Pierre, the terrace server, brought the last of the tables and chairs out.

"Just how warm do you think it will be?" Albano asked Pierre.

"At this time of the year, there is enough heat stored in the city's walls that it never quite cools down at night," Pierre responded gruffly, as though Albano were to be held personally responsible for this. "What will you have today?"

"Black coffee and toast, thank you, Pierre," Albano answered.

"No more butter; we used the last of it yesterday," Pierre said. "Only margarine. And now we have to charge extra for jam."

"I will do without," Albano said.

He leafed through the newspaper, a pointless act he insisted on out of habit rather than with expectation to gain any real insight from a news agency that continued to portray the British, Canadians, and Americans as the enemy. German and Italian armies were now at Egypt's border, he read. Hitler was closing in on him and his family. He scrutinized the pages for mentions of the accusation emanating from the BBC that over six hundred thousand Jews had been killed throughout Europe. No mention either of the other terrible rumor: the alleged convoys that moved Jews imprisoned in Drancy and Pithiviers to Dachau, a German internment camp with conditions so dire that many did not survive.

He leafed through the pages hoping for insight on the Vel' d'Hiv events. Rumor was that the roundup of Jewish families had not been ordered by the Nazis, but that it had been desired, planned, and implemented by Vichy. The most pessimistic people, even those who spoke of a deliberate act of genocide, of plans of mass extermination of the Jewish people – although most did not want to believe such a thing was possible – did not believe the French government capable of taking it upon itself to surpass the Nazis in zeal. But Albano had seen enough in his life not to discount the insanity of men. Through the centuries, insanity periodically seemed to grip men, irrespective of their race, their country, or their religion. Yes, one could point the finger to a single leader, Hitler, Mussolini. But nothing could happen without the participation of men. Humans, with their violent, hateful nature, would always find justification to follow their basest instincts. Give humanity evil leaders, and men eagerly followed.

He had been careful to keep the news surrounding the Vélodrome d'Hiver events from Lucienne. Her psyche was too fragile, he felt. But rumors found their way through the cracks underneath doors; rumors traveled in the wind. He feared Lucienne would panic and try to telephone or write acquaintances in Paris, even though he kept explaining to her that people could listen in on phone conversations or open mail and that for a few Algerian francs anyone could turn into a spy. But Lucienne had trouble remembering. His children, too, refused to face the situation, moving through this treacherous time, this foreign country, as though it were all a game. They did not realize that in the game of war there were no rules and no decency. Innocents weren't spared. Pity did not exist. Civilians suffered the most. Justice did not prevail. He had never told them what he knew, what he had seen in Smyrna, what people had done to each other. In his heart,

Gustave and Marceline were children, and he could not bear to burden them with such horrors.

Pierre brought his coffee and set it on the table. Albano did not ask for sugar, partly because Pierre seemed in a sour mood. He might as well get used to being without sugar, he thought. He returned to the newspaper. The sports events had been reduced to nothing. No Tour de France this year. No rugby championship. No soccer World Cup. Only horse races, but he had scant interest in that. Absorbed in his paper, he did not notice the man standing next to him.

"Pardon me, Monsieur," the man said in French. "Is this chair available?"

In the same instant, Albano's mind split into two. Part of his mind wondered why a stranger would ask to take his chair when the terrace was nearly empty. The second part of his mind was seized with a hollow sense of panic as he recognized the man's voice. He lifted his face and opened his mouth, but the only thing he found to say was, "Hagop!"

As stunned as if he had come face to face with a ghost, Albano watched Hagop sit across from him. Hagop's face was filled with such joy and mirth that for an instant Albano felt joy too, a fleeting emotion immediately replaced with dread.

Hagop was in Algiers. Hagop had found him.

"Are you happy to see me, old friend?" Hagop asked in a pleasant, jovial tone. "Oh, but how could you be, when you took such care to lose me?"

In shock, unable to speak, Albano took in Hagop's appearance. His face was gaunt, his cheeks hollow. His suit was dirty and tattered and torn at the knees and elbows. This was the suit of a man who had been sleeping in the streets. But what gave Albano the most anguish was the absence of his dentures. It wasn't only that without teeth Hagop looked twenty years older, it was the insanity, the drunkenness, the loss of control that would bring a man to lose an item so indispensable to self-esteem, physical comfort, and social belonging. Without his dentures, Hagop nearly gave an impression of helpless benevolence. But all it would take for rapaciousness to return to his face was a set of expensive false teeth. Albano tried to slow his breathing. He needed to appear calm. Whatever emotion he expressed, Hagop would find a way to use against him. "How did you find me?" he asked in the most even-quelled way he could.

"I always knew where you were," Hagop chuckled. He was speaking in Armenian now. "You thought you had lost me, didn't you? But you cannot, dear friend, no matter how hard you try." Hagop smiled with the open satisfaction of a man who has patiently hunted his prey and caught it.

Albano decided to appeal to Hagop's vanity to learn more. "It must have been difficult. How did you manage?"

"You told me where you would be yourself!" Hagop snapped with triumph. "That first day in Nice, when I came off the boat. That day you told me where your uncle was." Seeing Albano's confusion, he beamed. "You do not remember, do you? You told me that pig lived in Algiers." He said the word pig without anger, as though it was a natural way to refer to Uncle Moshe. "You told me this, and then you forgot. But I was paying attention! You underestimated me because my body was weak." He smiled sheepishly and lowered his voice, as though he were retelling a detective story. "But all the while, my mind was sharp. Already, back then in Nice, and even before, when you thought I was lower than dirt in Aleppo, you were already caught in my net like an unsuspecting sardine." He laughed out loud at the image.

Albano was baffled by his own folly. "I told you this?" In the warm feelings of that day in Nice when he had welcomed Hagop from the boat, he must not have thought it necessary to hide anything. In his excitement and trust, he must have said too much. He had no recollection of this.

"Of course, you were too busy thinking what a wonderful benefactor you would be to me." Hagop paused and thought. "You were too preoccupied with buying my affection. You had not started with all your lies quite yet. You forgot that you were speaking to your old friend, Hagop, the man who listens, and thinks, and forgets nothing."

Albano felt the warmth of the rising sun on him, harsh already. At the terrace tables around them, six or seven people were ordering breakfast, opening their newspapers, the waiter and busboys moving from one to the other with efficiency. "Why are you here?" Albano asked. He tried not to sound accusatory.

Hagop looked at him with amusement. "The money was running out, so I decided to go where the money was."

Was this what it was about? "Money has run out here as well," Albano said through tight lips.

Hagop laughed, too loudly. "Of course, it didn't. Not for a Jew it hasn't! Jews have a way with survival. Or rather what Jews call survival, which is more akin to thriving at the expense of others." He was saying the word Jew loudly, and the man at the next table peered at them.

Albano looked out into the street where the first of the automobiles were beginning to appear. Only expensive cars and taxis could function through the rationing and rising costs of gas. "Why did you not stay in Nice?" he asked. "You had a good life there?"

"A good life where your best friend and your own sister run away from you under cover of night?" Hagop was not bothering to smile now. Perhaps the excitement of the hunt had waned and what remained was cold anger.

"We were running from the Nazi threat," Albano protested without conviction.

"But you left me to face it alone?"

"I am sorry," Albano said, looking down at the pavement. He meant this. And yet faced with the same choice today, he would do the exact same thing. As he watched Hagop and listened to him, Albano was furious with himself. Had he interpreted the facts correctly, had he taken Marceline's words and Xandra's intuition seriously, he could have taken them all out of Algiers and moved to

Oran or Casablanca. He would not be right here, apologizing to and agreeing with Hagop. Because what else to do when facing a crazed man but agree, to gain time? There was no doubt in his mind now, and perhaps he was admitting this to himself for the first time, that for whatever reason, because of whatever seed of madness having sprouted over time, or due to whatever terrible torments he had witnessed and endured, Hagop had become insane. And his insanity was now single-mindedly powered by an obsession with him. "How long have you been in Algiers?" Albano asked with feigned casualty so that Hagop would not know that Marceline had seen him. "And how did you find me in this big city?"

"It took no time at all," Hagop said, his voice thick with contempt. "My dear friend, you are nothing if not predictable. Waking up early, sitting at café terraces the moment they open, your coffee, a single cube of sugar, your dear French newspaper, your little habits of comfort." He added meanly, "Don't forget, I know you better than your own wife does. I only had to walk around the French areas until I found you. I am a very patient man. Patient and discreet." He added with a smirk. "Invisible even to my own sister."

If Albano had any notion that Hagop did not know that Xandra was in Algiers, that hope vanished. He felt the beating of his pulse rise to his temples. As the sun now lit the buildings, heat oozed out of the walls. Hagop had been following him for weeks, perhaps months. He knew where he lived. He had followed Marceline and most likely Xandra, Gustave, and Lucienne as well. And yes, he was excellent at it if even Moshe's men had not been able to spot him. Albano realized his stupidity. The teeth! He should have mentioned to Moshe's men that the individual they were looking for might have no teeth.

"But I am tired now, I must admit," Hagop said, lighting a rolled-up cigarette and sitting back in his café chair. "I cannot keep up with some of you. Your daughter is all over town." He made a sound of disapproval through his teeth. "Tt, tt, a free spirit that one. Marches to the beat of her own drum, much like her papa."

Despite himself, Albano could not help but react. "I forbid you to intimidate my children or even cross their paths!"

Hagop feigned surprise. He displayed emotions like a second-rate actor, the seething anger and the threat leaking through each word he uttered. "I never saw you this emotional about Xandra, but make a single light comment about your daughter, or that boy of yours, the forlorn one. What does he have to be so upset about, your boy, I wonder? A life of nothing but privilege, yet he is always moping, always keeps to himself. He could use a friend is all, a real man in his life whom he could look up to. And that wife of yours? Does she still not know about Xandra, a mistress in her own house? Perhaps that could explain how sad she looks. That is the look of a woman betrayed."

"I am warning you," Albano growled.

Hagop stared at him defiantly and said in an innocent voice. "Warning me of what? What is it I am to fear? Being abandoned in the middle of a war? Well, that was done to me already, and I am not the worse for wear."

"I could cause you harm," Albano said, regretting his empty threat immediately, showing his cards when he still knew nothing of Hagop's plan.

Hagop answered, his words dripping with sarcasm. "It must be true that I am nothing and you are a powerful man. It is not as though I could reveal to the Vichy police that you are a foreign Jew, here in Algiers living under a false name."

Albano came closer to him, whispered in the hope that Hagop would start doing the same. "You are just as much an illegal immigrant in a country that doesn't welcome you as I am."

"Only you are a Jew." Hagop let the word hover between them. In his mouth, it sounded like a disease, a deformity. "And as such you are doubly unwelcome." As he spoke, Hagop's face twitched and contorted into peculiar emotions, one replacing the other in rapid succession with no rhyme or reason. The face of a madman. "And you are rich. With money stashed away somewhere, that could undoubtedly be appropriated by the authorities. As to me? What have I to fear? I am nothing to them – a vagrant, a drunkard. They think of me as one of those Arabs, so far below them. Oh, I loathe imagining what they would do to you. Arrest you? Almost certainly they would, wouldn't they?" He feigned outrage. "That's what they do to Jews these days." Now he was shaking his head with affected pity. "And would that not be a great shame? To think that a single word from me and suddenly there is no one left to protect this charming and unsuspecting family of yours, the two children ... the two wives." Now Hagop made a show of acting as though he were speaking to himself. "How long before they are destitute and lost? It would only be natural for them to want the support of the next strong man. Certainly, as your closest friend, it would be my responsibility to take over for you. Your flock, your sheep. Yes, I would do this for you. I would. All they need is a shepherd, and the responsibility would fall to me in the name of our friendship."

Albano's mind flooded with savage thoughts. Murder. That would be the only sure way to get rid of Hagop. Move. Leave the country. Blind him. Cut off his tongue. Maybe Moshe knew people who could do this. "Leave my family alone," he said. "I am warning you!"

"Do not get upset, Albano. You know I am being facetious."

"What is it you want?" Albano asked icily.

"What do I want?" Hagop sighed, and for a moment he was sincere. "It is the same thing I always wanted. Peace. But my demons will not allow for it. I cannot sleep. And when I am awake, my mind is cruel to me. It goes to and fro, to and fro, incessantly. Only wine allows me some respite."

"I can get you wine."

Hagop immediately gestured to the waiter and ordered a pitcher of wine in perfect Arabic, making it clear to Albano that he could easily pass as Algerian if he wished. "I was wondering when you would offer me something to drink." He sat back in his chair, looked around, looked up. "Sunshine at long last!" he exclaimed. When the waiter brought the wine, he said with a wink, "Sunshine in the sky, and now sunshine in my glass. What more could a man ask for?" He brought the wine to his lips and drank avidly, emptying his glass.

"If it is money you want, I will help you the best I can," Albano said.

In an instant, Hagop's expression changed to sour. "Money, money. It was always about the money to you Albano, wasn't it?" He raised his voice. "Yes, I was robbed that day when I left the cave with the satchel! Will you always hate me for it?"

"Of course, I don't," Albano said. "You've twisted everything in your mind."

Hagop wasn't listening; he had turned sullen and melancholy. "Years of hard work we did, selling those newspapers. We were filled with schemes and dreams for a wonderful future you and I, weren't we?"

"We were indeed."

"Do you remember that day on Smyrna's quayside, when you sold your first newspaper? You were shaking like a leaf. You were a weakling. You reminded me of the way your son looks, wide-eyed, eager, ignorant. And look at you now. Powerful. Rich. Only one of us got to fulfill those beautiful dreams."

"I'm not—"

"Because that never affected you, did it, that our hard-earned money went straight into the coffers of the Turkish police?" He added so loudly that people nearby turned to look at them. "Bringing wealth to my tormentors."

Albano could not believe this. "Can't you remember how I begged you not to leave the cave?"

But, as if all the reminiscing had burst a dam in Hagop's psyche, he could no longer restrain himself. Now he was sitting forward as if ready to throw himself at Albano. His face was red; he was nearly shouting, thank goodness in Armenian so that the people on the terrace did not understand what he was saying. "Had you not done the filthy things you did with my sister, the money would have remained in the cave and me with it! The gendarmes would not have arrested me. I would not have been robbed, and beaten, and taken to a slow death across the Syrian Desert!"

Pierre came to their table. "Messieurs, a little calm please, or I will ask that you take this elsewhere."

Hagop gathered himself quickly – too quickly, as though yet another man had entered his body. He smiled at the waiter and answered sweetly in very good French. "I am sorry, I was only telling my friend the plot of a motion picture film I saw." Pierre left, and Hagop continued in a wistful, whispering tone. "Who knows, had all this not happened, I might have a good life by now. The money would have helped me start an honest business. I am thinking a bakery. It was in my blood. It would have honored the memory of my father. Although I never much liked all the shelling he gave me to do, that bastard. I would have a wife perhaps, children, grandchildren."

It was hot now, uncomfortably so. Albano looked at his watch. Gustave and Marceline must be awake by now. Lucienne would rise later, usually around eleven. The terrace had filled up. In the street, people were going about their morning amidst the clanking of trolleys. The beggars had found their spots in the shade. The shoe shiner had set up his stand. The street sellers had displayed their merchandise in neat piles.

Albano would walk to Moshe's and see what could be done about leaving the country. How long would it take to pack what they had? "I can give you enough to be comfortable," he told Hagop. "You would not have to work."

Hagop seemed to consider this. "My needs are humble: a place to sleep, a few francs a day for a meal, perhaps a few bottles of wine. A new suit I would need so that I do not get arrested. What would help are identity papers, a doctor's letter explaining that I cannot enlist."

"I will get you all this," Albano lied.

Hagop called the waiter and ordered another pitcher of wine. "I like this city," he said. "The people are friendly. The climate reminds me of the old country. Yes. I could be at peace here with your generosity."

"As long as you stay away from my family and Xandra."

"You deny me the joy of seeing my own sister?"

"She is afraid of you."

Hagop had a sinister smile. "As well she should be."

Albano felt a terrible sadness drape over him. Hagop's reasoning and restraint, the ability to see things in shades of gray, were gone, his capacity to view the world from another person's standpoint washed away. Hagop had survived by clutching to notions of injustice and revenge, and he had made Albano the center of his paranoia. Trying to appeal to his reason would be a futile pursuit, and yet he tried one last time. "Please, believe me, Hagop. I never meant to hurt you or disrespect you."

"Oh, but you have," Hagop growled. "You did; you did both those things. And you know it."

"What can I do to repair the harm you feel I did to you?"

"Start by returning my sister to me."

Albano stared him down. Hagop had shown his cards, and now he had no choice but to reveal his. "Xandra is not your thing to have," he said. "Or mine. I do not own her that I can return her, as you say." He reached into his pocket, took out his wallet, and retrieved a few hundred-franc notes. "This is all I have with me. I will help you with money, but that is all I am willing to do. If you go anywhere near Xandra or any member of my family, I will do what I have to do to protect them." Hagop pocketed the money without a word. There was a cold light in his eyes. Anger, detachment, and maybe something else Albano could not read that gave him a chill. "Tell me, where are you staying?" Albano asked. "When can we see each other again to discuss details?"

At that moment, a trolley stopped a few meters from the terrace in a screech of metal on metal. A bell clanged, and a dozen people stepped out, French men in suits, Arab women carrying baskets, children in school uniforms. The trolley emptied, and new people pushed their ways inside. Just as the trolley was about to leave, Hagop got up from his chair and without another word made ten steps toward it and hopped onto the platform as casually as if he had done this his entire life. An instant later, he was gone.

Albano expected Hagop to return to the café the next day. He did not. The rest of July was a string of restless days and sleepless nights as Hagop stopped giving signs of life. Albano returned to the same café at the same time every day, but Hagop did not come. He could not find it in himself to tell Xandra that first day. He thought he would tell her the next day, once he knew how things were evolving. But day after day, Hagop did not turn up, and Albano postponed telling Xandra. This continued throughout August, with the secret he kept from Xandra turning into a festering sore, less the lie by omission it originally was and more a sign of his own cowardice and powerlessness.

The men he and Moshe hired to find Hagop learned that he had been seen among the homeless of the city, but that he had since disappeared. This could mean that Hagop was no longer in Algiers, but it also could be that he had found refuge in the Kasbah. If he were there, they would never find him. Despite the scrutiny of the French police, political refugees from every country, deserters of every army, criminals, madmen, people without identification, nationality, or religion could become invisible in the Kasbah. Hagop looked like many other men of indistinct race and age. His pale, olive skin could turn dark when exposed to the sun. Like Albano, Hagop spoke half a dozen languages, all of them with an indeterminate accent. He could blend into the crowds of the Kasbah as easily as a rattlesnake among desert rocks. When he realized this, Albano found it even more difficult to tell Xandra that her brother not only was here but that he had lost track of him.

And then, in late August, on the night of the twentieth anniversary of his marriage, everything that had kept Albano up at night was legitimized.

The last two anniversary dates had come and gone unacknowledged by him or Lucienne, but Marceline had coaxed him into making an effort. She had suggested that he should get opera tickets for the evening. This kind of tender attention was very much unlike Marceline, but instead of being suspicious, fool that he was, Albano had been touched by her thoughtfulness and congratulated himself on the change in her now that Xandra shared a room with her and on how fine and thoughtful a daughter she was turning out to be.

While they were at the opera, Marceline had escaped to meet up with a boy. Gustave, taking to heart his mission to keep an eye on her, a mission Albano himself had senselessly assigned, had followed her all the way to the foot of the Kasbah where he had been attacked and brutally beaten by a group of kids. The hospital had called them at the apartment. Xandra had answered the telephone and managed to reach them at the opera house. He and Lucienne had rushed to the hospital where the details of Marceline's preposterous story had been revealed to them: the manipulation of the opera tickets, Marceline dressed as an Arab woman, Gustave following Marceline all the way to the Kasbah, the Muslim young man Marceline was meeting, the assailants stopped just in time by the young man who was unjustly taken to jail while the assailants disappeared into the night.

As he sat by Gustave's hospital bed, Albano's heart felt as though it would burst with sadness at the sight of his boy hurt so badly. Also, from the moment he heard the attack had taken place near the Kasbah, he knew with certainty what had happened. And what had happened was far graver than his children's mischief and ill-conceived strategy. This was not a random attack. Hagop, he knew it, was at the root of this! Hagop had orchestrated this. Hagop had hired the group of kids who had done this to his boy.

They left Gustave to spend the night at the hospital. In the taxi back to the apartment he, Lucienne, and Marceline did not exchange a word. When they got home, Xandra, her eyes red from crying, was waiting for them by the door. "Gustave will be alright," he told her, as Xandra wept with relief.

"You!" Lucienne screamed, pointing her index finger inches from Xandra's face. "What business do you have crying? You are the one who did this! You were supposed to watch my daughter. She was your responsibility! You let Marceline leave, and you caused Gustave to be harmed. He could have died, and it would be your fault!" Xandra put her face in her hands. "Pack your things!" Lucienne shouted. "I want you out of the house this minute!"

"But, Lucienne!" Albano protested.

"She is not spending another night here. I don't care if she sleeps in the gutter."

Xandra sobbed. Albano looked from Lucienne to Xandra, and his heart broke in tinier pieces still. He said, "Lucienne, please don't be this way."

"This way?" Lucienne shouted. "I tell you what way I am. I will jump off this balcony! That is the way I am!"

"Mother!" Marceline said, trying to take her arm. But Lucienne shook herself free. Her eyes were red, her skin pale and blotchy.

"You have poisoned this family!" Lucienne shouted at Xandra.

"Mother, it's not Xandra's fault, it's my fault," Marceline implored.

But Lucienne would not stop. "I will kill myself, Alban! I will throw myself down five stories if she is not out of here in an hour! Then it will be clear. You will have made your choice." Lucienne ran to her room and slammed the door.

"Come," Albano told Xandra, and they went into the kitchen, leaving Marceline on the other side of the door.

"She is right," Xandra sobbed. "I saw Marceline leave. I said nothing."

"It is only one person's fault, and I will get to the bottom of it. There was nothing any of us could have done."

"What do you mean?"

"For now, all I know is that Lucienne is mad enough to endanger herself or draw even more attention to us than this episode already has."

"Do you think she would jump?"

"It's not her I want to protect," he admitted. "It's you."

"What do you mean?"

"Pack your things, and I will take you to a hotel. We'll leave in one hour. I will take you to a hotel, so he won't know where you are. Lucienne will think it is because she fired you."

"He? Who do you mean?"

"There is something I need to tell you. But not now. Now you need to pack your things, and we will go."

"Albano, I think Lucienne will never let me back in."

"Maybe it is for the best."

"But the children? How will I see the children?"

"You can see the children."

In a small voice, she said, "When I'm gone from their lives, will they ever think of looking for me?"

Albano's heart sank. "It will change nothing," he assured her. But he didn't believe his own words.

Xandra shook her head, dabbed her eyes, and in a tone that was clear-headed and without a trace of bitterness said, "The children don't need me anymore."

It was past midnight when Albano and Xandra arrived at the hotel. He asked for a room and paid for a week in advance. The manager asked him to write down his name and address and sign the register, then he took his money without looking at either of them and retreated to his office. Albano held the pen above the page, wondering what name to give, and then decided to write down his own first and last name.

This was in no way the kind of expensive hotel he could have afforded before the war, and there was no bellman to help with the luggage, no elevator. Albano grabbed Xandra's bags and walked up the three sets of stairs with Xandra following a few steps behind. The stairwell smelled of tobacco and strong detergent, masking the odors of human filth. Until he found something better, Albano felt Xandra would be safe here and comfortable. But this was not home. She was losing her home and the only family she had. She was being fired from her own family, by her own family. Thank God, she did not know how the children felt. They did not deserve her. He did not deserve her.

Albano opened the door to the hotel room. It was modest but clean, and the wallpaper and bedspread appeared to be in good condition. Xandra went from the bedroom to the bathroom, turning on lights, inspecting. "This is good," she said with her usual pragmatism.

Albano placed the bags atop the dresser, and Xandra began to take her things out, placing them inside the drawers. He saw her hold the cloth that contained the knife and said nothing when she placed it in the drawer of the nightstand. He admired her lovely silhouette, the thick braid of her hair. Xandra owned so few things that they took up hardly any room inside the dresser. "Your daughter is in love," she said as she folded the last of her shawls and placed them in the drawer.

Albano shrugged, "She knows all too well she can't be with a Muslim."

Xandra faced him. "If she loves him, she should be with him."

Albano frowned, confused. "But her life would be too difficult."

"A loveless life is more difficult."

"Lucienne wants so much more for her."

"So much more than love?" Xandra asked with a smile. "What else of importance is there?"

Albano went to sit at the single chair that faced a tiny desk. At least this was a room with real furniture. He tried to take in what her life would be in this room. She, so industrious, would have nothing to do. The most important part was to hide her from Hagop. Again, he felt that terrible guilt in his belly. He needed to tell Xandra the truth. "Marceline has a bright future for herself after the war," he said. "She cannot throw her opportunities away."

"There was no future for us, and yet we are together," Xandra said as she took out something white folded between sheets of thin paper.

"Do you know if she is promiscuous with this boy?"

"I would think yes, but I don't know."

Albano sighed, discouraged, but not finding himself angry or surprised. "How long have you known this?"

"Women are changing, along with the world," Xandra said. "They are doing what they please, not caring about who will judge them."

"You sound like Marceline."

"Modern women want to follow their hearts and do not care about notions of decency invented by men."

"It does not scandalize you?"

She smiled. "What scandalizes me has changed."

He could not help but tease her. "Hmmm. I so wish this was true."

Xandra gave him that playful smile she used just with him, which had the power to lift him out of just about any mood.

She went into the bathroom. Albano stood up from the chair and patted the bed. It was a good bed. Not too soft, not too firm. He wondered about the kinds of things he might need to buy to make the room more comfortable. In the bathroom, there was the clanging of glass jars as Xandra placed her things on the shelf above the sink: the one oil she used for her hair, her soap, all elements that contributed to the alchemy of Xandra, the scent Albano equated with love mixed in with unrequited lust. And suddenly he felt embarrassed. Or shy. Yes, shy was more like it. It was only the two of them in this hotel room, past midnight, Xandra in that bathroom, and Albano standing by the bed. "This room is only until I find an apartment," he called. "Something with a nice window and a balcony." The water was running; he was not sure that she had heard him. After all that had happened today, would it be insensitive to try to kiss her, he wondered? No, of course, he must not. Not with the war, and Gustave in the hospital, and Lucienne's morbidity, and Xandra being fired, and his daughter on a nightly rendezvous with a Muslim in the most dangerous part of town. Kissing was out of the question in such circumstances, regardless of how amorous he might suddenly feel.

His thoughts came to a halt when he saw that Xandra was standing by the bathroom door, smiling at him. Her hair, now unbraided, floated down alongside her body. She had changed into a thin white gown that left her shoulders, neck, and arms bare. She looked like a sumptuous goddess. "You look ... extraordinary," he said. His throat constricted suddenly. It was all too much. This desire felt as wild as it had been when he was a young man, and she was a young woman, and they had lived together in the cave.

Defying any possible scenario his imagination could have conjured up, Xandra came to stand right in front of him, took his hand, and placed it on her belly and said, "I am worried, Albano."

His hand on her, he felt her warmth through the thin gown. Her hair. Her body. So close to his. "You ... you are worried?"

"About letting you see my body."

"I ... I'm not worried about that," he stuttered, suddenly understanding that something had shifted.

"I am burned."

"I am in love with you and your burns!"

Xandra laughed, "You cannot love my burns."

"I love them!" he exclaimed. "I love all of them!" And to illustrate this, he began to kiss her burned hand and kiss every inch of her burned arm, all the way to the side of her neck and burned cheek.

"But I am more worried that there will not be a tomorrow," Xandra murmured, taking his head between her hands and placing it against her chest. She kissed the top of his hair. "The world is collapsing around us, and I don't want to be afraid of the same things anymore."

And so, Albano, trying to absorb it all, took her wonderful, warm body in his arms. When they began to make love, it was as though no time had passed since the cave at all.

Afterward, they stayed in bed, their bodies entwined. Albano held Xandra in his arms, not moving for fear of breaking the spell. But after a while, he could not wait any longer. "I have not been truthful with you. Please forgive me. I was only trying to spare you this until I knew what to do but … there is something I must tell you."

"Hagop is in Algiers," Xandra said.

"How did you know?"

"You did not believe it, but I knew it was him from the moment Marceline told me about the man she saw. I have been expecting this. And then you were tormented the last few weeks. So, I knew."

"I was only trying not to frighten you."

"I know."

"He came to me at the end of July," Albano said, sitting up in bed. "He had lost his teeth; he looked bedraggled like he had been sleeping in the streets. He was emotional, but not in any kind of normal way." Albano hesitated. "He looked deranged, Xandra."

"Did he say how he found us?"

"It was because of my carelessness," he admitted. "I guess I had told him that Uncle Moshe was in Algiers when I first saw him in Nice. I don't even remember saying this to him."

"You could not have known the future."

"Moshe and I hired men to look for him, and when they did not find him, part of me wanted to believe he wasn't here. But even now that I have seen him and I know for a fact that he is in town, our men can't find him. He is somewhere in the city, my darling."

"Did he say what he wants?"

Albano sank back on the pillow, and turning toward Xandra so their faces nearly touched, he said, "I think he was involved in what happened to Gustave."

Xandra blinked, fright and anger washing over her face at the same moment. "How?" she asked.

"The police said that this felt like an organized attack. These kinds of things don't usually happen otherwise, they said. Gustave was ambushed at that bridge. This was a planned attack. Someone paid those boys."

"Hagop did this?" Xandra said in a hollow voice.

"Who else would wish my family harm? Hagop knows where we live. It's possible he followed Gustave all the way from our apartment to the Kasbah. While Gustave waited at the foot of the Kasbah, Hagop hired a mob of boys and paid them."

"Do you believe him so full of hatred?"

"Full of hatred or insane."

"To hurt an innocent boy like Gustave. That pig!" Xandra's face was hard with anger.

"We were lucky because the young man who was with Marceline knew those kids, and the kids knew him. The moment he intervened, they ran away, when they could have easily overpowered all three of them."

"The Muslim boy Marceline loves?"

"Without him, Marceline could have been hurt as well. And Gustave could have been hurt even worse."

"If you are correct about this, Hagop must be stopped."

"Even if we knew where he is, how would we stop him? I cannot call the police on him, even if I have proof, because he knows too much about us. And where would I even find him? I don't think he has papers or even an identity card. Already he can blend into this city so well that even you and I cannot recognize him when he follows us. No, the only way is to reason with him. Appease him. Give him whatever money I have. Keep him drunk. I don't know."

"And what if he cannot be appeased?"

"That is one of the reasons I think it is better you are here instead of the apartment. It is for you I fear the most. That's why I did not fight Lucienne when she fired you. I want you in this hotel. For the time being, you are safest here."

****

Through the end of summer and early fall, as Gustave's cuts and broken bones healed, and Lucienne sank deeper into her depression, and Marceline was forbidden to leave the apartment, Albano and Xandra spent entire, wonderful afternoons together as lovers.

As the weather cooled and found its way through the wooden shutters into the hotel room, they ate in bed, took baths, rediscovered each other's bodies, and forgot the world. His love for Xandra burst out of him. He could not have enough of her presence, of her touch, of her scent, of her body. Now the apartment did not feel like home to Albano, but like work that he must return to each day, going through the motions until he could run back to Xandra. He felt differently about his family. Seeing Gustave's bruised face, he should have felt sadness for his son, but instead, he felt annoyed by his fragility. The emotion he felt with Marceline was no longer pride and amazement but resentment at her impulsiveness, her unwarranted sense of superiority over them all, and her indifference toward Xandra. As for Lucienne, he should have felt compassion, but instead, he felt impatience and irritation.

When Albano wasn't with Xandra, he worried about her safety. He was terrified that Hagop would follow him and find the hotel. He took the utmost care not to be followed. Walking back and forth between the hotel and the apartment, he took long, circuitous routes, stopping at shops and cafés along the way, checking behind him every few meters. He took an hour to get there when the hotel was ten minutes away. He wore a disguise. He wrapped himself in a burnous to walk to and from the hotel. He would leave the apartment, find a café's bathroom to change into, and walk to the hotel dressed as an Arab man. He made sure to have his hood covering his eyes, which he knew to be his most distinct feature. On the way back, he would do the same in reverse. If Hagop could disappear into an Algerian crowd, so could he.

Perhaps it was a ridiculous disguise, one that might fool only the French for whom everyone with Semitic features looked the same. But would it fool Hagop for long? And was Hagop even still in Algiers? For all he knew, he had left the country. Moshe's men had not ceased sifting through the city, but Hagop had not given any sign of life since that morning in July, over three months ago. As time went on without any sign of him, Albano found himself wondering if he had not imagined Hagop's involvement in the beating. Perhaps he had overestimated Hagop's desire to harm them or his ability to do so. Could the attack on Gustave have been a random act of hatred by a random group of kids? Hagop had no connections, had little money, and had to avoid the police for fear of being thrown in jail for not having papers. If he had wanted something from him, money or favors, would he not have come to him by now?

One afternoon in late October, Albano left the apartment and made his convoluted route to the hotel, stopping at a café to change into his burnous. Once at the hotel, he walked past the clerk who never paid him any attention, across the tiny, dark lobby and up to Xandra's room, and as usual, he knocked at her door.

Xandra did not open. He knocked again. After knocking several times and wondering what was wrong, he heard the door unlock and saw it open. Xandra now stood at the door with unusual stillness. She did not open it all the way. Her face was taut. Immediately he read in her eyes a command not to enter. He put his hand on the door, expecting Xandra to let him in, but she made a barrier with her body, and so he nearly had to push past her to enter the room. "What is happening?" he asked.

What he saw inside took the air out of his lungs.

Hagop was sitting on Xandra's bed, his back resting against the pillow, one leg casually crossed over the other, his shoes on. He was dressed elegantly, in loose breeches and a white shirt. In his hand was a gun aimed at them.

"It is me!" Hagop said jovially. "*I* am what is happening!" Albano looked from Hagop to the gun in his hand to Xandra, who remained absolutely still as if she was crossing paths with a scorpion. "My sister and I were waiting for you." Hagop waved the gun loosely. "You," he told Xandra, signaling to a spot on the floor beneath the window to the left side of the bed, "sit by me." Xandra obediently went to the bed and sat on the floor. Now she crouched below the window in the narrow space between the wall and the bed, and her face was at the level of the mattress. She looked up at Albano. She was afraid, but calm, her eyes deliberately without expression.

"What do you want from us?" Albano said when he was able to make a sound. He was standing between the door and the bed as Hagop sat on the bed, his legs extended, his back propped by a pillow as if he were waiting to be served breakfast in bed.

"Why are you so hostile?" Hagop said with a honeyed voice. "I am just a brother visiting his sister."

"Then put down that thing."

Hagop waved the gun as though it was a toy, making big arm gestures as he spoke. "This, you mean? I bought it with the last of the money you gave me. A man cannot be too prudent in this treacherous city."

From the cadence of his speech, the way he bobbed his head slowly, Albano thought that perhaps Hagop was drunk. But it could just as well be an act. When it is coiled, and still as stone, the rattlesnake is still an instant away from striking. "What is it you want from us?"

"What a hospitable man you are; thank you for asking, brother. Do you have wine here? I am parched. And food?" He turned to Xandra and said harshly, "Have you any food, woman?"

Xandra looked at Albano, who nodded to indicate it was best to oblige. "I have some food in there," she said softly, pointing to the drawer of the bedside table, the drawer that held the knife. Albano's stomach dropped. He held his breath as Xandra foraged through the drawer, and breathed again when she only retrieved small packages wrapped in paper. She unwrapped them. One contained dried fruit, the other one, bread. She set those on a tray, which she placed on the bed. Hagop held the gun loosely in his hand, as though he had forgotten it was even there. With his other hand, he picked at the food. He laughed. "Look at me, reclining and dining like an Ottoman prince." He turned to Xandra. "You, sit back down." Xandra returned to crouch on the floor to his left of the bed. Why was she crouching and not sitting Albano wondered briefly?

Albano stood by the door, motionless, his head still covered by the woolen hood. There was no air in the room, and yet the sweat that poured down his neck felt like ice. Was the gun loaded? Hagop loved being dramatic.

Whatever it was Hagop wanted, he was in no hurry to tell them. He was enjoying himself or at least wanted to give that impression. "Was this food for the two of you?" he cooed. "You know what this room reminds me of? It reminds me of the cave, that cozy little love nest you had made for yourselves, where you waited for me to have my back turned so that you could do your filth." He said this last word with rage and then tore at the bread with his teeth, savagely. Because now the teeth were back, white and gleaming. That day at the café, the gummy mouth, the hollowed-out cheeks, that air of indigence and weakness, it all had been another game of manipulation.

But then, in the stifling heat, as Xandra crouched by the bed, and Hagop made big smacking chewing sounds, Albano could not wait anymore. "Did you have something to do with my boy being attacked?" he said.

Hagop gave him a hurt look. "Come on now; why would I do such an evil thing to a boy?"

"So, you know about it?"

"How could have I orchestrated such a thing? Does it not seem too complicated for someone like me?" He shook his head in self-admiration. "That would be the work of a mastermind." He popped a nut in his mouth with unmasked contentment. "Imagine my surprise when I saw your boy by his bicycle at the foot of the Kasbah. I had not planned on anything. And here he was, waiting and waiting, that stupid boy. Asking for it, really. A scraggly boy. A Jew among Muslims. I waited and watched him, and then night fell, and he was still there! I could hardly believe he would be so foolish, and for what? To protect his sister? Is that what he was trying to do? Is that why he was there? Because that boy would not know how to protect himself if a kitten wanted to scratch him."

Xandra and Albano briefly looked at each other. "It was you. I was right. You paid those boys to beat my son?" Albano only asked.

Hagop smiled modestly, as though he were being recognized for a remarkable deed and was too humble to accept praise. Anger rushed to the tips of Albano's fingers, a wild tingling. His neck throbbed with the desire to pounce. Albano, attuned to Xandra's emotions, felt in her a surge of anger and desperation that matched his. Her eyes burned with such an intense fire that he wondered if she might be about to be sick. He felt like he was about to be sick. Xandra's head was inches away from the gun. It would be madness for Albano to make the slightest move. "If someone had not interfered, my son might have been beaten to death!" Albano said between clenched teeth. "Is that what you wanted?"

Albano's anger only resulted in Hagop sitting upright in bed and pushing the tip of the gun to Xandra's face. Albano and Xandra froze. Hagop was pale now, his smile gone. "I never pretended to be a good man. That's the difference between you and me, Albano. When I commit a crime, I might lie about it so as not to get into trouble, but I do not lie to myself. I believe this makes me a better man in fact. A more honorable one."

His eyes on the gun, Albano hoped to appeal to Hagop's reason and asked softly, "A boy of seventeen who did nothing to you? A child. If you wanted to hurt me, why did you attack him?"

"Think about this, my brother. If I were to kill you, it would be the end of your suffering. Whereas if I hurt those you love, your suffering would only increase." Xandra and Albano exchanged a look. Filled with melodrama and bitterness for his circumstances, Hagop added, "I thought for a long time that I was the one who should die. It would serve no justice, but perhaps then my suffering would stop." Hagop, deeply moved by his own words, forgot to aim the gun at Xandra. As soon as the metal no longer touched her skin, Albano relaxed, and he could think again. Hagop's eyes filled with tears of self-pity. "Easier said than done. Though I might wish for death at times, it simply won't happen on its own. This old body won't quit. And it has needs, this body," he said, thumping his heart with his fist. "It has *wants*. No, it is my soul that is tormenting me. An obsession. Yes. You could call it that." Hagop's voice broke. "Oh, my brother, why do I love you so and hate you so? Why are you to me crueler than any Turkish jailor?"

Albano blinked, trying to take in the absurdity of the accusation, the profession of love, the quick succession of bizarre emotions. "You know I am not trying to be cruel—"

"You are!" Hagop shouted. "By your mere existence, you are. Your handsome face, your wealth, your good fortune at every turn. And then, luring my sister into a life of servitude and sin! And she is too mesmerized by you to even rebel." He shook his head. "She is under your spell, Albano, as I am. But to her it is pleasurable, and to me, it is relentless torture."

Xandra looked at Albano intently. Something electric passed between them, the meaning of which he did not decipher. She was telling him something – a warning. "I will give you whatever money I have," Albano said. "There is money in the apartment. I have diamonds. Not many, but I still have a few. Please put down this thing."

"Good!" Hagop snickered. "I want all of it. All of it, you hear me? Your diamonds, your gold. Let your family live under bridges and sleep on beaches. How about that for a change?"

"Anything you want. Now please, let Xandra go."

"You go fetch the money first," Hagop said impatiently. He pointed to the door with his gun. "What are you waiting for? Go! Hustle up!"

"Xandra will go to my apartment," Albano said hurriedly. "She knows where to find it. She'll get the money and bring it back here." This was a lie. There was little money at the apartment, and the diamonds were at Moshe's. But once Xandra was out of the hotel room, Albano would pounce on Hagop. He would punch him, grab the gun, and throw it out the window; from there he would find a way to overpower Hagop. "Keep me here as hostage," he added, "while Xandra goes to get all the money."

"No! Not that!" Hagop loudly whined like a toddler on the verge of a tantrum. "You go, and she will be my hostage." Saying so, Hagop leaped at Xandra, grabbed her by her hair, and shoved the gun hard into the flesh of her neck.

"I will go. Please don't hurt her," Albano murmured.

Hagop only yanked Xandra's hair harder, brought her head closer to his, and smiled like a demon.

Had Hagop been less self-admiring, he might have noticed Xandra's sudden pallor, the combustion in her eyes, the grip of her hand even as she, like a prey who knows that resisting is futile, appeared to go limp under his touch. She looked as though a thousand springs had wound up at once inside her body.

Albano read the message in Xandra's eyes. She was telling Albano what to do. She was telling him to go.

Now that Xandra had given her that command, Albano knew he would go and fetch every bit of fortune he had left and that he would trade it for Xandra. He would imperil his family, render them destitute, all to rescue her.

But had Albano not been so afraid for Xandra, he would have remembered that a woman capable of surviving a stillbirth, a fire, and the destruction of a city all on her own, a woman who was unrelenting as she searched for him, a woman who endured years of another woman's contempt and raised that woman's children nonetheless, a woman who would resist his sexual advances until she reconciled them with her sense of right and wrong might not need rescuing. Such a woman was in fact formidable. But at that moment, Albano did not remember this, or perhaps he did not know what she was capable of. Because when a situation calls for fight or flight, there is no telling which constitution will choose which. Sometimes the strong man will run, and the quiet woman will be the one to coil and strike.

One moment later, Albano was in the hallway and had his ear against the door. Now that Xandra and Hagop were inside and he was outside, the thought of walking away even for an instant when Xandra was in a room with a madman waving a gun was beyond his strength. Hagop might try to rape her. He might decide to make good on his threat to hurt her in order to hurt him. Albano placed his ear on the door and listened in, his pulse beating hard against his temple. The hallway was empty. It was cooler there than inside the room and very dark. He could not budge, as though both his feet were nailed to the floor. He listened. He heard Hagop's order. "Give me more food, woman."

Albano sensed in his bones what was about to happen, and yet his reason rejected the idea: the knife.

He heard something. He did not know what he heard. Rustling. Gurgling. Sighing. All very strange noises that he probably imagined because it was all very quiet at the same time. This was followed by a minute of complete silence when he heard only the sound of his heartbeat. And then there were footsteps. The door cracked open, and it was Xandra opening for him. "Albano," she murmured.

"I didn't go yet."

"Come inside," she said.

That's when he saw the blood on her dress. "Xandra!"

"It's not my blood," she whispered as she pulled him inside and shut the door behind them. What he saw, Albano could not believe. He fell to his knees with shock. Hagop was on the bed. His eyes were open. Blood came down in a slow rivulet along the left side of his chest; the gun handle rested in his open palm. There was a knife planted in his heart. Xandra was pale and still as a tree. "There was no other choice," she said.

If Hagop had a chance to fire it, he had not taken it. It seemed to have happened in an instant, in silence, without a struggle. "What have we done?" Albano said in a voice barely above a murmur.

"I did this," Xandra said calmly. "Not you."

"But how … how did this happen?"

"He asked me for more food, and so I went to the drawer and took the knife. I was so scared, Albano. But I was more afraid of him than I was of killing him. And so, I did it."

"By God, Xandra! How could you? How did you?"

"The blade went in," she said, not believing it herself. "It just did, between his ribs, into his heart. He had no time to do anything. Or else he didn't choose to fight me." She paused and looked up at Albano.

"Mon Dieu," he whispered.

"I had thought about it before," Xandra said. "Where to strike. Between the ribs. Into the heart."

In disbelief, Albano echoed, "Into the heart."

On the bed, Hagop, dressed in white against the white sheet and the white wall, the small crucifix just above him, had his dead eyes fixed on nothing. He looked as though he were enacting a scene in a Caravaggio painting. The only sign of life in the scene was the expanding crimson blotch on his chest and the mattress. It struck Albano how Hagop's face, his body, gave a feeling of relaxation, as though the demon that possessed him had drained out of him and what was left was a lovely sense of peace.

As though she could read his thoughts, Xandra said, "It was fast, but in his eyes, as he expired, I could see that my brother welcomed death." Xandra went to Hagop and, placing her palm gently on his face, closed his eyes shut. She said a prayer and, looking at the crucifix above the bed, signed herself. Albano felt a profound hollowness in him. He felt confusion, paralysis, but no sadness. Just relief, for now. No matter the future, they were freed from Hagop.

"We will go to the police together," Albano said. "We'll say he attacked you and so I stabbed him in self-defense."

"I did this," Xandra said, turning to him. "I am unhurt, and he is dead. No one screamed. No one called for help. I am a murderess now."

Albano looked at Hagop's body, and the immensity of what had just taken place hit him at last. He turned frantic. "We'll topple furniture! We'll tear your dress so that it looks like an attack! You'll scream, and then people from the other rooms will come, and I will tell them I came in and defended you. We can move his body to the floor. Some of your hair could be in his hands … They will fetch the police and—"

Xandra was perfectly calm. "No police," she said. "You saw what they do to innocent people like this boy who helped Gustave. We will leave the body where it is. In a few days, it will start smelling. This gives me time to run away. You make sure that no one sees you leave, and you return to the apartment. The only time people saw you here in regular clothes is when you first brought me. But there is an explanation for that. You were helping me move in. The other times you came dressed as an Arab man. If the police come to you, tell them you have not seen me since you dropped me off."

"Uncle Moshe will help us hide you."

"I cannot hide anywhere in this city. Everyone in this hotel saw my scars."

"Then Moshe can smuggle us out of the country."

"Us?"

"To Greece, or Corsica, or Cypress."

"Wherever I go, you cannot come with me, or people will assume you are guilty. No, you must stay."

"I'm not letting you run away to some strange country while I stay in Algiers."

"If I go to jail, you won't be with me there either. And if you are crazy enough to accept the blame, then you will be sent to prison, and your family and I will be without you."

"I don't … I can't—"

"Listen to me," she said imperiously. "I did this because someone had to, and I didn't want it to be you. I did this so that you would not go to prison."

"I don't know that I could have killed him. I don't think I would have been capable."

She caressed his cheek, lovingly. "I know," she said.

****

Albano stood on the balcony looking at another balcony on the building on the opposite side of the street where a middle-aged French woman in incongruous pearls and curlers was tending to chickens in a cage. She took their eggs and gave them something to eat. In wartime, people did what they had to do.

He was trying to calm down. Inside the apartment, Lucienne had just taken one of her pills for nerves, and Gustave and Marceline were on separate ends of the living room, red in the face and disheveled. There had been another fight. This time, Gustave had thrown himself at his sister, and Albano had to jump in to separate them. It was as though the war outside also raged in their heart. Rather than rally against a common threat, they mistook the enemy for each other.

The Allied invasion was imminent. An American general had arrived via submarine and conversed with top-ranking Resistance organizers. Now they all waited for the date. In a matter of weeks, perhaps days, the Allied forces would attempt to take the country. Marceline did not know how dangerous the times were, but regardless, she had once again disobeyed and lied. She had taken a train to the Agha prison to see that Muslim boy. Someone he knew had spotted her and called Albano right away.

If Albano could not do the simple thing of helping his children be reasonable, what hope was there? He raised his eyes to the implacably blue sky. Xandra, he asked the sky, do you feel as lost without me as I am without you?

He wished it would be more of a comfort to him to know that Xandra was safe, protected by friends of Moshe. It was only three days since Hagop's death, three days since she had taken the boat to Portugal. A lifetime. An eternity. Portugal was for the moment neutral in the war, and he and Moshe had Jewish friends there, taking refuge. The same fishing boat that had brought Albano and his family from Nice to Algiers was always moored at an Algiers fishing dock, ready to smuggle people in or out of the country at a moment's notice, in case the Allied invasion failed, or if things got too dangerous in Algeria. Xandra had been whisked onto the boat and out of the country in a matter of hours. Three days without Xandra, and already Albano could not bear the distance between them. One moment he had been on his way to spend an afternoon with the woman he loved, and the next moment she was gone, possibly forever.

Since Hagop's death, Albano had hardly left the apartment. He was waiting for a telephone call from Xandra, although Moshe had told her not to make contact for now. But mostly Albano needed to be present when the police came knocking at their door.

Because the police would come; of this he was certain. He had signed the registry the day he had checked Xandra into the hotel. He had disguised himself, made sure to cover his tracks, but the police would link Xandra to his family sooner or later. He wished he could warn Lucienne and the children, explain to them what had happened, tell them that the police would invariably come, and what story they should all stick to. But it occurred to him that real ignorance was preferable to a feigned one.

What had happened replayed in his mind without mercy: Hagop on Xandra's bed, the knife in his chest; he, haggard and reeling, stepping out of the hotel in broad daylight dressed as an Arab man, hiding his face, and then melting into the noon crowd. He had walked in circles in the city, hiding in entryways every few blocks to make sure no one followed him. After an hour, he had entered a public urinal and stepped out looking once again like a Frenchman in a white shirt and wool pants. He had tossed his djellaba and burnous on a pile of trash and had climbed on the first bus. From there he had taken a second bus and a third. He had sat on garden benches and pretended to look at merchandise at the outdoor market. He had sat at cafés. He had had conversations with people in the street so that there would be a trace of his whereabouts that day. Two hours later, he had, at last, walked to Moshe's apartment and told him everything.

Meanwhile, Xandra, following their plan, had waited in the hotel room, steps from her brother's dead body. She had removed her bloody clothes, packed a few possessions, and waited for nightfall. At night, she had wrapped herself in black and walked to the fishing dock where Moshe's boat awaited her.

Albano had not seen Xandra off as he had promised her. Moshe had not let him, insisting that he needed an alibi and must at once rush back home and make sure everyone saw him there. The police would have a hard time figuring out the exact time of death, but he could not risk being away for another minute; neither could he be seen at the fishing dock. There were spies everywhere, and they could not take the chance of divulging their escape strategy.

He and Xandra had not said goodbye. They had not made a single plan for the future.

Across the street, the chickens on the neighbor's balcony pecked and fought for the food. It was only a matter of another day, two at the most, before the stench of Hagop's decomposing corpse would find its way below Xandra's hotel room door and through the open window, and the process of alerting the authorities would be set in motion. Perhaps Hagop's body was already found, and the police were on their way.

Albano was trying to come up with a plan to see Xandra, but he could not think straight. When had his plans ever made a positive difference? Over the course of his life, how much control did he have over fate? Every encounter, every action of his life had led to Hagop's body rotting ignominiously in that hotel room. Everything that had happened to him and everything that was about to happen now seemed inevitable: Smyrna, Uncle Moshe, Hagop, Xandra, the baby, the fire, the rescue, France, Lucienne … his children. Even his children had not been shaped by him. They were creatures firmly planted in this mad century and had been shaped, no, distorted, by the world's xenophobia, anti-Semitism, Hitler, the war, as well as the years of abundance and entitlement before the war. Albano had been a fool to think he had power in any of this. Their story, and his story, had long been written by God, who writes every story. Each time Albano had attempted something, each time he had believed himself in control, he had had as much influence over his existence as a bit of straw tumbled by the wind, and God had laughed.

An evil man wanted to conquer the world and destroy his race. His beloved friend had become demented. His wife was suicidal. His children risked their lives and tore each other apart. The woman he loved was a murderer. The police would come any moment to arrest him for the crime. And he had a decision to make, a decision that did not involve a futile attempt at controlling other people's destiny, only his own.

"Tell me, God. What should I do?" he asked the sky.

There was a sound like a flag flapping in the wind, a wide shadow came across the sky, and a powerful gust of air ruffled his hair. He jumped back, startled. A massive pelican had appeared, flown straight at him, and nearly touched him with his wing, and now, with a few more beatings of its dinosaur-like wings, it hovered above him a few feet away. The vision was so extraordinary that Albano opened his mouth to call the family. But before he could utter a single sound, the bird soared above the building and, in an instant, disappeared.

"Did you see that?" he called out to his family inside. But no one heard him.

Had God meant to speak to him alone?

His anger at Marceline and Gustave vanished. Air entered his lungs for what seemed to be the first time in days. Yes, Marceline was lying again. Of course, she was. She lied because she was pulled by her fate, unconscious of it, as they all were. His children, like him, were nothing more than cogs in the gears of life. Who was Albano to decide what they should do or not do, whom they should see, what they should say, where they should go, whom they must love when God's grand design was all that counted?

Albano looked down at the street. A police automobile had come abruptly to a stop in front of the building. Two men, one in police uniform, the other in civilian clothes, hopped out and hurried inside. Albano felt the dread of being caught. He had only a few minutes to regain his composure before they knocked at the front the door.

He turned on his feet and entered the living room. His eyes adjusted to the dim light. Gustave and Marceline were just as he had left them, each on opposite sides of the living room like boxers ready for their next round. Lucienne was fanning herself, looking absent or overwhelmed.

The knock at the door was so loud that they all jumped, even him.

His mouth dry and palms wet, Albano walked across the apartment and went to open the door.

On the doorstep was the policeman in uniform accompanied by the man in a suit and hat. But instead of handcuffing him, they removed their hats and asked if they could come inside, and Albano understood that they were not here to arrest him. This was an investigation.

The detective sat in one of the armchairs. The policeman stood. Both had thick mustaches. Someone offered them water. Albano put all of his concentration into appearing normal.

A man had been murdered in Xandra's hotel room, the detective explained. Xandra was nowhere to be found and thus was their prime suspect. The hotel records showed that Albano had paid for her room a month in advance. What exactly was the nature of their acquaintance with the suspect?

Albano did his best to match his family's reaction and painted his face into an expression of dismay. He hoped the children and Lucienne paid attention to the lies he was about to give the detective. They all needed to corroborate to keep the secret of their identity intact. It would not take much for an overzealous cop to start digging into their past and find inconsistencies. Xandra was Armenian, he told the detective. They did not know where she was born or how long she had lived in Algeria. She had answered an advertisement and had worked for them for two years. She had lived in a maid's room upstairs. From there, Albano went on with the truth. She had moved into the apartment to sleep in her daughter's room. But their daughter had run out at night, had broken curfew to see a boy, and Xandra had been fired for letting her. Albano went on to describe the attack at the Kasbah. There was a police report; the detective could look this up. That same night, Albano explained, he had taken Xandra to the hotel, paid for a month in advance, and given her a sum equivalent to a month's wages, and they had not heard from her since.

The children were shocked and swore of Xandra's innocence, although her disappearance wasn't anything they could explain to the police. Even Lucienne admitted that Xandra was incapable of murder. More things were said. Marceline was arrogant and feisty. Albano meant to tell her off, but he thought that perhaps it would be better, more authentic, if he appeared to be a weak father.

"A man was seen visiting her hotel room," the detective said, squinting and looking at each one of them slowly as he spoke, his eyes always lingering on Marceline.

"The man who died?" Albano asked.

"Another man. An Arab. Or most likely a Kabyle. Light eyes." There was no clear description, the detective went on to say. "He came and went at various hours. We assume he was her lover. He too was not seen since the murder, so he might be an accomplice, if not the murderer himself. Is it possible that the murder was rooted in a lover's dispute?"

They all shrugged off the notion of Xandra being caught in a love triangle. Had the police come just a few minutes earlier, Lucienne would have been strident, but now all she could manage was a weak pique at Albano. "Her sexual proclivities were not of interest to me," she said.

Marceline interjected, "Mother! Sandra lived with us. When would she have the time? Or the opportunity?"

To this, Lucienne agreed cryptically. "If she did have a lover, I suppose I would be the last one informed."

"What about you?" The detective asked, turning to Albano. His gaze was attentive, measuring.

"Me?"

"Do you have any idea who the dead man might be? And why he was killed? Do you have any theories of what might have happened?"

Albano had no time to come up with a plausible theory that might satisfy the man. What would an innocent person answer? "Perhaps he was wounded and found his way into the hotel, and into her room … somehow."

The detective scoffed at this. "Monsieur, with all due respect, the man was found with a knife planted in his heart. Not exactly the kind of wound that allows much meandering."

Lucienne put a hand to her mouth. "Goodness."

"What I will say with certainty is that we can all vouch for Sandra's character," Albano told the detective. He wondered if he seemed to care too much. Xandra was supposed to be nothing more to him than an employee he fired. The detective had a few more questions and Marceline said a few insolent things that nevertheless made it apparent that she knew nothing. From the corner of his eye, Albano noticed that Lucienne was dozing off. "We are glad to assist you in any way we can," he said at last as the detective got up to leave.

"Very well; I will leave you to your day." The detective turned to Lucienne. "Au revoir, Madame." And looked taken aback when he saw that Lucienne, although still sitting upright had her eyes closed, her chin, down and her mouth slightly ajar. He turned to Marceline, polished his mustache with a coquettish turn of the finger and said, "Mademoiselle." With this, he planted his hat back on his head and left, followed by the policeman. But just as the door was about to close behind them, he spun on his feet to look at them, his gaze steady on Marceline, Lucienne, Gustave, and finally Albano, and said, "Please do not leave town in the eventuality we need to call you in for further questioning."

That afternoon, Albano went to Moshe's to tell him about the police visit.

"You were not identified! This is fabulous news," Uncle Moshe said. "And there is nothing they can do about Xandra. Under normal conditions, the International Criminal Police would seek her out, and because of her physical description, they would rapidly apprehend her. But now the communication between countries is difficult at best. The world has more pressing issues than the fate of a woman of no consequence murdering a nameless man for undetermined reasons in a second-rate Algiers hotel room."

"They might still decide to arrest me. I am right at their fingertips. If they see that our papers are false, they will have grounds to, even if they cannot link me to the death."

"Once the Allies are here, Algiers will no longer be ruled by Vichy," Moshe said. "It is only a matter of days."

"If the Allied invasion is successful, how long do you think before Xandra can return to Algiers?"

Uncle Moshe raised an eyebrow and shook his head. "Albano, she did kill her brother. There is a warrant for her arrest. You must understand that she can never come back to Algeria."

Albano felt no hesitation. "If that is the case, I have made my decision. I will meet her in Portugal."

"You want to move there, the whole family?"

Albano thought for a long moment, wondering how he could explain this to Uncle Moshe. "I've decided," he said, "to do something that may shock you."

"Shock me?"

"My wife hasn't been a wife to me, or I a husband to her, in years," he began. "Lucienne is ill. In fact, my love for Xandra is precisely what is ailing her. My children are grown, or nearly, and they are set on doing whatever they please."

Moshe frowned. "What are you saying?"

"I will leave the money for them. All of it. After the war, you can help them recover our assets in Swiss banks."

Moshe looked shocked. "You want to run away with Xandra?"

Albano took a quick breath and nodded. "I have made my choice," he said.

Moshe crossed his arms. He was a smart, cool-headed man who found solutions to the most difficult problems. But now Moshe was shaking his head. "If you run away, it will make you guilty in the eyes of the police."

"Let the police think whatever they want."

"But what would your family think, Albano. Could you live with that?"

"I would write a letter explaining about Hagop."

"I can understand you would leave Lucienne, but to abandon your children—"

"What about Xandra? How can I abandon her?" Albano erupted. "The children have had me. They've received my time, my energy, and love, and care. They've had their turn. Whereas Xandra continued to get nothing!"

"They would think you didn't love them. Is that something you can live with?"

"But I do. I love them so very much! Even Lucienne, I want her to have a good life. I want them to be happy." He looked at his uncle imploringly. "But I need Xandra. I need her, and she needs me, more than I need my children and more than they need me at this point in their life." At once, the absurdity of his logic beset him. "But if the children see that I chose Xandra over them, it would destroy everything they believe to be true about me, or about her. They would know I have lied to them all these years. They would hate me for what we did to Lucienne."

"If you disappear," Uncle Moshe said, "the police will think that you were the one who murdered Hagop or that you were Xandra's accomplice. When this happens, the government is likely to confiscate the money you have."

"They would have no grounds."

"How long before they learn that you are Jewish? They would find any loophole in the law. If they succeed, how would your family cope? How would they survive? Not only that, but it would draw attention to your identity and your family's. And they would surely put their nose in all your activities, which might lead them to me and what we're trying to do here."

Albano slumped in his chair, as discouraged as he'd ever felt. "There is no solution," he said.

"Are you certain that you are willing to run away with Xandra?"

"Yes," Albano said.

"Even if that means you might become permanently estranged from your children?"

Albano stayed quiet for a minute, and then he said, "If they can be safe and protected without me, my answer is yes. But I can see how that is not possible. If I run away, they will be vulnerable. There is no solution to this."

"Actually, there might be one." Moshe hesitated. "One you will not like."

"What is it?"

Moshe got up from his chair and began pacing the room. "Let's speak from the standpoint of pure practicality. Imagine that you are dead."

"Dead?" Albano echoed.

"Imagine you died. The murder investigation against you would stop. Your family would be left alone."

"Yes," Albano shrugged. "But I am not dead."

"Lucienne and the children would have enough money to last in Algiers if they continued to live conservatively. When the war ends, provided Hitler is defeated, which will happen now that he had the fatal arrogance to turn on the Soviet Union, you know my certainty on this, Lucienne would gain access to the money in Switzerland. Eventually, the house in Paris might even be returned to her as well."

"But I am not dead and—" Albano interrupted himself, suddenly struck by the understanding of what Uncle Moshe was saying. They looked at each other. The solution appeared to him vividly. When people died, their loved ones moved on. "I believed that Xandra was dead," he muttered.

"And when you set fire to the boat off the coast of Cannes, no one questioned that you had all perished."

"And people went on with their lives," Albano said. The boat had burned down, they were missing, and there had been no further discussion on the matter, no investigation. People without fame came and went unnoticed in this life, especially in times of war. Uncle Moshe was right. If Albano died, it would mark the end of the police investigating him.

All he needed to do was to pretend to die.

Numbed by this realization, Albano looked at his hands. There would be very little time to prepare. In a matter of days, the Allied troops would be at Algiers's door. The dawn of the day after the Allied invasion might see Algeria free from the Nazi threat and Pétain's government, and Lucienne, Marceline, and Gustave would be safe in liberated French territory. "Only it matters to me that I see my children," Albano said in a fog. "How could I not be in their lives?"

"If they imprison you for murder, you will not be in their lives either," Moshe said. "They are old enough to start their own lives. Perhaps even without you. You said so yourself."

"In fact, they already have," Albano said. If they believed him dead, Marceline and Gustave would be devastated. They would mourn him, and they would grieve. But in a few weeks, a few months, a year, they would start anew. In Moshe's plan, their memory of him would remain intact. They would not feel betrayed. They would not once doubt he loved them. From a practical standpoint, it worked too: at the end of the war, they would inherit the assets hidden in Swiss banks. It would be a terrible betrayal, but they would never know about it. "Either I betray them and live without them," Albano said. "Or I betray Xandra and live without her,"

"What betrayal?" Moshe said impatiently. "You would be ensuring their safety and future, while sacrificing yourself." Moshe paced faster, talked faster. Albano could see all sides of Moshe at work: the big-hearted man, the warrior who already was planning the logistics of Albano's escape, and at the same time, the rug salesman, convincing himself as he tried to convince Albano. "You are the reason your children and wife weren't in Paris when the monsters rounded up our people in the Vel' d'Hiv. You are the reason they weren't trapped in the South of France when they started imprisoning Jews there. You are the reason there will be a considerable amount of money waiting for them at war's end. They will remember you as the man who gave them their life through his quick-thinking, his decisiveness. What is better? Tell me. Is it better for your children and their children and grandchildren to think of you dead but heroic or rotting in jail for the murder of a vagrant?"

"But the lie…."

"So now you owe them the truth? Isn't it too late for this, Albano? Ask yourself: would their lives be improved by the knowledge that their father ran away and abandoned them for the woman they thought of as their nanny?"

Albano was thinking in even broader strokes. If he was gone, the children would have no choice but to turn into adults, and it was about time. They would have to care for Lucienne. Marceline would have to stop endangering herself. His daughter had a good head on her shoulders when it came to getting things done. And Gustave would become head of the family, and it would give him a function and a purpose. As the new head of the household, Gustave might be allowed to stay away from combat. This alone could guarantee his safety. "The children would have to grow up and stick together," he said.

Moshe stopped pacing and softened his voice. "Moreover, your love for Xandra would remain a secret from all, and so their respect for you both would be intact. Those are all things that matter to you."

"Although," Albano said, "this would be leaving Lucienne in her most fragile moment."

Moshe shrugged. "Lucienne can remarry if she finds a man foolish enough to have her."

"I asked Xandra to sacrifice everything for my children," Albano murmured. "And she has." He could see it now; it was his turn to make a sacrifice for Xandra, even though she would never ask him to – *because* she would never ask him to. He thought of his beloved, alone and exiled. He imagined himself with her, free, starting a life somewhere in Portugal, in Greece, in Palestine perhaps. "But I would never see my children again," Albano said numbly.

Moshe placed his fleshy palm on his heart. "You will always know what is happening to them, as long as I live. On my honor, I will do this for you."

"They will marry; they will have children." Albano's voice broke into a strangled sob. "Grandchildren I will never know."

Moshe sat down heavily on a chair. His forehead was moist with sweat. "You must do what you think is right," he said. "I have given you the wrong advice before." They both knew that Moshe's plan was no loss to him. Moshe never liked Lucienne. He would get to see Gustave and Marceline whenever he wanted.

"Every advice you gave me served God's purpose," Albano said. "I never could reconcile my beliefs and my actions, my heart, and my reason. Each time I do one thing, it brings a result that seems worse than the original problem. I suffered when I thought I had lost Xandra, and then when I found her, I suffered even more. And now I am about to suffer in yet a new way." His throat constricted; his decision was made. "I want to do this for Xandra," he said. "I want to start anew with her. That is what I want."

Moshe smiled sadly. "God knows the saintly woman has earned it."

Albano had seen his uncle do this time and again, the way he set aside emotional components, including fear, and came up with a plan. "The day of the Allied operation will be mayhem," Moshe said. "That's the day to do it. We'll manufacture your death and whisk you out of the country."

"How?" Albano asked.

Moshe blurted out ideas as they came to him. "An event. An explosion. A fire. A mission where you set up explosives … somewhere. And something goes wrong. We produce charred remains. I know someone at the morgue. We get a body and burn it beyond recognition. And then we place it where you would have been. You, dead as a Resistance hero, which by the way you are. Your reputation preserved, beyond reproach."

"What if the Allied operation fails? My family would be left in Algiers to fend for themselves. I simply won't do this to them."

"Then we hide you in the chamber for a few days, and we watch what happens," Moshe said.

"The chamber," Albano repeated. That musky room where they had hidden countless people already. Food, water, a windowless, soundproof place hidden from sight to take refuge in for a few days.

"If the landing fails, you can always reappear a few days later," Moshe continued, "saying that you were trapped somewhere. But if the landing is successful, and your family is safe, then you head off to Portugal. We will get you and Xandra a new identity as husband and wife."

"As husband and wife," Albano echoed, mesmerized by the sound of it. They would no longer have to hide their love. They would not have to lie. And at the same time, they would be hiding forever – lying forever.

"I will help your family in every way they need," Moshe said, his hand on Albano's shoulder. "I will be the liaison. You will know of their whereabouts. I will tell you everything. One day you could come back to them if you chose to, and explain why you did this."

"Fake my death only to reappear years later? What kind of man would do this?"

"A man who, through a dark twist of fate, has found himself in an impossible predicament," Moshe said, indignant that Albano would entertain any other thought. "A generous man. A loving man. A man willing to sacrifice himself."

The simplicity of Uncle Moshe's solution, its finality, were as if an almighty giant hammer of judgment had descended from the sky onto Albano's head. Like a death sentence, and at the same time, like salvation. Albano was overwhelmed.

This was not a road that could be walked back in the opposite direction. But suddenly, more than anything, he longed for his life to take this new turn. "I promised Xandra that when the children grew up, she and I would be together," he said. "Now the children are grown. Marceline might be headstrong, but she also has real strength."

"More than most men I know."

"As for Gustave, my presence is almost an impediment to his becoming himself. Lucienne deserves her freedom as well. Maybe she will get a chance to remarry."

"Without the embarrassment of a divorce," Moshe noted.

Albano closed his eyes. He had heard of a place, a small Greek island, where people had dug an entire city out of the mountain. A place with nothing to do but rest one's eyes on blue sky, blue sea, and walls painted in white lime. A place where, when the war was over, a man and a woman could live a simple life in peace.

When he looked up at Uncle Moshe, his face was pale, and he was shivering, but his eyes were dry.

"And so, it is yes?" Moshe asked gravely.

"It is yes," Albano answered.

****

November 8, 1942

Inside the secret chamber, Albano listened in for the sounds of gunfire, but he heard nothing. Back at the apartment, his children and his wife were asleep when he had gotten out of bed and left this life with nothing other than the clothes on his back. He had walked to Uncle Moshe's place, making sure no one saw him. He had left his family for the last time without being able to say good-bye, or ask for forgiveness.

Had the Allied forces already entered the Algerian sea? From inside this room, he had no way to know. Had the invasion begun? Would it be successful? The Resistance was in place. Outside, people might already be risking their lives for freedom while he stayed in hiding.

If the invasion failed, he would return home to his family.

If it was a success, he would take the fishing boat to Portugal and be reunited with Xandra.

At the bridge, which was set to explode in just a few minutes, two of Moshe's men had taken a corpse of bulk similar to Albano's from the morgue. That corpse would be set in flames at the time of the explosion. Albano's wallet, his hat, and his handkerchief would be left nearby, proof that the unrecognizably scorched body was, in fact, his.

His family would have a good life – a life without him. He wiped his tears; there would be many more. He would never hold his children again. He would never again see them or meet his grandchildren.

And then he felt a flutter of happiness. Xandra. Soon he might be with her again. She would know that he was choosing her over them this time. Their life, which had been interrupted by fate twenty years before, would begin again. A fire had stolen their future, and now another fire would return it to them.

CHAPTER 7

The Curator of Broken Things

On the plane to Los Angeles, Cassie had a dream. Her father was in it. In the dream, she was the mother, and he was the child. She held his hand firmly. They wanted to cross a street with cars zooming in front of them. On the other side of the street was an island with white houses built on a cliff. Suddenly the boy let go of her hand and leaped to the other side of the street. She woke up.

****

At the airport, Peter was the first person she saw after she passed through security. It was a different Peter she faced. Or else she was the one who had changed. "How is your father," he asked.

"Like you care now?"

"Don't make me out to be a monster because I asked you to come home early," Peter said.

"You're not the reason I came early," she said. "And I don't want to talk about my father."

"Oh boy, I sense a mood," Peter said.

They were on the 405 freeway. The Porsche smelled of Jessica's perfume. Thin palm trees reached for the hazy blue sky. The anchors to Cassie's life had become unmoored. Now it was her life in Los Angeles that felt unreal. Would her time in Paris recede just as easily? Would memories of Hervé, the hospital, her dad, and Marceline fade until they had no more corporeality than a dream?

Peter asked, "Have you had a chance to—"

"Work on the screenplay? No."

"I sent you a tablet at great expense."

"About that tablet ..."

"You broke it!"

"I gave it to someone."

"What?" Peter yelped.

"To my aunt. I needed a parting gift."

"For God's sake, Cassie, it cost six hundred bucks!"

"Six hundred dollars for you is like six dollars to a normal person," she said. They did not speak again until they were driving up Laurel Canyon, when Cassie said, "I can't work until I get some rest. Can you come back in a couple of hours?"

Peter dropped her off at her house. She let herself in. Everything was exactly as it was eight days ago when she had received that phone call from Sabine. It might as well have been eight years ago. She could hardly remember the person she was then. The cardboard boxes intended for the Salvation Army were still stacked near the front door, awaiting pickup. They were still overflowing with Peter's and the kids' bric-a-brac: an old tennis racket, beach towels, bad art, that frame with the broken glass and a key mounted against velvet, a pair of ice skates used once. Before leaving for Paris, she knew she needed a change, but spring cleaning had been as far as her imagination stretched. That's what she did: she swallowed feelings; she reacted to trivial things but let the big ones slide. She had bickered with Peter when what mattered lay dormant like hidden abscesses.

If Paris had been on the fence about deciding between winter and spring, here in Los Angeles, it was summer. When wasn't it summer in Los Angeles? The sleek architectural kitchen in which she never cooked basked in natural light. Outside the bay windows, the mountain was peppered with multi-million-dollar houses with infinity pools, and indoor-outdoor kitchens with sandstone countertops and flower arrangements dropped off twice weekly, and maids that picked up dirt before it could hit the floors. Sabine would get a kick out of that. But for Cassie, the charm had waned.

Part of her longed for her ignorance of a week ago, before Paris, before Hervé, before Marceline, when her defenses had worked pretty well for the job of living her existence. How she saw her life, how she saw her marriage, how she saw her family, and how she saw herself: all of that was gone. What would replace it? She tried not to think about Hervé, but thoughts of him were creeping in through the back door, and each time they did, her throat constricted. Disappointment. In him. In herself.

She sat on the couch, curled up on her side, rested her cheek on a throw pillow, and sank into a deep sleep.

Two hours later, the sound of a key opening the front door awakened her. "Look what Santa brought!" Peter said in a thundering voice. Peter had never once respected her sleep. He plopped down on the couch heavily, sitting on her foot.

"Ouch!" she yelped. She sat up, her head in a fog.

"It is Christmas in April, yes, it is!" he exclaimed, unpacking a laptop. "Here it is! A brand new 15-inch, complete with screenwriting software! I know a guy, don't thank me." Cassie grunted and put a throw pillow over her face. "Wake up sleepy head," he continued. "We're open for business!" Cassie rubbed her eyes. Every molecule in her brain told her to get back to sleep. She dragged her feet to the kitchen sink and splashed cold water on her face. She prepared coffee on automatic pilot, a confused part of her wondering how it could be so bright out when, in her brain, it was the middle of the night.

Later, they sat across each other facing their respective laptops, the same way they always did, and she dipped her lips in her coffee. "Do you have fresh Oreos," Peter asked. "Those from last week must be stale."

"That's the beauty of processed food, Peter," Cassie grumbled. "It can't go stale because it was never food to begin with."

They opened a shared document. Peter was in a chatty mood. He went on, and on, and ON: about the screenplay, about Jessica, about the baby. He moved his arms, his eyebrows, his mouth. It all felt like gibberish. She wanted silence. She could not focus on what he was saying or on the page in front of her. She looked at Peter and his moving mouth and suddenly had the vision of herself hurling the content of her mug across the table to make him SHUT UP. Instead, she focused on the page in front of her. Her mind was blank. Across from her, Peter was chatting happily and typing up useless sentences, pretending to work. Really, he was doing as he always did: he was waiting for her to do the thinking. But the only thinking she was capable of was that she did not want him to be there. She did not want to hear about the producer, the film, Jessica, or their stupid baby.

"Chop, chop. You're off your game, Cassie," he said.

"Why don't you come up with an idea for a change?" She put her hands in her lap as they turned into fists. *Peter was a user and a manipulating jerk, and she did not want to hear another word from his lying mouth.*

She drank her coffee, typed a few words, erased them. The coffee was starting to work. Or was it really the coffee? Her skin buzzed. She erased a sentence Peter had just written, then a whole paragraph. Seeing what she was doing, he looked up at her. "What are you doing? You're not supposed to do that. That's not how it works!"

"No, you're right. How it works is that you write crap, and I try to make you think it's gold and change it anyway. This goes faster."

"I can see that France awakened the bitch within," Peter said. He looked good in his V-neck T-shirt. Not Hervé-good, but handsome nonetheless. She realized that she was feeling this without the usual pinch of wistfulness.

Things did have a way to work out for Peter, didn't they?

Don't, she told herself. But she could tell it was too late. Peter looked at her, handsome and unperturbed while everything in her life was going to shit. "There is something I've meant to ask you," she said, grabbing the empty coffee mugs from the table. She went to the sink and turned on the faucet.

"Go ahead, sweetie," he said, closing his laptop and stretching lazily on the chair.

"I'd like you to answer truthfully," she said. She rinsed the mug, her back turned to Peter, gathering strength.

"O-kay," he said, separating the syllables to indicate his misgivings about any conversation that might require truth.

She needed to look at him, or he would find ways to elude her. Elude her. That's what she had allowed him to do for too long. Courage. She breathed in, filled her lungs, turned around, leaned against the sink, wiping her hands on a cloth to appear casual. "When did it really start?" she asked in the most detached tone she could muster.

"Start what?" he asked. He unpeeled the top of the Oreo package, took out a cookie, and put it into his mouth.

"With Jessica," she said. "When did the two of you start your thing?"

Peter stopped chewing, then started again, slower, as though the cookie had turned to sand in his mouth. "What thing?"

"You didn't meet her after we separated," she calmly said. "You met earlier. Much earlier."

Peter swallowed but did not reach for a second cookie. "I'm not sure what you're talking about."

She stayed at the sink. She needed to lean against it for support because what she was about to do demanded more courage than she thought herself capable of, and at the same time, it required her to be sneaky. Very sneaky. Peter-sneaky. "You and I have a good relationship," she said. "We work well together. I've grown to appreciate Jessica. We're all a big family now." He was staring at her, making his face expressionless. It took everything she had to appear conciliatory. "We're grown-ups. I'm just curious, that's all. I think it's time to come clean. Put this all behind us."

"We met when I said we met," Peter said. Now he was sitting upright in his chair, everything about his posture and his tone on guard.

She returned to the kitchen table and sat down close to him, like a trusted old friend, and leaned toward him. Too much depended on her calm. She could not back down. If she did not get the truth from him now, she never would. "The twins remember Jessica showing you houses when they were five years old."

He looked surprised. "They said that?"

"You met Jessica twelve years ago. You know that; the twins know that; Jessica knows that, and I know that." She added, honey in her voice, "Don't you think for the sake of our relationship you owe me to verbalize it?" She patted him on the arm and said sweetly, "Don't worry. I won't get mad." She pushed the box of Oreos soothingly toward him. He looked at her hand and at the box of Oreos, took a cookie, and put it in his mouth.

"I was looking for houses, and you didn't want to come," he said. "And there she was. She showed me a couple of houses. The children were there. I was not trying to do anything behind your back." He added, accusatorily, "you were invited to be part of this. I asked you a hundred times, but you refused to entertain the idea."

"I didn't come along, and there she was," Cassie said. She made herself sound motherly.

"And there she was," he repeated, as though things from there were self-explanatory.

"And after a while, you continued house hunting, but you didn't bring the kids anymore."

"They got tired of it; you know kids."

"And you started an affair."

He shook his head, "Cassie...."

"I'm way past this, Peter." She said this with a smile and so casually that she should have been offered an Academy Award on the spot. "Come on. Just tell me. Get it off your chest. You'll feel better."

Peter was uneasy about the whole thing. "I was extremely devoted to you."

"It's okay," she said, magnanimously. "A man is only a man."

He looked relieved. "I've wanted to tell you this so many times. But I did not see the point in hurting you."

"But that affair. It went on for a while, didn't it?"

"Yes," he said, shrugging. For the very first time in forever, Peter's eyes were telling the truth.

"For years if I'm correct."

"You promise you won't get mad?" Peter said guilelessly.

"Honey, I already know. I just need to hear it from you." She was lying. Still now, and even though she should have known, she did not know. She had not wanted to know. And now she needed to know as though her life depended on it. Had Peter looked at her at that moment, he would have sensed the hairline fractures in her tone, the cracking varnish of her composure. Instead, he peered into the box of Oreos, hunting for the perfect one.

"Twelve years ago. Yeah, that sounds about right. Yes. What can I say; we fell in love."

Cassie drew a silent, sharp breath. "So, in all fairness to me, wouldn't you say that the affair was the reason you were not into me anymore?"

"I was into you," he assured her. "I loved you both. Each in your own way."

Cassie let that sentence float between her ears. It was vague and amorphous and unsettling. "On the one hand, I was the mother of your children, but on the other hand, Jessica was hot."

"You were hot too," he said, chivalrously.

"Wasn't it hard on Jessica, that you wouldn't leave me? I mean, she was in her prime; she probably wanted children quite badly and, well, to be the other woman must not have been easy. How long did she have to wait until you finally left me? Let's see; the kids were five. We divorced when they were thirteen, so that's what? Seven years? Eight?"

"It was hard for her. And don't think Jess didn't feel guilty. She felt real shitty about it. You know how she's got this huge heart."

"Poor thing," Cassie said, her jaw clenched to the breaking point. "And then I decided to take time apart, and so you jumped at it. You moved out, and 'officially' met her for the first time."

"It was your decision to separate," Peter said, defensively, but at the same time dully, like an automaton that repeats itself one time too many. "I wanted to stay married for the kids. And you better believe that Jessica was pressuring me to leave you. But then you wanted to separate, and the children were older by then, so it happened, organically."

"Except…." Cassie had to pause. The image of Marceline came to her, and it stopped her from dissolving into tears. "Except, the only reason I mentioned a separation was that you didn't love me anymore."

"Unconsciously, you gave me my freedom," Peter said. Even this was a concept he must have repeated to himself.

"It's interesting how the subconscious works," she said. She was silent for a moment. "Eight years. Wow. That's quite something," she murmured to herself. "You had a mistress for eight years out of our twelve-year marriage."

"I'm sorry, Cass," Peter said. She could tell that he meant it.

"You know what's funny about it?" she said, "It's that if you add up the years and include the overlapping, Jessica's was with you longer than I was when we divorced."

"I didn't do the math," he said, irritated now.

"You know what's even funnier?"

"What?"

Her voice changed pitch. "What's funny is how the two of you can look me in the eye, invite me for dinner, invite me to your wedding even – and I came! And how she brown-noses me constantly. And how you use me, day after day, after day, to further your career. Of course, you didn't want to lose me. I would have stopped writing for you!"

"Writing with me," he corrected.

She took this in the solar plexus. Still, in the middle of this, he maintained the alternate reality, the brainwash. This was enough to send her to the other side. She was yelling now. "Oh, this was so perfect for you! You had me, the unsuspecting idiot, raising your children, working like a horse in the shadow, making your career possible. This is not something you would want to fuck up even for an unforgettable piece of ass like Jessica!"

"You said you would not get mad!"

"Well, I fucking lied!" she screamed.

"She was in love with me!" he screamed back.

"So was I!" she said, tears erupting from her eyes. "I was in love with you. I was in love with you from the day we met until long after our divorce. I'm probably still in love with you now!"

He bent his head and shook it with real sadness. "But I'm in love with her," he said. He had tears in his eyes, the big oaf. "I'm so sorry, Cassie. I do adore you.

I care about you. You are a friend, very dear to me. And I have the utmost respect for you as the wonderful, selfless mother of my children. I never wanted to hurt you. Not then, not now."

Cassie felt something collapse in her. It was over. She knew the truth. She had to let go not only of the fantasy that she could get him back but of the hope that he had loved her.

Tough. To be tough was a quality, not a flaw, Marceline had said. This was where the courage part started. Cassie needed to learn to live without clinging to the hope of her father's love, and she needed to learn to live without Peter's. The very fabric of her soul had been shaped by cultivating those illusions. She did not even know how to live without the hope. "I'll have to live with this," she murmured.

"Can you forgive me? Cassie! You have to forgive me."

"I can forgive you for loving her. I even can forgive you for not loving me." As she said this, she knew it was the truth or that it would become the truth one day. She inhaled deeply and added coldly, "But I can't forgive you for the deception."

"Cassie, come on...."

She spoke slowly. "You say I'm your dear friend, but to you, I am nothing but a means to an end."

"How can you say such a thing?"

"It's not your friendship with me you're trying to protect. It's your ass."

"Cassie, you know that's not true."

"But I'm done with this."

"With what?"

"With all of it. For one, I'm done doing any kind of writing for you, or with you."

She saw a flash of anger on Peter's face, but he controlled it. "But, Cassie," he said. "Work is an entirely separate issue."

"All those years you denied me the credit I deserved. You knew my weaknesses. You banked on the fact that I would allow myself to be hidden from sight."

Now the anger in him was here too, bare and unbridled. "Here we go again. If it is writing credit that you want, you can get the credit. I can't believe you would be so egotistical."

"I'm egotistical?"

He was in attack mode. "Your ego needs feeding. Is that what it comes down to? Your name on a billboard? Sad, really."

"But when your name is on a billboard, that's not egotistical? Screwing a woman behind my back for years, that's not egotistical? Keeping your wife silent and unloved, that's not egotistical?"

"I'm done with this argument. It goes nowhere when you get hysterical."

"When you're angry, it's righteous, and when I am, it's hysterical. You know what, here is the good news. You won't have to put up with any more hysterics. I swear to you right now that I will never write another line for you. With or without credit."

"That's nonsense," Peter said. Somehow, at that moment, buried deep in the recess of her heart, she longed for him to tell her that she was wrong, that he loved her best, that his continued relationship with her was with no strings attached. But instead, he said, "You *have* to work for me. Per our contract!"

She looked at him and burst into laughter. She tilted her head back and laughed for a long time, freely, and without anger, while he stared at her, puzzled and furious. This fell so short of the declaration of love she had longed for. But perhaps, it was better. This was the truth she needed to hear. He did not love her, had not in over twelve years, if ever, and he was not about to start loving her now. But he *needed* her. He needed her for her skills, which meant she *had* skills. It was an admission of the importance of her work, the validation of her talent. "Consider this a breach of contract," she said, and with those words, she was drained of any residue of hope, expectation, or illusion. She was free of him.

At that moment, the front door opened. It was Jessica letting herself in. Waltzing in without even knocking first, as though it were her right, as though she were welcome to do so since, after all, Cassie had allowed her to steal her husband's heart and had let her insert herself into every moment of her children's life.

When Jessica walked into the kitchen, did she not see Cassie's and Peter's pale faces and shining eyes, the clenched jaws and fists? "Hi, you guys!" she chirped. She was dressed for horseback riding, lithe and tight in her close-fitting pants and tall black boots.

"Oh, Jessica," Cassie said, "I brought you a little something back from Paris." She caught the warning glance Peter gave Jessica, which only served to fuel her energy. She marched to her tote bag, marched back to face Jessica, pulled put the Monoprix plastic bag, and shook its contents out onto the floor. Out came all four of Jessica's exquisitely wrapped packages. They landed with small thuds, dusting the wood floor with glitter. With Jessica watching in mute shock, Cassie, with four sharp blows, stomped once on each with all the force she could muster. The packages burst in quick succession. Bam. Bam. Bam. Bam. In one fell swoop, Cassie kneeled, scooped up the mess of broken packages, put them back into the Monoprix bag, and thrust it into Jessica's hands. "My father, mother, and sisters thank you warmly and ask you to stay the hell away from them from now on," Cassie said.

In an instant, Jessica and Peter were out the door.

Cassie stood in the middle of the room panting. She felt a wave of relief beyond any kind she thought possible. From there, she ran to the couch, grabbed a throw pillow, and buried her sobs in it.

An hour later, she called Sabine. In her rush to get out of Paris, she had not told her sisters that she was leaving. "It's me," she said when Sabine picked up.

Sabine sounded frantic. "Cassie, where have you been? We've been trying to reach you. They said you checked out of the hotel. Are you staying with that guy?"

"I'm so sorry; I should have found the time to tell you. No, no more of that guy. He was just a fluke. Peter needed me for work, and well, after the circus at the hospital, and Mom, and Odile, and well, I was disgusted. Exhausted. Fed up with all of them, so I went home."

"Home ... *where*?" Sabine moaned.

"Back in Los Angeles. I took the night flight."

Sabine had a sharp inhalation "Oh no, Cassie."

"What?"

"It's Papa...." She left her sentence hanging, perhaps counting on Cassie to fill in the blanks.

"What?"

"He didn't make it, Cassie. Papa passed away during the night."

Cassie felt the room swirl around her. Her knees buckled. "That's not possible! I *saw* him! Just hours ago." On the line, Sabine was silent. "He was awake," Cassie insisted. "He spoke to me. I just ... don't understand."

"Can you come back?" Sabine said in a tiny voice.

"I'll be on the next plane out."

"Can you stay with me this time?" Sabine asked pitifully. "I don't want to be alone."

"I'll head straight for the airport. Just hang on for a little while."

After hanging up the phone, Cassie realized that none of her limbs worked. Her legs were limp. She sat on the first chair she found. This could not be! She and her father were not finished yet! He still needed to tell her what she needed to hear to feel whole! She waited for a feeling of reality to reenter her body. What did this mean? What just happened? *You didn't tell me your father was dying*, Hervé had said. And yet after hearing him say this, Cassie had left the country. Just how delusional had she been? Just how incapable was she of seeing things as they were? Maybe her mother was right: she was a liar. And the person she lied to the most was herself.

She sat on the couch wondering what to do next. She was numb. She needed a bag, a suitcase of some sort to shove in some clothes into. She looked at the pile for the Salvation Army. Was there something there she could use?

Something about the boxes piled near the door was at the tip of her consciousness and at the same time vague and urgent. What had Peter said before she left for France? It was something about her dad. What was it? What were they talking about? They were arguing about the kids. No, not about the kids: about the things she wanted to throw away. "Alex found that key, and your father said he could have it," Peter had said. "Alex put it in a frame because he liked the look of it."

A key?

Cassie flew to the pile of boxes. "Please, please, please," she repeated. She found it immediately: a small gilded frame, cracked glass, and, behind the glass, a key mounted on black velvet. This key was an object she had known her entire life! First, growing up, it had been in a drawer in the kitchen among batteries, chopsticks, and flashlights. One day, when he was perhaps six years old, and they were in France visiting her parents, Alex had found it. It looked cool to him. Her father said he could have it. Not only that: it was the very same key that Marceline had amongst the trinkets and pendants she wore around her neck. Keys to the safety deposit box had been in their possession the entire time! Marceline wore one around her neck, and Cassie had nearly thrown hers away!

She broke the glass hastily and turned it over between her fingers. It was heavy for its size. Engraved in the metal were three letters. B. S. G., Banque Société Générale.

She called Air France and made a plane reservation for that same night.

After that, she called Odile and her mother.

When she was done with that, she called Marceline.

CHAPTER 8

The Vault

Cassie slept on the plane for eleven hours straight. When she landed at Charles de Gaulle Airport, she had to explain to the border officer why she had flown out of Paris, to the United States, and back in under forty-eight hours. "My father passed away," she told the stranger, and for the first time since she learned the news, she burst into tears.

"Please take me to the Societé Générale Bank on Boulevard Haussmann," she told the taxi driver.

At the bank, she tapped her foot on the mosaic floor as she waited in line at the circular counter in the center of the room. When it was her turn, she presented the account number and the key.

She was taken to the entrance of a vault guarded by a metal sculpture of entwined snakes, and then to a massive, circular, esoteric-looking metal door, all gleaming steel and copper, like a giant wheel that made her think of the entrance to the Nautilus. Inside the vault, she was taken to the third underground level via a small elevator. Finally, she was in the room that contained the safety deposit box. The room was covered wall to wall with built-in metal cabinets. The clerk unlocked one of the cabinet doors and slid it open, revealing a series of small drawers. He verified the number one more time and let her insert the key. He pulled the drawer out from the casing and set it on one of the several small copper desks that had sides built in opaque glass for privacy. Cassie sat down at the desk, took a deep breath, and opened the box.

It fell open like a ripe fruit.

Inside were two envelopes and five photographs.

Three of the pictures, yellowed in places and brittle, were black and white. Two of them were color. On each photograph was the same smiling couple. Each photo appeared to be of the couple in a different decade: in their forties, in their fifties, sixties, seventies, and eighties. The background was always the same: the sea with islands in the distance. In the back, of each photo always the same mention, Oia Santorini, and a date: 1945, 1952, 1963, 1974, 1985. Cassie recognized the man instantly. She had only seen a photo of him once when she was five or six, but it was him without the shadow of a doubt: handsome, like a silent movie star, well-aligned teeth, an aura of gentleness, and on the color photographs, that peculiar golden eye color they shared. This was Albano, her grandfather. But how could it be? The math didn't work. How could there be photos of him in the fifties, or eighties, when he had died in 1942 at the age of forty?

The woman beside him was very short, petite, with long black hair in the early portraits, which became gray, then white in subsequent photos. Her eyes were grave, dark, and beautiful. Cassie took a closer look. On the right half of the woman's face, below her eye, alongside her temple and her cheek, and down her neck, there seemed to be some sort of disfiguration, as though her skin had melted terribly.

Cassie felt a chill run through her body.

Sandra, the nanny?

Astonished, she turned the photos, looking at them from every angle, trying to understand with her eyes what her heart already knew.

She took out the first letter, unfolded it. It was addressed to Uncle Moshe and signed by her grandfather.

Oia Santorini, Greece, December 1977
Dear Uncle Moshe,

Xandra and I cherished every word of your last letter. On the picture of Gustave's family, baby Cassandra looks like Marceline at the same age, don't you agree? And little Odile looks so serious! Xandra and I think she takes most after her father. Will Gustave and Raymonde have a third child you think? As always, your letters and photograph fill us with utter joy.

The wind knocked out of her, Cassie stopped reading. Albano's letter was written several months after her birth and twenty years after he was supposed to have died. And he knew her name. And Odile's. And her mom's!

Xandra and I continue our happy life as troglodytes. This year, Paco took the reign of the family construction business, and I am thankful for the rest this allows me. We just celebrated my seventy-fifth birthday, and it is taxing to walk up and down the steep, uneven alleys of the city even if the donkeys are the ones doing all the carrying. Now I let Paco handle the physical work, and I oversee the stucco. I like to think that Oia Santorini keeps getting more beautiful every day, partly thanks to our work. Paco, always the attentive son, took it upon himself to dig deeper into the hillside and expand our bedroom to one side. This gave us a window. Now Xandra and I can watch sunrises from our bed! Since my last letter, Paco and his wife welcomed a second child. His name is Alyes, and he is the apple of our eyes.

Our joy can never be cloudless. Alyes, like his sister Eva, will never know that they have French cousins about their ages. Just as Paco will never know of Gustave and Marceline, or that they are his half-brother and a half-sister. The constant weight in my heart is the punishment I must suffer.

Some nights, it feels as though the only thing alive in the universe is my own mind, filled with regret and guilt. This year will mark thirty years since Operation Torch; thirty years since

Xandra and I left Algiers. When I lay awake at night, I focus on my children's good lives. That Gustave and Marceline have become so close is perhaps my greatest comfort. Will you soon send the picture you promised of both their families together?

Xandra had a wonderful idea: You must celebrate your 90th birthday here in Oia. They have direct flights from Paris, and I promise that once you are off the airplane, all you would have to do is drink ouzo, eat Xandra's pastries, and rest your eyes on our incomparable sunsets.

Here is a photograph of Xandra and me that Paco took recently. She and I have aged, I know. But we're still as much in love as when we were children.

Please come and visit us. Xandra and I miss you very much.

Yours,

Albano.

Cassie read the letter again and scrutinized the pictures until the fog in her mind cleared up and the understanding burst through, but slowly, almost painfully, with a mixture of pain and joy, like a birth.

She opened the second letter. It was signed by Uncle Moshe.

Paris, July 2nd, 1987

Dearest Gustave and Marceline,

If you are reading this letter, it means that I am gone from this earth. It also means that you were able to piece together the riddle that led to the safety deposit box.

I am the one who had the finials engraved, one with the code to the vault box, the other with the bank's address, just as I am the one who gave you the two keys without telling you what they were for but to keep them because you might one day find out. The rest was up to you, or rather, up to God. I am leaving things up to fate. I could not make myself the arbitrator of what you should know, so I have created this riddle. If you are reading this letter today, it means that God wants you to know your father's secret.

Today, I must inform you of the truth. Your father, Albano, was not killed during Operation Torch. He did not die at 39 in the explosion of a bridge in Algiers. He died a month ago, at the age of 85, after a long, peaceful existence spent in Greece with the love of his life.

In 1942, under my advice and with my help, we staged Albano's death. A few days later, once Algiers was liberated and he knew the two of you and your mother would be safe, he fled to Portugal where he was reunited with Xandra, the woman you know as Sandra, the caretaker of your childhood.

"Oh my God," Cassie said out loud. She settled her breath and read on.

There is more to the story than Xandra appearing into your life when you were children. In truth, she and Albano knew each other long before you were born, and long before he ever married your mother. They met in 1913 in Smyrna when they were children, and fell in love then. Theirs was not an ordinary infatuation, but the kind of deep love one should only dream to experience in a lifetime. However, it was a dangerous and forbidden love between two people of different religions at a very precarious time and place in history. They had no choice but to conceal their love. When Smyrna burned to the ground in 1922, Xandra and Albano were accidentally separated, and for years believed the other one dead. When you were five and seven years old, in 1930, eight years after the fire, Xandra was found alive. But by then, your father had started over in Paris and was married to Lucienne.

Xandra was a very principled and deeply religious woman. She never thought to break up your father's marriage, which was sacred in her eyes. She agreed to live at your house and take care of you on the condition that their secret love remained a chaste one. Perhaps it was madness on Albano's part to have Xandra join your family as your nanny, but what is a man to do who loves and wants to protect two families?

In 1942, when you lived in Algiers, Xandra was accused of killing a man. We believed the police would soon apprehend Albano as an accomplice. At the time you were seventeen and nineteen, and Albano had to make a choice. The circumstances of the man's death are not important. What is important is that your father and Xandra, had they not left the country, would have been arrested and surely accused of his murder. There would have been a trial, and your family's identities would have been revealed, putting you all at terrible risk. Staging Albano's death solved all the problems. By then you were adults, or nearly. At the time, it seemed the only solution. Operation Storm, I told him, was just the diversion he needed. He knew what this sacrifice entailed. He would thereafter live in hiding and would never again see his children. There was little time for him to make this terrible choice. The police had already begun their investigation.

The night of the Allied invasion of North Africa, we met at the bridge that was set to explode. My men set up the explosion. Albano's hat and some of his clothes and personal belongings were put on a corpse, while Albano escaped by car and was taken to a boat, and eventually abroad where Xandra awaited him. If you remember, I was the one who identified the body so you would not have to.

Over the many years, your father was never out of touch with your lives. Each time I visited you, I took photographs, as you might remember. I reported everything to Albano and gave him your photographs. I told him all the happy news. He knew that the money hidden away in Switzerland had allowed Lucienne to return to her family home and to live in material comfort. He learned about Marceline's life as a modern woman, about Gustave's three beautiful daughters. But I could never tell him the entire truth. How could I have told Albano that his children's rivalry had hardened into hatred? I could not do this to him. Over the years, I did all within my power to help the two of you reconcile, but you never ceased to be inexplicably thick-headed and full of bitterness toward each other.

As I write this letter, I am 97 years old. Xandra and Albano should have outlived me, but it seems that few people do. It was Albano's deepest wish that Gustave and Marceline have a close relationship. He died believing this was the case. I am at peace with the fact that I lied to him, and I don't regret my actions which allowed for Albano and Xandra to be together at last. For 42 years, they lived in peace on the island of Oia Santorini. Their miracle was that Xandra, who had been told that she could not have children, became pregnant soon after leaving Algiers. Paco was born. They had two grandchildren by the time Xandra passed away abruptly at age 85.

When this happened, Albano buried his beloved. After that, he did something he had attempted to do sixty years before in Smyrna when he thought he could not live without her; he swam out to sea and let the waves take him.

    Yours truly,

    Moshe

Cassie put down the letter, disconcerted to find herself at a small desk inside a bank vault. Everything Marceline had told her over the last few days was turning on its head. The locations and events from Marceline's account matched: Paris, Cannes, Algiers, Xandra as a murder suspect, Operation Torch, the bridge explosion. But the story was something else entirely.

She looked at the photos of Albano and Xandra. They stood, their bodies tight next to each other, he with his arm around her waist, or draped over her shoulders. They smiled radiantly in their adoration for each other.

What they had done was unforgivable. They may or may not have been involved in a murder and wanted to run away, but Albano had pretended to be dead and abandoned his children and wife! He had conducted a love affair with the nanny for nearly the entirety of his marriage to Lucienne.

And yet, after listening to Marceline's side of the story for the last few days, part of Cassie understood Albano. She rooted for him. She also understood, as she was reading the letter, that she would never tell Marceline any of this. And had her dad been alive today, she would not have told him either. Her head spun with the ramifications, the altered course of so many lives and Gustave and Marceline burdened with shame and guilt they did not deserve, and entrenched in resentment that had no legitimacy. But it would be a terrible thing for Marceline to learn that Albano had abandoned and betrayed them, and so she would say nothing.

She put the envelopes and the photographs back in the box, closed it, and rang for the clerk to return the box to the vault.

Outside the bank, she hopped in a taxi and headed for the Montparnasse cemetery.

The taxi stopped outside the cemetery gate just as Marceline's limo pulled up. The chauffeur came out and walked around to open Marceline's door. The old lady looked regal but frail in a structured black coat and hat. Cassie came to greet her.

"I wish I could have met your family on a less somber occasion," Marceline said.

"We're all very thankful that you're letting my dad be buried in the family sepulcher."

"Why would Gustave not be? This is where he belongs. Our mother is here, as well as her father and mother and her two brothers. Sadly, Father's remains were buried in Algiers."

"We' re happy that you came," Cassie said, in case her mother and sisters omitted to say it. She saw that Maurice had walked around the car to open the door to another passenger. To her surprise, Marceline's gardener emerged from the car. Why on earth would he come to her father's funeral? The old man was dressed to the nines and stood, light on his feet and distinguished in his suit. His hair was bright white and contrasted handsomely with his tanned skin. His kind eyes smiled at Cassie, and he came to her and took her hand in his. "I am sorry for your loss," he said in his North African accent.

"Thank you. My name is Cassandra, by the way," she said. "I'm afraid I don't know your name."

"Don't be absurd," Marceline said, as she clutched the old gardener's arm.

Cassie widened her eyes, understanding. "You can't be … are you …?"

"I'm Khaled," the man said, shaking Cassie's hand.

"I thought you were—"

"The gardener?" Khaled asked.

Marceline laughed. "Of course not! He's my lover."

Khaled smiled playfully and said, "I tend to all Marceline's gardens."

"Well, that's rich!" Marceline exclaimed. "How was it not evident? I've been yapping away about him for days as he was right in front of us."

"I never made the connection," Cassie said, astounded at her blind spots.

Marceline shrugged with irritation, "I thought it was quite obvious."

"I asked if you and Khaled ever married," Cassie said, "and you said no, so I assumed—"

"I did not think you would be so provincial as to assume that marriage is the only way to have a relationship," Marceline said.

"So, you two did have a happy ending!"

"What ending?" Marceline said. "There is no ending in sight as far as I am concerned."

Khaled took Cassie's hand in his again. "I met your father just once."

"When you saved his life."

"He was a gentle young man," Khaled said.

"Thank you."

"Have you written my biography yet?" Marceline asked her as they walked inside.

"It's only been a few days," Cassie said, flustered. "It will take months. Years."

"You better get started soon, then."

"How did you and Khaled get together at last?" Cassie asked.

"Well, there was the Second World War. And then there was the Algerian war," Khaled said. Minus his ladder and crumpled trousers, and in his well-cut suit, Khaled was a regal, handsome man. And now that Marceline stood by him, putting her hand on his arm, his identity was, as Marceline had said, obvious.

"It's a very long story," Marceline said. "I will tell you about it someday. It's ripe with drama. You'll love it. In fact, I think you should write it."

Cassie could not help herself; she was beaming. "As long as in the end love conquers all," she said.

"Did you give Gustave the finial?" Marceline asked.

"I tried."

"You failed, you mean?"

"He was delirious at the time. Or hostile towards me. Or you; I will never know. He still had you and me mixed up."

"He rejected the finial?"

"I don't even know if he saw it." Cassie thought of stopping there but then decided that if one person would understand, it was Marceline. His rage at them was one thing they had in common. "I think he resented me until the end. I could never impress him quite in the way I hoped, even when I brought him the finial. I was naïve about ever gaining his approval. I guess I can say that I tried, so that might be worth something." Cassie took a deep breath. In the hospital room, in the middle of the mayhem, she had told her dad that she loved him. She was convinced now that he had turned away on purpose, that he knew it was she who was in the room, and that he had held back his affection until the end. But she would never know for certain, and it was better that way.

"Perhaps," Marceline said, "what you are naïve about is not whether he could not approve of you or not, but why."

"What do you mean?"

"It was not because he found you inadequate, darling, but because he found you impressive."

"Impressive? Me?"

"Well, yes," Marceline said. "It scared him. It made him feel insignificant. Wasn't that his reason for hating me all along? He made a sort of amalgam between us two, for whatever reason I don't know. But believe me when I say that he wasn't upset that you weren't good enough. He worried about how remarkable you might turn out to be. He worried about your potential. With all due respect to your departed father, he seems to have made every effort to suppress in you any sort of ambition of greatness."

"But why?" Cassie exclaimed.

"For fear that you would turn into me."

She faced Marceline, blinking. What if her aunt was right? Yes, it was very possible that her father had wanted, consciously or not, to smother Cassie's *spark*. What if the parts of herself Cassie had smothered to please her dad — and later to please everyone else — were, as Marceline pointed out, her *best* qualities? He had called her annoying when she was excited, arrogant when she showed determination, a know-it-all when she was passionate, bossy when she was confident. She had, over the years, learned that creativity, ambition, the desire to shine were somehow shameful and better left hidden from sight. He had redrawn the map of who she was, who she could dare aspire to be. And now came the curious concept that those traits weren't flaws but gifts – attributes that should not be squashed but fostered and nurtured.

It was as though her dad's fixation on Marceline had compelled him to repair a perceived injustice through his daughters. She had played the role of Marceline, and Odile the role of Gustave. Only in this new scenario, Gustave came out on top, and Marceline was the one whom everyone dismissed.

Perhaps, in the end, Cassie had not failed her dad by missing some kind of mark. It was he who had failed her. Perhaps she wasn't unlovable, but rather he had failed at loving her.

****

Before the service started, Cassie introduced Marceline and Khaled to Sabine, Odile, and her mother. Odile's face and eyes were swelled up as though she had been crying for days. Raymonde was curiously dry-eyed. Perhaps it would hit her later. "I am very sorry for your loss," Marceline told her sisters and her mother. "Thank you for including me. Gustave and I may not have seen eye to eye, but we share the same blood."

"Thank you for letting my dad be part of the sepulcher," Odile said. "It means so much to be in such a beautiful place. To think that he belongs here is heartwarming. To all of us." She stopped herself to blow her nose. "I'm not sure why, but it feels as though burying him here honors him. It makes him belong somewhere special."

"We have four generations buried here," Marceline said. "Do you know that your father comes from a great Parisian family. Gustave belongs here. And so will you, one day." She added with a Machiavellian smile. "I am told that you did not know that Gustave was Jewish?"

"Well … we…." Odile stuttered. "He was not religious. Not at all."

"One can be Jewish without religion. Gustave was Jewish as a fact of history, not as a matter of choice. I'd love to explain to you how that works sometime."

They were interrupted by the start of the service. The room was much too large. There were Raymonde and Sabine, Odile, her husband and children, Marceline and Khaled, a few neighbors and old co-workers, several of Raymonde's friends. In all, about twenty people. Not enough to fill two rows of chairs. Odile had decorated a table with photographs of her father with her children and a few other photos of the family. There were no photos of Cassie's children, as though they had been erased from existence. There were flowers people brought, but in the vast room, they looked meager, insufficient. Odile gave a tearful eulogy. Neither her mother nor Sabine volunteered to talk. And so, without having planned what she would say, Cassie went up to the pulpit.

"When I was on the plane coming here, I scribbled a few thoughts," Cassie said. "It was not meant to be read out loud, but … I guess why not. Here it goes:

"We're all the product of our family's dynamic, which is bred from the generation before us, and that generation is filled with the issues and neuroses of the generation before that. In a way, we are fools to believe that we choose our lives." She paused, unsure. "Here is what this means to me: my dad tried his very best throughout his life while carrying the weight of his difficult childhood. He tried not to burden his family with it, but it was there … under the surface. I loved him very much. I tried to show this to him in every way that I could. I'm thankful that I got to do that because to love someone and express it fills the heart. I'd rather experience unrequited love than feel no love at all."

Across the room, Odile's face turned red, and Marceline nodded approvingly.

Later, when they emerged from the sepulcher into mid-day light, Cassie looked up, stunned. Standing in a black suit outside the sepulcher, holding an oversized funeral wreath covered in white gladiolus, was Hervé.

"Who is this?" Sabine whispered in her ear.

"That," Cassie said in disbelief, "is Prince Charming."

On unsteady legs and her heart thundering in her chest, Cassie walked toward him. In his suit and coat, Hervé looked incredible.

She took him aside. "How did you know about today?" she asked.

"I work at the hospital, remember," he said.

Steady your cardiac rhythm, she thought. "It's nice of you to come," she said.

"I never knew your last name, where you live exactly, or where to reach you," Hervé said. "I'm sorry to intrude in your family circumstance, but this was my only chance to catch you."

"Listen," she said. "Can we talk later?"

"When and where?"

"Later," she said evasively. "Somewhere. Not here. I mean this is not the time or place. At a café later, maybe?"

He shook his head. "Not a chance. You'll never show up."

"Why would I not show up?"

"Because you're afraid of me."

"I am not!"

"Afraid of what I represent."

"And what do you represent?"

"The future," he said.

She thought about this. "Can you stick around?" she asked.

Hervé followed her into a small reception room. Sabine grinned at her, and Cassie grinned back. A cold buffet had been set in the center of the room and Cassie watched the surreal spectacle of universes colliding: Marceline speaking to Hervé, her mother speaking to Khaled, Hervé speaking to Odile. Cassie thought of Albano and Xandra, how their secret had held separate universes intact. She felt Xandra's and Albano's presence with her, hovering, looking down at them.

At one point, Hervé cornered her near a window and said, "You look very pretty today."

"What are you talking about?" Cassie said. "I'm at my worst; I'm jetlagged beyond recognition, my dad just died, my ex-husband and his wife are … the point is, I look and feel like crap."

"Your worst is better than ninety-nine percent of the population's best," he said, and she giggled like a school girl.

It seemed that the whole room was looking at them with curiosity, except for Odile, who looked about to combust with anger. "I don't know what I am, at the moment," Cassie said. "A basket case, I think. I really can't focus on this right now."

"Understood," Hervé said. "I'll make myself discreet."

"Fat chance," she said.

She walked toward Odile. "I can see that you have a bug up your butt," she said. "What now?"

"What the hell was that?" Odile asked angrily.

"He's a friend. What, I'm not allowed to bring a friend?"

"I'm talking about what you said in there. About neuroses. You had to attack Papa one last time? At his funeral!"

"Really? Are you going to do that thing right now?"

"What thing?"

"That thing you do where you suffer more than me?"

"I *am* suffering more than you!" Odile cried out. "Here you are with your new boyfriend, and your little clique of new relatives, and I didn't see you shedding a tear. Instead, you do this bogus eulogy, like salt in the wound, blaming Papa."

"That was me trying to provide him with extenuating circumstances."

"For heaven sake!"

"Look, Odile. You can live in your bubble all you want, but I can't. Papa grew up as a Jewish kid in Paris at one of the most openly anti-Semitic times in history. He and his family ran for their lives, literally, to avoid being killed in the Holocaust. He then proceeded to legally change his last name, marry a non-Jew, cuts all ties with his family, raised his daughters Catholic, and never tell them about his past. He swore Maman to secrecy, as though being Jewish were either a terrible crime, a terrible shame, or both, and you don't think it had an impact? And then there is everything that happened that even Papa didn't know about."

"Like what?"

"His family had secrets, just like ours, and those secrets had secrets. All that is passed down as neurosis. That's what the eulogy was about."

Odile sighed. "You are exhausting, you know. For just this once, on the day of his funeral, could you have not stirred things up?"

"My whole life I tried to please Papa, but it was impossible. Just this week, I understood why for the first time. I could not please him because I reminded him of Marceline. There was nothing I could have done. I was marked from the start."

"How long do you plan on blaming him? Whatever he did to you, when you were a kid, you're more than happy to do it to yourself now."

"What are you talking about?"

"You're subconsciously finishing the job Papa started: beating yourself up for some masochistic reason."

"How so?"

"In your marriage. You did the same thing you accuse Papa of doing. You accused your ex of squashing your ambition and talent when, in fact, you're doing this to yourself."

"You have no idea of what you're talking about. You know precisely ZERO about my marriage or my work."

"It's so much easier to resent someone else and be the victim."

"You're such a BIG bitch, Odile!"

Cassie left Odile planted there and rushed to the bathroom. She avoided looking at herself in the mirror and splashed cold water on her face. Reverberating with outrage, she dug into her purse and found her lipstick. With a trembling hand, she applied the lipstick, hating herself and everyone with whom she had ever come into contact.

But when she finally looked into her own eyes in the mirror, she saw: Odile was absolutely right!

Why risk making the man you love insecure with your talent and ambition? She had muffled her soul and spirit in the hope of pleasing her dad and her husband, and in the process of making herself smaller and unthreatening, she had lost herself completely. She had spent a lifetime pretending to be someone she was not, to devastating results. Her last-ditch effort at self-preservation had been to move to the United States, but there she had re-created the same pattern with Peter, offering him a reduced version of herself and then waiting for his seal of approval. She had kept herself in the shadows, made herself small and angry but unthreatening to his ego. Success, strength, those were not safe paths. Anytime she sensed she risked being impressive, as Marceline had said, she squashed it in the bud for fear that it would make her unlovable.

That was the reason she had let Peter take the credit for her work. How could she not end up resenting him? How could she not push him away? How could she not drive him to fall in love with someone else?

What would she look like today had her genuine talents and traits been valued by her father? What would it be like to be more like Marceline? What would freedom feel like?

She walked out of the bathroom and to the cloakroom and asked for her travel bag. She reentered the reception room and headed toward Odile. "Here," she said. "This belongs to you." She opened her bag, uncovered the finial, and put it in Odile's hand. "You have the pair now."

"Me?" Odile said, stunned. "Marceline gave it to you. Why me?"

"Because Papa would have wanted you to have them."

"Why?"

"You are the person in the world he loved most," Cassie said. She said this without anger or bitterness. She said it because it was the truth.

Odile eyes flooded with tears. "Are you sure you want me to keep both?"

"They were always meant to be a pair, to be whole. And I think that you're right. You are suffering more than I am today. For you, Dad's loss is brand new. Me, I've had a lifetime of practice losing him."

When she was speaking with Odile, Cassie saw Sabine shoot her a look. They met a few minutes later by a window overlooking the cemetery. "What was that all about," Sabine said. "You're giving Odile *the finial?*"

"I don't want to be mad at Odile anymore," Cassie said. "Gustave and Marceline hated each other, and look at the results."

"Not to change the subject," Sabine said, "but Hervé is a frigging dreamboat."

Cassie laughed. "I know! Right?"

Sabine twirled a strand of her hair between her fingers, hesitant. "Do you know what you said about me taking a leave of absence from my job? I think maybe it's a good idea. Being elsewhere for a while might help me digest everything. I need to jumpstart my thoughts in a new direction. My doctor said he would prescribe a few months off. Does your offer stand about California?"

"Absolutely! When?"

"Soon."

"Fabulous! Although there is this one thing I need to do. One place I need to go. I can't explain. Sorry if I sound overly mysterious."

"Speaking of mysterious, who is this man with Marceline, the old guy with the white hair?"

Cassie repressed a laugh. The day should have felt somber, but it was all so slapstick and out of body. "He's Marceline's lover," she said. "Her lover with gardening benefits."

****

When everyone had left, Cassie and Hervé walked to a nearby café on rue de la Gaité. They sat across from each other at the corner table. The place smelled of espresso and croque monsieur. Outside, it had begun to rain. It felt right to be there; it was their environment: she and Hervé in a Parisian café, sharing a small table.

"I have your boots by the way," Hervé said. "Your red boots; you forgot them at the hotel."

"How in the world?"

"I went to look for you. They told me you had checked out and forgotten your stuff. I said I'd return them to you."

"I had left them there on purpose. They're not really me."

"They're exactly you: hot-blooded and American."

"Is that how you see me?"

"Isn't that how you are?"

"I don't know what I am. The version of me I've stuck to my whole life is changing by the minute."

"You convinced me to make a change in my life," Hervé said. "I'm quitting my job. You were right. It was bad for the soul."

"What will you do now?"

"I'd like to go back to traveling, and to actual medicine. Doctors without Borders, something like that. I'm a few months away from recovering my license."

"Well, I'm glad for you. Congrats," she said coolly. "And thank you for coming. It was very considerate." She took hold of her purse.

Hervé put his hand on hers. "What's the big hurry? Do you have a better place to be? A plane to catch? Other love interests to push away?"

"I do have a plane to catch. Eventually."

"Why didn't you tell me where you lived?" he asked.

"Why didn't you tell me you worked at the hospital?"

"I thought I had. Looking back on it, where I worked must not have come up in the conversation."

"Okay," she conceded. "I guess that's possible."

"I was not trying to hide anything, but I'm pretty confident that you were. Why didn't you say anything about your dad being in the hospital? You told me everything else you were going through."

"I was looking for all kinds of reasons why it wouldn't work between you and me," she admitted. "I didn't want to be hurt. I didn't want to be disappointed."

"So you hurt me and disappointed me."

"That's because I didn't think anything would come of us. We had one date and then another. I knew I was leaving. But mostly, I think I was afraid of rejection if you knew I'd be gone a week later."

"Look, I don't collect women. I don't chase them looking for a boost to my ego. I'm just as afraid as you are to get my heart broken."

"You told me you were planning on traveling," she said accusatorily. "You said, and I quote, this was just a fun thing between us. By the second date, I thought that if I told you where I lived, you would see I had been deceptive. I thought … well, I thought I'd be gone before we'd have time to start to like each other."

"The first moment I saw you steal my table at La Jument Bleue, the harm was done," Hervé said. "I already liked you very much."

"You liked me for the time being. But it would have been temporary."

"Everything is temporary!" Hervé said. "I don't know the future. I might drop dead. You might drop dead."

"That's not exactly reassuring."

"I'm willing to take a chance with you."

She looked at him in amazement. "Take your chances with a liar who writes crappy movies?"

He smiled. "Who also happens to be sexy, and smart, and fun."

"My children are in college in the U.S., and I have a house there. In Paris, I have nothing. I can't put all my eggs in the same basket. I've been burned before."

"I have now experienced it."

"What?"

"The burn."

"Well, that's not me," Cassie said. "At least not usually. I am usually dreadfully reliable. I am the most boringly reliable person you will ever meet. When I make a commitment to someone, I stick to it. Believe me, I'm still trying to untangle myself from my relationship to my ex-husband, and he's been with another woman for twelve years, most of it when he was still married to me. That's why I lied to you. I needed to protect myself from my forever mentality."

"I can't commit to forever. No one honest can do that."

"And I'm afraid of temporary, so there you go. What if I gave myself to you, heart and soul, and then you tired of me? I'm afraid that there would be nothing left of me after I gave it all to you. Do you understand how terrifying that is? Not to mention how much pressure's put on you? And there is something else you need to know about me."

"Another big secret?"

"The biggest secret of them all."

"What is it?"

"I'm not tough."

"What?"

"That's the crippling narrative. That's how my family sees me. *Cassie is tough. She falls back on her feet.* You don't know how many times I heard that said about me. So, I act tough. I act as though I don't need anyone. I act as though things don't bother me. I act as though it doesn't matter to me if my kids forget my birthday, or if the man I love doesn't know my favorite flower, or if my mother doesn't call me to see how I'm doing. I might look as though all I need to be happy is to dispense love and care and remember other people's favorite flowers, and birthdays, and call them and anticipate their needs. But it's all an act. I need to feel known; I yearn for someone to anticipate my needs. I want to be the object of small kindnesses as much as the next person."

"That seems perfectly reasonable. I agree to all conditions."

"You what?"

He reached across the table for her hand. "Where do I sign up?"

"Well … I don't even know how to get started."

"With me?"

"With anything."

"How about we take it a moment at a time?" Hervé said, squeezing her hand.

Cassie looked at Hervé. "How do you do that?"

"You start with a good espresso machine – the crappy kind. And then you put good espresso coffee in it. And water. Then you pour it, and you take the sugar and the milk. None of that fat-free nonsense. And good bread, and good butter. And while the coffee is brewing, I take you in my arms and hold you very tight." He got up from his chair and came to sit beside her. "Like this." He took her in his arms. "And we have one good breakfast, and then we make love."

"Not love first?"

"Either way will be fine. But you can only be in one place at a time because if all you do is fret about the next moment, you miss out on this one."

CHAPTER 9

Epilogue

Oia Santorini, Greece. 2013

Barefoot and in a white cotton bathrobe, Cassie stepped out onto the terrace of the hotel room.

How easy it was for her to side with her grandfather for this terrible thing he had done. He had done it for love. He had lied and deceived and abandoned his family, and yet all she could think of is that he had not had a choice. This was a case of momentous double standard, to take the side of the adulterer. Because, in her own story of hidden love, she had played the role of Lucienne, the unloved, betrayed wife.

Love was love, and you didn't get to choose who you fell in love with. With luck, you fell in love with a person who loved you back. But what were the probabilities of that perfect synchronicity? She could see now that Peter, like Albano, had had a difficult choice to make. His choice to lie to her to preserve the family intact was messed up but had intrinsic value.

Falling in love, was, as it turned out, a free fall. It *happened* to you. It knocked you off course and transformed you. It made you act and think profoundly out of character. It made you throw caution to the wind. Now that she understood this, she could start to forgive Peter.

Everything she wanted to become was at her fingertips. She was done altering herself in the hope of being loved. With a little moxie, she could, at last, harness the power she had always suppressed. She could wear red cowboy boots or feathery boas and no bra. She could become a field nurse, climb high peaks, write epic novels, dabble in espionage, or be someone's lover. She could laugh too loud and have lipstick on her teeth and drink champagne for breakfast. She could sell the Godforsaken house and its spiral staircase leading to a narrower and narrower version of herself. She could dwell in hotels around the world and never set foot in another kitchen or lift another laundry basket. She could let the wind decide where she should live next.

She stepped out onto the terrace and into the bright morning. Oia Santorini was indeed one of the most beautiful places in the world. An entire city dug out from a hillside, all gleaming white-washed walls and dome-shaped roofs painted blue, and as a backdrop, the Mediterranean. Hervé, in a bathing suit and barefoot, was reading the paper at the table. Breakfast had been set under an umbrella. He folded the newspaper and looked at her. "What a vision you are," he said. "Are you nervous?"

"Terrified."

"All right then," Hervé said, folding his newspaper. "Let's go meet those Greek cousins of yours."

The end of The Curator of Broken Things Trilogy.

*****

A note by the author:

Dear reader, nothing makes me happier than the thought that you took a leap of faith when purchasing the first book in the Curator of Broken Things trilogy, and then that you went on to read book 2 and 3. So a huge thank you for coming along for the ride!

I hope you will kindly leave a review, or attribute starts on Amazon or where you purchased the book. This will help nudge the series toward greater visibility.

*If you detected typos, or just to say hello, don't hesitate to send me an email at **corinegantz@live.com**. I love to hear from my readers.*

*You can also sign up for my newsletter at **www.corinegantz.com** to received updates and promotions.*

Thank you so much!

Corine Gantz

ACKNOWLEDGEMENTS

Thank you to my first readers, Joanna Kamburoff, Katherine Kohler, Catie Jarvis, Peggy Schmouder, and Betsey Parlatore, for kindly and carefully sifting through versions of the books when they were still a mess. Thank you to Isabelle Bryer and Jan Schafer for their keen eye for post-publishing typos (no doubt saving me from mortal embarrassment by detecting that my characters at one point 'circled *the glove*'). I am incredibly thankful to Donald Berman, a man with the soul of a writer, for his precision in English *and* French and for his support for the novels. A great thank you to Lisa Yoo for her creative talent and expertise in design. Most of all, thank you to my husband Joe for his tireless editing, his honesty, his intuition, his kindness, his ebullient optimism, and for not wavering in his belief in me in the past 30 years.

ABOUT THE AUTHOR

Corine Gantz was born in France where she spent the first twenty years of her life. She studied Contemporary Art at the Sorbonne and worked in advertising and marketing in Paris, San Francisco, and Los Angeles. Her first novel, *Hidden in Paris*, was published in 2011 and has been translated in nine languages. She is the mother of two sons and lives near Los Angeles with her husband.

Email her:
corinegantz@live.com

Visit her website:
www.corinegantz.com

For information, email:
corinegantz@live.com
www.corinegantz.com

All rights reserved
Copyright © 2018 by Corine Gantz
The Curator of Broken Things Trilogy

Carpenter Hill Publishing

ISBN-13: 978-0-9834366-7-6
ISBN-10: 0-9834366-7-3

Proofreading and copyediting by Donald Berman
donaldberman@hotmail.com

COVER ART

Cover illustration by David Navas
www.davidnavas.com

Cover design by Lisa Yoo
www.yisaloo.info